W9-BVC-480

HP
MY
SK

"DELANEY, IS IT YOU?"

He stepped into the light, and happiness burst within Allie. She threw herself against him, holding him close. "I knew you couldn't leave without saying good-bye! I ached without you, Delaney. The ache wouldn't stop, no matter what I tried."

Delaney's eyes were blazing. "Damn it all, you've made me a cripple! I don't feel whole without you, and I don't like it!"

Allie could feel him trembling, and a warmth kindled inside her. She wanted to hold him. She wanted— "Oh, Delaney, you're part of me, just like I'm part of you," she breathed.

"Do you want me to kiss you, Allie?"

Allie's heart fluttered. "Yes."

Delaney's lips touched hers, and the joy of all that was Delaney swept over her, filled her. An incredible exhilaration came alive inside her. . . .

WINGS OF A DOVE

Books by Elaine Barbieri
from Jove

TARNISHED ANGEL
WINGS OF A DOVE

Elaine Barbieri

WINGS OF A DOVE

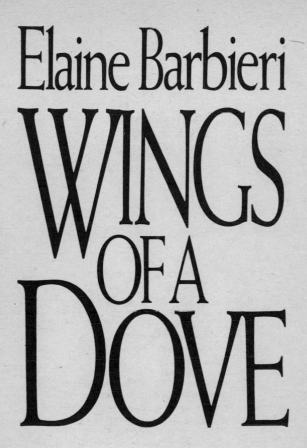

JOVE BOOKS, NEW YORK

WINGS OF A DOVE

A Jove Book / published by arrangement with
the author

PRINTING HISTORY
Jove edition / January 1990

All rights reserved.
Copyright © 1990 by Elaine Barbieri.
This book may not be reproduced in whole
or in part, by mimeograph or any other means,
without permission. For information address:
The Berkley Publishing Group,
200 Madison Avenue, New York, New York 10016.

ISBN: 0-515-10205-9

Jove Books are published by The Berkley Publishing Group,
200 Madison Avenue, New York, New York 10016.
The name "JOVE" and the "J" logo
are trademarks belonging to Jove Publications, Inc.

PRINTED IN THE UNITED STATES OF AMERICA

10 9 8 7 6 5 4 3 2 1

To the new little man in my life,
Michael Robert Settineri.
I love you, baby.

1856

THE QUEST

chapter

one

ALLIE JUMPED BACK with a gasp, dodging the flailing fists of the two young fellows who barreled past her, locked in a furious struggle. Her eyes widened as the boys fell to the deck with a loud crack, scattering other passengers of the *Issac Newton* as they continued to exchange hard, pounding blows.

"Fight! Fight!"

Allie retreated, backing up against the boat's rail as excited members of their group of traveling orphans and street children circled the combatants, showing no clear favorite as they cheered them on. Her heart pounding, she realized Mr. Smith had gone to attend to last minute details of their journey to Albany before the boat got under way and was nowhere to be seen. Someone must stop them!

Allie gasped. Blood! The darker-haired boy's mouth was bleeding. A familiar taste of bile rose to her throat. She remembered blood trickling from the corner of Mama's mouth like that, but this boy was not weak and pale as Mama had been. He was tall and strong, his face flushed from violent exertion.

Appearing suddenly behind the boisterous group, Mr. Smith pushed his way into the center of the circle and separated the boys with harsh words of admonishment. The dark-haired boy's startling light eyes were hot with fury as Mr. Smith stood resolutely between him and his adversary. His response to the older man's words rose over the excited babble around them.

"I don't care! He got what he had coming!"

"That's not the attitude I had hoped to see you display as a part of our company, Delaney." Turning to include the lighter-haired fellow in his reprimand, Mr. Smith continued sternly, "We are embarking on a serious venture that will affect not only the futures of the children present, but the futures of those who follow. Yet, this vessel has not left the dock and you are already behaving intemperately. We did not embark upon this endeavor to make a spectacle of ourselves. Whatever the cause of your dispute, I tell you now to put it aside for the general good of our company. This is only the first leg of our journey. If you cannot agree to get along peacefully with each other, both of you are free to return from whence you came. You, Sam, to the streets, and you, Delaney, to—"

Mr. Smith paused, his brow creasing as he chose not to complete his statement. His keen eyes moved between the two boys once more. "Well, what is your decision?"

Not a word was spoken in the attentive circle of children surrounding the two young offenders. The dark-haired boy, Delaney, wiped the blood from the corner of his mouth with the back of his hand. His hard eyes intent on the other boy's face, he finally spoke. "All right. Whatever you say."

Mr. Smith's narrowed gaze revealed his momentary suspicion of the young fellow's abrupt about-face. Turning toward the other, he cast an inquiring glance, which was met with a brief, concurring shrug of the boy's shoulders. Mr. Smith's relief was apparent.

"It's over and done, then. Fine. I suggest you both brush yourselves off. We want to present as respectable an appearance as possible when we meet the captain."

The two boys followed his directions, and Mr. Smith turned toward the silent circle around him.

"All right, children, line up. That's right, in twos. Follow me."

Stepping obediently into her place in line, Allie did not miss the quick heated glance the boy called Delaney darted in his adversary's direction. Her heart skipped a beat. She was old enough and wise enough to know what it meant. All was not yet settled between the two of them.

Allie took a deep, shuddering breath and straightened her shoulders in an attempt to disguise her anxiety. Her apprehension had soared the moment the boat got under way an hour earlier. They had been summoned to the upper saloon by the captain, and now standing with the other children, she cast a glance toward Mr. Smith. His thin figure erect, he stood beside the youngsters from their group who held the attention of the other passengers gathered there with their lively recitations. But their youthful voices grew faint in her ears as she attempted to recall the short speech Mr. Smith had delivered prior to boarding.

"You will depart on the most important journey of your young lives today, children. You'll travel west to new homes, new families, and surroundings more generous than the streets of New York. Hold tight to your Bibles and your blankets, and keep your chins up. And smile, children—smile!"

But Allie did not feel like smiling as she assessed her surroundings again with a brief glance. The group, forty-six children in all, had boarded the *Isaac Newton*, bound for Albany and, eventually, for new homes in Michigan. Allie had not had a peaceful moment since. In all of her ten years, she had never been outside the city of New York; and despite the misery and uncertainty of the last few months, she found herself thoroughly undecided about leaving behind her last link with the past.

The past. The past was one person. Mama.

An aching heat burned under Allie's eyelids and she took a deep breath. With great firmness she blinked it away. She was finished with crying. She had cried when Mama lost her position as Mrs. Van Houten's personal maid because of accusations, which Mama swore were not true. Her tears had fallen again when Mama was unable to find another position and when their funds slipped so low that they were forced to move to one of the immigrant neighborhoods of New York. She had tried to ignore the nasty children who called her names because she did not have a father. She had not believed their vicious taunts.

She had restrained her tears and used all her strength to take care of Mama after she fell ill. Then she had been strangely unable to cry when pneumonia quickly snuffed out Mama's life.

After her mother's death, she had found her way to the orphan asylum that had been her home for the past few months. In all that time, pride had not allowed her to cry. She had been out of place among the children there, who were all so wise in ways she had not yet begun to understand. She had learned the hard way to use caution in her dealings with them, and the memory of their cruel taunts had prevented her from forming any close bonds.

Her physical appearance had done little to ease her situation. Undersized for her age, she had always been thin; and in the time since her mother's death, she had grown thinner still. She remembered Mama's annoyance when Mrs. Van Houten had commented on her "sickly appearance." Later, in the privacy of their room, Mama had reassured her that she was not the least bit frail. It was true, for she was seldom ill, but that knowledge had done little to ease her distress.

She had asked Mama then why her hair was so fine and pale, and not dark and shining like hers, why her skin was so light and colorless when Mama's was so bright and clear, why her own eyes were brown instead of Mama's brilliant blue, and why she was plain when Mama was so beautiful.

Mama had not laughed at her questions. Instead, her eyes had misted as she whispered in a slightly shaky voice, "You look like your papa, Allie, and you should be happy about that, not sad, because your father was very handsome. He was tall and blond, with loving brown eyes. Some day, when you become a woman, you'll be very beautiful. I know it, and you must believe it, too. And anyway, it's the beauty in your heart that really matters." Mama had kissed her lightly then and whispered, "You're already beautiful there."

Allie had brought those words back to mind many times since Mama died, and although she knew she was still small and plain on the outside, she had tried to remain beautiful inside. It was not easy.

She had learned much after coming to the orphanage, but the greatest lesson she had learned was that she must not cry. To cry was to be weak, and she was determined to be strong, at least on the outside. She would not allow the others to think her upbringing had been lacking in any way.

So Allie had hidden her fear and uncertainty behind an unblinking facade and, dry-eyed, had stared down her tormentors. It was a pretense, a deception she still practiced, and it had earned her the respect of the others. But she had cried inside. She had not wanted to be there, in that cold, unfamiliar place. She had wanted to go home—but she had no home to go to.

Allie recalled the day the children began to whisper about the man who had come to the asylum. ''Placing out''—she remembered the speculation those words had caused. The man was going to select some children between the ages of seven and fifteen to take west to new homes where they could work and be part of a family that wanted them.

Mary Louise was eleven. She had shuddered and had vigorously shaken her head when she was asked to join the group. Slavery—she had whispered that they would all be sold into slavery.

Maggie, who was ten, the same age as Allie, had hissed that they would be taken away to a strange place and left with people who would work them from morning to night and starve them. She had said they would never be seen or heard of again.

Stella was fourteen, and she had just smirked and shaken her head, saying she knew what that man wanted to do with girls like her, and she wasn't about to slip back into that life again.

Mrs. Sutton had calmly accepted those girls' refusal to go, but when it was Allie's turn, the soft-spoken matron had been patient and untiring in her effort to persuade her to join the Reverend Mr. Brace's group.

''You mustn't be afraid to go, Allie. Reverend Brace will see that you find a good home. You can't stay here forever, and this may be the best chance you have for a good life, just as your mother would have wanted for you. You'll have no problem finding someone to take you in. You can read and cipher, and you speak well. The people who take you must sign a paper stating they agree to continue your education and treat you like one of their own family. As a part of the agreement, we must hear from you by letter, personally, twice a year. If they don't keep to the terms of the contract, you can just write us and you'll be free to come back.''

Fear surged anew as the echo of Mrs. Sutton's words whirled inside Allie's mind, mixing with the memory of Stella's harsh laughter and the frightening, confusing comments she had made about Allie's ''lily-white'' skin. The lump in Allie's throat tightened painfully and she swallowed firmly against it. She looked to the young faces around her and saw not a trace of fear in their eager expressions.

Allie raised her chin a notch higher. She could not conquer her fear, but she was resolved. *She would not cry.*

Instead, Allie forced her attention back to the children as they listened intently to one boy's lively recitation of the circumstances that had brought him to the *Isaac Newton* as a part of their group. It was obvious that William's spirits were high; like the rest of the group, he considered their journey to the West a great adventure. It was also obvious that he was enjoying the attention he was receiving as he regaled everyone with amusing stories of life on the streets, and the great things he would do once he was settled in the West and had a horse of his own.

Allie had heard all these stories before. The majority of their group had spent some time on the streets before coming to the asylum. Ten of the boys had been recruited directly from the docks, where they slept in empty packing crates, warm doorways, or whatever spot appealed to them for the night. They had supported themselves by begging and petty thievery, by peddling matches or apples or newspapers, or by gathering rags and bones on the street to sell. Others had even resorted to robbery for the bare necessities of life.

Two of that group, Willie and Barney, had slept in nearly all the station-houses in the city at one time or another. Another, Carl, had been born in Chicago and abandoned in New York by his drunken brother. A friendless, quiet boy named George had been completely alone when he made his way to the Newsboys' Lodging House. There were also Dick and Jack, brothers whose father, a jobless drunkard, had given them up in the hope that by going west they might find a better life than he could give them.

Allie eyed the crowd of interested passengers who had gathered around the children. The older boys had raised three cheers for Michigan when the boat left the harbor on the first leg of their journey. The cheers had caught the other passengers' attention, and it appeared interest in their group had not yet waned.

Allie took another deep, steadying breath. All the other children were engrossed in the show the older boys seemed only too happy to provide the passengers, with their enthusiastic singing and their lively recitations. They were all smiling, excited. They were all—

Allie's slow surveillance of the children stopped abruptly, catching and holding on the tall, dark-haired boy who had been fighting earlier. He was the one who had been delivered to join their party just before they left the orphanage, and she had found out since that his name was Delaney Marsh.

No, not *all* the others were smiling.

Silent since arriving in the upper saloon with the rest of them, Delaney Marsh continued to shun attention of any kind. He was one of the oldest, but he had not joined the other boys in their lively exchange with the captain and passengers. He had been unnaturally silent; and now, when he obviously believed no one was paying him the slightest attention, he stared with true venom at Sam, with whom he had been fighting earlier.

Allie had heard the whispered rumors repeated by the others when Delaney Marsh's back was turned, and a chill passed down her spine. Unexpectedly, as if the boy sensed her thoughts, he snapped his heated, light-eyed glare in her direction. Jumping with a start as its unexpected intensity raked her face, Allie immediately turned away. She could feel his eyes burning into her back for long moments afterward, but her gaze did not stir again from William as his conversation with the captain drew to a close.

Her heart racing, Allie closed her eyes. Oh, how she wished these last terrible months, when she had been frightened and alone and when even God had seemed deaf to her prayers, were all a terrible dream. How she wished she would awaken to the morning light and find herself far from this place, with Mama alive beside her.

Abruptly, with great determination, Allie brought her thoughts to a halt. It was stupid to keep on thinking this way. She had learned only too well in the long months since Mama went to live with God that wishing accomplished nothing at all.

Allie walked quickly, maintaining her place in line as the children moved rapidly through Albany's crowded train depot. She stumbled over the trailing end of the blanket she clutched close to her chest and, frowning, scooped it up to scramble forward once more. She tightened her grip on the Bible she held in her other hand. A Bible had been issued to each of them prior to leaving the orphanage, along with a blanket and traveling clothes, but this Bible was strange to her, offering little of the comfort intended.

The whistle of a departing train screeched and the babble of loud voices in an unfamiliar tongue turned Allie from her thoughts to a large, frantic family streaming past them. The father was bent low under the weight of large bundles secured to his back with shoulder straps. Several older children scurried anxiously alongside him. Trailing behind them was an obviously exhausted and apprehensive woman, struggling with the weight of the baby in her arms and the smaller child clinging to her skirt. The crowd thickened rapidly as that same scene was repeated time and again in dizzying numbers, the only variation the languages the anxious immigrants spoke as they rushed and pushed toward their destinations.

Dodging the advance of a heavy luggage cart rumbling past as the relentless tide of humanity threatened to separate her from her group, Allie hastened her step, making certain to keep close to the heels of the girl ahead of her. Confusion and disorder seemed everywhere apparent, in the great piles of baggage, the stacks of unclaimed freight, and the clusters of vendors hawking their wares as the ragged line of children continued on through the bustling terminal.

Bringing their group to an abrupt halt in front of a short uniformed gentleman, Mr. Smith addressed him quietly, only to react with a sharp exclamation to the man's response.

"Six hours! You can't be serious!" His thin face flushed, Mr. Smith paused briefly before addressing the middle-aged conductor again. "Sir, these children and I have been all night in steerage on the *Isaac Newton*. I don't think I need tell you that the accommodations left much to be desired in the way of comfort. The children have not uttered a word of complaint, but to ask them to wait six hours more in their state of exhaustion before boarding the train is truly too much to ask."

The conductor shrugged his rounded shoulders, showing little regret. "Too much to ask or not, sir, the train for Buffalo won't arrive for another six hours, and if you're wanting to go on from here, you'll have to wait.''

Mr. Smith withdrew his watch from his pocket with obvious distress. A nervous flutter moved in Allie's stomach as he then shook his head in obvious resignation.

"You say the train will leave promptly at noon?"

"That's right, but I'm advising you and your charges to be ready on time. This is an immigrant train you're taking, you know. There'll be a mad rush for places in the cars."

Mr. Smith's frown deepened. "Sir, we were told we would have a separate car so the children might spend a comfortable journey."

The conductor's wiry brows rose expressively as he turned to survey the small faces turned attentively in his direction. "That so? Well, I'll do my best for them, but I'm making no promises."

"All right. We'll be ready." Mr. Smith's face tightened, and the nervous fluttering in Allie's stomach increased as he turned to address them.

"You heard the conductor, children. We have an extended wait for the train that is to take us west." Mr. Smith's small eyes moved along the line, dwelling on the older boys in the rear as he continued. "I would prefer that our group remain close together for the duration of that time. However, my function is to serve as guardian, not guard. You are all of a reasonable age and I do not expect to maintain a constant watch to ensure that no one strays. I feel it is important at this time to make one point very clear to all of you: We have been delayed, but we *are* going to Michigan; and any of you who want to come along *must* be here when the train arrives. Is that understood?"

A chorus of youthful voices responded in agreement as Allie turned toward the rear to observe the reactions to Mr. Smith's statement. She saw eager expressions keen with anticipation, except for the stone-faced Delaney Marsh. Sam turned toward him with another low-whispered word, and anger blazed anew in Marsh's peculiarly light eyes. Allie snapped her attention back toward Mr. Smith. Sooner or later there was going to be trouble again.

Allie moved hastily into step behind the girl in front of her as the line again surged forward. She so desperately wanted to go home, wherever that was going to be.

* * *

"Marchin' in line like a bunch of lambs to the slaughter!"

"Yeah, lambs to the slaughter, that's what you fellers are!"

"All them pretty clothes and that book you got in your hand ain't goin' to do you no good when you're slavin' from dawn to dark."

"Take a deep breath! It's goin' to be one of the last breaths of free air you fellers'll be takin'!"

The shouted taunts of Albany street boys rang in Allie's ears as Mr. Smith led them back to the depot after a brief walk. Unwashed, with long, matted hair, stained, cast-off clothes, and the uncertainty of the next day staring them in their dirty faces, they continued their harangue as the westward-bound children continued walking. But their jeers did not go unreturned by the street boys in Allie's group.

"What would you snoozers know about where we're goin'? We're goin' west to find our fortune!"

"Fortune! Yeah, a yoke around your neck and a whip crackin' over your head!"

"We'll be ridin' on our own horses, and we'll be sittin' every night at a table where there'll be as much food as we can eat. Seconds, if we want. Thirds, even!"

"Yeah, yeah . . ."

Unexpectedly, Allie felt a sharp tug on her freshly cut pale hair swinging against her neck. Turning in protest, she met the eyes of a tall, light-haired, adolescent girl within the group of tormentors.

"Goin' west, girl? I'm thinkin' I can find easier work for you than workin' on a farm. Fellers take a real likin' to them girls that got yeller hair, especially if they're young and willin'."

Stella's reference to her "lilly-white" skin flashed back into Allie's mind. Controlling a shudder, she struck the girl's arm, freeing herself with a loud smack that turned the girl's expression abruptly ugly.

"You'll be sorry you did that! You won't be so sassy a couple of weeks from now after some feller uses you!"

Closing her ears to the girl's taunts, Allie directed her gaze forward and raised her chin. She fixed her eyes on the girl ahead of her, ignoring the painful knotting in her stomach as their wavering line continued marching past the State House and down the hill toward the waiting train.

She had been distinctly relieved when Mr. Smith finally called the group together after their extended wait and had begun to march them toward the depot once more. Surprisingly, not a one of their group had ventured far, including the older boys with whom she was certain Mr. Smith expected to have the greatest difficulty.

The hours of waiting had been long. She was uncomfortable in the clothes she had been issued before leaving New York. The rough wool of her skirt and jacket irritated her delicate skin, and the collar had already begun rubbing a sore red line around her neck. The thin cotton of her shirtwaist did little to protect her from the abrasive fabric that lay atop it, and the hot September sun had increased her discomfort yet another notch.

But Allie's greatest source of discomfort stemmed from a problem of an entirely different kind. Allie glanced with growing desperation toward the depot as they drew nearer.

Oh, dear, she so desperately had to piddle!

Walking with a short, restrained step calculated not to put any further strain on her already heavily burdened bladder, Allie brushed the perspiration from her forehead with the back of her hand. As they entered the depot, she searched the area for the appropriate sign but saw none. She glanced toward Mary Clark who walked beside her. Mary had disappeared for a few minutes a little while ago. Why had she not followed?

An ear-piercing whistle interrupted Allie's thoughts. She needed to find a place soon or her humiliation would be complete.

Waiting only until Mr. Smith halted the orderly line and set out in search of the conductor he had spoken with earlier, Allie left her assigned position and struck out on her own. Only a few minutes—she would be right back.

Greatly relieved a short time later, Allie raised her hand to brush back the sweat-dampened wisps of hair clinging to her cheek. She made a short grimace of despair as she started back in the direction from which she had come. Even newly cut, her hair refused to behave. The pale, flyaway wisps, bleached lighter still from recent exposure to the summer sun, had a mind of their own and she had long ago accepted that no matter the trouble Mama or she took, her hair would never look neat.

Mama had so valued neatness. Her hair had lain in a dark, gleaming cap against her head, and her eyes had seemed all the more blue in contrast. Allie fingered the lank strands lying warmly against her neck. She had inherited the coloring and features of a father she had never known, a father Mama had discussed only when persistently pressed to do so. But she remembered the softness that had sprung into Mama's eyes each time she mentioned his name. She knew Mama had loved him dearly.

Allie's fine lips narrowed into an angry line. It made little difference what those nasty children had said, the names they had called her when she and Mama moved into that terrible room where Mama died. She knew none of it was true. Mama had loved her father. She had loved him very much, and Mama had loved her, too. Allie didn't care about anything else.

Uncertainty again touched her mind. She was going to Michigan where she would meet people who wanted to take children into their homes in exchange for good honest work. But who would want a girl who was small for her age and thin besides, whose hair was colorless and never neat, a girl who looked frail and who could not seem to make herself smile? Of all the girls in the group, she was surely the one least likely to be—

Allie stopped abruptly in her tracks. Deep, hoarse sobs were coming from a point nearby, behind a great pile of unattended freight in the corner of the yard. Someone was crying.

Reacting instinctively, Allie took a few quick steps toward the sound, her heartbeat escalating as the low sobbing grew louder, more intense. She had almost reached the spot when she heard a hard, familiar voice cut into the tortured moans.

"You're not calling me names now, are you?" Silence, and then a harsher prompting, "*Are* you?"

The response was a single, gasping "No."

She heard a short, grating laugh and then the familiar voice continued, "You won't be giving me any more trouble, will you?"

"No . . . no."

"Say it again, brave man!" A low, grunting sound ensued and the familiar voice prompted more harshly, "I said, say it again!"

Another low sob was the only answer.

Allie stepped around the piled crates to stand immobile at the sight that met her eyes. Delaney Marsh and Sam were sprawled on the floor. Sam, his face flushed, his mouth bleeding, was lying on his stomach as Delaney sat on his back twisting Sam's arm cruelly behind him. Still waiting for Sam's response, Delaney tangled his free hand in the boy's blond hair and jerked his head viciously backwards.

At the sound of her step, Delaney Marsh turned sharply in her direction.

"Get out of here! This is none of your business."

Allie remained motionless, unable to move. As if from a distance she heard Delaney give her another harsh command. It also went unheeded, but the violent scene she had stumbled onto was not the cause of her numbed silence. Her gaze was fixed on Delaney Marsh's heaving chest. She stared at a silver chain that had worked loose from underneath his shirt. The religious medal suspended from it hung dangling over Sam's back, catching the light.

Sam sobbed anew, succeeding in breaking Allie's mesmerized stare. Tearing her gaze from the medal, she looked into Delaney's cold, light eyes as he spoke again in a low, warning voice.

"I told you to get out of here."

Allie frowned, shaking her head. "M-Mr. Smith is talking to the conductor. We're going to board the train any minute. You'll be left behind."

"*I'm* not going to be left behind."

His words little more than a weak gasp, Sam pleaded with a sob, "Let me go, Delaney. I won't say nothin' no more. I promise."

A cruel smile flickered across Delaney's lips as his gaze dropped back to Sam, and he gave a short triumphant laugh. Allie watched, realizing she had been right from the first. Delaney Marsh was trouble. But she wasn't ready to leave yet. She had to ask him if he—

Delaney looked again in her direction. His eyes narrowed, his voice a low, warning growl, he barked, "I'm only going to tell you one more time. If you don't get out of here right now, you're going to be sorry."

Allie did not wait for Delaney to say any more. Turning, she ran as fast as her feet would carry her.

Breathless, she drew herself to a halt beside the line of waiting children a few moments later and raised her eyes to Mr. Smith's relieved frown.

"There you are, Allie!" His tone was admonishing. "A few

more minutes and we could have left without you. What would you have done then?''

Not waiting for her response, Mr. Smith motioned the line forward. An unexpected panic gripping her, Allie shouted over the din of the congested depot, ''Mr. Smith, we can't leave. Not everyone has returned yet.''

Mr. Smith's narrow face tightened. ''Only two fellows are missing now, Allie, and it is my thought that if those two have not returned by this time, they will not return at all. In any case, I will not wait any longer. The cars will be loading any minute.''

''But, Mr. Smith—''

''Follow me, children.''

Mr. Smith motioned the line onward and Allie's heart began to hammer in her chest. He had to wait!

Allie cast another anxious glance over her shoulder as she stepped forward. Her heart leaping, she caught sight of two lanky boys running through the depot. A wave of relief swept over her trembling frame as she saw Sam's frantic, bruised face, and then Delaney's tight, tense expression bobbing through the surging throng. Within seconds they had caught up and attached themselves to the end of the line.

Allie looked forward, unconsciously releasing a short, tense breath as she maintained her step. She only hoped Sam would be smart enough to keep his word. She knew Delaney Marsh would not let him off so easily again.

Allie coughed and choked in the stifling rail car. She struggled for breath as the floor rocked and swayed unsteadily beneath her and the din of the wheels clicking over the rails echoed in her ears. She looked toward the great sliding doors, the only source of ventilation in the windowless boxcar, but not even the slightest gust of fresh air circulated past the passengers crammed into the limited space between her and the opening.

Allie shot a short glance toward Mr. Smith's sleeping figure, remembering his discouraged expression as they had boarded. His protests had been vigorous as the car designated as theirs pulled up in front of them, only to be filled by waiting immigrants. The conductor had shrugged at the uselessness of attempting to convince the frantic, uncertain people that they must step down and seek other accommodations.

The children had finally boarded the crowded car and taken whatever space remained—some standing, some sitting on laps, some seated on the floor beneath the crowded, backless benches. The day had passed slowly as the train progressed from one stop to another. The only break in the monotony of their journey was the bawdy songs a group of Irish immigrants sang as they passed a bottle among them, and the unrelenting crying of babies reduced by discomfort to constant fretfulness.

As night had begun to darken the interior of the car, Allie heard Mr. Smith's low exclamation when the conductor appeared to announce, "Passengers furnish their own light." She had cast a quick glance around her, grateful that a few meager lights were raised in the growing darkness.

Allie had remained rolled up in her blanket, unable to sleep, when the train came to a shuddering stop and the conductor's shout, "Utica!" echoed in the sudden stillness. Relieved of a number of passengers, the car was moving again, and Allie raised her head. Her eyes watering from the choking tobacco smoke that emanated from the pipes of dozing male and female passengers, she cast a searching glance into a darkened corner of the car.

Finally coming upon the object of her search, Allie hesitated. Motionless, sleeping on his side as if the hard floor offered all the comforts of home, lay Delaney Marsh.

Allie took a short, anxious breath, her mind returning to the scene she had witnessed in the depot before the train departed. The gleaming silver chain and religious medal dangling from Delaney Marsh's neck had been on her mind ever since. She swallowed tightly. She remembered that medal. She knew every detail of the figure carved onto the small silver disk: the soft expression on the Lady's beautiful face, the smooth, flowing veil that covered her hair and shoulders, her simple but graceful garments, the serpent crushed beneath her small bare feet, the way she held her arms, slightly raised, palms upward.

She wanted that medal desperately.

Allowing herself a moment more to assess the steady rise and fall of Marsh's chest, Allie slowly began inching her way toward him. With great care and a sharp eye on Mr. Smith's slumped figure, she worked her way among the sleeping passengers. She continued crawling stealthily until she was within a few feet of Delaney Marsh.

It was then that she hesitated, doubt and no little fear creasing her brow. She remembered the coldness in those eyes now closed in sleep, the pain inflicted so heartlessly as Marsh had twisted Sam's arm tighter.

Allie took a short breath, her determination failing. Perhaps she should not try to—

An unexpected jolt shook the car as it continued onward. Momentarily losing her balance, Allie righted herself in time to see that Delaney Marsh had shifted his position. A small gasp escaped her lips. The silver medal and chain were again visible inside his unbuttoned shirtfront.

Her heart hammering, Allie gave a short, unconscious nod. She had to have it.

Silently, Allie slipped to Delaney Marsh's side. She paused to study him again. She had not realized how big he was, how very broad his shoulders were underneath his worn shirt, despite his boyish thinness. But he did not seem so frightening in sleep, now that his cruel eyes were closed and his mouth was not issuing threats. She followed the strong curve of his profile as he turned onto his side. He had a surprisingly pleasant face when he was not frowning or glaring.

Allie took another deep breath. Carefully, she extended her hand toward the medal. A flickering shaft of light from a nearby lantern caught its carved facets, and it sparkled appealingly. The Lady was calling her.

Delaney Marsh was suddenly fully awake. His hand snaking out, he grasped her wrist, holding her prisoner with a painful grip as he hissed, "What do you think you're doing?"

A jolt of fear shook her at his menacing tone, and Allie pulled back. She opened her mouth to cry out, but Marsh was too quick for her. With a quick, agile movement, he clamped his other hand over her mouth and pulled her down beside him. Holding her motionless with his superior strength, he whispered harshly into her ear, "Be quiet! I can't afford any more trouble, understand? I'm not going back to prison, not for you or for anybody else!"

Allie's eyes widened. The rumors were true! He *had* come from the city prison!

Marsh flicked a brief glance across her frightened face. Slowly he lifted his hand from her mouth.

"That's right, prison. You made a mistake when you tried to steal from me."

Finding her voice, Allie shook her head in denial. "I—I wasn't trying to steal your medal. I just wanted to borrow it for a while."

Delaney Marsh's low, scoffing laugh sent a flush of anger surging to her face. Allie attempted to pull herself upright, only to have his hold tighten even more restrictively than before. Wincing against the pain, Allie was mortified as she felt a tear squeeze out the corner of her eye.

"Crying won't do you any good."

"I'm *not* crying!"

Marsh's expression registered impatience at her denial. Furious at her helplessness, she continued hotly, "You shouldn't have that medal, anyway. You're too mean to pray! If I had it, I'd pray for it to be mine instead of yours, and that you'd go out west where you want to be, so you wouldn't be here, making trouble and hurting people."

Delaney Marsh's light eyes narrowed.

"Only weak people pray—people who are too afraid or lazy to do things themselves. And then they cry when their prayers aren't answered!"

Shocked at his reply, Allie pulled back. Regretting her movement as his grip tightened further, she managed a reply. "If you really believe that, why do you keep the medal?"

"For the same reason you tried to steal it. Because it's valuable. When the right time comes, I'm going to sell it."

"Sell it!"

Allie shook her head, incredulous. Mama would *never* have sold her medal! Allie lowered her gaze to the medal lying against his chest. Her throat tightened, and her voice was a choked whisper.

"I wish *I* could buy the medal from you. If I had it, God would hear my prayers."

Delaney's short, mocking laugh pushed Allie beyond the bounds of fear, and she raised her chin defiantly.

"My mother said God *always* heard her prayers when she held the Lady's medal in her hand, and Mama wasn't weak *or* lazy!"

"Is that so? Where's your mother now?"

An almost indiscernible flicker of pain moved across Allie's face. "Mama went to live with God."

"Where's your father?"

Allie was suddenly angry. "That's none of your business!"

Marsh's expression was all too knowing, and Allie's anger turned to fury. Suddenly she was struggling to be free of his imprisoning hold. She didn't care how much he hurt her! She wasn't going to let him call Mama or her names!

Easily subduing her, Delaney Marsh held Allie immobile a few moments later as he looked down into her flushed face. His expression flickered a second before he loosened his grip on one of her wrists. He hesitated only a moment longer before guiding her hand toward the medal, his skepticism obvious.

"For all the good it's going to do you . . ."

Allie looked at the medal, which was now only inches from her hand. The dim light in the swaying car again glittered on the carved figure and a familiar warmth came alive inside her. The Lady *was* calling her.

All thought of the intimidating Delaney Marsh slipping from her mind, Allie took the medal into her hand and held it tight. She remembered the many times Mama and she had prayed together. She had asked Mama why she held the medal when she prayed. Mama had smiled and said that when she did, the Lady sent her prayers on the wings of a dove directly into God's ear.

Allie clutched the medal tighter. It was still warm from the heat of Delaney Marsh's body, and Allie hesitated. Finally closing her eyes, she began to pray with all the fervor in her young heart. She prayed that her uncertainty would soon come to an end. She prayed that she would find a home and someone to love her as Mama had loved her. She prayed that she wouldn't be afraid anymore.

At an unexpected sound behind her, Allie opened her eyes and saw Marsh's face stiffen. She followed his gaze and saw Mr. Smith moving through the darkened car as he checked the sleeping children. Glancing back to Delaney, she saw his expression change again before he pulled her closer, shielding her from Mr. Smith's view with his broad shoulders.

Allie lay perfectly still, suddenly grateful for his protection. She was not yet ready to give up the medal and the serenity that had touched her the moment she took it in her hand.

She again closed her eyes to pray. She was tired, but she was strangely at peace. For the first time in many months, both Mama and God seemed very close.

* * *

Delaney lifted his head from the blanket and furtively inspected the shadowed, silent forms in the crowded rail car. Mr. Smith was sleeping soundly, and except for the car's rhythmic creaking and jolting as the train moved steadily forward, all was motionless and quiet within.

Turning, Delaney peered into the face of the sleeping girl lying beside him. She was such a pale, scrawny little thing. His gaze moved to her hand where it curled loosely around the medal suspended from his neck. He forced away the almost forgotten sadness that touched his mind.

He had seen the fear in her eyes when he first caught her looking at him. It had not been difficult to read her thoughts: prison boy. His anger had been instinctive, and it had flared even more hotly when that fool, Sam, had taunted him. Well, Sam wouldn't taunt him anymore, and for all her fear, this puny little girl had faced him with more courage than Sam had.

Delaney cast another cautious glance toward Mr. Smith, who was now lying down. He was well aware that taking a "prison boy" on this trip was an experiment. Not everyone agreed that it was wise to include him as part of the company. But someone had marked him as "reclaimable" and decided to give him an opportunity to make a fresh start in the West. He was determined to take advantage of that chance. There was nothing left for him in New York but trouble, and he had made up his mind never to spend another day behind bars.

He had meant what he said to this girl. He couldn't afford any more problems that might turn Mr. Smith against him. He had been too smart for his own good in the past when he had been ten years old and destitute and no one wanted to hire him for honest work. He had found other ways to support himself. But he was going west now, and he was going to put in a day's work for a day's pay. And he was going back to school, at least for another few years. Pa would have liked that. When he turned eighteen he would be free to go out on his own. He'd have decent clothes and a full stomach, and there would be no stopping him from there. He'd show them all.

Delaney's handsome young face creased in a frown. He was certain of one thing. Nobody would ever take advantage of him again. He was too old, too big, and now he was on the right side of the law.

His thoughts returning to the little girl sleeping beside him, Delaney frowned again. Small, obviously lacking in street experience, she was a prime target for those who preyed on homeless kids. He had seen what happened to her kind. She had a lot to learn, and she'd probably learn it the hard way. The truth about the medal and "the Lady" would not be the least of those hard lessons.

Delaney's frown deepened and he shrugged away memories of countless unanswered prayers which still filled him with pain. He had stopped praying after Pa was killed, but despite what he had said to the girl, he knew he'd never sell the medal. Pa had given it to him, and he had loved his father too much to ever give it up.

Unwilling to pursue his thoughts any further, Delaney lowered his head to the blanket. The girl's small hand twitched in sleep and he hesitated for a brief moment before curving his body toward her. He was somehow unwilling to force the sleeping child to relinquish the medal any sooner than was necessary. He could afford to give her that much, at least for a little while.

Allie awakened to a stifling closeness, suffocatingly stale air, and the rattle and shaking of the floor beneath her. Momentarily disoriented, she strained to see into the unfamiliar semidarkness. She felt a warm breath on her cheek and turned her head toward the shadowed form curved toward her in sleep. Delaney Marsh. She paused, her gaze dropping to the chain hanging around his neck, only inches from her upturned hand.

She looked up again, studying Delaney Marsh's sleeping face for long, silent moments. A smile flicked across her lips and she allowed her eyes to drift slowly closed once more. Mama had been right about the medal. One of her prayers had already been answered: She was no longer afraid.

chapter

two

"WHAT'S ALL THEM red things out there on the trees, mister?"

Loud squeals of laughter followed the question, succeeding in bringing Allie abruptly awake to the new day within the swiftly moving rail car.

"Them's apples. Apples growin' on trees, that's what!"

Allie opened her eyes and gasped. Mr. Smith was grabbing one of his young charges as the boy leaned from the door of the rail car, arm outstretched in an attempt to snatch the apple-laden branches as they flashed past. She pulled herself erect and glanced around, momentarily disoriented. The loud, screeching whistle, the clicking of the wheels against the rails beneath her, dozing immigrants raising sleepy eyes to the commotion the boys were making, and flashing glimpses of a brilliant sunlit landscape through the open doors of the rail car brought back the reality of her situation.

Allie looked down. Her blanket lay at her side, but Delaney was gone. She glanced up toward the open door as Mr. Smith attempted valiantly, but with little success, to move the children gathered there to a spot that posed less risk. Delaney stood behind them, exhibiting none of their excitement or enthusiasm. His expression unrevealing, his eyes were slits of blue as he stared at the passing orchards.

Turning, Allie attempted to fold her blanket, only to find her Bible tucked safely beneath it. A spot long cold and dead inside her stirred to life as she completed her task and drew herself to her feet. She started hesitantly toward the open door of the rail car as exclamations started anew.

"Oh, yonder! Look! What's them?"

Squeezing herself into the excited crowd, Allie could not help echoing the gasps of those around her. Fields, great, golden fields as far as her eyes could see were coming into view, replacing the burgeoning orchards of a few minutes before. Scattered on the ground in endless rows were big, orange—

"*Mushmillons!* That's what them are! Mushmillons!" And then the ecstatic question, "Mr. Smith, do they make mushmillons in Michigan?"

The chorus of laughter that followed little Peter's shouted question did not allay the excitement in his wide eyes as Mr. Smith replied with an almost indiscernible twitch of his lips, "Pumpkins, Peter. Those are pumpkin fields, and yes, I'm certain Michigan has its share of pumpkins."

Feeling no inclination at all to join in the laughter, Allie continued staring out through the open door. She blinked incredulously. She had often stolen into the vegetable patch that Mrs. Van Houten's gardener had maintained for the household, and she had marveled at the beautiful melons growing on creeping vines and the tall green stalks that produced juicy red tomatoes. But this—she had never seen the likes of this before!

Feeling the weight of someone's gaze, Allie turned to catch Delaney Marsh's eye. Startled at his coldness as he abruptly turned away, Allie felt the small spot of warmth within her shrivel and die. He was the old Delaney Marsh again, the one with the cruel eyes. It was as if the night before had never happened and he . . .

No! Catching herself as she began to slip back into her former fears, Allie raised her chin determinedly. The night before *had* happened. She had held the Lady's image in her hand, and she had felt the Lady's strength and courage touch her. Her prayers had flown directly into God's ear, just as Mama had said they

would, and her fear had faded. She would not let the Lady down
by allowing those fears to return. She didn't care about Delaney
Marsh and his cold eyes. It was the Lady and her image on the
medal she wanted and needed. She wished . . .

Halting the rapid progression of her thoughts, Allie gave her
head a short, determined shake. She was being stupid again.
How many times must she remind herself that wishing, no matter how very hard she wished, did not make it so?

The smell of the docks was strong and pungent in her nostrils,
and Allie grimaced. Mama had once told her that ships and the
sea often got into a man's blood, and when that was so, a man
would sometimes abandon all he held dear to follow the sea for
all of his life. Allie had seen sadness in Mama's eyes then and
had accepted her statement without question. But now, in this
place—with the confusion of loading lake boats, the complaints
of disgruntled passengers, and the ever-present odors that seemed
to accompany both—she was uncertain how that could be true.

The sudden forward surge of their group brought Allie sharply
back to the present, and she stumbled in an attempt to stay close
behind the girl ahead of her as they made their way along the
dock. Righting herself a moment later, she darted a quick glance
toward the streaming throngs that threatened to overwhelm them.

Buffalo. Somehow that name did not conjure up teeming
wharves, endless confusion, and the stench of fish. How very
much she preferred the countryside they had passed through only
hours earlier, but those burgeoning fields and orchards had
yielded only too soon to this unappealing port on this great lake
that stretched out endlessly before her eyes like a huge, open
sea.

Mr. Smith had accepted the news of another delay with grace
when he was informed earlier that morning that there would be
a nine-hour wait for the lake boat that was to take them to the
next stop in their journey. He had turned the older boys out on
their own, with strict instructions as to the time to return. During
the long hours when the younger members of the group had little
to do to entertain themselves, Mr. Smith had explained to them
that the boat would take them across Lake Erie to Detroit, Michigan. They would board a train in that city and proceed to a little

town called Dowagiac, where he expected to meet with the people who would find them their new homes.

Many of the children imagined Michigan to be filled with fields and orchards like those they had recently passed through, a land of plenty where they could pick the fruit off the trees, but Mr. Smith had cautioned them against wild dreams. He had informed them that not all the children would be placed on farms, that many would go into the homes of professional men, possibly doctors, teachers, or men of the cloth. Others would go into the homes of business people—storekeepers, tinners, and the like. But he had promised that not a one would go into a home where he or she did not wish to go. For that reassurance Allie had been immensely grateful.

Determined to hold fast to her courage, Allie had spent the day with the children her age, with nary a glance toward the dark, unsmiling Delaney Marsh. Along with the other older boys, he had disappeared for the greater portion of the time they had spent in Buffalo, returning only a short half-hour before the appointed hour. But now, as their wavering line again made its way through piles of unclaimed freight and around loudly complaining livestock waiting to be loaded, Allie felt her determination slowly slipping away.

With a cautious step, she followed Mr. Smith's lead as they boarded the ship, crossed the deck, and descended the companionway to the steerage cabins. With each successive level they reached, Allie's trepidation grew. She did not like abandoning the sun and fresh air above to descend into the foul-smelling darkness of the lower decks. One glance at Mr. Smith's face revealed he shared her dismay at the filth of the berths and the coarse mattresses provided on the remaining floor space in the open deck accommodations.

"A thousand passengers before us, and doubtless not a change of linens or a clean cloth passed over a single surface." Mr. Smith's muttered comment lifted Allie's gaze to his face. Sensing her scrutiny, he forced a smile.

"But we will survive, will we not, children?"

Along with the others, Allie nodded to Mr. Smith's question, but her response lacked conviction.

The crashing of hooves against the deck above them a short time later, and the realization that the livestock she had seen on the dock were being loaded over their heads, seemed to shrink their crowded, rank quarters even more.

But it was only after the ship was under way and darkness had reduced their deck to wavering shadows that the plaintive cries of the animals took on an almost human sound, the creak and groan of the ship gained an ominous tone, and the sounds of convulsive retching filling the darkness around her became a personal assault.

Allie cast a short glance at the other children and swallowed tightly. Most of them were asleep. She envied them their escape from this frightening world of shadows, for despite her greatest efforts, her eyes would not close.

Delaney turned restlessly in an attempt to get comfortable, but sleep continued to elude him. There had been a shortage of bunks, and he had found himself, along with some of the other older boys, provided with nothing more than a vermin-filled mattress and a spot on the deck in which to lay it. Adjusting his position, Delaney shrugged. He would be glad to be away from this ship, but, in truth, he had endured worse circumstances in the past.

Turning, Delaney looked around the crowded steerage cabin. It was a repetition of the previous night, only worse. Even the darkness was not still. Weary immigrants, filling every nook and cranny between and around the children's group, moved steadily in the shadows—some women washing clothes, some men smoking in silence, some drinking and mumbling to themselves. Others, judging from the grunting, almost animallike sounds emanating from the far corner, were seriously involved in another business entirely.

As it had countless times during the long day, Delaney's gaze touched unconsciously on the small, pale-haired girl who had approached him the night before. She had pulled herself upright on the bunk, her posture rigid. His frown darkened. He remembered her face when she had awakened that morning and glanced toward him for reassurance, and he remembered her startled glance at the coldness with which he had turned from her mute appeal. But he also remembered the strong sense of caution that had returned to plague him upon awakening. He had been angry with himself, regretting his softness of the night before. He did not need the complication of a frightened little girl following at his heels, no matter how brave the front she attempted to present. His future would be decided within the next few days, and he did not intend to make any more mistakes. There was only one person for whom he was going to be responsible, and that person was himself.

His decision made, he had stuck to it, but he had not forgotten the expression in the girl's eyes. The memory of it even now caused him discomfort. Her eyes big and brown in her small, thin face, she had looked for all the world like a wounded fawn he had seen in a picture book when he was younger. It gave him little peace knowing he was responsible for the most recent wounding of a fawn that had been wounded too many times before.

Delaney moved restlessly, annoyed by his preoccupation with the frail-looking orphan who sat rigidly on her bunk a few feet away. Toughened by the streets, he no longer needed the solace of the medal he wore around his neck, the same medal the girl had held with such reverence the night before. He didn't need anyone, but he was uncomfortably aware that such was not the case with that little girl.

Delaney gave a short, unconscious shake of his head. The girl was obviously out of place in this group of orphans, snoozers, and copper pickers. The mother whom she had defended so vigorously the night before had left her ill prepared for the hardships she faced.

A small shudder shook the girl's skinny frame, bringing Delaney's wandering thoughts up short. If he didn't miss his guess, the girl didn't want to lie down on the mattress because it was crawling with bugs and smelled of sweat and filth. He remembered a time when he had suffered the same revulsion, but he had long since overcome it.

She brushed something from her arm, shuddering again, and he could almost see the tears brimming in those big, lost eyes.

Unfamiliar, warring emotions assailed him and Delaney clamped his teeth tightly shut. With great deliberation, he turned his back. So the girl was unhappy. It was no business of his.

Allie brushed anxiously at her arm once, and then again. Panic was beginning to overwhelm her. She was tired, but she didn't want to lie down on the mattress. It was infested with bugs. She had sat up when one crawled across her forehead, and she still shuddered to think that it could have found its way into her hair to nest there. The memory of her own bed at home returned, the one she had shared with Mama, and Allie took a deep, pained breath. The linens had been clean and white; Mama had prided herself on keeping them and the room spotless.

Abruptly drawing her thoughts to a halt, Allie closed her eyes. It would do no good to torment herself with memories of the past. She needed to concentrate on her unknown future and try to become the kind of woman Mama had wanted her to be.

An unexpected sound in the semidarkness made Allie turn apprehensively in its direction. She gasped as Delaney Marsh appeared out of the shadows and wordlessly sat beside her. He was frowning, and when he spoke, his voice was a low whisper.

"Your name's Allie, isn't it?"

Startled by his question, Allie nodded. His eyes narrowed as he returned her stare. The startling color was surprisingly light in the dim glow as he gave a sarcastic snort.

"Allie. What kind of name is that for a nice little Irish girl?"

Allie flushed. She was familiar with tormenting.

"I don't like people to make fun of me."

"I wasn't making fun of you. I was asking a question."

"You weren't. You were making fun, and I don't like it."

"What if I don't care what you like?"

"Then I won't answer you."

"And if I said I don't care if you don't answer me?"

"I'd say that's stupid."

"Stupid?"

"Yes. You wouldn't have asked a question if you didn't want an answer." Allie snapped her lips tightly shut. Adopting the same defense that had worked so well for her in the past, she allowed her gaze to cool and her expression to become aloof. She would not allow Delaney Marsh to get the best of her.

But Marsh was not put off.

"All right. I'll put it another way. What's the name you were baptized with? No girl who believes in 'the Lady' was baptized with a name like Allie."

Her anger mollified at the mention of the Lady, Allie re-

sponded with polite stiffness. "Mary Alice Pierce is the name
on my birth papers, but Mama called me Allie."

"I think I'll call you Mary Alice."

Delaney's response made Allie flush more hotly than before.
He *was* making fun of her!

Allie stared into his face in a manner she hoped was supremely haughty. "Then I won't answer you."

Delaney shrugged. "That's too bad. I just thought that nice
little Irish girl, Mary Alice Pierce, might want to borrow my
medal again."

Allie's defensive posture slipped as her eyes darted to Delaney's chest. A spark of hope came alive inside her. Did Delaney
Marsh really mean what he said, or was he just teasing her more
cruelly than before?

Biting her lip in anxious confusion, Allie was about to respond when a sound nearby caused her to glance toward Mr.
Smith as he drew himself to his feet. Gripping her arm unexpectedly, Delaney pulled Allie off the bunk and onto the floor,
out of Mr. Smith's sight. By way of explanation he offered softly,
"I don't think Mr. Smith would understand about the Lady."

Allie nodded in agreement. No one had understood about the
Lady after Mama died—no one but Delaney.

Within a few moments Allie was again holding the medal in
her hand, a familiar warmth suffusing her. She squinted, unable
to make out the Lady's face in the limited light, but it didn't
really matter. The darkness was no longer so ominous, or the
strange noises so frightening, and the sting of her earlier exchange with Delaney Marsh had faded.

Still clutching the medal, Allie looked up at Delaney with
new insight. Her whispered question was offered with an attempt
at a smile. "Delaney Marsh : . . Why in the world would a nice
Irish boy like you have two last names?"

Moving quickly, the ragtag line of children ascended the companionway to the main deck. Her heart pounding heavily in her
chest, Allie gasped as the first ray of sunlight touched her skin
and she took a deep breath of fresh air. A sharp push from
behind propelled her forward as those in the rear made their bid
for a share of the morning sun.

Allie moved closer to the rail and paused. She was feeling

much better this morning. She cast a quick glance behind her as Delaney emerged from the companionway into the sunlight. She saw him squint and take a deep breath, and she realized that fresh air and the realization that their group was only a short distance from its destination was not the only reason for her sense of well-being. She had a friend.

Glancing once more toward Delaney, Allie smiled. She was not truly certain when it had come to her that Delaney was her friend. He had never even smiled at her, and when he appeared at her side last night, her reaction to him had been far from friendly. She had awakened this morning to find herself alone, with her blanket wrapped around her, but the flame of friendship that had been kindled inside her the previous night still warmed her. Without reasoning why, she knew Delaney cared enough to share the Lady with her, and she was thankful for that.

Delaney rounded the deck to her left, and Allie caught his eye. She was not deceived by the frown he flashed in her direction. The prison boy, Delaney Marsh, was surly, hard, and difficult. He did not want a girl tagging at his heels. But somehow he was still her friend.

Allie turned toward the nearing lakeshore. For the first time the conviction was strong within her that she would soon be home.

chapter

three

WEARY TO THE bone, Allie squinted into the predawn darkness. Yawning, she pushed a wisp of hair from her eye and glanced back at the departing train from which the group of children had disembarked only minutes before. A loud, screeching whistle its parting sally, it disappeared into the darkness. Allie turned her attention back toward Mr. Smith, not in the least sorry to see it go.

"All right, children, quickly, into the train station."

Sitting wearily on the floor beside her young fellow travelers a few minutes later, Allie listened to Mr. Smith's exchange with the perplexed stationmaster.

"But surely you see these children cannot go on now. They are exhausted."

"It's out of the question, sir. This is not a lodging house. They can't sleep here."

"It is three o'clock on a Sunday morning! What else do you expect them to do? I tell you, no rules of any consequence will be broken if you allow these poor young travelers the simple comfort of sleeping on the floor. They ask for no more. I cannot see how you can refuse."

Allie's attention strayed from the intense conversation to the rear of their group, her eyes touching on Delaney as he wandered toward a corner of the waiting room. She watched as he lay down on the floor, rolled his jacket under his head for a pillow, wrapped his blanket around him, and closed his eyes.

Ignoring the continuing exchange between Mr. Smith and the stationmaster as it progressed in muted tones, Allie proceeded to do the same. She marveled inwardly at the supreme comfort of the hard wooden floor in the last moments before she drifted off to sleep.

"Where are we, Mr. Smith? Have we arrived?"

Allie awoke to the morning with a start, Isabel Turner's eager question echoing foggily in the back of her mind. Turning automatically toward Mr. Smith, she awaited his answer, still attempting to blink sleep from her eyes.

Mr. Smith's brief announcement—"We are in Dowagiac, Michigan"—was met with eardrum-piercing cheers from the suddenly jubilant children around her. Abruptly wide awake, Allie got to her feet. They had arrived!

Turning, Allie glanced quickly around the crowded train station. The younger children were busily collecting blankets and jackets, jabbering excitedly, but not a single one of the older boys was to be seen. Frowning, Allie bent down to scoop her blanket from the floor. She had folded it roughly and was picking up her jacket and Bible when Mr. Smith called them to attention once more.

"All right, children, that's right, form a line. I don't think it is necessary for me to tell you how very important this day is. It is essential that we make as presentable an appearance as possible. To that end, I will expect that each of you will take special care to wash your hands and face and to groom yourselves as well as may be expected under these rather difficult circumstances. In the meantime, I will negotiate breakfast at the American House Hotel, which the stationmaster advises is the establishment that will best suit our needs." Mr. Smith paused, his bearded face alight with anticipation. "Ready, children? All right, forward, please."

Excitement leaving her slightly breathless, Allie quickly fell into line at Mr. Smith's urging. She looked around the quiet depot as they moved through the doorway and out onto the street. Warm sun, the silence of early Sunday morning, a nearly deserted street. She took a shaky breath. They would all soon have homes.

A short time later, Allie stepped away from the outdoor washstand to which the hotel manager had directed them and dried her hands and face on a damp cloth used by several others before her. She walked to the tree where she had left her belongings and paused to glance around her. Violet, one of the older girls, was jealously guarding the comb with which she groomed her long red-gold hair. Violet was a beauty, as well as a strong, hardy girl. Allie had no doubt Violet would be one of the first to find a home.

Allie ran her hands through her pale, tangled locks in an attempt to modify the disarray, then winced as her fingers became enmeshed in stubborn snarls. Eyes watering, she abandoned the effort as useless a few moments later. Making one last futile attempt to smooth her stained and wrinkled shirtwaist and skirt, she donned her jacket and joined the others as they began walking toward Mr. Smith.

As the children walked around to the front of the wooden structure bearing the brightly painted sign, "The American House," hooting laughter and sounds of great hilarity sounded from behind. Turning, Allie saw the older boys returning in a state of great excitement, laden with souvenirs of their exploration.

"This sure be the land of plenty, Mr. Smith!"

Biting into a bright red apple, carefully polished to impress the others, George grinned in appreciation as Sam passed him up to glance scathingly at his finds.

"You ain't seen nothin' like I seen, and you ain't found nothin' like what I got."

Holding out his hat, Sam proudly displayed several ripe, juicy peaches. "Found a right nice pond for swimmin', too. Clear, sweet water, it was, and a few steps away were a whole stand of trees just waitin' for somebody to do some pickin'. And them peaches taste even better than they looks. I can tell you that for sure. I already et three!"

Mr. Smith waved an impatient hand. "In line, boys, now. Breakfast is waiting, and afterward we are expected at church."

Nervous giggles sounded from the girls around her, but Allie wasn't smiling. Everyone knew what "being expected" meant. The time had just about come. Who would be the first to be chosen?

Their ragged line had started up the wooden steps of the hotel when Allie turned again to survey the rear. It appeared all had returned, with one exception. Delaney Marsh was noticeably absent, and Allie's heart dropped to her toes. It was too soon for him to leave. She still needed . . .

Catching a sudden movement out of the corner of her eye, Allie turned toward the side of the building in time to see Delaney walking leisurely toward them. Stopping in her tracks, Allie took a deep breath. Delaney had obviously found that pond Sam had spoken of and had put it to better use. Where Sam's blond hair was wet and sticking untidily to his head, his clothes in general disarray as they adhered to his still-damp body, Delaney had apparently taken a few more moments to present an appearance of an entirely different sort. True, his clothes were wrinkled and showed the effects of travel as did those of the others in the group, but his person was spotlessly clean. His thick, heavy hair, neatly combed, fairly glowed and his skin was touched with becoming color after a short hour of exposure to the morning sun's rays. His peculiarly light eyes appeared almost translucent, eerily so against his newly tinted skin as he walked silently erect, unsmiling in sharp contrast with the physical disarray and jubilant enthusiasm displayed by the others.

Allie swallowed as he approached. Delaney Marsh was very handsome, despite the coldness of his light eyes, and Allie suddenly knew he would be one of the first to be chosen.

Bearing Mr. Smith's censuring glance without flinching, Delaney paid little attention to the continued excitement of those around him as he assumed his place in line. Allie frowned. For all his earlier kindness to her, Delaney Marsh was again cutting her out coldly, as if he regretted their previous exchanges.

A sudden nudge from behind pushed her forward, and Allie stumbled on the first step of the wooden staircase. She glared at Violet Marks as she tittered mockingly. Allie was acutely aware how difficult it sometimes was to remain "beautiful inside" when it came to that vain, annoying girl.

Gritting her teeth with new determination, Allie ascended the staircase.

* * *

The last, hearty refrains of "Come Ye Sinners, Poor and Needy" were still echoing in the unfamiliar church as Allie cast a nervous glance around its crowded interior. Having arrived early, Mr. Smith had seated the children in the front pews and then proceeded to lead them in a nonstop series of hymns. Turning to the rear, Allie was surprised to see teary eyes and the liberal use of handkerchiefs by some of the less controlled matrons as the vigorous singing came to an end.

But Allie did not join in the enthusiastic singing, nor was she touched by the refrains. Instead, she continued to study her surroundings with a small frown as the unfamiliar service progressed. She had never seen a church quite like this one before. Where were the beautiful colored-glass windows? Where was the holy water with which to bless herself when she entered? Where were the pictures on the wall—the beautiful scenes that brought to life the Bible stories Mama had read to her? Where was the altar with its crucifix, tall candles, and flowers? Where were the statues of the saints with their peaceful faces? Where were the small candles in glass cups, which Mama and she had lit to keep their prayers bright before God's eye? And where was the statue of the Lady with her arms raised in welcome? Kneeling beside Mama in church, Allie had never found it difficult to pray and to believe God heard the words she whispered to him, but here . . .

Allie gave a low, trembling sigh. It was different here. In this church the walls were white and bare, and no one knelt to pray. Nothing in this church was in the least familiar. She did not even know the hymns the others sang, and she was all the more lost for the comfort some of the others seemed to feel.

An abrupt movement in the front of the church drew Allie from her thoughts as a man who had earlier introduced himself as Reverend Martin called Mr. Smith up front and presented him to the congregation. Disconcerted, uncomfortable, Allie barely heard Mr. Smith's brief explanation of the aims of the Society and of its hope that this would be but the first of the groups of orphaned and abandoned children who would find homes in the West. She turned toward the sound of a few short sniffles in the rear, surprised to see some matrons openly crying. Her throat filled up and she resisted the desire to display a similar weakness. Instead, she drew herself to her feet with the rest of the children when directed by Mr. Smith, and followed him toward a large meeting room in the rear of the church.

Her heart pounding, Allie assumed a seat in the corner of the meeting room, relieved to have the attention of the congregation diverted by some of the more gregarious children. She sat erect, as Mama had taught her to do, her chin raised proudly, but somehow she could not make herself smile.

Swallowing tensely, Allie watched as a young couple approached little Roger. The man gently touched Roger's tousled yellow hair as his wife knelt beside the boy and started to speak. When Roger raised his clear blue eyes to her, the woman's face creased into a tearful smile that said more than words. The flushed young woman enfolded Roger in her arms and hugged him warmly. Allie knew instinctively there was not a possibility in the world that the smiling couple would leave without him.

She watched as the man spoke with Mr. Smith, who then said a few words to Roger. Within a few minutes, the papers were signed and Roger, no more than seven years old, left with his new family.

Then it was Violet Marks's turn. A slender red-haired woman approached Violet almost immediately after entering the room. She touched Violet's hair and whispered something to her, a small smile on her face. Allie was startled to see tears spring into Violet's eyes, and for the first time she felt a flash of warmth for the vain, selfish older girl. She supposed Violet would not be so annoying in a household with that red-haired woman and her smiling husband to love her.

And then it was Harry's turn . . . and Robert's. Gathering her courage, Allie finally looked toward the far corner where the older boys had gathered. As she had suspected, several serious-looking farmers were talking to Delaney. Her heart sinking, she looked away. She knew she would not be able to bear watching him leave.

And then it was Margaret's turn to go, and John's. Allie raised her chin a notch higher.

Unsmiling, Delaney answered yet another question posed to him by the tall, sober-faced farmer to his right. He was getting impatient, but he knew it behooved him to remain polite and respectful during the man's inquisition.

Eyeing the first farmer intently, Delaney attempted to see the man behind the full, sun-reddened face. Without a trace of conceit, Delaney had known it would not be difficult to find a family to take him in. The farmers were all looking for the same thing, cheap labor for their farms, and he had no quarrel with that as long as they upheld their part of the bargain. Delaney was also aware that he was exactly what most of them wanted. He was young and strong and of an age where he could be expected to pull the weight of a fully grown man. He was intelligent and had gotten a primary education beyond that of the average boy in their group. He also knew that he was good-looking, and he had taken pains to present a good appearance.

Unconsciously drawing his young, broad-shouldered frame up more stiffly, Delaney listened as the first farmer openly discussed him with Mr. Smith. He saw a flicker of doubt move across the man's florid face when prison was mentioned. The other farmers were cautiously watching the man's expression, and Delaney had no doubt that if he did not take him, the second or the third farmer would. He wasn't worried. He knew he could take care of himself wherever he ended up.

Delaney cast a surreptitious glance toward the opposite corner of the room. Milling couples momentarily blocked his view, and he felt a flash of impatience before a well-rounded farmer stepped to one side, giving him the view he sought. Sitting in the corner—totally ignored, her chin bravely raised as it had been since she entered the room—was Allie Pierce. An indefinable emotion tugged at Delaney's gut and he frowned. At an awkward stage, she was neither an appealing little girl, nor old enough to perform a woman's tasks on a farm, and she looked so frail. In this crowd of boisterous and active children, she was easily overlooked.

Suddenly noticing a couple linger near Allie, Delaney watched as the woman turned a hopeful glance back toward her husband, only to have the man shake his head and divert his wife's attention toward a dark-haired girl sitting nearby. The man's reaction did not go unnoticed by Allie. Delaney's stomach twisted painfully as Allie's proud chin rose a notch, her small mouth twitching revealingly.

Delaney turned his attention back to Mr. Smith as he started to speak.

"These gentlemen are interested in offering you a home, Delaney. I've informed them of your history, and they have a few questions to ask you. Do you have any objections to answering them?''

"No, sir."

The farmer with the high coloring addressed Delaney directly. "You're of an age my wife and I are looking for, boy, but I'm concerned about your history. I would like you to answer me truthfully. Do you intend to honor your contract if we agree to take you on?"

Delaney's lips tightened. "As well as you honor yours, sir."

The man's expression reflected his surprise at Delaney's response. "You're telling me that you think I may have come here today, with my wife and in the presence of these good people, to enter into a contract that I did not fully intend to honor? Are you accusing me of being dishonest, boy?"

"No more than you're accusing me, sir."

"I'm not accusing you, boy! I'm merely asking a question!"

"And I've answered it, sir."

His florid face flushing even more deeply, the farmer turned abruptly and walked away. Mr. Smith flashed an embarrassed glance toward the two men remaining.

"I'm sorry, gentlemen. I'm certain the boy didn't mean to offend. He merely responded as honestly as he could to Mr. Carlisle's question."

"You needn't apologize for the boy, Mr. Smith. I admire his forthright answer." Turning toward Delaney, the second farmer, a thin man with a deeply lined face and graying hair, extended his hand with a smile. "My name is Willard Grimsley. I have more room in my house and more work on my farm than I know what to do with. I have three children, and I'm looking to find a fourth here today." His smile broadening as Delaney accepted his hand with a firm shake, the man continued, "I don't intend to waste time asking you about your past. I figure you did what you had to do to get along. On my farm, I would expect you to do the same. My only thought would be to ask if we're what you've been looking for, boy, since this contract will be a two-way street. I'll be expecting you to answer that question as honestly as you can. But first, I'll tell you a little about us. My wife, Millicent, and I have been married for seventeen years and we own a farm that once was a part of the . . ."

Willard Grimsley's voice continued on in earnest recitation. Delaney listened with half his mind as the other half remained strangely distracted. His first thought was that this farmer appeared to be as fair a man as he could expect to find, but he had long ago learned the difficult lesson that appearances were deceiving, that an honest face and a steady eye often disguised a man of an entirely different type. He also knew he would get no guarantees with any contract entered into, and a choice would soon have to be made. This man appeared to be offering exactly the situation he had been looking for. He doubted he would get a better opportunity than this. He did not honestly think he could expect more.

Allie's thin shoulders twitched. She kept her gaze forward, intensely aware of the man who stood a few feet away. She had felt his eyes on her from the first moment he entered the room. She did not like the feeling, and she did not know why. The man was pleasant-looking and well dressed. His frock coat and matching trousers were as stylish as those of any of Mrs. Van Houten's callers. The fair-haired, noticeably younger woman standing at his side was well dressed, too, but she did not appear to be at ease.

The man came closer, moving cautiously through the crowded room and Allie felt her throat tighten. Within moments he was standing beside her chair.

"Stand up, child. Mrs. Crosley and I would like to get a better look at you."

Allie stood obediently, her eyes traveling up to the soft-spoken gentleman's face. His face was smooth and clean-shaven except for a narrow, well tended mustache. His features were fine, almost to the point of appearing feminine, and his thin lips were curved into a smile, but Allie felt none of its warmth. Instead, she was immobilized by his dark eyes, which appeared to dissect her as he touched her hair with his soft pink hands.

"It appears to me that she is exactly the girl we have been looking for, isn't she, Meridith, dear?"

Allie looked at the woman who stood slightly behind Mr. Crosley. She was startled by the anxiety apparent in the woman's expression before she averted her head and murmured, "Yes, she is, Albert."

"Look at *me*, child." The unexpected sharpness of the command snapped Allie's attention back to Mr. Crosley as he took a step closer. "That's better. Now turn around . . . yes, completely around."

Following the man's commands, Allie turned in a small circle, her pale face flooding a bright pink. She was embarrassed by the man's manner, and her skin crawled at his intense scrutiny.

"Ah, now I have embarrassed you, haven't I, dear? Well, you mustn't be shy. Mrs. Crosley and I came here today hoping against hope that there would be a child in this group who would appeal to us. You see, I first came into contact with my darling wife in much the same way."

At Allie's obvious confusion, Mr. Crosley's smooth face creased into a wider smile. "You see, the first Mrs. Crosley and I adopted Meridith seven years ago. My dear Patricia died a few years later. In the time following, Meridith grew into the fine young woman you see here today, and she is now my loving wife. She is so appreciative of the life that I have been able to give her that the moment she heard of your group's arrival, she expressed a desire to afford another child the same opportunity that was afforded her."

Pausing, Mr. Crosley ran his long, smooth fingers across Allie's cheek in a brief caress. "Ah, yes, I do find pale-haired children especially appealing." Cupping her chin, he raised it so that she could no longer avoid his eyes.

A chill passed down Allie's spine, and Stella's reference to her "lily-white skin" flitted across her mind. She drew back, repulsion whitening her small face even further.

"No, child, you mustn't be frightened. Meridith and I will provide you with a very good home. You are obviously intelligent. I saw that at first glance. Mr. Smith informed me of your name and background, and that you can read and cipher, and that is an added plus. I am a banker, you see, and a man in my position must have an intelligent family around him, a bright, obedient daughter whom he can train to reflect well upon him. You will have much to gain by becoming that daughter—the finest clothes, just as have been given to Meridith—and I will personally see to it that your education is continued in a vein suitable to the position you will hold in life. You cannot ask for more than that, can you, dear?"

Abruptly releasing her chin, Mr. Crosley reached down to take her firmly by the hand. "Come now. We'll find Mr. Smith and tell him we've made a match, shall we? And then Meridith and I will take you home."

Allie shook her head. An unexpected fear seemed to have frozen her throat, but she stepped back in protest and attempted to pull her hand free. A light flush moving over his delicate features, Mr. Crosley gripped her hand all the more tightly. His dark eyes held hers captive with their intensity.

"Come, Allie. You must not appear ungrateful. Mr. Smith will not understand your reluctance to come with us when we have so much to offer you. He might even be angry and punish you quite severely. Your attitude will also reflect on the other children, and the good people here may refuse to accept another group such as this because of your adverse behavior."

Allie pulled back more strongly, her frozen throat still refusing to allow words to pass, and Mr. Crosley whispered harshly, "I tell you now, girl. Persist in this contrary behavior and you will suffer the consequences. I do not intend to allow you to upset my plans . . . my dear wife's plans. You *will* come with us."

"No."

That single word escaping her throat, Allie attempted to withdraw her hand from Mr. Crosley's crushing grip without drawing the attention of those around her. She did not want to spoil things for the other children, but she would not go with this man.

A low hiss escaped Mr. Crosley's fine lips as he took a step closer, drawing her hand firmly against his side. "I am a very influential man in this community. I am sure you are not too young or too foolish to realize how I might affect your future and the future of your group if you persist in this behavior. You will come now, without further protest, and you will—"

"No, she won't."

Allie turned just as a heavy hand came down on Mr. Crosley's, breaking his grip on her wrist.

Delaney!

Allie stepped back. A hot flush covered Delaney's stiff features, contrasting vividly with the ice in his gaze. He took her hand and held it tight in his.

"Allie doesn't want to go with you. She has the right to refuse your offer."

Mr. Crosley's face became mottled with anger, and Allie backed up firmly against Delaney for support. Trembling, she remained silent as the banker hissed low in his throat, "But she does want to come with us, don't you, dear? Tell this fellow. *Tell* him!"

Delaney's color heightened as he turned toward Allie. "Yes, tell me what you want to do, Allie."

Her eyes darting to Mr. Crosley's livid face, Allie struggled to speak.

Realizing her difficulty, Delaney spoke again, his voice unexpectedly soft. "Allie, do you want to go with him?"

"I . . . I want to stay with you."

A low choking sound issuing from his throat, Mr. Crosley pulled himself sharply erect. Turning a brief, scorching glance in her direction, he took his silent wife's arm and ushered her stiffly toward the door without speaking another word.

Her eyes remaining fixed on the doorway long moments after the Crosleys' departure, Allie finally turned back toward Delaney. The hot color of a few minutes before had all but drained from his face, but he appeared even angrier than before.

"A smart girl like you should know you can't let people push you around, no matter how much they threaten. You're going to have to learn to speak up for yourself. I won't always be around to do it for you."

Confused, Allie shook her head. "Are you mad at me, Delaney?"

Delaney's stance remained stiff. His frown darkened as his eyes flicked over her face.

"No, I'm mad at myself for bothering with something that's none of my business." He paused, then continued harshly, "If you think the Lady is going to protect you, you're wrong. She's nothing more than an image carved on a piece of silver. She can't do anything for you that you won't do for yourself. If I hadn't interfered, that low-down bugger would have been dragging you out the door right now!"

Allie nodded. "I know."

Obviously surprised by her response, Delaney remained silent as she continued. "The Lady is nothing more than an image carved on a piece of silver—unless you trust her. I trust her, and she helped me."

"*She* helped you?"

"That's right. I prayed to the Lady, and just like Mama said, she sent my prayers into God's ear. And then God sent me a friend. He sent me you."

At her soft statement, Delaney's lean frame went suddenly stiff. His lips parted as if to speak but no sound came forth. Unexpectedly dropping her hand, he turned without another word and strode back to the two farmers.

Hot tears gathered in Allie's eyes as he deliberately turned his back. Swallowing with considerable difficulty, she sat down, stiffly erect as she studied the couples still mingling in the room. With the exception of a few who were talking to the older boys, it appeared they had all found a child to suit them. Nevertheless, about fifteen girls and a like number of boys were still without homes.

Allie brushed a strand of hair back from her face and clamped her lips tightly shut against their trembling. No matter what Delaney said, she knew the Lady was watching over her. She would go on with Mr. Smith and the rest of the children, and she would find a family to love her. The Lady would see to that, too. The Lady had already sent her Delaney, hadn't she? It didn't matter that he was presently angry for some reason and had turned his back on her. He was still her friend.

With that thought in mind, Allie raised her chin and blinked back the tears that were still threatening.

The church meeting room was silent except for the sound of shuffling feet. Disappointment inhibited conversation between the children remaining as the last of the congregation finally trailed away. Attempting to inject a note of hopefulness into the desolate glances turned his way, Mr. Smith raised his voice into the silence.

"All right, children, take your places in line. We have a very successful morning behind us. Many of our number have found homes, and tomorrow, before we take the train to the next stop, we may yet find homes for more. In time, you will all find a place to your liking."

His small eyes assessing the reception his words of encouragement had received, Mr. Smith mentally counted the heads in his greatly diminished flock. He nodded and turned to smile at Reverend Martin. "Our sincere appreciation, Reverend. You have truly done God's work this morning."

Pausing only to accept an invitation to a church supper that evening, Mr. Smith waved the children on. As they marched solemnly out of the church and back up the street toward the hotel, he tapped the broad shoulder of the boy in front of him.

Delaney turned at his touch.

"I feel it is my duty to speak seriously to you, Delaney. It is the conviction of the Society that none of our children should be placed in a home that is not to their liking, and I concur with that policy. I do not, however, sanction the actions of any of our group who sees fit to insult good people by turning down the offer of a home without true cause." Pausing so that his stern words might be absorbed, Mr. Smith studied Delaney's unreadable expression.

"You do realize how very fortunate you were, Delaney, that two men of superior reputation and circumstances offered to take you into their homes. Two, mind you—two! It is doubly impressive that both these men saw fit to put aside all thought of your history. And for that generosity of spirit, you rewarded both of them with a refusal to accept their offers. Delaney, I am incredulous at your lack of foresight as well as your ingratitude!"

Delaney's dark brows drew into a familiar frown.

"I refused, and they took someone else. What difference does it make?"

Mr. Smith's expression tightened.

"The difference is that you might have had reason to turn down one of those men, but to turn down both without even a word of appreciation or regret to either? Just what are you looking for, Delaney? I doubt you will find circumstances at any of the stops farther along the line that are any better than those you refused today."

Observing the boy closely, Mr. Smith noted the almost indiscernible tightening of Delaney's lips.

"The decision was mine, Mr. Smith. And I'll pay the consequences, won't I?"

"Yes, but—" The sobriety of Delaney Marsh's question halted Mr. Smith in midsentence. Suddenly realizing the futility of pursuing the subject, he shrugged. "All right, Delaney. I hope you know what you're doing."

Dismissing Delaney with a wave of his hand, Mr. Smith watched as the hard-eyed boy turned and walked toward the hotel. He knew what those farmers had seen in the boy. A keen intelligence was reflected in that boyishly handsome face, and there was strength in his slim, youthful frame and in shoulders already excessively broad for a fellow his age. But there was something else that Mr. Smith found difficult to pinpoint. Was it determination, ambition, a sense of purpose? Or was it plain ruthlessness? He had the feeling the boy had already committed himself to something, but he had no idea what it was.

Shrugging his narrow shoulders once more, Mr. Smith raised his hand as the first of his charges reached the front steps of the American House.

"Stop here, children!"

Delaney Marsh dismissed from his mind in the presence of more pressing matters, Mr. Smith hurried forward.

As he caught up with the others, Delaney gave a short, harsh laugh. Mr. Smith had said he was incredulous that he had turned down offers from both those farmers. Well, he was incredulous, too. He supposed it was ironic that his antagonist, Sam, had been offered and had taken the contract that Farmer Grimsley had first proposed to Delaney. As far as the other farmer was concerned, he had never considered his offer for a minute.

He had counted—sixteen from their group had gone off to their new homes. As it turned out, that number had come mainly from the ranks of the oldest and the youngest in their party.

Delaney felt a surge of anger. Damn that Allie Pierce! She had no right to look at him the way she did, burdening him with her trust. She was a stupid, gullible little girl who still believed in fairy tales. Well, she had made a mistake when she had included him in them. She had no right.

Getting a glimpse of a small, pale head midway down the line, Delaney gave a low snort. Her mother, whoever she was, had done the girl a real disservice, but the harsh realities of life would soon wipe all that foolishness about "the Lady" from her mind. Admittedly, he had made a mistake, too, encouraging the girl with his medal, but it had all seemed harmless at the time.

Delaney's well-drawn lips twitched in annoyance. Well, he had learned two things the hard way, the way he had learned everything else in his life. The first thing was that he was not helping the girl or himself by putting off the inevitable. The girl would have to face the truth about "the Lady" sooner or later.

The second thing he had learned was that he was not as smart as he thought he was. He had forgotten the basic rule that had helped him to survive in a hard world: Survival was for the smartest, the strongest, the fastest—the man who put himself first. He had turned down Farmer Grimsley's offer today, but he would not make the same stupid mistake again. The girl was Mr. Smith's responsibility.

The pale head midway down the line turned unexpectedly in his direction. He frowned as he looked at the small face dominated by those intense brown eyes, and the small head snapped forward once more as the line began moving up the steps to the hotel.

Mr. Smith began an earnest conversation with the proprietor, who met him at the door. Within moments the line was moving inside the hotel, with Mr. Smith in the lead. Allie Pierce, however, remained stationary while the other children filed past her. When Delaney came abreast of her, she turned in his direction.

His disagreeable stare caused a momentary dimming of the girl's tentative smile. Obviously unwilling to be overheard by the others as a few curious heads turned their way, she whispered softly, "I'm sorry those farmers took Sam and Tucker instead of you, Delaney, but you'll find someplace better tomorrow."

It came to Delaney with a start that the girl thought *he* had been rejected, not the reverse! He would have laughed and set her straight, but he was afraid the truth might encourage her. Instead, only too keenly aware that it was time for Allie Pierce to learn a hard lesson, he turned away from her with great deliberation and, without a word, walked into the hotel.

Vastly relieved to find the old Delaney Marsh was not completely lost to him, Delaney walked into the dining room and assumed his place at the table.

chapter

four

THE DISAGREEABLE SOUNDS—the harsh clicking and scraping of the wheels on the railway tracks, the jolting of the car as it sped through the darkened countryside, the whistle's screech punctuating the long night hours while Allie attempted to sleep— were finally drawing to an end. Despite the discomforts, she was not eager to reach their destination.

The bright light of dawn had crept through the windows of their rail car almost an hour earlier, and Allie had pulled her blanket up higher on her shoulders in an attempt to shield herself from the growing light. Their accommodations on this train far surpassed those of the immigrant train that had carried them from Albany to Buffalo, but she had little thought for the comfort of the cushioned seat on which she slept. Instead, the first sliver of dawn had reawakened a familiar apprehension.

There were thirty children left in their party, and Mr. Smith had solemnly promised them the previous night that he would not return to New York until each and every one of them had found a home. That thought brought Allie little consolation. She knew there would be countless towns where strangers would compare and assess—and find her lacking. Would there be another Mr. Crosley waiting at one of those stops? More frightening still was the realization that Mr. Smith had been unaware of Mr. Crosley's manner with her. He had been too busy with other couples to see. Only Delaney had noticed. Only Delaney had come to help her.

Feeling queasy, Allie closed her eyes and took a deep breath. Shamefacedly, she realized that despite the sympathy she had expressed, she was actually glad those farmers had decided to take other boys instead of Delaney. She was being foolish, too, for he would surely be one of the first to find a new home at the next stop. Even if he was not, he had gone to great pains to impress upon her that he did not want to be bothered with her anymore.

Maybe that was her punishment for being so selfish. Or maybe Delaney was right, and all this had nothing to do with the Lady. Maybe he had just taken pity on her and now all his pity was used up. Maybe it had just been wishful thinking that the Lady had sent her a friend.

But Allie knew that she could not hold back the dawn of a new day and everything it would bring. When the train drew up to the next stop, she would have no choice but to follow Mr. Smith with the rest of the children.

With that thought, Allie squeezed her eyes tightly closed and tried to sleep. For the time being, she would think no more.

The sunlit car was screeching to a slow, grinding halt when Allie joined the other children at the windows and peered out at the crowded platform. Her heart pounding, she shot a quick glance toward Mr. Smith as he raised his voice over the eardrum-piercing din.

"Look, children, there is Reverend Masters." His smile broadening at his first glimpse of the group of adults standing behind the young minister on the platform, Mr. Smith continued with great conviction, "Many of you are close to finding your new homes at this very minute."

Mr. Smith's enthusiastic words set the mood for their group and an excited buzzing ensued among the girls surrounding Allie, accompanied by many valiant attempts to smooth wrinkled clothes and tousled hair. But Allie's trembling fingers refused to

Elaine Barbieri

cooperate, and she was only too aware that her own efforts at
hasty grooming proved useless.

A slow trembling began in her limbs as the train drew to a
full halt and Allie's mouth suddenly went dry. She glanced outside again as the line in front of her began moving toward the
door, panicking as the crowd behind the young minister appeared to have grown even larger. She could feel their eyes upon
her. She willed her feet to move, but her frozen limbs would not
obey her command. At that moment Allie realized that for all
her brave intentions, she could not do it.

She could not move.

"Hurry up, Allie, Mr. Smith is waiting." Elizabeth's low
entreaty was unsuccessful in freeing Allie's lifeless limbs. With
a low sound of disgust, Elizabeth pushed her aside to follow the
quickly moving line as she hissed, "Mr. Smith is going to be
mad."

The end of the line was trailing past and Allie glanced up in
desperation as Delaney Marsh's broad-shouldered figure came
abreast of her. Her heart dropped to her toes as Delaney continued on without a glance and followed the rest of the group out
onto the platform.

Within a few moments, Mr. Smith's thin face was pressed
against the window of the car as he spoke with controlled impatience.

"Allie, we are waiting."

They were all looking at her, staring into the car in an attempt
to determine the cause for her delay. They were frowning. She felt
their disapproval and again willed herself to move, but she could
not.

Through her despair, the faint voice of reason sounded in the
back of her mind. Where were her courage and faith? Had the
Lady really forsaken her, or had she forsaken the Lady?

Beset by confusion, Allie closed her eyes. "Lady, I need your
help," she murmured. "I'm afraid. Please whisper into God's
ear for me."

Familiar words came to her mind and she recited silently,
"Hail Mary, full of grace, the Lord is with thee. Blessed are
thou amongst women—"

"Come on, Allie."

A familiar voice interrupted Allie's prayer and she knew whose face she would see when she opened her eyes. The Lady had heard her prayer and had acted to dispel her doubts once and for all. She was ashamed that she had doubted the Lady even for a minute. She would never, never doubt her again.

A small smile twitching at her pale lips, Allie extended her hand toward the one Delaney held out to her. The warmth that had fled her body returned as Delaney's callused palm touched hers. Her heart joyful, she turned to follow Delaney's lead, silent words of gratitude filling her mind. Thank you, Lady. Oh, thank you for giving me back my friend.

Mr. Smith smiled approvingly as the milling couples in the church meeting room began approaching the children of their choice. His keen eye appraised the conversation under way between children and adults, and satisfaction moved warmly through him. Oh, yes, Reverend Masters had brought him an extremely receptive group. He had no doubt that the number of his charges would be cut at least in half by the time the day was out.

Mr. Smith's appraising glance continued to skim the crowd, abruptly drawing to a halt as his graying brows merged into a frown. While he watched, Delaney Marsh, his expression grim, responded to the short, well-dressed farmer who had addressed him. The farmer expressed surprise and glanced down at Allie Pierce, who had not left the boy's side from the time Delaney had, startlingly, taken it upon himself to help her overcome her reluctance to leave the railway car.

Shaking his head, the farmer then turned toward another older boy, and Mr. Smith felt a familiar annoyance. Realizing that it was neither the time nor the place to address that annoyance, he put it aside. He would look into the situation later, and he would get to the bottom of it, once and for all.

Delaney sensed, rather than felt, the inner trembling of the young girl at his side, and a familiar anger assailed him. As he had expected, he was one of the first in the group to be offered a home. His second conversation had produced the same result as the first, and he was once again waiting.

Delaney looked at the top of Allie Pierce's pale head as she stood silently beside him. She had not said a word since he had led her out of the train. She had self-consciously dropped his hand when they stepped down on the platform, but she had continued to walk beside him as they approached the church. Her chin high, her face composed, she had not budged from his side in the time since.

Strangely, he did not remember making a conscious decision to go back into the car to get Allie. Even now, he was a bit incredulous at his actions, which contradicted his decision of the night before. But somehow, watching Allie Pierce learn her hard lessons, one after the other, caused him more pain than he was willing to bear.

Allie's desperation had been obvious to him from the moment they pulled into the crowded station; he had seen it in the tensing of her limbs, her sudden pallor. With fierce determination, he had ignored her silent plea as he had walked past her, but those steps had been costly. He was still uncertain whether he had finally gone back into the car to relieve her distress or his own.

He had continued to surprise himself. When approached in the church hall, his response to inquiries had been a question that had been startling even to his own ears: "Are you willing to take both of us?"

The prospective parents had not been willing.

It occurred to Delaney that, for the first time in recent memory, he was putting someone else's welfare before his own. What was more, he was acting in contradiction to his own rule of survival. It also occurred to him that somewhere along the line he would probably pay for his stupidity. Well, it would not be the first time. The only thing he was certain of right now was that he was at ease with his feelings for the first time since Allie Pierce had clutched his medal and given him her trust.

Delaney's frown darkened. Yes, he would probably pay for this some day, and very dearly.

Allie stood silently beside Delaney in the church hall. She had seen several children walk off with smiling couples and had heard some of the older boys voicing agreement to proposed contracts. She did not want to acknowledge, even to herself, that Delaney had turned down two offers because those offers had not included her. The realization that she was selfishly allowing Delaney to make that sacrifice for her nagged viciously at her mind. Even more vicious, however, was the prospect of being alone again.

The persistent feeling she was being watched suddenly turned Allie from her thoughts to scan the crowd in the small room. It did not take long for her to see that a small woman standing a few feet away was studying her intently. Strangely, the woman's gaze did not discomfort her in any way. Her gray eyes were comforting, and Allie responded with a small, hesitant smile.

The woman did not approach her, allowing Allie the time to study her in return, and it occurred to Allie that the woman did not look at all well. She was very thin and pale, and when she raised her hand to the man standing beside her, it trembled weakly. The concern in the burly fellow's expression seemed to confirm her suspicion, and Allie remembered Mama during those last days before she left her forever.

Determined to put those unhappy thoughts behind her, Allie looked at the other two in the woman's party—a pretty, dark-haired adolescent girl and a boy several years older. Allie guessed they were brother and sister, and since they both resembled the burly fellow, she concluded they were a family.

The woman smiled in her direction, and Allie felt the warmth of that smile glow within her. Abruptly, the woman turned toward the man at her side. Her whispered remark made him glance in Allie's direction. Then he gave a short negative shake of his head.

Allie flushed and stepped to one side, unintentionally bringing herself up against Delaney's arm. He looked down at her, and she knew he had missed little of the disagreement progressing between the sweet woman and her reluctant husband.

Her attention diverted by Delaney, Allie was not prepared for the warmth of the sweet face looking down into hers as the woman suddenly appeared beside her.

"I think it is time we became acquainted, my dear. My name is Margaret Case." Turning slightly, she continued. "This is my husband, Jacob Case, my daughter, Sarah, and my son, James. Now, may I ask your name?"

Allie's voice was just above a whisper. "Allie, ma'am. Allie Pierce."

"Allie dear . . ." Pausing as her eyes filled with tears, Mrs. Case attempted a smile. "Mr. Case and I came here today for a very special reason. You see, my youngest child, Annie, and I were stricken with the fever several months ago. I was fortunate enough to recover, but my poor Annie was not. It occurred to me that the Lord would not have taken dear Annie without a specific purpose in mind, and when I heard that your group was coming to town, I hoped I had found that reason.

"I spent a long time walking about this room, Allie. There are many lovely girls here, but my heart did not call out to them. You weren't standing with the rest of them, and I momentarily despaired. But then I saw you." Her gray eyes moistening further, Mrs. Case whispered in a breaking voice, "My heart called out to you, dear. Mr. Case and I would very much like you to join our family if you are willing."

Her own eyes filling, Allie was unable to speak. In the time since she had lost Mama, no other woman had touched her heart in the same way this frail lady did.

A movement at her side alerted Allie to Delaney's stiff posture. She glanced up, for a brief moment catching and holding his narrowed gaze. Yes, this woman touched her, but not in the same way Delaney had touched her. Her feelings for Delaney were different. With Delaney she felt a kinship—a bond. He was special to her, and he had a special place in her heart.

Allie slid her hand into Delaney's. There was a moment's hesitation before his hand closed around hers, and taking a determined breath, Allie responded, "Will you take both of us, ma'am?"

"Both?" Obviously startled, the woman glanced toward Delaney. "Is this boy your brother?"

"No, ma'am. He's my friend."

"Your friend—and you will not part from him?"

"No, ma'am."

Delaney's hand tightened around hers, and its warmth gave Allie strength as the woman turned again to her husband.

"Jacob, if we had another hand we could plow the north field."

Her husband shook his head, frowning. "I wasn't expecting to plow that field for another year, Margaret."

"We could plow it a year earlier. We're both getting older, dear. We don't have much time to waste, and another strong arm will help."

"It'll also mean another person to feed and clothe."

"Jacob, we have more than enough."

At a sound to their left, they turned their attention to Mr. Smith as he extended his hand toward the uncertain farmer.

"If I may be of help, sir. My name is Smith. It is my pleasure to have brought these children here."

Jacob Case accepted Mr. Smith's hand and introduced himself. "It was our intention to come here today and take one of your group, Mr. Smith. We did not intend to take two."

"Two? We are placing one child at a time, sir."

"But the girl will not come unless we take the boy."

Glancing down at Allie in surprise, Mr. Smith raised his brow. "Is that so, Allie?"

Allie felt Delaney's warmth at her back as she moved closer to him. Her reply was soft, but firm. "Yes, Mr. Smith."

"And you, Delaney?"

There was a long, silent moment before Delaney gave a short nod.

His expression revealing his astonishment at Delaney's response, Mr. Smith shook his head. "I admit to being surprised at this. These children are related by neither blood nor circumstance and to my knowledge have nothing in common except the venture on which our group has embarked. However, it is the policy of the Society not to allow a child to be taken into a home without his or her consent. Since it appears neither will give consent without the other . . ." Mr. Smith's voice trailed away as he raised his shoulders in a shrug. "But before you make any decisions, there are some things you should know in the way of background information."

Mrs. Case's voice was soft as she replied. "We care very little about background, Mr. Smith."

"Of course. But if you will be so kind as to oblige me. Mr. Case?"

Taking Mr. Case's well-muscled arm, Mr. Smith drew him a few steps away and began talking in earnest. Allie's stomach tightened, but her discomfort was not for herself. She remembered Delaney's rage at Sam's name-calling, and she felt his anger rise as Mr. Case glanced sharply in his direction and then rejoined their group. Directing his words to Mrs. Case, he spoke gently. "Margaret dear, I'm afraid I'm forced to disappoint you. We cannot take these children."

Obviously confused, Mrs. Case searched her husband's expression. "I don't know what this gentleman said, but I tell you now, Jacob, nothing will shake my conviction that Allie is the child the Lord meant for us. And if she is determined not to accept us without our accepting her friend also, I can only think the Lord meant him for us, too."

Mr. Case's voice dropped a notch lower. "Margaret, you don't understand."

Delaney spoke up clearly. "Your husband is trying to tell you, ma'am, that I was released from prison to join this party, and he does not want a prison boy in his home."

Mrs. Case's surprise was evident. She was silent as she glanced toward her husband. Reading confirmation of Delaney's statement in the senior Case's face, she turned back to Delaney once more. "And what are your thoughts, Delaney? Do you feel you would be out of place with us?"

Delaney responded in his low, young-man's voice. "It was in prison that I was out of place, ma'am. I didn't belong there. I don't make excuses for myself, ma'am, or apologies, but whether I go with you or with someone else, I'll never go back to prison or to my old ways again. I've set my mind to that—and to much more."

Mrs. Case paused. "You have set yourself a goal in life, then?"

"I have, ma'am."

"May I be privileged to know what that goal is?"

"I'm sorry, no, ma'am."

Low gasps indicated to Allie that the others considered Delaney's response insolent, but Mrs. Case merely smiled.

"No, *I'm* sorry, Delaney. That question was an intrusion on your privacy. I hope someday you'll trust me enough to confide in me."

"Margaret . . ."

Margaret Case turned toward her husband, her smile bright with conviction. "Jacob, these are the children we came for. Please, let us conclude this discussion and take them home. I find I am tiring."

Appearing to note his wife's pallor for the first time, Jacob

Case turned toward Delaney. "I will ask you one question, boy: Do you intend to honor your contract with us and to deal with us honestly?"

Allie felt Delaney stiffen. His frown did not soften as he held the man's eye. "As honestly as you will deal with us, sir."

"Jacob dear, do let us go home—*all* of us."

Appearing to consider Mrs. Case's soft request for a moment, Mr. Case turned finally to Mr. Smith. "My wife is tired, sir. Might we get the paperwork out of the way?"

Allie did not hear the remainder of Mr. Case's remarks. Enfolded in Mrs. Case's warm arms, she briefly shut her eyes, closing out all else but her joy. Stepping back a moment later, she watched as Mr. Case extended his hand to Delaney. He accepted it and shook it firmly, but she did not miss James Case's harsh expression or the peculiar fascination with which young Sarah Case stared at Delaney.

Taking Delaney's hand once more, Allie experienced a surge of untarnished joy. She had a home, and she had a friend. Could she ask for more?

chapter

five

THE WAGON RATTLED along the deeply rutted road as Allie and Delaney progressed toward their new home. Low clouds of dust settled a gritty residue on the silent travelers as they continued steadily forward, but Delaney was unconscious of discomfort. He glanced toward Allie, seated beside him on the wooden flatbed. Exposure to the afternoon sun was beginning to cause a small strip of pink under her eyes and across the bridge of her nose. It was the only color in her face.

Intent on the passing countryside, Allie was not aware of his gaze, and Delaney turned his attention to the other occupants of the slow-moving conveyance. Mr. and Mrs. Case and their daughter were seated up front and had been silent for most of the ride, but he had been suffering hostile glances from James Case, who rode his mount beside the wagon, since they had started out. It occurred to him that his future within this family was going to be much bumpier than the road they presently traveled. He also recognized that things would probably be far different if he had not put himself in the position where he had been offered a home merely because of a little girl's attachment to him.

He was still uncertain when he realized that he could not

abandon Allie. Perhaps he felt he owed this all to the memory of his father before drink had changed him, or to Allie's dead mother, whoever she was, or to the Delaney Marsh who no longer existed. The only thing of which he was certain, was that there had to be a place in the world for Allie's trusting innocence, regardless of how temporary it might be. He was determined to see that it was not taken from her as harshly as had all else in her life.

Acknowledging that determination for the first time, Delaney turned toward Allie once more. He noted her fascination with the rolling land through which they traveled, just beginning to take on the colors of fall, and her rapt attention to the house just coming into sight in the distance, the first they had seen in over an hour. Wonder, anticipation, apprehension, and a touch of uncertainty moved across her small face, and Delaney's frown darkened. She was too open, too vulnerable.

As he watched, Allie looked quickly at James Case. Catching the young man's eye, she offered him a tentative smile. His expression hardening, James Case turned and urged his horse forward, totally ignoring her.

Managing to control his anger at the intentional slight, Delaney quickly averted his gaze. Out of the corner of his eye, he saw Allie turn toward him as he had expected she would, her color high. She seemed relieved that he had not witnessed her embarrassment, and then turned back to the passing landscape, but Delaney did not dismiss the deliberate cut as easily as Allie apparently had. As he had done many times in the past, he stored the incident in the back of his mind until an opportunity to even the score presented itself. Delaney was very good at evening scores.

Movement from the front seat of the wagon diverted Delaney's attention in time to see Mrs. Case turn a warm glance toward both passengers in the rear. She pointed at the house just coming into sight.

"Over there—that's our house. We're on Case land now, children. You'll both be home soon."

Mrs. Case flashed Allie an encouraging smile, and Delaney saw Allie's face flush again, this time with pleasure. She turned toward him a moment later, anticipation bright in her eyes. He wished he could tell her not to expect too much, that people often were not as good as they pretended to be. He wished he could tell her that she would never find a home like the one she'd had before, that no one would ever love her again like the mother she remembered, that for all this family's good intentions they would probably never truly accept either one of them as their own.

Delaney was only too aware of those hard facts of life, and he accepted them. He had never expected more than to be housed and fed in exchange for an honest day's work, and he had no illusions. But he knew that this little girl with pale hair and lost eyes silently hoped for something that would never be.

Annoyed with the direction his thoughts were taking, Delaney brought them to a halt and fastened his gaze on the house in the slowly diminishing distance. Neither the facts of life nor the inevitable could be changed, and in the end little Allie would learn that, too.

With the abrupt recognition that this reality was the crux of his torment, Delaney took a deep breath and stared resolutely toward the horizon.

Allie attempted to control her rising anticipation. She sent a short glance toward Delaney as the wagon made the last turn and began a direct approach to the house. She had been unable to take her eyes from the small structure since Mrs. Case had pointed it out in the distance. Now, at closer range, welcome seemed to be written in its low, comfortable lines, the broad porch in front, and the gingham curtains at the clean bright windows.

Oh, the house was small, to be sure, and it was not as impressive as Mrs. Van Houten's New York residence, but it reflected clearly the personality of the small woman who had made it a home. In that way it was almost pleasantly familiar, and Allie was grateful.

Her eyes quickly scanning the area as the wagon drew closer, Allie noted a small garden barely visible at the rear of the house and a large, well-kept barn a short distance away. Several small coops stood on a rise beyond the barn. Around them chickens pecked at the ground.

An unpleasant memory returned. It had been her daily duty to feed the chickens and to collect eggs from the coops that stood a respectable distance behind Mrs. Van Houten's residence. It had been a difficult task, with the irritable, protective hens sometimes unwilling to allow her near their nests, but she had neither given up nor complained. Her diligence had never earned her as much as a smile from the impatient, ill-tempered Mrs. Van Houten, but her satisfaction had come in helping to alleviate the heavy burden of chores Mama performed. Mama's appreciation had been enough.

Purposefully drawing her mind from bittersweet memories of the past, Allie forced a smile. She was pleased she was experienced at some of the chores that would be expected of her. She sewed a very fine stitch, and with a little instruction, she was certain she would be able to help out with the mending. She had often worked with Mama and was well acquainted with cleaning and polishing. Cook had also taken a fancy to her and had taught her to make really fine biscuits. Cook had promised to teach her to bake pies, too, but before then they had been forced to leave.

Taking a deep, determined breath, Allie raised her chin. She was certain she would learn quickly here. She was older and smarter in many ways, and she would not allow minutes to slip away as she had in the past, when she had believed the good days were in no danger of coming to an end.

Determinedly, Allie directed her attention to the fields with their narrow cultivated rows, the orchards a short distance away, the cows moving out of sight behind the barn. A small gray cat walked across the porch, its tail raised high in welcome as it rubbed against the railing. She could almost hear it purring, and a small sound of delight escaped Allie's lips. She had had a kitten of her own when she lived at Mrs. Van Houten's house, but Mrs. Van Houten had not allowed her to take it with her when Mama and she had left so hurriedly.

Bringing another disagreeable memory to a halt, Allie turned toward Delaney. He had been silent for the duration of the ride. She could tell by the expression on his face that he was deep in thought, and she respected that silence. But she was certain Delaney did not suffer the doubts and uncertainties that tormented her. She knew Delaney was strong and confident, and would always be able to do exactly what he expected of himself.

Allie also knew Delaney's frown and chilling eyes hid unexpected kindness. She was aware not many others were allowed to glimpse that part of Delaney, and she was supremely grateful to the Lady for having revealed that quality to her.

The wagon was drawing to a halt and Mr. Case turned to whisper to his wife. Allie could not hear his words, but she saw Sarah's head turn sharply in Delaney's direction. Mr. Case stepped down from the wagon and lifted his wife to the ground with utmost care. He was turning to lift his daughter down as well when Delaney slipped to the back of the wagon and stepped down.

Allie followed Delaney's lead. Scrambling to the back of the wagon, she jumped to the ground. Landing rather unsteadily, she shot Delaney a sheepish glance and turned to retrieve her blanket and Bible. She noted the ease with which Delaney reached over her head and snatched up his belongings, tucking them under his arm as he turned to Mrs. Case's summons.

"Allie, Delaney, please come here."

Her small features reflecting even more clearly than before a fragile beauty faded by years and illness, Mrs. Case beckoned her family forward also, her eyes suspiciously bright. Her voice quivered with emotion as she took Allie's and Delaney's hands in her own.

"With my family around me, children, I want to welcome you to your new home. I want you both to remember that you are a part of this family now, as truly as if you were born into it. The Lord has acted in your coming to us, and his will be done. I know that no one can ever replace your own parents in your minds, but it is my wish that you will call me Mother Case from this moment on as, in my heart and mind, I will call you daughter and son. Is that agreeable, dears?"

Her heart too filled to respond, Allie nodded briefly. Shooting a short glance toward Delaney, she saw his frown had softened, and her heart was warmed. Mother Case had touched him, also, and she was glad.

Allie's and Delaney's acquiescence brightened the damp glitter in Mrs. Case's eyes. Leaning down, she kissed Allie lightly. It occurred to Allie as the sweet woman's lips touched her cheek that she was the first person to kiss her since Mama died. She had not realized how very much she had missed that small gesture of love.

A similar gesture was not as easily accomplished with Delaney because of his height, and Mother Case swayed as she stood on tiptoe. Delaney reached out to steady her, and a small laugh escaped Mother Case's lips.

"I shall have to practice if I expect to do this again, but right now, Delaney, may I prevail upon you to lean down so that I might kiss your cheek?"

Delaney wordlessly accommodated Mrs. Case. The smiling woman's lips touched Delaney's cheek, and Allie was struck with the feeling that the kiss had touched her own cheek as well. Obviously pleased, Mother Case then turned and took Allie's hand. Smoothing back a flying wisp of pale hair from Allie's damp cheek, she smiled down into her eyes.

"Now I see why you were reluctant to part from this fellow, Allie. He is a dear boy, and it is no wonder that you love him. But now I think it would be best for us to leave and allow Delaney to become acquainted with Papa Case and James. It's time to attend to women's work."

Mother Case turned toward her daughter. "A ham from the smokehouse should do, Sarah. Allie and I will gather some greens from the garden."

Uncertainty touched Allie as she was forced to part from Delaney for the first time. Her short, anxious glance did not go unnoted by Mrs. Case.

"Delaney is a capable fellow, Allie. I am sure he doesn't need you right now. Shall we leave him to become acquainted with the men? They have much to learn about each other, just as do you, Sarah, and I."

Allie cast an apologetic glance toward Delaney before shaking her head with a soft reply that came straight from the heart. "It isn't Delaney who needed me. *I* needed him."

Mrs. Case's response was a smile touched with emotion as she met Delaney's sober glance. "An excellent testimonial, indeed, Delaney."

Observing that Delaney's silent reassurance freed Allie to follow her with full confidence, Mrs. Case urged Allie toward the house. "We have much to talk about, Allie, but for now we'll just enjoy the fact that we are a family."

"I'll take care of the wagon, Pa."

James's harsh tone drew Delaney's attention away from Allie

and Mrs. Case as they disappeared into the house. His mouth tightening, Delaney turned slowly toward the sandy-haired young man. It didn't take much to see that Margaret Case's sentiments were not echoed by the male members of her household.

The thought struck Delaney as he glimpsed James's stiff demeanor that Mrs. Case and Allie were probably the only two who were satisfied with the situation. He hadn't been able to strike from his mind the expression on Allie's face the moment she saw Mrs. Case. A strange emotion had touched him when Allie's tension had lessened in a way only his presence had previously been able to accomplish. Allie was as happy as he had ever seen her, and he was going to make sure that resentment within the family did not threaten that happiness.

Mr. Case frowned as he responded to his son's offer with a negative shake of the head. "No, James, I'll take care of the horses. This old mare is having problems with her leg again and I think I should attend to her."

"All right, Pa." Shooting a sharp glance at Delaney, James secured his horse's reins to the back of the wagon. "I'll show this fella around."

Delaney suspected that James intended to do more than show him the farm, but he fell into step behind the older boy anyway. He wasn't worried; he had no doubt he was up to anything Case had in mind.

James's step quickened and Delaney followed suit. He noted with satisfaction that a few years and an inch or so in height were the only advantages James Case held over him, for in direct contrast to his father's almost corpulent physique, James was thin. In muscle tone and breadth of shoulder, Delaney was superior, and Delaney had no doubt the same held true for his knowledge of self-defense. He seldom lost a fight. He was ready to face James Case with his fists if it came to that, and instinct told him that it would come to that sooner or later.

But, for the first time in his life, Delaney hoped he would be able to avoid such a confrontation. He recalled Allie's anxious glance before she had followed Mrs. Case into the house. She was depending on him to ease her into this new home. A fight with his new "brother" a few minutes after his arrival would do little toward that end.

When their rapid pace had taken them a distance from both

the house and the barn, James turned unexpectedly. Halting abruptly, Delaney shifted his weight, settling it evenly on his feet as he unconsciously braced himself for an assault. His hands curled slightly as James spoke, his narrowed gaze raking his face. "You're a cunning bastard, aren't you?"

Anger tightened his waiting fists as Delaney responded in a low voice. "Let's get one thing straight, right from the start." His light eyes cold as ice, he continued with a thread of menace, "I don't like being called names. I'm not a bastard any more than you are, and unless you're looking for trouble, you'd better remember that."

"I'm not taking orders from you, prison boy! I heard everything the chaperon told my father about you. You're trouble! You came from prison, and you were a problem from the minute you joined that group of orphans he brought here. Smith said he thought you had good things in you, that the right home would make the difference, but you and I know better, don't we, prison boy?"

"I told you I don't like being called names."

Ignoring his comment, James continued hotly, "Don't think Pa and I aren't wise to you. You had trouble getting placed, didn't you? So you latched on to that little girl and told her you'd protect her. You figured some soft-hearted lady like my mother would feel sorry for her and take you along as part of the deal. Only you didn't figure on somebody like my Pa and me being in on it. My Pa and I aren't stupid, and if it wasn't for my mother being so sick, and her heart being broken by little Annie's passing, my Pa never would have agreed to take an orphan in the first place.

"But that doesn't mean you're going to get away with anything here, and I'm telling you right now, *don't even try*. I saw you take my mother's arm. You keep your hands off her! She doesn't need your help. Any help my mother needs, she'll get from Pa or me. And while I'm about it, I'm telling you to keep your hands off my sister, too. Pa and I will be watching you every minute."

His anger at James's unwarranted attack barely under control, Delaney responded slowly, "Your father agreed to a contract that says I get room and board in exchange for work on this farm until I'm eighteen years old."

"And that contract also says if you turn out to be trouble, you go back to where you came from. Understand?"

His control beginning to slip, Delaney unconsciously squared his stance more firmly. His fists tightened. "I'm not going back anywhere."

"Then you'd better be all my mother is expecting."

"And while we're talking about what we're expecting, I'll tell you what I expect. I don't expect to listen to any red-faced country boy telling me what to do."

James Case's face turned a true red, and he took a threatening step forward, only to be halted by a deep voice. "That's enough, James!"

Jacob Case's sharp admonition alerted both young men to his unexpected appearance.

"I was just telling this prison boy—"

"I said that's enough!"

Taking a few long strides closer, Jacob Case waited until his son's thin lips snapped tightly shut before turning toward Delaney. His eyes searched Delaney's unrevealing expression, holding his frigid gaze for long seconds before he spoke again.

"I haven't said much to you, and I suppose I'm to blame for letting James get to you before I could set the matter straight for both of you. Well, here's the truth of the situation, boy. James was right when he said none of us, including Sarah, was in favor of taking an orphan into our home. It was too close to our losing Annie and we . . ." His lined face twitching revealingly for a silent second, Mr. Case swallowed and continued with a new firmness, "And we were against taking you along with the girl. We didn't want one orphan, much less two, and a boy with a bad record at that.

"But I want you to know this, boy, here and now." Turning, Mr. Case directed a brief, meaningful look into his son's tight face. "Now that you're here, we expect to fulfill that contract we signed. We'll treat you like one of the family as far as working and eating and everyday living is concerned. And as far as schooling, well, that's up to you. Nobody can make another fella learn, and that's the truth of it." Jacob Case paused for a deep breath. "But you're a member of the family now and we—"

"Pa, you're making a mistake if you get soft with this one!"

"James, we made a bargain, and we'll keep it. Now that's the finish! We'll forget the bad blood between you two and we'll go on from there. I don't expect anything like this to happen again, understand?''

"Pa—"

"Do you understand, James?"

His fair face flushing, James hesitated only a moment before giving a short, jerking nod in response.

Turning so that his narrowed gaze touched on Delaney's stiff face, Jacob Case continued. "Just a simple word of warning, boy. Mrs. Case is a good woman, and I'll not stand for you or anybody taking advantage of her. It's also my thought that the girl will follow your lead. She looks at you like you're one step down from God. She trusts you. I'll be expecting you to be worthy of that trust and not lead her astray."

Delaney's unrevealing facade cracked.

"How I treat Allie is my business! And while we're setting things straight, I have something else to say: The way you treat Allie is my business, too."

His eyes narrowing into slits, Mr. Case assessed Delaney's anger, openly revealed for the first time.

"All right, I suppose you have a right to make yourself clear. I'll answer you by saying I hear you. Now I want to know if you heard me, too."

His cheek ticking tensely, Delaney nodded.

"All right. As far as I'm concerned, all's been said that need be said." Jacob Case turned to his son. "I'm thinking you should go back and take care of the horses and the wagon after all, James. I'll take Delaney around the farm. I'll see you back in the house when your ma calls us for supper."

His expression tight, James strode away without another word. Jacob Case watched his son's stiff figure until he disappeared from sight. He turned back to Delaney with a silently measuring gaze.

"All right, let's get on with it, then. I don't know how much you know about farming, but I expect you'll learn easy enough. You'll be expected to do your fair share of the work around here, and there's plenty to be done. As for the plowing, we do it with oxen on this farm. We have two horses, old Maggie, and the gelding James was riding, and we take good care of both. Most of the crops've been taken in already this year, but that doesn't mean we lack for things to do. Starting tomorrow, I'll be expecting you to pitch right in.''

Delaney followed Jacob Case back toward the barn in silence. This was not going to be easy.

Allie looked down at her plate. The meal she had been eagerly anticipating had gone tasteless in her mouth, and her appetite had disappeared. She cast a quick glance around the table. Mrs. Case's attempt to ease the tension that hung over the dinner table had been unsuccessful. Something was dreadfully wrong.

Mr. Case made an effort to respond enthusiastically to his wife's conversation, but it was obvious that his mind was taken with other things. Perhaps those other things had to do with James's silence and the way he kept his eyes glued to his plate, lifting them only for an occasional glance. Allie felt the weight of James's gaze a time or two. She attempted a smile but received only a glare in return. But most disturbing of all was the anger in James's expression when he looked at Delaney. Tension tightened into a knot in Allie's stomach. She did not understand what was going on.

Delaney contributed little to the conversation except short, polite responses to direct questions. He caught her eye several times during the meal, and although he did not smile, she was comforted to know that his thoughts were with her.

As for Sarah . . . Allie lowered her eyes guiltily. It was not her place either to approve or disapprove of the real daughter in her new home, but Sarah was a disappointment. Having been an only child, Allie had been truly excited at the prospect of having an older sister, but she had learned only too soon that the distance between Sarah and herself was not to be measured in years. It had not taken her long to realize that Sarah was far too interested in herself to have time for anyone else. The small mirror in the corner of the kitchen had gotten more attention from Sarah than any of Mrs. Case's repeated instructions while they prepared supper. The only other person Sarah turned her big green eyes toward with any real interest was Delaney.

Annoyance tugged again inside Allie. Perhaps that was the reason for Mr. Case's silence and James's unfriendly manner. Sarah was flirting outrageously with Delaney, and Allie sup-

posed the girl's behavior was as much of an embarrassment to
her new family as it was to her.

But Allie knew she could not blame the tension entirely on
Sarah. Mother Case's soft reprimand had returned Sarah's eyes
to her plate on several occasions, and surely that should have
ended the tension. But it hadn't. No, there was something else.

Allie's throat abruptly closed. Despite all her high hopes,
things were not going well in her new home.

With great determination, Allie raised another forkful of ham
to her mouth, slipped it between her lips, chewed, and forced
herself to swallow. She had been taught never to waste food, to
eat everything on her plate, and to remember that she was fortunate to have had a meal placed before her. In the short time
before she had become situated after Mama's death, she had
learned her mother's teachings contained true merit. But even
that realization could not make her enjoy this food, no matter
the love with which it had been prepared.

"Allie . . .''

Her head snapping up at the sound of her name, Allie met
Mrs. Case's smile.

"I'm sorry if I startled you, dear. I suppose we are all a bit
more tired than we realized, and I'm sure neither you nor Delaney slept very well while traveling.''

"Yes, ma'am—Mother Case.'' Flushing at the unfamiliar
name, Allie added, "I didn't sleep well until . . . until—''

Stammering to a halt, Allie belatedly realized she could not
expect any of the people around this table to understand the fears
and sense of displacement she had suffered. Neither could she
expect them to understand the consolation Delaney had afforded
her by bringing her close to the Lady again. She continued
roughly, "Until I realized that I wasn't alone anymore.''

Her brief glance toward Delaney was apparently more revealing than she had intended, and Allie was startled by the low
snort of impatience that came from Sarah's fine lips the moment
before she spoke. "Mama, do we have to stay at the table? I
want to go up to my room. Mrs. Preston told me to finish some
papers before school starts again.''

"If the papers have waited this long, dear, I'm sure they can
wait until we've put the kitchen in order.''

Glancing sideways at Allie, Sarah shrugged. "I thought Allie was going to do the kitchen work."

"Sarah!"

Giving her husband a look that effectively halted his reprimand, Mrs. Case responded quietly, "Yes, Allie will be doing the kitchen work—along with you and me."

"If Allie helps you, you won't need me, Mama."

"Perhaps I won't need you, dear, but I will expect you to do your fair share of the work."

Heavily fringed lids dropping over brilliant eyes, Sarah looked down at her empty plate, adequately rebuked for her behavior.

Mr. Case's voice broke gruffly into the silence that followed as he drew himself to his feet.

"The women will take care of the kitchen, Delaney. James will put the cows out into the back pasture while· I settle you into your sleeping arrangements. We didn't expect to bring home two children today. I hope you won't find sleeping in the barn loft uncomfortable until we can make other arrangements."

Delaney's expression barely changed. "No, sir. That will be fine."

"All right, girls. Shall we clear the table?"

Responding immediately, Allie picked up her plate and began collecting the others, turning her back to the men as they left the kitchen. She did not glance toward Sarah's pouting expression or at Mother Case, but busied herself with her task.

The last of the dishes had been washed and stacked and the table prepared for the morning meal when Allie lifted her hand to her mouth to cover a yawn she could not suppress. She glanced quickly at the window. Twilight had turned to night. She was not certain of the hour, but she knew the evening meal had been delayed because of the unusual events of the day. She was tired.

"Yes, it definitely is time to put an end to this day, isn't it, Allie?"

Allie turned at Mrs. Case's soft statement and smiled. She had worked with the greatest pleasure at Mother Case's side, drying the dishes as the older woman washed them. It had been comforting work that had given her a sense of belonging.

Mrs. Case extended her hand toward Allie.

"Come. I'll show you the room you'll share with Sarah."

Allie stopped in her tracks. She shook her head. "But . . .
but Mr. Case said I would be sleeping in the barn loft."

The thought appeared to amuse Mrs. Case, and she gave a
short laugh. "No, dear, not you. Delaney will sleep there for
now. You'll sleep with Sarah."

Her expression sober, Allie gave a short negative shake of her
head. "If you don't mind, I would rather sleep with Delaney."

Sarah laughed aloud, turning Mrs. Case's head sharply toward
her. Covering her mouth with her hand, Sarah continued to laugh
annoyingly as Mrs. Case turned back to Allie.

"No, I'm afraid that would not do, Allie."

"But . . . but Delaney and I—"

"I'm sorry, dear. I'm certain you'll like Sarah's room. She
shared it with Annie, and now she'll share it with you."

"Yes, ma'am." Nodding, Allie took the hand Mrs. Case held
out to her, her troubled mind causing her to continue softly as
she took her first step forward, "But why must I sleep in the
house if Delaney is sleeping in the barn?"

"Because there are two beds in the room you'll share with
Sarah. James has a much smaller room. Delaney wouldn't be
comfortable in there. He'll only be sleeping in the barn temporarily. By the time the winter cold sets in, we'll have made other
arrangements for him."

Nodding again, Allie walked to the staircase. Aware that Sarah
was following behind, still snickering audibly, she raised her
chin. She didn't care about Sarah. Delaney was her friend, and
she would rather be with Delaney than anyone else in this house.

Looking behind her quickly as she reached the second floor,
Allie caught Sarah's superior glance, and her annoyance turned
to gloom. She was beginning to believe Sarah would never be
the sister she had hoped for, and in that moment it came to her
with an instinct deep and true that Sarah would never even be
her friend.

Allie twisted in the soft bed and turned once more toward the
window and the brilliant moon that flooded the small room with
silver light. She fingered the narrow edging of hand-tatted lace
on the sleeve of her nightgown, glancing down at the long white
garment once more. She had been lying abed for an endless

time, and she was certain she was the only person in the whole house who was not sleeping.

In the bed closest to the wall, Sarah was snoring softly, moonlight illuminating her features. Allie didn't want to look at Sarah at all, especially during the long hours of a sleepless night.

Closing her eyes, Allie admitted with shame that a part of her dislike of her new sister arose from jealousy, for Sarah was very pretty.

She was not pretty like Mother Case, with small, delicate features and light skin. In truth, Sarah resembled Papa Case, and that puzzled Allie, because Papa Case was not a very pretty man. Sarah had Papa Case's dark hair, but it was thick and shiny. It was almost as beautiful as Mama's had been. Her skin was a warm peach color that made her green eyes seem all the brighter and made the thick, dark lashes that she had been fluttering so annoyingly at Delaney seem even longer. Her face was narrow, like Papa Case's and James's, but it was pleasantly feminine and beautiful. She had well-shaped lips that smiled often, white teeth that were straight and even, and a deep dimple in one cheek that she went to great pains to display.

Allie frowned again. Sarah had bragged that she was fourteen, four years older than Allie and only a year younger than Delaney. But Sarah was years and years older than she in many ways. Allie had not been certain what the girl meant by many of the things she had whispered in the darkness of the room after Mother Case had put out the lamp and closed the door behind her.

Allie felt puzzled again as she remembered how Sarah had laughed mockingly and said, "So you'd rather be sleeping with Delaney than sleeping in here with me. Well, I don't blame you, 'little sister.' I'd rather be sleeping with Delaney, too."

Allie had become angry then and had muttered, "Delaney let me sleep with him because he's my friend. He doesn't let everybody be his friend, and he wouldn't want you to sleep with him."

Sarah had laughed all the harder. When she finally got control of herself, she had whispered in a low hiss, "Oh, but Delaney will be my friend, you'll see. He'll be a better 'friend' to me than he is to you. It isn't hard at all for me to make friends."

Allie had turned on her side then, away from Sarah, but the

girl's laughter had followed her. Sarah had fallen asleep a short time later, but Allie was still awake. She did not think she would ever be able sleep in this room with that hateful Sarah sleeping so close by.

Guilt suddenly overwhelming her, Allie felt dangerously close to tears. How ungrateful she was. Her prayers had been answered. She had a home and a family, and she had so much more. She had never had such a beautiful room, even if she had to share it with Sarah. There were lace curtains at the windows, clean white linens that smelled of soap and fresh air on the bed, a soft pillow under her head, a fluffy mattress underneath her, and at her feet was a beautiful pink coverlet, identical to the one on Sarah's bed. On the floor between Sarah's bed and hers was a soft woolen rug to protect her feet from the cold when the weather began to touch the mornings with a chill. It was a beautiful rug, in light shades of pink and yellow and blue, and Mother Case had woven it herself.

Her eyes moving to the small wardrobe in the corner of the room, Allie remembered the tenderness with which Mother Case had opened the door and shown her four lovely dresses hanging there that were now hers alone: three for daily wear and one for the Sabbath. Mother Case had then taken her to the dresser and pulled out the second drawer, telling her that the nightgowns and dainties within were now hers. Allie had not needed to be told that all those beautiful things had once been little Annie's, and her heart wept for the little girl who had been called home so very young.

Remembering a time when she would have thought her present circumstances as close to heaven as she could come, Allie closed her eyes in despair. She wasn't happy. She wasn't. She felt strange, uncertain, and uncomfortable. She was powerless against her new sister's unexplained resentment of her. Here on this farm, where her only friend was out of her reach, she felt more alone than she had ever felt in her life.

Closing her eyes, Allie tried, as she had several times before, to pray, but the Lady seemed deaf to her whispered appeal. In her mind she saw her prayers floating up into a dark, silent void, only to become lost in the echoing shadows there.

The threat of tears even heavier than before, Allie brushed a strand of pale hair back from her face. With newly formed re-

solve, she glanced again toward the other bed. Satisfied that
Sarah was still sleeping, she sat up, swung her legs over the
edge of the bed, and put her small, bare feet down on the rug,
not bothering to slip into the sturdy slippers waiting there.

The bed creaked when relieved of her weight, and the sound
reverberated in the silence, turning Allie toward Sarah's bed once
more. Sarah continued to snore and Allie made a small grimace.
She wondered if Sarah knew she snored. It was not very pretty
to snore.

Within moments Allie was at the door to the hall, and then
she was moving toward the staircase.

Her heart thumping in her chest, Allie took a last look back
down the darkened hallway. She stared toward the door to Mother
and Papa Case's room. Beyond it, the door to James's room was
in shadow. She knew they would be angry with her if they knew
where she was going. For some reason James seemed to like
Delaney even less than he liked her, and Mother Case had made
her wishes very clear about remaining in her room.

Allie swallowed tightly. She would never have disobeyed
Mama like this—but while Mama was alive, she never needed
anyone else.

Carefully, Allie put her foot on the first step, and then the
second, and the third. Within seconds she was at the bottom of
the staircase and reaching for the knob to the front door.

She ran breathlessly across the yard toward the barn, grimacing as small pebbles cut her tender feet. A few moments later,
her heart pounding, she stood at the door. With a deep determined breath, she pulled it open.

The dark cavern of the silent barn met her eyes, and Allie's
heart hammered more heavily in trepidation. It was so dark in
there. Soft, unidentifiable sounds met her ears: a slow, steady
thumping; a scratching, as of tiny feet; a low, eerie whine. Her
eyes slowly becoming accustomed to the dim light, she squinted
toward the loft and saw the faint glow of a lamp in the rear. In
the shadows ahead of her, she spied a ladder leading to the loft.
A cool night breeze lifted the pale, limp strands of her hair, and
chills raced down her spine, but Allie knew those chills were
entirely unrelated to the change in temperature. Summoning her
courage, she plunged through the darkness toward the ladder.

Allie's feet met the first wooden rung, and then the second.

Suddenly more frightened to go back than to go ahead, she climbed faster, her hands trembling as she reached the top. Hesitating as she reached the loft, she squinted into the semidarkness.

There in the flickering shadows created by the small lamp hanging on the wall was Delaney. He was asleep on a bed of straw in the corner. Bed linens from the house lay folded and unused beside him. Instead, he had chosen to cover himself with the blanket provided by the Society, the same blanket that had served them both during the long journey from New York.

Relieved at the sight of him, Allie crept across the loft floor. Again hesitant, she paused. Would Delaney be angry? Would he tell her to go back to the house?

Delaney moved restlessly in his sleep, and Allie stared a moment longer. His face was younger, more boyish in repose. He did not look like the Delaney whose fierce expression had become so familiar to her, whose light eyes, often so chillingly cold, could smile in reassurance even when his lips did not. Allie took a step closer, her long white gown brushing the tops of her bare feet, catching the straw on the floor as she walked. Delaney turned once more, the chain around his neck, visible in his open shirtfront, catching the light.

Abruptly he was awake. His reflexes startlingly quick, he sat up and stared at her. His low voice was clear, without a trace of the fogginess of sleep.

"What's wrong, Allie?"

Allie was unable to respond. How could someone who was sufficient in himself, who knew no fear, understand that she . . . she was lost.

"Allie . . ."

Still she hesitated.

Delaney raised a hand toward her in invitation. He had but a moment to wait before Allie rushed to his side. Curling his arm around her, he drew her down beside him. His expression was sober as he looked into her colorless face.

"Tell me what's wrong, Allie."

"They . . . they put you out here, and they put me in there—with Sarah. I'd rather be with you, Delaney. I told Mother Case and Sarah that I'd rather sleep with you than in the house, but Sarah laughed. She said she'd rather sleep with you, too, and I told her you wouldn't want her with you because she wasn't your friend. Sarah said she was going to make herself a better friend to you than I am. She says it's easy for her to make friends."

Delaney was silent, his light eyes startlingly visible in the darkness as they searched her face. Allie did not realize she was crying until he raised his hand and brushed the tears from her cheeks. Suddenly ashamed of her weakness, Allie drew back against his arm. Her voice was a low whisper.

"I prayed to the Lady, Delaney. I tried to talk to her, to ask her to help me, but she didn't hear me. The words left my lips, but they didn't reach God's ear."

Silent and still for long moments, Delaney slowly reached inside his shirt and withdrew his medal. Frowning, he took her hand and placed it in her palm. He squeezed her hand tightly shut around it.

"Allie, don't worry. Everything will be all right. Sarah is vain. She thinks she can fool everybody with her pretty face, but she can't fool me. I've seen too many girls like her before."

Finally expressing the thought that had caused her the deepest misery, Allie whispered again, "Nobody wants us here, Delaney, nobody but Mother Case."

"She's the most important one, Allie. Mr. Case will do whatever he can to make her happy, and when he gets to know you, he'll be just as happy as she is to have you here."

"But James is angry."

Allie felt Delaney stiffen.

"He'll get over it."

Allie lowered her eyes. "I prayed to the Lady, but . . . but I don't think I'll ever like Sarah."

A hint of a smile touched Delaney's lips. "You're going to have to pray real hard on that one."

His smile contagious, it turned up the corners of Allie's lips as well, and then Delaney's smile came full and bright. It lit the darkness inside her with its warmth as his arm tightened around her with a small squeeze.

"You can stay a little while, Allie, but you have to go back to the house. You wouldn't want Mrs. Case to know you came out here, after she told you not to."

Relaxing against the straw, Delaney urged her to lean back

with him. She thought she saw him smile again as he turned toward her so that she could hold his medal with more ease.

"You're going to have to pray quickly tonight, Allie. The Lady isn't tired, but I am." He took a short, weary breath and allowed his eyes to drift closed. "Remember, only a few minutes."

Allie closed her eyes as well, a familiar peace touching her senses as she held the medal in her hand. She could feel the Lady close to her. She could talk to her now, and know the Lady would send her prayers flying into God's ear. And when she prayed, she would not pray only for herself. She would pray for Delaney, too. She would pray that Papa Case and James would like them both, and she would pray that Sarah . . .

Allie's warm thoughts came to an abrupt halt and she tried again. She would pray that Sarah . . .

Her light brows working into a small frown, Allie took a short, firm breath. She would have to save that prayer for another time.

An uncharacteristic frown drawing his light brown brows together, James pulled on his boots and stood up. He had not slept well. He had opened his eyes to see the first streaks of dawn mark the night sky, and his mind had begun working again.

Things had not gone well on the farm in the past months, and it appeared that the Cases were in for more of the same. The fever had hit Annie so unexpectedly. She had been such a happy little girl, everyone's favorite with her dark, shining curls, her laughing eyes, rosy cheeks, and infectious smile. She had seemed to have an endless capacity for loving. Unlike Sarah, who had been self-centered and vain as long as James could remember, Annie had seemed to take her happiness from giving joy to others. Pa had often said the Lord had saved them the best for last.

No one had expected Annie to die, and when it had become evident that she would not rally, disbelief had swept the family. In all too short a time, Annie was gone. They had barely had time to gain control of their grief when Mama, too, was stricken with the fever.

James could not remember a time when he had ever been more frightened. He had not wanted to see Mama slip away as Annie had, and he had been truly uncertain if Pa could have sustained

Mama's loss without losing himself. But Mama had pulled through, even if they were not certain how long she would . . .

Biting down sharply on his lower lip, James took a deep breath. Mama had pulled through, but, somehow, the realization that she had been saved while the Lord had seen fit to take Annie had seemed unbearable to her. That thought had plagued her mind, inhibiting full recuperation; then had come the notice about the orphan train.

They had been true, those cruel words he had hissed to that hard-eyed prison boy the day before. No one in the family wanted to take another child into their home in Annie's place, because they knew no one could replace her. But Mama was adamant that the Lord worked in mysterious ways. She was certain she would know—that God would speak to her in some way if a child in that group was meant to be chosen by her.

Clamping his teeth tightly shut, James took a deep, angry breath and tucked his shirt firmly into his trousers. One look at that forlorn little Allie Pierce and the brave front she had tried so unsuccessfully to present, and Mama had been lost.

James took a short, angry step toward the door to his room and pulled it open. If he could only be sure. If he could only be certain that the look in the little girl's eyes was sincere. Somehow he could not believe it was so. He had heard about children who lived by their wits on the city streets. He had heard how they learned to take advantage of the goodness of others. He could not truly believe the innocence in that small, pale face was feigned, but . . . No, the girl could not be as innocent as she pretended to be, if she was so attracted to that prison boy she had foisted upon them.

"Birds of a feather flock together."

That old adage going through his mind, James walked quietly past his parents' room. The girl was probably as corrupt as her friend, or well on her way in that direction, and he was determined that this family would not suffer at their hands. No, he would go out to the barn now and shake the truth out of Delaney Marsh.

At a sound to his right, James turned just as the door to Sarah's room drew open. He slowed his step, a soft murmur of surprise escaping his lips at his mother's unexpected appearance in the doorway. The alarm on her pale face stopped him in his tracks.

"Mama, what's wrong?"

Mrs. Pierce stepped into the hall and pulled the door closed behind her. "She's gone, James."

"She? Who's gone?"

"Allie. Little Allie is gone! I've already checked, and she's nowhere in the house. Sarah said she awoke during the night and saw the bed empty. Accustomed to seeing it that way, she said she didn't think anything of it until I shook her awake a few minutes ago and asked her where Allie was. It appears Allie has been gone most of the night."

"She can't have gone far, Mama."

"Your father is already up and working. He doesn't know Allie is missing. Before you find him and tell him, go out to the barn and talk to Delaney. Maybe he knows where she is. Maybe he—" Her words caught in her throat, and she was unable to continue.

James took her arm with a firm but gentle hand. "Don't worry, Mama. We'll find her, wherever she is."

Turning, James started down the steps at a run. Within minutes he was across the yard and drawing open the door to the barn. Entering, he paused for a brief moment to listen to the sounds of early morning stirring within. He heard nothing unusual.

Glancing up toward the loft, James saw a dim light glimmering in the shadows there. Moments later he was climbing toward it. He had reached the top rung of the ladder when he stopped short at the sight that met his eyes.

Sleeping deeply, Delaney Marsh was lying on the hay, his face averted from sight. But it was not Delaney Marsh who caught and held James's attention. Lying beside him on her back, her small face turned so that it caught a slim ray of dawn that entered through a crack in the wall, was Allie Pierce.

It came to James in a short moment of revelation that Allie Pierce could not be the conniving street urchin he had suspected her to be. The small, thin face revealed in the meager light was almost angelic. Why was it he had not before noticed the dainty perfection of her small features, the innocence in those slender lips, slightly parted in sleep? Her fine silver-gold hair had originally appeared colorless and without life, but in the slender rays of dawn slanting into the loft, it glimmered like a pale halo about her face.

A small, pained grimace slipping across his lips, James recognized the fine lawn nightgown the child wore. It had been Annie's. He shook his head, his brows drawing into a frown. His mind returned the vision of Annie to his mind, her dark bouncing curls, her dancing eyes, her vigor, the enthusiasm and joy that were so much a part of her and that seemed to endow even the clothing she wore with life.

James's brows tightened further. Not so this child. Small and frail, her meager frame all but lost in the folds, she gave the appearance of a celestial apparition in the white, lace-trimmed garment. Her childish vulnerability fully exposed to his eye for the first time, James felt shame touch his mind. He had not been fair to this child. This child had done nothing to excite his resentment. She was merely unfortunate enough to be in need. And then, in another of what must have been a long line of misfortunes, she had met Delaney Marsh.

Oh, Delaney Marsh was smart, all right! He had taken advantage of Allie Pierce's need, and the child had been totally taken in by him. How the girl managed to find solace in those cold eyes and comfort in his hard countenance, James could not quite understand. She was certainly too young to be taken in by the fellow's handsome face, as had Sarah.

Annoyance flashed across James's mind, and he corrected his thought of a moment before. Sarah had not been taken in by Delaney Marsh's handsome face. She had merely disregarded the welfare of others and the threat to the family Delaney Marsh presented. She hadn't given a moment's thought to the strain Pa and he would be under with a boy of his character on the farm. Nor had she contemplated the disillusionment Ma would suffer when she realized the Lord had not sent Delaney Marsh to them, but that her overwhelming grief had allowed her to be taken in by an opportunistic street rat who had nowhere else to go.

Sarah had not thought of any of these things. As usual, she had considered only herself and the pleasure she would derive from Delaney Marsh's company. Sarah was fool enough to believe she could twist Delaney Marsh around her finger, as she had every other young fellow in the vicinity, but James knew instinctively that she was wrong. His instinct also told him that in any relationship that developed between the handsome prison boy and his sister, Sarah would come out the loser. In this way, even more pressure was being exerted on Pa and himself by this newcomer's presence. Protecting Sarah against herself would not be an easy task.

Appearing to sense his scrutiny, little Allie Pierce moved, her light brows drawing together in a frown as she resisted awakening. A few low, indistinguishable words escaped her lips, and James tensed as Delaney Marsh turned in his sleep. Curling himself on his side, he was facing Allie when the child started to open her eyes. Not realizing she was being watched, the girl stared at Marsh's face, obviously determining that he was still asleep. She then reached out toward the boy's chest, toward a chain the boy wore around his neck.

At that moment a voice from below startled James from his thoughts, snapping his head toward his father as he called up to him in a loud voice.

"James! Did you ask Delaney if he knows where the child is?"

His eyes jerking back toward the two lying in the loft as his father's voice echoed in the barn's stillness, James saw Delaney Marsh snap to a seated position. Instantly alert, Marsh's eyes darted to the girl at his side before darting back to James as he stepped up into the loft.

"James!"

"I didn't have to ask him, Pa. The girl's up here. Tell Mama she's all right and she'll be down in a minute."

His father grunted in response and left the barn, and James was momentarily grateful. He needed this short moment of privacy with these two new additions to his family. He needed it to make some things very clear.

Delaney and the girl were now standing. The girl was visibly quaking, her eyes wide in the growing light, her face paler than James had ever seen it. He realized she was frightened of him, and he regretted that, but he did not attempt to soften the reprimand in his voice as he addressed her.

"My mother was very worried when she went to your room and found your bed empty, Allie. She imagined all sorts of things might have happened to you when she couldn't find you in the house and then realized you had been gone for the greater part of the night. I think you should show more consideration for the woman who is responsible for giving you a home.''

The girl's eyes filled with tears, but James did not relent. He did not want there to be a repetition of this incident, and if guilt was the manner in which to accomplish the task, he was not above using it.

''My mother has just lost one daughter. It was very cruel of you to make her think that she might have lost another. She was very disturbed when I saw her, and she—''

''All right, I think you've made your point.'' Slipping his arm around the girl's trembling shoulders, Delaney Marsh stared at James, his light eyes narrowing in silent warning before he turned and addressed her. ''Allie, you'd better go in the house now.''

The girl looked up into Marsh's unsmiling face. Her expression was sober as she responded in a whisper, ''I'm sorry, Delaney.''

''You have things a little confused, Allie,'' James said, his voice harder than he intended. ''My mother is the person you should be apologizing to, and I think you should get to it right away.''

Surprising him, the girl looked at James and shook her head. ''No, I . . . it's my fault that you're angry and that Mother Case was worried. I didn't mean to . . .'' Biting her lip nervously, she paused before continuing with obvious resolution, ''I felt alone. Delaney told me I shouldn't have come. He told me I had to go back to the house, but I fell asleep.'' She shook her head. ''Don't be angry with Delaney, James. He didn't do anything. It was all my fault, and I'm sorry if you—''

''Don't apologize to him, dammit!''

Delaney's angry words came in a low growl, and James took a step forward. He didn't like cursing, and he knew it would not be tolerated in their home. It was further proof that Delaney Marsh had no place in their family.

Marsh gripped Allie's shoulder and turned her to face him. ''You don't have to apologize to him, Allie. He's a bully. He likes pushing little girls around and frightening them. But he doesn't have the guts to talk that way to somebody big enough to look him in the eye.''

The girl looked back at James, and he could feel his face flush as she spoke in soft appeal.

"Please don't be angry with Delaney, James."

"Go in the house, Allie." Delaney's gruff command turned Allie again in his direction as he dropped his hands from her shoulders.

She shook her head.

"I said go in the house. Mrs. Case is waiting for you."

Allie looked toward James and back again. She shook her head for the second time. "I want you to come with me, Delaney."

James managed a harsh laugh. "So, I'm a bully. Big talk from a brave fella who hides behind a little girl's skirts. Yes, go inside with her, Marsh. You don't have to be afraid. Allie will protect you."

Delaney took two charging steps forward, and James squared his stance. Oh, yes, he would like that very much. He was just aching to wipe the arrogance from that prison boy's face.

Within a moment Allie was between them, her eyes wide with panic. "No, you can't fight! James, Mother Case will be angry!"

Immediately realizing her plea had had little effect on James, Allie turned her anxious gaze toward Delaney. Her next words were filled with despair. "Delaney, we were going to be a family."

Allie's whispered appeal drew Delaney's attention to her colorless face. The cold fury in his eyes flickered briefly as he held her gaze.

Unexpectedly affected by the girl's words, James felt the heat drain from his anger. He took a deep breath, using the time to bring his temper under control. What was wrong with him? Instead of protecting his family against this intruder, he was rapidly sinking to Delaney's level. He was frightening this poor, unfortunate child whose only mistake was in trusting someone unworthy of her trust.

"We were going to be a family."

That was all too true, James realized. The worst of it was that if he managed to rid his family of Delaney Marsh, he would be unable to save the relationship between himself and his surpris-

ingly brave little "sister." Somehow that thought was too dis-
comforting for him to ignore.

But James was spared the need to respond when Delaney
Marsh looked up from the girl's face.

"I don't know what you had in mind when you came up here,
Case," he said, "but you're not going to get your way. Whether
you like it or not, I'm going in the house with Allie right now,
and you can't do a damned thing about it. Your mother is waiting
for her, and she'll be expecting an explanation. Allie will give
it to her, and I'll be standing at her side when she does. Nothing
you say or do is going to change that. So I'm telling you now,
get back down that ladder, or get out of our way."

A heated flush rising to his cheeks, James gave a low, angry
laugh. "Just who's protecting who here, Marsh?"

Satisfied when restrained anger darkened Delaney Marsh's face
once more, James gave another short laugh. He turned to Allie
and spoke more softly. "I think we're agreed that you should go
inside and talk to Mama. She and Pa are waiting."

Allie glanced quickly at the two young men, and James was
struck with the thought that this frail little girl would neither be
threatened nor cajoled into doing something she did not want to
do. There was more spirit in her than was evident to the eye.

As he watched, Allie turned back to face him. She attempted
a conciliatory smile. "If you'll go down first, James."

Unexpectedly aware that he envied Delaney Marsh the loyalty
he had won from this brave little orphan, James turned toward
the ladder.

Touching down on the barn floor a few seconds later, he raised
his eyes toward the small figure descending behind him. Reaching up when Allie was a few rungs from the bottom, James lifted
her to the ground. His mind unconsciously registered the frailty
of the girl's frame. The child was undersize and underweight,
but he suspected those were the only ways in which she was
lacking. For the first time it came to him that Mama had chosen
well. No one could take Annie's place, but he was suddenly
certain this little girl would carve a place of her own in their
family.

At the sound of Marsh's descending step James looked up.
He met Marsh's cold-eyed stare and silently amended that last
thought: Allie would carve a place for herself in this family *if*

she could rid herself of her attachment to this unwanted baggage
she had picked up along the way. James took a deep breath. He
was determined she would.

James offered her a smile. "Come on, Allie. Mama's waiting."

Before Allie could respond, Delaney Marsh touched her
shoulder lightly to urge her forward. Allie started unhesitatingly
toward the house, and James realized that the confidence with
which the girl walked had little, if anything, to do with his
friendly overture.

Walking slightly behind them as they approached the house,
James reaffirmed his decision. He would rid Allie of this opportunistic prison boy if it was the last thing he ever did.

Mrs. Case looked down into Allie's small face in silence. Her
gray eyes studied the little girl who had walked through her
kitchen door only minutes before, her chin held high, but trembling visibly. This small, lost child had so touched her heart.

Margaret was uncertain why she had known that this child,
of all the children in the church hall, was meant for her. She
had at first thought it was the need she had seen in Allie's eyes,
the loss. It had reflected so clearly the need and loss that she
had felt after Annie's death.

Certainly, it was not a physical resemblance to Annie that had
drawn her to the girl, for no two children could have been more
dissimilar. She had originally thought that lack of resemblance
extended to personality as well, but now she was unsure, because she didn't know what new facet of Allie Pierce's surprising
character she would discover next.

She had seen the gentleness in Allie from the first—the sensitivity—and had sensed a kindred spirit. She had felt love swell
within her, and she had known instinctively Allie Pierce was
capable of returning that love.

But Margaret Case realized that she had been mistaken in
considering the child timid. It was not a timid child who walked
so bravely from the barn, her friend at her side and a scowling
James taking up the rear. It was not a fainthearted child who
had approached her directly, without hesitation. The child had
shown no timidity when, despite her trembling, she had assumed
all blame for the fright she had caused her new mother. And

despite the remorse in Allie's eyes, Margaret had seen the pride that would not allow her to apologize for seeking out her friend in a moment of uncertainty.

Looking at her now, Margaret wondered if the child was trembling with fear for Delaney Marsh or for herself, so worried did she appear over the fate of her friend.

Glancing quickly toward James, who was scowling even more darkly, toward Jacob, whose angry concern was concealed for her benefit, and toward Sarah, of whom she had begun to despair, Margaret realized the child's unconscious evaluation of the situation was far too accurate for comfort. The boy was truly on shaky ground with her overly protective menfolk, and he would have to tread carefully around her vain and selfish daughter.

Margaret resisted a laugh. Somehow, observing the clarity of the child's gaze and the intensity of feeling exhibited within it, she believed Allie Pierce would be a match for them all. But it would not be an easy battle, and the little girl would need an ally.

Margaret took a deep breath. The child had that ally in her, but some things needed be made clear from the outset.

Realizing Allie awaited her response, Margaret raised a trembling hand to her brow in a gesture she often used when she was disturbed. She did not notice that both James and Jacob frowned as she addressed the child directly. "Allie, dear, surely you realize you could have come to me with any uncertainties that assailed you during the night. We are a family, and we are here for each other."

Allie's pale brows knit in a frown. How could this dear lady understand? She was certain this family did not know of the Lady, and would not understand Allie's closeness to her. Nor would they understand that Delaney, who no longer believed in God, helped send her words into God's ear. How could she explain that Delaney, with his cold eyes and unsmiling face, who cared so little for anything at all, cared about her? How could she explain that he had been her family when she was most alone and, for that reason, would be forever in her heart?

"Delaney and I . . . ." Biting her lip, Allie hesitated for a brief moment, only to have Delaney take up in her stead.

"Allie came out to the barn to talk to me for just a few minutes, but we both fell asleep. It won't happen again, Mrs. Case.

Allie wouldn't want to make you unhappy.'' Turning to Allie for agreement, he waited only for her nod before continuing, ''You needn't worry. As for any other concerns, Allie—''

''Allie isn't a baby. Why don't you let her talk for herself?'' All eyes turned toward James as he interrupted Delaney's softly spoken statement. His glance intense, he continued in a clipped tone, ''It seems to me you've had too much say where Allie's concerned. She's a part of this family now, and there's no reason she can't answer Mama herself.''

''James . . .''

At Mrs. Case's soft admonition, James turned in her direction, but his expression did not soften.

''You spoke to Allie, not him,'' he said.

Delaney interjected harshly, ''I told you, what concerns Allie concerns me.''

His expression livid, James turned to face Delaney with anger held barely in check. ''And I told you I don't care what you said. Mama wasn't talking to you, and if you don't know your place, maybe somebody should teach it to you.''

Delaney took a step forward, and Allie gasped. Everything was going wrong!

''All right, that's enough from both of you!'' Mr. Case's low voice shattered the tense tableau as he continued roughly, ''Mama and I run this house. We're the ones who give the orders *and* teach the lessons here! I think it's plain enough to see that Allie didn't mean for her and Delaney's first day to start off on the wrong foot, and I think we can safely say she won't be going out to the barn anymore during the night.'' Pausing, Mr. Case turned to Allie. ''Is that right, Allie?''

Unable to speak, Allie nodded.

Apparently satisfied, Mr. Case continued in a softer tone, ''Then I think you should go upstairs and get dressed now, Allie. The morning is wasting, and I don't know about the rest of you, but I'm ready for breakfast. Mama?''

Appearing relieved, Mrs. Case gave a short nod. ''Of course, Jacob.'' Sarah, standing near the hallway entrance to the room, had remained silent throughout the whole exchange, and Mrs. Case turned in her direction.

''Sarah, dear, bring some fresh bacon in from the smokehouse like a good girl. I think we've all worked up a sizable appetite this morning.''

Her expression revealing only too plainly that she disliked being ordered about in such a manner, Sarah turned to follow her mother's directions.

Turning toward Allie who had not yet moved, Mrs. Case said softly, "Get dressed now, dear. There's much work to be done.''

Waiting only until both girls had left the room, Mr. Case turned to Delaney. "All right, boy. Since the womenfolk have started on their chores, I suppose it's time we got to work, too. Mrs. Case will call us when breakfast is ready.''

Watching as her husband and Delaney walked across the yard and into the barn, Mrs. Case released a low, relieved sigh. Aware that her son had not yet moved and was watching his father and Delaney Marsh as intently as she, Margaret turned toward him. She searched his face with obvious concern. "What is it, James? Why do you dislike the boy so much? He hasn't done anything that should have upset you so.''

"Maybe he hasn't, but he's not going to get the opportunity, either.''

"James . . .''

"He's trouble, Mama.''

" 'Judge not, least ye be judged,' James.''

"It's not me who did the judging. You heard that Mr. Smith. Marsh is straight out of prison.''

"And he wants to make a better life for himself.''

"Not at our expense.''

"James, you're being unfair.''

"Me, unfair? What would you call his using that little girl to wangle a place in this house? You wouldn't have taken him if it hadn't been for the girl's attachment to him, and you know it.''

"That's right, but we *did* take him, James. We made a commitment to him.''

"He has some kind of hold on her, Mama. I don't know what he told her or what he did, but he has her convinced that he's God Almighty.''

"She's attached to him because he helped her when she needed someone.''

"She's only a little girl. She doesn't see past the act he puts on for her benefit. But I do, and so can you, Mama, if you'll be honest. That fella hasn't a speck of humanity in him. His eyes are as cold as ice. He doesn't feel anything for that girl, not like he'd like us to believe. He's using her just to get us to accept him. He's not what he pretends to be. He'll use any one of us the same way if we let him.''

"James dear, Allie loves the boy. Trying to come between them now, when she's so insecure, will only hurt her. Surely you can see that. If what you say is true, she'll see what he is sooner or later. We all will. But in the meantime, we've made a commitment to the boy, and we must honor it.''

"And he made one to us. I'm just going to make sure he stands to the letter of that commitment.''

Concern darkening her soft gray eyes, Mrs. Case shook her head. "James, I meant what I said to those two children. We've taken them into our home, and I intend to treat them with the same love and care I give Sarah and you.''

"I don't think you'll have any trouble with little Allie—unless Marsh comes between you, but he won't let you get close to him. He won't let anybody get close to him. You'll see.''

"That will be his choice, dear. But I tell you now, I will not put up with anger and abuse of any kind in the bosom of my family.''

"The abuse won't start with me, Mama.''

"Do I have your word on that, James?''

His mother suddenly sounded tired, and James paused, scrutinizing her lined face more intently than his anger had allowed moments before. The past hour had added immeasurably to the exhaustion always visible there, and James stifled his response. If anybody was going to add to the weight of her cares, it would not be he. And he was determined it would not be Delaney Marsh, either. Reaching out, he touched his mother's frail shoulder.

"Yes, Mama, you have my word.''

Realizing there was no more to be said, James turned and walked out into the yard. Steering clear of the barn, he headed toward the fields and the last remaining crops to be tended. He would wait to deal with Delaney Marsh. He would give him enough rope to hang himself. He didn't expect he'd have to wait long.

chapter

six

ALLIE STEPPED OUT of the kitchen into a bright, clear morning. Standing silently for a few moments, she closed her eyes and savored the sweet scent of earth and sun that filled her nostrils. She had been in her new home for three weeks, but she had not yet become used to the natural fragrance of this beautiful land.

Suddenly conscious of her posture, her eyes closed, her head back, her small face raised to the warm morning sun, Allie opened her eyes and glanced quickly around her. She was distinctly relieved to see that no one had witnessed her foolish preoccupation with that which everyone else appeared to take for granted. Of course, Mother Case and Papa Case had settled in this place years before, and they were accustomed to its natural beauty. James and Sarah had lived here all their lives, and Delaney's natural caution did not allow him to become attached to anything.

That thought turning her mind to Delaney, Allie smiled. Yes, he had heartily resisted extending her his friendship, but now that he had, he was closer to her than anyone she had ever known, except Mama. His friendship was securely hers. She had been reassured of that often since they arrived on the farm. Not in spoken words but in the way he seemed to read her thoughts, sensing when she was upset over some failure, and in the way he seemed to know when a light touch on her shoulder or a covert squeeze of her hand would restore the courage that had temporarily deserted her, and in the watchful eye she knew he kept on the treatment she received from her new family. She felt his protective presence around her, and she thanked the Lady nightly for his friendship. It was the greatest gift she had ever received.

But although Delancy was concerned about the warmth extended to her in this new family, he appeared to care little about the friendly overtures extended to him. He had spent his first three weeks performing well the tasks asked of him, while continuing to hold himself aloof. She knew that was true, because she had overheard Papa Case talking to Mother Case only the night before.

"The boy does a good job with just about everything I ask him to do," Jacob Case had said, "but the truth is, I don't know him one bit better now than I did when he first came here. He's holdin' back, Margaret, and I have to admit I don't trust him because of it. He's a strange boy, very strange."

Mother Case had protested his comment, and Allie had wished that she could enter the room and tell Papa Case that Delaney was not strange at all—even though she supposed it was partly true.

Delaney seldom smiled and seldom spoke, except when directly addressed or when Allie sought him out after the evening meal to tell him the events of the day, as had become her custom. He listened to her intently then, and he smiled when she told him about her silly mistakes, too, and quietly teased her until she also smiled.

The only other softness he displayed was the few brief words he occasionally spoke to Mother Case. They were usually spoken so low as to reach Mother Case's ear alone, but Allie had seen the mistiness in Mother Case's eyes, her smile, and the way she squeezed his arm with true warmth in return. There was no strangeness there.

Delaney did not talk much to Allie about his own adjustment to the farm and his new family, but she knew he spent much of his free time in the hayloft with the books Mrs. Preston, the schoolmistress, had given him. She was uncertain if the other members of the family were aware of Delaney's surprising dedication to learning, so distant did he remain from them, and it troubled her.

But Allie had to admit she found particular satisfaction in knowing that Delaney also kept Sarah at a distance, despite her advances toward him. She knew Sarah's pride was offended, and that each rebuff only made her more determined than ever to break him down.

Sarah's offended pride had resulted in angry, jealous verbal attacks on Allie in the silence of their room at night. Allie had defended herself as well as she could against them, but there was no protection from Sarah's mockery. Nor did she have a defense when Sarah told her she was plain and Mother Case had only taken her in because she felt sorry for her, because Allie knew that was true. Pride had kept her from telling Delaney about Sarah's vicious remarks. She could not bring herself to call to his attention a comparison between Sarah and herself, because she knew in such a comparison she would be found lacking. She did not ever want to be found lacking in Delaney's eyes.

As for the treatment she received from the others, Mother Case was ever loving and generous, and the sweet woman had stirred within Allie a true love in return. Papa Case was kind to her, but she feared he remembered Annie with too much pain to allow her a place in his heart. As for James . . .

Allie's light brows worked into a frown. She was confused and uncertain about James. His unrelenting dislike of Delaney did not seem to include her. To the contrary, he was often considerate, evincing concern for her, but the antagonism between Delaney and him kept her from responding. She was not certain what to think of James. She wondered if she would ever truly understand the way he studied Delaney and her when they were together and his obvious disapproval of their friendship.

Her sober thoughts had stolen some of the warmth from a morning that had given her so much enjoyment only a few minutes before, and Allie picked up the wooden bucket resting on the ground beside her. She walked toward the chicken coops some distance behind the house, determined to put aside her concerns and concentrate on the task at hand.

It was time to bring the fowl feed and collect the eggs. It was a disagreeable task that Sarah had gladly surrendered when Allie volunteered to take it over. She knew Sarah had thought her a fool. Her lips twisted in a small grimace. But then, Sarah rarely had a good opinion of anyone but herself.

The familiar unpleasant odor of the coops assaulted her nostrils as Allie drew nearer. She gave a small sniff and attempted to dismiss the odor from her mind as she reached into the bucket and began scattering feed to the hungry birds flocking around her. Chickens were insatiable. Her stomach rebelled as she recalled the startling way she had discovered they would even eat each other if provided the opportunity. She had lost her fondness for them then, but that dislike had not stopped her from volunteering to take care of them. She had been anxious to show Mother Case that she was an asset on the farm, and she was glad she had taken that opportunity, because she had not been successful in her other endeavors thus far.

When the bucket was empty, Allie looked around her. Her quick perusal of the yard failed to turn up any sign of the particular bird she sought, and Allie heaved a short, resigned breath. That nasty hen was still on her nest—and probably waiting for her.

Suddenly flushing, Allie was embarrassed by her own cowardice. Afraid of a little chicken. How Sarah would laugh at her if she knew.

Unconsciously, Allie glanced down at the gouges on the back of her hand. She grimaced, remembering the way that particular hen's beady eyes had watched her approach the nest yesterday. Refusing to budge despite Allie's most energetic attempts to frighten her off, she had forced Allie to reach under her for the eggs. The bird had then attacked her, pecking and scratching so viciously that she had drawn blood. When Allie refused to give up, the enraged fowl had flown at her eyes, and to her silent shame, Allie had fled in defeat.

Allie took another deep, firm breath. That was yesterday. It would not happen again today. With renewed determination, Allie pulled open the door to the coop and stepped inside.

Working her way toward the rear of the coop, Allie took the

warm eggs from the nests and carefully put them inside the bucket. She anticipated Mother Case's pleasure when she saw the size of some of the eggs. Mother Case had said she would make a cake if there was an abundance of eggs that morning, and Allie was certain that several of the eggs she had collected were double yolks. Mama had always said double yolks made the best cakes.

Abruptly stopping in her tracks, Allie faced the last row of nests and the beady eyes of her nemesis. Her heart began racing, and annoyance at her own cowardice raged anew inside her. She would not let that nasty bird get the better of her!

With a firm step, Allie started forward. With each step she took, with each nest she emptied, the vicious hen's agitation became more visible. Suddenly within a few feet of her and faced with the task of emptying that last nest, Allie set her bucket on the floor and took a firm hold on her courage.

"Shoo! Get off! Shoo!"

Waving her arms, Allie frowned as she attempted to make the hen vacate her nest, but the old bird was determined to stay where she was. Obviously preferring to fight rather than move, the bird stretched out her scrawny neck, flapped her wings, and pecked until sharp, stinging wounds forced Allie to draw back.

Allie gasped, her eyes darting to the fresh cuts on her forearm and the back of her hand. They were bleeding, and she rubbed them in an attempt to assuage the pain. Tears flooded her eyes.

"Nasty, nasty bird! You want to keep all your eggs, and you can't! But you won't win this time. I'll get those eggs! I'll get them and take them back to Mother Case, and when I do—"

But Allie did not have time to finish her statement. Stirred to fury by Allie's threats, the bird abruptly began flapping its wings once more, this time leaving its nest and hurling itself directly toward Allie's head. Allie took a quick step backward and threw her arm over her eyes as the chicken attacked her. Abruptly snatching up the bucket, she beat a hasty retreat, slamming the door behind her even as the vicious bird flew against it in a last brazen attack.

Her back against the door, Allie took a deep breath, and then another in an attempt to control her tears. She glanced at the bucket in her hand and was relieved to see that the eggs inside were not broken, but that did not stop her humiliation—or her pain.

Raising a scratched and bleeding hand to her head, Allie touched her scalp tentatively, wincing as she felt another stinging wound there. Drawing her hand away, she saw her fingers were stained with blood, and tears welled more hotly than before. The fresh cuts burned miserably.

James paused on his way back from the rear pasture to watch Allie as he had many times in the past weeks. She was so slight, almost lost in the gingham dress that had been sewn for Annie's sturdier figure. Her pale hair and skin, glimmering in the bright fall sunlight, and her slightly oversized clothing with thin but strong limbs showing created an appearance of fragility that he knew was deceiving. But it was somehow endearing, nonetheless, as she trudged with unrelenting enthusiasm up the rise toward the chicken coops.

A smile touched James's lips, and a flicker of warmth stirred inside him. Three weeks had passed since Allie's arrival at the farm, and those weeks had confirmed his thoughts when he had seen her asleep in the loft that first morning. Allie had looked innocent, almost angelic, and the passage of time had proved that she was, indeed, all she had appeared to be.

Mama was pleased with Allie. James had not thought anyone could fill the void Annie had left in his mother's heart, but he knew now this pale little stick of a girl, who bore not the slightest resemblance to their bright, robust Annie, was well on her way to doing just that. As for Pa, well, it was going to take longer than three weeks to convince him that Allie was meant for them.

It was clear to James that the child loved the farm and appeared to find delight in the simplest things. If there was any reason for Annie's passing, it had to be that this little girl was not meant to have her loving sweetness wasted in a city orphanage where there was no one to love her. And if James was certain of anything, it was that little Allie was meant to be loved and to give love in return. He had seen her response to Mama. He had observed her desire to please, and he had noted the way she hid Sarah's meanness from Mama, so Mama would not be upset. He had attempted to speak to Sarah about her unreasonable resentment toward the girl, but the exchange had been a disaster, which he suspected had only turned Sarah more firmly against Allie.

Allie reached the coops and began to scatter feed to the chickens who had flocked toward her in a great, squawking swarm as James's thoughts had continued to wander. He supposed Allie's need to be loved was the cause of her attachment to Delaney Marsh, but how could she find consolation in a boy who had no love to give? That friendship was a mystery to James. And it was a mistake. Delaney Marsh was hardened beyond redemption by the streets and by the bars that had imprisoned him before he joined the Society's orphan train. He was biding his time, awaiting an opportunity to do something. What that something was, James wasn't sure. He was certain, however, that when the opportunity appeared, Marsh would forget his feigned concern for Allie, his contract with Pa, and everything else that got in his way.

Anger again touched James's mind, and his light brows furrowed into a deeper frown. Sarah had refused to listen to his warning about Delaney. She was impressed with his good looks and intrigued by the air of mystery about him. James refused to believe Allie was touched by that type of foolishness. Instead, Allie seemed to think only *she* understood Marsh, and stranger still, that only *Marsh* truly understood her.

James felt a familiar frustration. How many times in the past weeks had he seen Allie turn a glance toward Marsh in a bond of silent communication that excluded everyone else? The realization that Marsh fed upon Allie's gullibility caused James's frustration to grow.

He was determined to uncover the hold Marsh had over the girl. He would then dispel the myth Marsh had managed to perpetuate in her mind that he was her friend—her *only* friend. James would protect the child against Delaney Marsh, whether she wanted to be protected or not. And he'd do the same for Sarah. For all her selfish disregard of anyone's feelings, Sarah had not Delaney Marsh's experience, and she was James's sister. He did not want to see her hurt.

Allie had emptied the bucket and turned toward the coop. She paused at the door and then stepped inside to collect the eggs. James had been in the kitchen on one occasion when she had brought the eggs to Mama. She had been so proud of her accomplishment that Mama's eyes had misted. She had leaned down and hugged Allie, and he had not been able to forget the expression on the child's face.

James gave a short laugh and, lifting his worn hat, ran his long freckled fingers through his hair. He had not realized, when he first saw little Allie Pierce, that he would become so concerned about the child's welfare that he would neglect other facets of his life. In the three weeks since her coming, he had not once ridden the gelding over to see Jeanie Lowe, as had been his custom in the few months past. He had seen Jeanie in town only the day before, and she had let him know that she did not take his neglect kindly. He supposed Jeanie was right. She was, after all, sixteen years old and the prettiest girl in the county, excluding Sarah. There were plenty of fellows waiting to call on Jeanie, but James knew she favored him. But somehow, although he was seventeen years old, he could not seem to concentrate on Jeanie Lowe when matters at home were so unsettled.

This family needed to be rid of Delaney Marsh, and then everything else would fall into line. He supposed it was just a matter of time. Marsh would make a mistake soon, and James had no doubt that Pa would take the first opportunity to send him back where he came from.

His gazed fixed unconsciously on the coop Allie had entered a few minutes before, James was suddenly brought from his rambling thoughts by her abrupt exit. Slamming the coop door behind her, she leaned back against it with all her strength. He watched with growing concern as, still holding the door with one hand, she put the bucket carefully on the ground and took a deep breath. He attempted to read the expression on her face more clearly. Something was wrong.

Returning his hat to his head, James started toward her. He was a few feet away from Allie when he saw that she was trembling. A few steps closer and he saw that her hand was streaked with blood.

"Allie, what happened?"

At the sound of his voice, Allie looked up suddenly, a multitude of emotions visible on her colorless face. Embarrassment abruptly flooded her pale skin with color, wiping away the pain, the anger, the frustration he had viewed there only seconds before. She slipped her injured hand behind her back, but she could not avoid his scrutiny that easily.

Crouching down beside her, James drew her arm from behind her and examined it closely. He frowned, his light brows meeting over his freckled nose.

"Did that old hen get you?"

Allie lowered her eyes. Obviously too embarrassed to respond, she nodded her head. The short, jerking movement brought his eyes to her scalp and the wound still oozing blood there.

Taking her head gently between his palms, James tilted it forward to examine the cut. He released a short, angry breath and then tilted up her chin so she again met his eyes.

"You'd better go into the house and let Mama put something on those cuts." His callused fingertips touched her cheek. "You have a scratch on your face, too. That bird's nasty—too nasty for her own good. We've been having trouble with her since she started laying eggs. She came at me a few times, too."

Realizing he would only further embarrass her by relating the ease with which he had handled the angry hen, James brushed a wisp of hair back from Allie's face. "You'll get used to her. You have to be firm."

"I tried!" Speaking for the first time, Allie shook her head. "I told myself I wasn't going to let her get me again today, but she flew after me—chased me right out of the coop!"

"I'll tell Mama, and she'll—"

"Oh, please don't tell anyone, James. I'll do much better tomorrow."

Suddenly realizing Allie had considered his comment a threat, James frowned. "That old hen has given every one of us trouble at one time or another. Nobody will think less of you."

"Please, James."

The intensity in her dark eyes only too revealing, James paused before responding. Tilting her head forward once more, he examined her scalp more closely. He shook his head.

"You should put something on this, Allie, or it'll fester. Mama'll find out then, and she'll wonder why you didn't want her to know."

"It'll be all right, James. I'll take care of it myself, tonight."

"And when she sees the scratches on your face and hands?"

Allie bit her lower lip nervously. There was pain in her whispered response. "Everyone will laugh at me."

"I didn't laugh."

Allie met his eyes in silence.

Abruptly, James stood up. "All right, I won't tell anyone, even though there's nothing to be ashamed of. But you'd better come with me. There's some alcohol in the barn. It might smart a bit, but it'll clean out that cut real well, and it'll stop the bleeding, too."

Gripping her hand, James turned toward the barn, realizing Allie had no recourse but to follow his rapid step.

Withdrawing his handkerchief a few minutes later, James frowned even more darkly. He shook his head. "Mama would've used a clean cloth, but we don't have much choice here, do we?"

Motioning her to be seated on an overturned pail nearby, James crouched down beside her and moistened the handkerchief from the bottle in his hand.

"This will sting, Allie."

His narrow face pulled into a frown of concentration, James touched the cut on Allie's head slightly. She made no sound, and he pressed the alcohol-soaked cloth more firmly to the cut. Allie jumped, a low sound escaping her throat. His whispered "I'm sorry, Allie" came from the heart.

Realizing that the first sting would be the worst, James worked quickly, cleaning the gouge on her scalp. It occurred to him as he did so that in the three weeks Allie had been on the farm, the sun had lightened her hair so that it was now even paler than her original color. But exposure to the sun had also tinted her complexion, and the contrast of tanned skin against silver-blond hair was surprisingly appealing.

Finished with that first wound, James raised Allie's chin to examine the scratch on her cheek. He dabbed at it lightly, noting the way she forced herself to remain still until he was finished. It occurred to him then as he perused her sober face that Allie had begun to look considerably different from the pale, sickly looking child who had first come to them.

Suddenly realizing that Allie was studying him as well, James abruptly took her small hand and concentrated on the cuts that marked it. He shook his head. "Some of these are old cuts, Allie. They've already begun festering."

"Th-they'll be all right, James."

Her nervous stammer touching his heart, James gave a short nod and continued his ministrations. She remained perfectly still, although he knew the wounds burned painfully, and James was silently impressed with her grit.

Finally done, James released a low, relieved breath.

"All right. I'm finished, but what are you going to say to Mama if she asks you how you got so scratched up?"

Allie paused, obviously giving the question weighty consideration. She was frowning slightly when she responded. "I'll tell her it's nothing. It *is* nothing, James. You said yourself that hen has gone after everybody at one time or another, and—and I won't let her get away with it next time. I'll be firm, just like you said."

James nodded. He didn't tell her that hen had never cut anybody as badly as it had cut her. He knew it would only upset her more, and he didn't want that. To the contrary, he sincerely wished he could put a smile on her small, sober face.

A thought he had considered only fleetingly a short time earlier suddenly returned to his mind. "All right. But before you go back into the house, I have something to show you. Leave the eggs here for a minute. Come on."

Taking her hand, James pulled her to her feet. He was aware Allie was puzzled as he led her into the rear stall of the barn. He watched as she scanned the stall in uncertain silence until a sound from the shadowed corner caught her attention. Within seconds she was on her knees beside a small straw bed there, staring at the tiny squirming kittens that moved with soft, mewing sounds as they sought to suckle the gray female cat lying there.

A low gasp of pleasure escaped her throat.

"Oh, they're beautiful!"

Reaching out, she stroked the smooth, newborn fur, her voice low with fascination. "Four of them—two black and white, one striped, and one gray, just like Shadow."

Allie turned in his direction, and James saw a suspicious brightness in her eyes. "I had a kitten once," she said.

"Pa doesn't like to keep the kittens."

Allie averted her head abruptly, but James continued slowly,

"But I already told Pa that we should keep one this time. I thought you'd be willing to take care of it."

Allie turned toward him with surprise. He saw incredulity flash across her small face, and he saw something else, too, in the moment she hesitated before nodding.

"I . . . I'll take care of it."

"You'll have to be responsible for it completely, Allie, because it'll be yours."

Allie hesitated again. "Mine?"

James gave a short nod, a slow warmth beginning to pervade him. "You do want one, don't you?"

"Oh, yes!"

"Then I think you should decide which one you want to keep."

"I'd like to have the striped one."

James gave a short laugh. "It didn't take you long to decide."

"I'll call it Mischief."

"All right, I'll tell Pa."

Allie turned back to the kittens once more and James resisted the desire to run a caressing hand over her straight, pale hair. Instead, he urged softly, "I think we'd better leave Shadow alone for a while so she can finish feeding them. You can come back later."

Allie rose obediently. He extended his hand to her, and she took it without hesitation. The warmth inside him rose to a glow as Allie turned to walk at his side. Suddenly pausing, she looked up, her brow knotted. Her softly spoken question was touched by a note of confusion. "Do . . . do you like us now, James? Are you happy Mother Case brought us here?"

Allie's childish candor brought an unfamiliar tightness to his throat, adding a husky note to James's response.

"I've always liked you, Allie."

Allie appeared to consider his statement for long silent moments. Her solemn gaze remained fixed on his face. "Thank you for the kitten, James."

Unable to think of a more fitting response, he replied with corresponding formality. "You're welcome, Allie."

Her small hand still enclosed in his, she walked with James to the barn door where she picked up the bucket of eggs. All thought of the cuts on her hand and the defeat they represented fled her mind as they walked hand and hand into the yard, where Allie turned to look soberly up at him once more.

"I'll take good care of the kitten, James. I promise."

Disengaging her hand as he nodded in response, Allie started toward the house at a rapid gait that gradually escalated to a cautious run. There was joy in that step, a joy that was suddenly mirrored in James's heart.

He turned, the smile on his face freezing as he met Delaney Marsh's cold stare. Allie's candid question of a few minutes before returned to his mind, as did his evasive response: "I've always liked you, Allie."

Whether Allie had realized it or not, the word "you" had not included the street vagrant now staring at him so boldly, and he knew it never would. But he had taken the first step in freeing Allie from her dependence on Marsh, and he would not be satisfied until she finally saw the youthful opportunist for what he really was. That day would not be long in coming.

Not bothering with amenities, James turned his back on Delaney and walked into the barn.

Allie worked quickly, her small hands gripping the dishes firmly as she returned the last stack to the shelf. Turning, she surveyed the kitchen once more. The men had left shortly after finishing their midday meal, and Mother Case, Sarah, and Allie had begun cleaning up. As usual, Sarah had disappeared after a few minutes, with one excuse or another, and Mother Case and she had completed the chores. The food had been covered and stored, the bread wrapped, the dishes washed, dried, and put away, and the beautiful black iron stove had been cleaned and readied for preparation of the evening meal. Turning, Allie retrieved the heavy vase filled with flowers she had picked in the field that morning, and placed it back on the center of the table. Yes, the kitchen was again back to rights.

Sensing a silent perusal, Allie turned to Mother Case's benevolent gaze.

"Yes, dear, everything is in order. I won't be needing you for an hour or so, so you may entertain yourself as you like. It's a beautiful day. Why don't you go outside?"

Allie nodded, an enthusiastic "Yes, ma'am" escaping her lips as she turned toward the door. Within minutes she was running across the yard, her eyes on the barn. Allie had not mentioned the kitten at the table, but now she wanted to see it again, to touch it and make sure it was really hers. And then she wanted to tell Delaney.

A frown flicking across her brow, she recalled the moment she had sat down for the midday meal and felt Sarah's keen eyes on her face.

"Whatever happened to you, Allie? Your face is all scratched."

Sarah's comments had turned the attention of everyone at the table in Allie's direction, and she had flushed as she had offered her prepared response.

"Nothing much."

"Oh, I'd say it's something. Considering your poor skin, it'll probably scar." Pausing, as if to give her last comment additional thought, Sarah added with a small shrug, "But I guess that wouldn't make much difference."

Allie's averted gaze did not allow her to see the dismay on Mother Case's face or the angry glances the others turned to Sarah. Allie kept silent, as Mother Case offered softly, "I'm sure those scratches will heal just fine, and Allie's skin will be as pretty as ever. They look quite clean and free of infection."

Allie had deliberately kept her eyes on her plate. She had not wanted to inadvertently glance toward James and reveal the part he had played in the rapidly healing cuts.

But even Sarah's hatefulness had not dampened Allie's buoyant spirits. A kitten—she had a kitten of her own again!

Reaching the barn doors, Allie was about to step inside when whispered words from within brought her to an abrupt halt. She hesitated, scanning the darkened interior of the barn, finally realizing that the voices came from the corner where the harnesses were stored. She squinted into the shadows to see two figures standing so close as to be almost touching. Then came Sarah's voice, louder this time and more easily identified.

"James is taller than you are, but your shoulders are so much broader." Allie could see that Sarah was stroking Delaney's chest. "I like touching you, Delaney. Wouldn't you like to touch me, too?"

After a short silence, Delaney responded, his voice so low that Allie could not make out his words. But whatever they were, they added an edge to Sarah's tone when she spoke again.

"But nobody will know! I won't tell anybody, and neither will you." Allie watched as Sarah took Delaney's hand, put it against her waist, and started moving it slowly upward. "All the boys tell me I'm pretty. They try to pull me behind the church house and kiss me. I won't let them, but I'd like *you* to kiss me, Delaney."

Unable to stand more, Allie turned and walked back out into the yard. Her heart was racing and tears choked her throat. Sarah was mean, but she was never mean to Delaney. No, she cooed to him just as Mrs. Bascombe had cooed to her baby when she visited the farm a week before. Delaney said he knew how Sarah was, but he had not pushed her away or told her to leave. He was still in there with her.

Turning away, Allie walked with a lagging step toward the apple tree that shaded the side of the house. She sat abruptly in the shadow of its wide, split trunk. She wanted to see her kitten, but she did not want to see Sarah and Delaney.

Her chin in her hands, Allie waited in silence, uncertain how much time elapsed before Sarah emerged from the barn and walked swiftly back into the house. Allie drew back so that Sarah would not see her. She could not see Sarah's face, but she could visualize the triumph visible there. She had no doubt she would be treated to Sarah's version of the scene later that night, after the lamps were turned off in their room and Mother Case thought they were asleep.

Slowly drawing herself to her feet, Allie again started toward the barn. Delaney had not emerged, and she hesitated in the doorway. A curt voice made her snap her head toward the far corner as Delaney walked toward her, a harness in his hand.

"What are you doing here, Allie?"

Allie winced at the lack of warmth in Delaney's tone. The fear that Sarah had already begun to turn him against her made her unconsciously take a step back.

"I'm sorry, Delaney. I didn't mean to come in when you were with Sarah."

Delaney's cool glance flickered momentarily. "Sarah doesn't give up easy." He had walked into the light, and Allie searched his expression. She saw no warmth there, and her heart fell.

"Are you mad at me, Delaney?"

"No."

Allie lowered her eyes at his tone. "Sarah is very pretty." Allie raised her hand to her scratched cheek, unconsciously revealing her thoughts as Sarah's comments at the table returned to torment her.

Delaney frowned and took another step closer.

"That scratch won't leave a scar on your face, Allie, and even if it did, you'd still be prettier than Sarah because you're prettier inside than she is."

A faint hope came alive within Allie. It pulled at the corners of her lips, coaxing them upward in a hesitant smile.

"Mama said it was better to be pretty on the inside than on the outside, because the outside gets old and the inside doesn't. I try real hard to be pretty inside when I'm with Sarah, but . . ."

A smile pulled at Delaney's lips as well. "I guess you'll have to keep working on that, Allie."

Delaney lightly touched the scratch on her cheek. His expression softening, he slipped his hand down to squeeze her shoulder reassuringly.

A disturbing thought abruptly took shape inside Allie's mind, then slipped off her tongue to hang on the air between Delaney and herself.

"Did you smile when you touched Sarah?"

Motionless for a moment, Delaney then crouched down beside her, again serious.

"I didn't touch Sarah because I wanted to, Allie, and I told her she was wasting her time. Whatever she says to you tonight, after the lamp is out, you don't have to believe a word. She's a pretty girl, but she's ugly inside, and that takes away her beauty."

Suddenly Delaney's smile was truly warm, his stiff manner of a few minutes before gone. He touched her chin playfully. "Don't worry, Allie. I told you Sarah will never be my friend, and I meant it."

It came to Allie in that second that Delaney was the one who was beautiful. Not only was his face beautiful—and it was, with his shiny black hair making his clear eyes seem even lighter, and with the smile that most people never saw making them glow—but he was beautiful inside, too, and he showed that beauty only to her.

Gratitude for all Delaney had given her suddenly freed her

from the bonds of shyness, and Allie took a step closer to him. Impulsively, she slid her arm around his neck.

"You're beautiful on the inside, too, more beautiful than anybody knows."

For the briefest moment, the bright blue of Delaney's eyes held hers in silence. Finally, giving a short laugh, he drew himself up straight.

"Well, we'll keep that secret between us, won't we, Allie?"

Allie nodded, the earlier joy of the day returning at last. Taking Delaney's hand, she excitedly pulled him forward.

"I have another secret, too, Delaney. I wanted to tell you first. Come on. I'll show you."

"Allie, Mr. Case is waiting for me."

"Only a minute. Please, Delaney."

Drawing him to the rear stall, Allie pulled Delaney to the corner where Shadow was again nursing her kittens.

"The striped kitten is mine."

Delaney studied her face, his expression again closed. "Yours?"

"James gave it to me. He said I could have any kitten I wanted, and I chose the striped one." Her voice dropping a notch, reflecting the return of a sober memory, she continued, "I had a striped kitten when Mama and I lived at Mrs. Van Houten's house. Her name was Mischief, too. James says I can keep this one as long as I take good care of it. I'll take very good care of it."

Delaney was silent. His narrowed gaze moved over her flushed face. "When did this happen?"

"This morning, after that hen pecked me."

Delaney glanced at the scratch on her cheek, then studied her more closely. His exploring fingers gently found the dried wound on her head. He smiled, but it was a strange smile.

"It was that speckled hen, wasn't it—the one who always chases the others?"

Allie nodded.

"Did James tend to your cuts, Allie?"

Allie nodded again.

Delaney dropped his hand. "He did a good job." He paused a moment before continuing. "So James is your friend, too, now."

Allie took a step closer, an inexplicable sadness touching her heart.

"James wants to be *your* friend, too, Delaney. I asked him if he liked us now, and he said he always liked us."

Delaney studied her sincere expression before he again crouched down beside her. The blue of his eyes held no trace of the ice often visible there.

"Allie, James does like you. I think he liked you almost from the start. But he doesn't like me at all."

The spot of sadness inside Allie grew. "I'll tell him about you, Delaney. I'll tell him about the Lady and how you helped me, and then he'll like you."

"No, Allie. He wouldn't understand about the Lady. He'd only dislike me more."

Remembering the church she had attended each Sunday since coming to the farm, Allie nodded, belatedly realizing that Delaney was probably right. No one here understood about the Lady.

"I'll pray harder, Delaney, and James will start to like you, too. I know he will."

Seeing the skepticism Delaney attempted to disguise, Allie reached toward his chest and found the outline of the medal lying under his shirt. She traced it with her finger as she said with heartfelt certainty, "The Lady will help me, Delaney."

"Allie . . ."

Realizing he hesitated to voice his disbelief for her benefit, Allie lowered her eyes. It was not fair to press Delaney when he did not feel free to answer her truthfully. She again met his gaze. "Will you be mad at me if I let James be my friend?"

Delaney gave a short laugh that had no joy in it. "No, Allie."

"You didn't let Sarah be *your* friend."

"I don't like Sarah. You *like* James."

Allie stopped to consider that, then nodded. "Yes, I like him."

"Then you should let him be your friend. I want you to be happy, Allie. And I don't want you to feel alone when I have to leave."

"Leave?"

Responding immediately to the panic he saw in her face, Delaney took her small hand in his. "You know I can't stay here forever."

"Why can't you stay? Mother Case wants you to, and I do, too."

"Allie, I have things I want to do. I don't want to be a farmer, and even if I did, I'd never be anything more than a hired man here."

"But Papa Case—"

"Allie"—squeezing her hand even tighter, Delaney continued— "Allie, do you remember the day we met Mother Case? I told her that I was never going back to prison again, that I had—"

"A goal. But you wouldn't tell her what it was."

"I'll tell you, if you'll promise not to tell anyone else."

Allie nodded. "I promise."

"I'm going to study very hard, like my pa told me, and when I'm ready, I'm going to the city."

"Back to New York?"

"No. I'm going to Chicago, and I'm going to be wealthy. I'm going to have so much money that I'll never have to worry about anything again. And I'm going to be famous, Allie."

Allie's eyes widened as her voice dropped to a barely audible whisper. "Famous?"

"Just like my pa"—Delaney's expression hardened into a frown—"before everything started going wrong."

Accepting all Delaney said without question, Allie finally broke the silence between them. "You . . . you won't be leaving soon?"

"No."

"Not for a long time?"

"Not for a while."

Allie was not happy with that response, but the look in Delaney's eyes halted the words that rose to her lips.

Touched with a sense of impending loss, Allie whispered fervently, "You'll always be my best friend, Delaney, always."

A sudden meowing from the corner interrupted the intimacy of the moment, turning Allie toward Shadow as she detached herself from her complaining kittens and walked away. Allie scooped up the tiny striped kitten, then raised her eyes to Delaney's sober perusal.

"Mischief will be *your* kitten, too, but I won't tell James."

Searching her face a moment longer, Delaney drew himself up straight. "I won't tell him either."

As sober as he, Allie watched as Delaney turned and walked

away. He picked up the harness and disappeared through the doorway into the yard, and Allie glanced back to her mewing kitten.

The sadness inside her conflicted with her supreme confidence and pride in Delaney as Allie whispered softly, "Delaney will be famous someday, just like he said. Delaney can do anything he wants to do, because he's brave and strong and smart. But you don't have to worry. He won't leave us for a very long time."

Pressing her cheek against Mischief's soft, warm fur, Allie added silently that she hoped that time would never come.

His anger growing with each step he took, Delaney clutched the harness in his hand. His knuckles grew white with his choking grip.

He was annoyed with himself. He had not meant to reveal the dream that had given impetus to his life since he was told he would be released from prison to join the Society orphans on their journey to Michigan. Put into the spoken word, the dream seemed far beyond him, even though he was determined to make it come true.

He was annoyed with himself for another reason as well. He was not certain why he had told Allie that he would one day leave her and the farm. His stupidity in frightening her needlessly infuriated him.

Delaney turned toward the back field where Mr. Case occupied himself fixing the wagon while he awaited Delaney's return. He strained his clear, light eyes toward the man's broad back, noting that James was approaching from the other direction, tools in his hands. His agitation increased.

A knot of an unfamiliar emotion tightened in his stomach, and Delaney ground his teeth tightly shut. He had seen the warmth on James's face when he looked at Allie, and he had little doubt James's overtures to her were sincere. He also had little doubt that James's efforts would be just as sincere when he attempted to sever Allie's attachment to the worthless prison boy who had thrust himself upon her and his family.

His eyes not leaving James's tall, spare figure as they both converged upon the wagon, Delaney felt a familiar heat rise inside him. Wherever James's intentions took him from here, Delaney was certain of only one thing. James had better not try to get to him through Allie. If he did, he would regret it.

Reaching the wagon, Delaney met James's eye stiffly. No words needed to be spoken. Enemies they were, declared or undeclared, and enemies they would remain.

His light, translucent eyes steady and cool, Delaney extended his arm toward James and placed the harness in his hand.

Her expression sober, Allie gave the table a last, cursory glance. A light touch on her shoulder turned her to Mother Case's smile.

"Everything is fine, dear. Sit down. We're ready to eat."

Nodding, Allie walked immediately to her place and assumed her seat, aware that except for Mother Case, she was the last to do so. She passed a quick glance around the table. Papa Case was talking to James, and Sarah was talking to Delaney. She was smiling broadly into his eyes, and Allie felt her stomach twist. Delaney had been right: Sarah did not give up easily.

"Jacob, dear, will you say grace?"

Mother Case's soft request turned all eyes in her direction, and it occurred to Allie that the only way her new family was completely united was in love for this dear woman.

Papa Case acknowledged his wife's suggestion with a nod. "Heavenly Father, we thank you for the bounty which you have seen fit to put upon our table. We thank you for . . ."

Her head lowered, her hands clasped together in prayer, Allie let her mind wander from the familiar blessing. The sadness that had dogged her since her conversation with Delaney had not lessened. She had surrendered the consolation of Mischief's warmth to Shadow when the conscientious mother cat returned for yet another feeding. Allie had then wandered aimlessly in the sun-drenched fields until a tantalizing fragrance had reached her nostrils, telling her that it was time to help Mother Case with supper.

"James, please pass the biscuits."

Mother Case's soft voice drew Allie from her thoughts, and she looked up, catching Delaney's curious glance. She attempted a smile, which was thoroughly unsuccessful, if she was to judge by Delaney's frown.

"Allie!"

An annoyed summons turned Allie toward Sarah's piqued expression. "Really, I've never met a girl who spends so much time daydreaming! Please pass the biscuits and the potatoes."

Sarah's comment brought embarrassed color to Allie's cheeks.

She quickly passed the biscuits down the table, unaware of the dark looks Sarah received from the other members of the family.

Allie's quick glance at Delaney revealed that his frown had intensified. She attempted a smile. Delaney had confided his ambitions to her, and she should be happy about that. If she persisted with this attitude, Delaney would regret having confided in her.

"Oh, I think Allie did a bit more than daydream, today." Attempting to soften Sarah's unfair criticism, Mother Case continued lightly, "As a matter of fact, Allie made the biscuits tonight, without any help at all from me."

Allie smiled at the compliments that sounded around the table, but her discomfort returned during the silence that followed. Her spirits low, she accepted a hearty helping of chicken stew and picked up her fork. She jabbed at the juicy meat and, ignoring the fact that she had no appetite at all, slid a small piece between her lips. It was delicious, as was all the food Mother Case prepared.

"This stew is delicious, Margaret." His voice unnaturally hearty in the pervading silence, Papa Case smiled at his fragile wife.

Mrs. Case smiled in return. "We have Delaney to thank for this stew," she said. Ignoring the curious glances sent his way, Delaney continued to devote his attention to his plate as Mrs. Case continued. "Delaney never ceases to surprise me with his thoughtfulness. He brought me the chicken for this stew, all cleaned and plucked and ready to be cooked. It saved me a considerable amount of work."

Papa Case made an appropriate remark, but it was lost to Allie's ears as a thought suddenly struck her mind. She stopped chewing abruptly and looked down at the savory food in her plate. She stared at the succulent pieces of chicken as if to identify . . .

She glanced up. Catching Delaney's eye, she held his gaze in silence for long moments until a small tug at the corner of his lips sent a jolt of absolute certainty through her mind.

Allie swallowed convulsively. The small piece of chicken slipped slowly down her throat as she was compelled by a force stronger than her will to look back down at her plate. She stared at the stew with a wide-eyed, incredulous gaze, then looked back up at Delaney.

She was still staring at him when a small bubble of laughter threatened to escape her throat. Blinking almost comically, she firmly forced it back. With sheer strength of will, she maintained her sober expression, the sparkle in her eye silently acknowledging to Delaney's innocent light-eyed gaze yet another secret that the two of them shared.

With great deliberation, Allie turned her attention back to the meal before her. She jabbed her fork into the largest piece of chicken on her plate and popped in into her mouth. She chewed energetically, all trace of her former sadness dissolved as she fought to suppress a smile. She would never have trouble with that speckled hen again. Her laughter emerged in a small hiccup.

Oh, Delaney . . .

His expression not revealing his amused satisfaction, Delaney walked back out into the yard after dinner. The picture of Allie's small face remained in his mind, her dark eyes wide, her mouth incredulously open, and he resisted the urge to laugh. The determination with which she had returned her attention to her plate and continued eating until it was empty stirred his admiration. Full of surprises was his little Allie.

His little Allie.

Another picture returned to his mind, replacing the humorous one of a few moments before. He remembered the spark in her deep, dark eyes when Allie had held his gaze at the table—the confirmation of yet another bond they shared. Somehow, in that fleeting moment, he had seen a glimpse of the Allie that slight little girl would someday be, and he had not yet recovered from the effects of that brief revelation.

Delaney had almost reached the barn when his wandering thoughts were violently interrupted. A rough hand turned him unexpectedly to James's tensely controlled expression. Anger replacing the softer emotions of a few moments before, Delaney felt a small muscle tic in his cheek as James growled, "You bastard!"

"I told you once before—"

"I don't care what you told me," James interrupted. "You had to do it, didn't you? You had to get the upper hand."

"I don't know what you're talking about."

"You know what I'm talking about, all right! Maybe nobody

else knows about that hen and Allie, but you and I do, and you proved what kind of person you really are by using her little secret to your own advantage. You aren't going to let go of that little girl, are you? You know she stands up for you, and you know that as long as she does, and as long as my mother feels that Allie wants you here, there's no way anybody is going to get you off this farm.''

Releasing a low grunt of disgust at James's accusations, Delaney attempted to turn away from him, only to have James's hand tighten on his arm.

''Well, it isn't going to work much longer, Marsh! That little girl trusts me, too, now. She's going to trust me more and more, and as soon as I can make her see you for what you really are, you'll be off this farm and out on your ear!''

His anger flooding to a full fury, Delaney controlled with the most strenuous effort the desire to smash his fist into James Case's livid, freckled face. ''Take your hand off me, Case.''

James was obviously unaffected by the threat in the cold, light eyes staring into his. ''Did you hear what I said, Marsh?''

His chest heaving from suppressed emotion, Delaney repeated, ''Did you hear what *I* said, Case? *Take your hand off me!*'' Suddenly dropping his hand from Delaney's arm, James gave a short laugh. ''Oh, no, you're not going to force me into a fight right here where Mama and Pa can see us. I'm not fool enough to give you the advantage by making them think I'm picking on you.'' James laughed again, a hard, joyless sound. ''No, bastard, I'm not that much a fool.''

Delaney's level gaze silently disputed that last statement, and James's flush deepened. James's low hiss followed Delaney as he turned away and walked toward the barn.

''Save yourself a lot of trouble, Marsh, and do this family a favor. Let us wake up some morning and find you gone. Because I'm warning you, you aren't going to get anything out of this family that you don't earn with the sweat of your brow. There's nothing for a fella like you here on this farm. Nothing, do you hear me?''

Careful to maintain a steady gait that did not betray the fury surging through him, Delaney turned into the barn and out of James Case's sight. In the shadows at last, Delaney paused in an attempt to control his rage as Case's words rang in his mind.

Why did he stay here on this godforsaken farm in the wilderness, taking abuse from a fellow he would have given the hard side of his hand without a second thought a few months ago? He could ask the Society to place him in a better home. He could be—

Abruptly halting the rapid progression of his thoughts, Delaney gave a short laugh. Who was he fooling? He knew the reason he had come here and the reason he was going to stay, for a while longer, at least.

That reason was Allie. She needed him, and while she needed him, he needed her. When that need was gone he would be free to leave, but until that time nobody, especially not a redneck farmboy he could beat with one hand tied behind his back, was going to get him out. And that was that!

Delaney strode toward the ladder and started climbing to the loft.

"Sarah."

Turning from the tense confrontation between her brother and Delaney, which she had witnessed unseen, Sarah faced her mother. Disregarding the worried lines that had become all too familiar of late, she responded in a tightly controlled voice, "Why do you let James get away with it, Mama? You saw him! He was picking on Delaney again, and Delaney didn't do anything!"

Mrs. Case looked over her shoulder into the kitchen where Allie was washing the dishes. She was grateful she had not sent the child into the yard on the chores that had allowed both Sarah and her to witness the sharp exchange.

"Sarah, please. I don't want Allie to hear."

"Allie, Allie, Allie! That's all I hear!" Her voice low, Sarah continued venomously, "Well, I don't want her to hear, either, because nothing that goes on here is any of her business! She doesn't belong here!"

Her expression pained, Mrs. Case shook her head. "Sarah dear, you know that isn't true. We have more than enough on this farm, and it's only right that we share our bounty with those who are less fortunate."

"We should've taken Delaney—only Delaney. He's practically a man, and he can work like one. Papa would be glad for his help if James wasn't so pigheaded. But we don't need her! She doesn't do anything but give us more work!''

"Sarah," Mother Case said despairingly, "you know Delaney wouldn't have come here without Allie. They've suffered similar tragedies, and there's a bond between them. Allie depends on Delaney, and Delaney cares about her.''

Her slender body going abruptly rigid, Sarah stared at her mother in silence. Her lovely face twitched unattractively. "No, he doesn't.''

"He does, Sarah. It's only natural.''

"Natural." Sarah took a deep, angry breath. "I'll tell you what's natural, Mama. Allie Pierce is a baby, but I'm not, and neither is Delaney. And I'm pretty, real pretty. All the boys tell me that. So it's natural that Delaney's going to start liking me better than he likes her.''

"Sarah!"

"That's right, Mama, Delaney's going to start liking me. I'm fourteen years old. I'm almost grown. Pretty soon I'll be ready for courting, and Delaney's going to start courting me. You wait and see!''

Mrs. Case cast a quick glance in the direction Mr. Case had disappeared only minutes before, but Sarah continued belligerently, "I don't care if Papa hears me, because I'm telling you, that's how it's going to be. I'm going to get Delaney for myself. You'll see.''

"Sarah!"

"He's going to forget Allie Pierce ever existed! And I'm going to marry him! Then I'm going to make sure he never even talks to that skinny little orphan again!''

"That's enough, Sarah. More than enough!" With unexpected sternness, Mrs. Case raised her chin uncompromisingly. "It's time you went to your room.''

"Mama . . .''

"Go now, Sarah, before I lose my temper. But before you do, I want to make clear that I will not tolerate another tirade like this.''

Sarah was taken aback by her mother's surprisingly sharp words. "Mama . . .''

"Do you understand?''

Her startled expression turning to one of defiance, Sarah nodded. Turning abruptly without another word, she walked stiffly back into the kitchen.

Shocked by Sarah's insolence, Mrs. Case was still in deep thought when a touch on her arm caused her to turn toward her husband's concerned expression as he spoke.

"I'm beginning to think those two will never get along."

Margaret Case turned in the direction of Jacob's gaze and saw that he referred to the confrontation between James and Delaney. She released her breath, grateful he had somehow missed witnessing his daughter's unexpected viciousness.

At Margaret's hesitation, Jacob turned to study her pale face. "Margaret dear, you mustn't let this upset you." Caressing her cheek with a light, loving touch, he berated himself softly, "I never should've allowed you to take those two children in. You're not well enough or strong enough yet. You don't need the responsibility of two more around here, much less children with problems."

"Jacob, I could not have turned them away." The truth of those words registering in her heart, Margaret Case felt a new strength gradually transfuse her. "It will work out, dear. The hand of the Lord is in all of this, so it must work out."

Turning, Jacob glanced toward the kitchen where Allie worked, unaware of all that was going on around her. His brows knit in a frown, he glanced back toward the spot where Delaney Marsh had disappeared into the barn, and then toward his son who was walking with a stiff, angry posture toward the back field. "I don't know, Margaret. Sometimes I fear for how this is all going to turn out."

Unable to respond, realizing the situation was even more difficult than he knew, Margaret tucked her hand under her husband's arm and leaned against his side, suddenly weary and grateful for his strength.

Jacob's words echoed in her mind as they walked toward the house, and Margaret thought of the years to come. Somewhere in her heart, she worried how this all would come out, too.

1859

❈

THE HAVEN

chapter

seven

DELANEY GRIPPED THE reins of the wagon with a firm, practiced hand as it rattled along the dusty road to town. He had learned to handle the reins the hard way, the same way he had learned everything else on the Casc farm in the last three years, the same way he had learned everything in his life. He uttered a short, sardonic laugh. He supposed he should be grateful. Hard-learned lessons were not easily forgotten.

His expression sober once more, Delaney frowned with impatience. The unrelenting August sun was hot on his back, and the air unusually heavy. He was sweaty, irritable, anxious to be off the road. Shifting the reins to his left hand, Delaney lifted his well-worn broad-brimmed hat and wiped his arm across his forehead. Replacing the hat, he made a clucking sound and slapped the reins gently against the old mare's back. She immediately picked up her pace, kicking up even greater clouds of gritty dust to settle against his damp skin as the vehicle shuddered along at a more impressive speed.

Delaney gave a low snort of reluctant approval. Bad legs or not, the old girl was as dependable as the sunrise, and completely impartial in her response to command. He recognized only too well that impartiality was a rare commodity, becoming more so each day.

He supposed that generalization applied as much to the country as a whole as it did to his personal life. The slavery question was drawing to a head, with northern states slowly drawing up sides against southern slave-owning states, and even their small Michigan town was not exempt from participation in the controversy. A few weeks before, a well-dressed rabble-rouser with all the skills of a professional had spent a few hours in town. His angry voice and wild gestures had gathered a crowd quickly as he had decried the cause of slavery. He had left a short time later to continue his crusade at the next stop on the rail line, but he had not been forgotten.

The town was generally in sympathy with the Union, but the country itself was torn apart. Delaney shrugged. He was against slavery. His own situation in life had taught him to sympathize with the slaves' plight. He believed every man should be in charge of his own destiny and be free to make his own way; but, in truth, he had not been as deeply touched by the progress of events in the country as others had. He had been too busy fighting his own war to pay much attention to the rumors circulating that the slavery question might come to just that—war.

His own war was one he waged daily against James's rancor and Mr. Case's long-standing resentment at having him foisted upon the family. He knew he would continue to wage that same war as long as he remained on the Case farm. However, unlike the undeclared conflict that raged between the North and the South, he now saw an end to his own personal war in sight.

Taking a deep breath, Delaney turned his attention to the passing countryside. He had traveled this road countless times during the past three years. Unpaved, deeply rutted, it wound through heavily forested patches and land dotted with bright sunlit meadows and pastures. Clear, sparkling streams were abundant, often forming small, deep pools which had cooled him when he was overworked, overheated, and nearing the end of his patience. It was land that rolled unmarred by the hand of man for long miles at a time, and its contrast with the city where he had spent the first fifteen years of his life could not have been more distinct. Delaney absentmindedly waved away a buzzing insect. He was not sure he considered this landscape an improvement.

His tight expression softening, Delaney allowed memories of an earlier time to sweep his mind. The first nine years of his life in New York City had been dramatically different from this simple life he was now living. Pa had more than made up to Delaney for the loss of his mother by exposing him to the advantages of city living, its excitement and diversity. As a boy, he had never been excluded from the groups that gathered in fashionable rooms for intense, serious conversations which he had not always understood. He had not suffered from neglect—not then.

The warmth of happy memories abruptly fading, Delaney's dark brow knit more tightly. He realized the turning point in his life and his father's had come when Pa lost his job. With it had gone all Pa's pleasant friends as well as their living quarters on the street where all the pretty matrons made a fuss over him and Pa. Their new home had been a furnished room, and the boys who attended his new school had been tough and mean. He had learned all too soon to defend himself with his fists, and he had not hesitated to do so.

Delaney attempted to shrug off the memories that followed— the recollection of Pa's alternating periods of despair and painful, frustrating hope; of Pa ranting that "those bastards have fixed it for me, all right—they've fixed it so no decent newspaper will touch me!" The memory of a policeman at the door, saying that Mr. Walter Marsh had been struck by a carriage and had died.

His vision shadowed by harsh memories, Delaney stared unseeingly forward. After his father's death, he had received a far more liberal education than the one Pa had so diligently imparted. Lessons learned on the street were taught by a hard, unrelenting hand, and Delaney had been a good student.

One of the earliest of those lessons had been that he was smarter than the average street boy and could live a reasonably good life if he used his superior wit ruthlessly. Another was that he neither needed nor could depend on anyone but himself.

Only later, when he was locked away, had he realized that he wasn't as smart as he thought—that he had succeeded in getting off the streets only by going to jail. But he was smart enough to recognize his mistakes. It had not taken him long to realize that he needed to direct his energies toward a goal. He had known immediately what that goal would be.

It had been difficult to accept the fact that he would have to bide his time, accept restrictions, for a while. Then—hard, bitter, wise beyond his years, and totally free of emotional need for another living soul—he had agreed to go west with the Society's company.

He had not been prepared, however, for the possibility that someone might need *him*.

An image of Allie's face rose before him, and the bitter memories came to a halt. He had long before admitted to himself that his concern for the little girl with the trusting eyes was a weakness he could not afford. With that admission, he had made himself a promise that he would not indulge that weakness a moment longer than was necessary.

Allowing his mind to remain on that thought for only a few moments longer, Delaney turned his attention back to the passing landscape. He had expected that Mrs. Case would send him on an errand to town today. These errands often followed a period of unusual tension in the family, and he supposed this was her kindly way of allowing him a short respite. Aside from Allie, Mrs. Case was his only ally in the Case household.

Delaney gave a short, bitter laugh. The Case family had met his expectations almost to the letter. The friction between James and himself had been instantaneous and mutual from the first moment, and relations between them had deteriorated from that point on. The numerous efforts exerted by Mrs. Case and Allie to bring them together had seen little success. As a matter of fact, it had sometimes made matters worse.

A small muscle in Delaney's cheek ticked with annoyance. If it wasn't so ridiculous, he'd think James was jealous of Allie's attachment to him. It galled him that James continually attempted to make him look bad to Allie. James had used every advantage he had as natural son of the family to do so, but for all her trusting innocence, Allie had not been taken in. Her confidence in Delaney never wavered, and although she had adjusted well to her new home, he knew she still needed him in a way she needed no one else.

Unconsciously, Delaney traced the outline of the medal lying against his damp chest in the same manner Allie was inclined to do when she was disturbed. There hadn't been much talk of "the Lady" between them since their early days at the farm, but

Delaney knew Allie's confidence in her had not faltered. He knew she avoided talking about the Lady because he did not share her belief, and she wanted to spare him discomfort. He felt a familiar guilt. He knew that in spite of that knowledge, Allie somehow associated him with the Lady in her mind, and he sometimes wondered just how much of Allie's attachment to him was due to that association. He had never encouraged her to think that way, but he had never discouraged her, either, and he didn't know why.

Of all the family, however, Sarah was the true thorn in his side when it came to the volatile relations between Mr. Case, James, and himself.

Sarah had reached the womanly age of seventeen a few months back, not long after he turned eighteen. From that point on she had been relentless in her pursuit. He didn't flatter himself that his charm was the reason she seemed to prefer him to the other fellows who flocked around her. To the contrary, he was convinced that she found him appealing because he wanted nothing to do with her. His life on the streets had introduced him to the pleasures of the flesh at an early age, and he could not count the times he had been tempted to take advantage of what Sarah offered him. But he wasn't about to repay Mrs. Case's kindness by lying with her daughter.

Delaney paused in his introspection. In one area, at least, his life on the Case farm had not been a total disaster. The schoolmistress provided for the district had been replaced by a strict, Scottish, maiden-lady shortly after he had arrived on the farm. Miss Ferguson had vigorously protested when Mr. Case, in accordance with the provisions of the Society's contract, had elected to pull Delaney out of school when he turned sixteen. Because of her adamancy, a compromise had been struck allowing him to visit the schoolhouse once a week to pick up books and to turn in lessons, and he would forever be indebted to the outspoken, feisty Miss Ferguson for her unrelenting dedication to his education. He had worked diligently toward the goal he had set for himself, and he was aware that the time had come to take his first step in achieving it.

The mare pulled the wagon around a curve in the road, and Main Street came into view. After drawing up in front of Bosley's general store a few minutes later, Delaney jumped down from the wagon and turned an assessing glance around him.

It wasn't much of a town, just a whistle-stop on the railway line. Near the store stood the Cass County Bank, the Farmers' Meeting Hall, where people from nearby towns conducted business, the office of the *Cass County News*, the area's biggest newspaper, such as it was, and several other establishments, including a post office, a barber shop, a leather-goods store, the Silver Dollar saloon, numerous little shops, and a church to which farmers from miles around flocked every Sunday.

Still deep in thought, Delaney lifted his hat to rake a callused hand through his hair and flexed his shoulder in an unconscious attempt to unstick his shirt from his sweat-soaked back. In doing so, he caught the attention of two young women passing by who had not missed the changes three years had wrought in his appearance. Maturity had strengthened the strong line of his profile and firmed the cut of his jaw, adding a new potency to the gaze of his translucent eyes. He grimaced with discomfort, flashing the contrast of strong white teeth against sun-darkened skin, unmindful that the total effect was devastating on the young women who watched him.

However, the past three years had wrought other physical changes in Delaney, of which he was acutely aware and which he thoroughly enjoyed. Standing a few inches over six feet, his frame had grown in proportion with his height, every inch of him firm skin and tight muscle. He had earned that muscle with the sweat of his brow, and it gave him particular satisfaction that he now topped James by at least two inches in height and far outsized him in breadth of shoulder. He knew it galled his rival to be forced to look up at him when he spoke, because he knew James looked down on him in so many other ways. He gave a short laugh. Nature had a way of compensating.

Delaney nodded to the few familiar faces he passed as he stepped up onto the board sidewalk and strode into the general store, but he did not bother to smile. Not many people warranted a smile from him, and he cared little for damaged feelings. He was, after all, just passing through.

Giving the merchandise he passed no more than a fleeting glance, Delaney walked directly to the counter and paused with obvious impatience while the clerk concluded his transaction with the customer ahead of him. A soft tittering from the bolts of material nearby made him turn toward two young ladies—the Tilson girls, Mary and Susan. Having succeeded in catching his eye, they smiled brightly. He nodded in return and turned away.

Lord save him from giggling females! Allie, for all her youth, *never* giggled. And as few as were Sarah's admirable qualities, even she didn't titter.

Averting his gaze, Delancy turned toward the far side of the store. His eyes carelessly took in the rack of ready-made clothes in the corner, the barrel of soda crackers nearby, the countless tables of miscellaneous articles covering every inch of floor space between, and the counter spread with miscellaneous knick-knacks in the hope of catching the female eye. The thought had struck him when he first entered the store years before that the casual display of these items would have made them prime targets for the quick fingers of the street boy he once had been. Delaney's expression tightened. He would never walk that track again.

A roll of pink ribbon obviously left on the counter by a customer caught Delaney's eye and Allie came sharply to mind. He recalled her wistful expression just the week before when Elizabeth Morley arrived in church, her hair tied back with a similar ribbon, and he remembered thinking then how much prettier that ribbon would have looked in Allie's fine pale hair.

"What can I do for you, Delaney?"

The high-pitched nasal voice of Elmer Winthrop cut into Delaney's wandering thoughts, and turned him toward the perspiring clerk. Reaching into his pocket, Delaney withdrew a slip of paper and placed it on the counter.

"Mrs. Case would like you to fill this order and put it on her account."

Elmer scratched his balding head. "This is quite a list you got here. It's goin' to take me a little while to put the order together."

"That's all right. I've got some other things to do. I'll stop back for it in a little while."

Not waiting for the clerk's response, Delaney left the store and strode to a shop at the far end of Main Street. There he hesitated, as he had so many times in the past. Realizing that his heart had begun a rapid pounding, Delaney gave a short, self-deprecating laugh. He wasn't going to walk away this time. He was as ready as he would ever be. With a firm step, he walked into the office.

The scent of printer's ink met his nostrils, and an unexpected rush of nostalgia brought a frown to his face. His frown did not soften as he met the eyes of the short, gray-haired fellow who turned toward him.

"Can I help you, boy?"

"You're Mr. Marshall, aren't you?"

"I am."

"I'm looking for work."

The man tilted his lined, heavily jowled face upward, assessing Delaney silently. "What kind of a job did you have in mind?"

"Whatever you have. I'm not particular right now."

"Right now, meanin' you got your mind set on somethin' else more positive for later on?"

Unaccustomed to suffering anybody's curiosity, Delaney replied in a clipped voice, "I'm interested in doing newspaper work, and I figured this would be a good place to start."

"Newspaper work, huh? I gotta admit, you got me guessin', boy. Aren't you the fella that Case family took in a few years ago?"

Delaney nodded.

"And aren't you under contract to them or somethin'?"

"The contract expired when I turned eighteen a few months ago. I'm free to do what I want now."

"Have you talked this over with them, boy?"

"No. There's no need. I know what I want to do. Besides, I figured you wouldn't have anything more than part-time work for me right now, since your newspaper comes out weekly."

"What do you know about this paper? What do you think you'd be qualified to do here?"

Delaney's cheek ticked as he strove to control his annoyance. "I've made it my business to read your paper every week, and I think I know the kind of news you're interested in reporting. I'm good at my letters. I can handle just about anything you'll need, and what I don't know, I can learn. With a little training I can help you set up type, proofread, or solicit ads."

The light of curiosity grew brighter in the keen eyes returning his gaze.

"You sound as if you've been around a newspaper before."

"My father was a newspaper reporter."

"He was, huh? Where was that?"

"In New York City."

"What's your name, boy?"

"Delaney Marsh."

"Marsh. New York paper, you say?" The older man's eyes narrowed into cautious slits. "What's your father's full name?"

"Walter Marsh."

"Walter Marsh, huh? Where's your father now?"

"He was killed."

"What was your mother's name?"

"Jean Delaney."

"Well, I'll be damned!"

Delaney's expression tightened.

"I'm sorry, boy. I gotta admit I had my doubts you were who you said you were, but I figure the average person wouldn't know enough about Walter Marsh to know his wife's name. I should've realized from your given name."

Delaney strained to keep his irritation under control. The effort was not lost on the gray-haired editor.

"Look, boy, it's kinda hard for me to believe that the son of Walter Marsh would walk into my office and ask for a job."

"Did you know my father?"

"No, but I read a lot about him. Your father was pretty famous for the work he did in exposin' shady dealin's in the construction of the railroads."

Delaney nodded, suspecting that if Max Marshall knew that much about his father, he probably knew more. He didn't have to wait long for confirmation.

"I heard he lost his job with the *New York Herald* because he started drinkin'. Then I didn't hear anythin' at all until the story about him bein' killed. Rumor had it that some pretty important people had it in for him, that they took their time about gettin' even, but when they did, they did a real good job. They smeared his name and—"

"Dead is dead, Mr. Marshall." Unwilling to allow this sharp-minded man to dredge up painful memories, Delaney continued tightly, "Do you have a job for me or not?"

Obviously annoyed by his abruptness, Marshall squinted at

him in silence. Delaney stared back in return. Max Marshall
was the first to break the impasse.

"You're a hard case, aren't you, boy?"

"I'm just looking for work."

"No, you aren't."

Delaney's light eyes narrowed.

"You aren't lookin' for work anymore because you found it."

Delaney remained silent, eliciting an impatient grunt from
Marshall as he continued, "That's what you said you came here
for, isn't it? Well, you're in luck. The young fella who usually
helps me around here just quit. Part-time is all I've got for you
but if you can come in three afternoons a week, I'll give you all
the experience you need." The editor narrowed his gaze. "You
won't be able to live on what I pay you, so don't get yourself in
trouble with that family or you'll end up starvin' to death."

Delaney nodded his head. "I'll take care of that."

"And let me know what days you'll be comin' in, so I can
be expectin' you."

Delaney nodded and extended his hand. "Agreed."

Surprised by the strength in the knobby hand that gripped his
firmly, Delaney paused before speaking again. "Thank you."

Mr. Marshall gave a short laugh. "You surprise me, boy. You
don't much look like the type to say thanks."

"I'm not."

"Well, in that case, you're welcome."

Pausing only a moment more, Delaney turned and walked out
the door.

Outside on the sidewalk a few seconds later, Delaney felt the
first flush of elation sweep his mind. He had done it! He had
taken the first step, and he was on his way. Dammit, nothing
was going to stop him now!

Striding rapidly down the street, Delaney glanced at the clock
in the post office window. Was it possible that only fifteen minutes had passed since he left the general store?

Unexpectedly, he laughed. Damn, he felt good!

Pausing, Delaney cast a speculative glance at the general store.
Elmer Winthrop was a notoriously slow worker. There was no
way he had filled Mrs. Case's order yet. If he went back there
now, he'd have to wait in that stuffy store, with silly giggles
grating on his nerves. He had better things to do with his time.

Delaney turned and a few minutes later climbed a familiar wooden staircase. He felt too good right now to let it all go to waste. Reaching the landing, he paused to catch his breath before knocking boldly on the door there. The sound of a light step inside preceded the slow opening of the door and a huskily voiced comment from the striking red-haired woman standing there.

"Well, if it isn't the farm boy back for an afternoon on the town. What happened? Did they need to get you out of the house for a while to cool things off?"

Delaney's smile faded. He didn't like questions, and he didn't like having keen eyes drawing answers from his silence in response to them.

"All right, Delaney Marsh, you can keep your secrets, and little old Lil will keep hers. Come on in, darlin'."

Pulling him forward, the woman tucked her arm through his and pushed the door shut behind them. She plucked off his hat and tossed it on a chair. The sound of a honky-tonk piano from the saloon below reached his ears as Delaney flicked a fleeting glance around the ruffled, fussy, but meticulously clean room, the center of which was a broad satin-covered bed.

The room reflected the personality of the woman standing in front of him in a bright red gown that lay against her generous female curves like a second skin, but Delaney knew this woman's heart was as generous as the full breasts that lightly brushed his chest. He raised his hand and touched her cheek.

"I don't have to start back for a little while yet, Lil. I thought of you and I figured I'd come and visit."

Lil's light eyes flicked over his face. "I done some thinkin' about you, too, darlin', since the last time you were here." Lil placed her palm against his cheek and slowly slid her fingers up into his hair. "You sure enough are one beautiful fella, you know that, Delaney Marsh?"

"If you say so, Lil."

Lil gave a short laugh and took a step closer, bringing her body warmly up against his. She laughed again as she felt him harden against her. "Yeah, I say so. That's why I crooked my finger at you that day you walked past me on the street and took you under my mature and experienced wing."

It was Delaney's turn to laugh before he lowered his head to brush her full lips with his. "Is that what you did, Lil?"

"Yeah, that's what I did, all right. And you remember what I said that day, after you showed me there was more to a young farm boy than meets the eye?"

"Yeah, I remember." Lil's persuasive fingers had slipped below his belt to caress him and Delaney paused with a short intake of breath. Lil laughed, her hand then moving freely against him.

"I said I'd always have time for you, boy, and that you were more man than most full-grown men I knew."

Delaney's head dropped to Lil's neck, and he moved his mouth against the white skin there. He remembered the musky scent of her flesh. It was all woman, just like Lil. He remembered a lot more, too. His hands moving to the narrow straps that supported the plunging neckline of her dress, he paused, drawing back to look soberly into her lightly flushed face.

"Lil, I don't have much money."

"You never needed money with me, boy, and you never will."

Her experienced hands made short work of the buttons on his shirt, then opened his belt buckle and the closure below it. Having freed him from his trousers, she caressed him warmly, growing breathless as she pressed her mouth against his chest.

"I don't feel much like talkin' now, boy."

"My name's Delaney, Lil."

A spark of annoyance lifted Lil's eyes to his. "I'm sorry, darlin'. It's not that I can't remember your name. Hell, I whisper it in my sleep."

Delaney gave a short laugh. "You're a damned good liar, Lil."

"Am I? Well, maybe I am and maybe I'm not. Anyway, darlin', I'm no damned good when it comes to patience."

Reaching behind her, Lil worked at the fastenings of her dress and then took a short step backwards. The silky garment fell into a bright circle around her feet, and a gasp escaped Delaney's lips. Clad only in black lace underdrawers and sheer black stockings, Lil began to stroke her full white breasts.

"Darlin', they're all yours, and they been waitin' to feel you touchin' them again. Come on, darlin'. I'm warm and ready for you."

Pulling Delaney with her toward the bed, Lil lay down, staring up at him as she slowly slid her underdrawers down her firm, full legs. She smiled as Delaney finished the task, and within seconds he was as naked as she. He stood looking down at her, and Lil made a small strangled sound.

"Dammit, Delaney, get yourself down here and put yourself inside me, you damned fool boy!"

"Yes, ma'am."

Delaney lowered himself over the soft cushion of Lil's womanly flesh. A low gasp escaped his throat at the moment of his body's contact with hers, and he covered her warm, hungry mouth with his. Her anxious, taunting tongue sought his, but he freed himself from her clinging kiss to follow a heated trail down her throat to the pale mounds that rubbed his chest. He covered the dark moons that ringed their crests with his mouth, drawing on them until she was gasping. He grasped her ample buttocks in his hands, kneading and cupping them as his mouth played against her skin.

Lil gasped, breathless. Her voice was a hoarse whisper against his hair. "Damn you, Delaney, I can't wait any longer."

His unspoken sentiments the same, Delaney raised himself and thrust inside her. She was ready for him all right.

With a brief laugh Delaney thrust again, his mind gradually losing count until the sudden explosion that went off inside his brain resounded in deep, convulsive shudders. He was motionless atop her, except for the breathless heaving of his chest, when he heard Lil's husky whisper.

"Delaney."

Raising his head, he was startled by Lil's sober expression as she raised her hands to cup his cheeks with her palms.

"There aren't many times when a woman like me puts business aside and forgets about money, but you're different from the rest of the fellas who visit me. You know what you are, Delaney? You're a present *to* me, *from* me, darlin'. A real indulgence. And I'm tellin' you now, I'll never give any man more, at any price, than I give you."

Touched by the sincerity in the light eyes looking into his, Delaney smiled. "I appreciate that, Lil."

"Now kiss me, darlin'."

Touching his lips lightly to hers, Delaney shook his head. "I have to go, Lil. My time's not my own yet."

"I said kiss me."

Drawing his head down firmly toward hers, Lil met him with a warm, opened-mouthed kiss that was slowly tantalizing. Releasing him at last, she whispered against his mouth, "That was just the beginnin', darlin', now that I got that first heat out of my system."

"Lil, I have to go."

Sliding her hand down between them, Lil cupped him caressingly, manipulating him with her expert touch in a way that brought a low groan to his lips.

"Let the sound out, darlin'. There's more to come, and then you can show me again the man you really are, just like you did before."

"Lil, I can't. I—"

"Give it up, darlin'."

Drawing his mouth down to her lips, Lil captured him again, and his protest went unspoken as he slid his arms around her, drawing her smooth, damp flesh close.

"All right. Just a half-hour more."

They were the last words he spoke.

Almost an hour later, Delaney strode across the bright sunlit street toward the general store. In a few rapid steps, he was inside. Elmer Winthrop looked up as he approached the counter, and a low grunt escaped Delaney's lips.

"Not finished with that order yet, Elmer?"

"Just puttin' in the last few things. What's your hurry?"

"I got things to do, and Mrs. Case is expecting me back."

"All right, that's the last of it." Placing one final sack next to the two previously readied, Elmer released a slow breath. "Will that be all?"

Halting as he reached for the first sack, Delaney turned abruptly toward the roll of pink ribbon lying on the counter. "How do you sell that ribbon?"

"By the yard. It's on sale, marked down because—"

"I'll take a yard."

His thick lips twisting into a knowing smile, Elmer picked up the roll and stretching out the ribbon in an expert manner, snipped off a length and wrapped it in paper. He was about to add it to the other items in the sack when Delaney took it from his hand.

"I'll pay for the ribbon." Slapping down a coin, Delaney waited for his change as Elmer's smile widened.

"Well, I'm guessin' I can expect to see Miss Sarah Case wearin' a pretty strip of pink ribbon the next time she comes to town. And I'm thinkin' you got real good taste in women, Delaney."

Stifling the comment that rose to his lips, Delaney took the change Elmer held out and shoved it in his pocket. "Expect what you like."

Scooping up all three sacks at once, Delaney turned to the door without another word.

A short time later, Delaney slapped the reins against the old mare's back and urged her to a modest pace as he drove back along the main street of town. A smile lifted his lips. He hadn't really expected to dally so long. He was a little tired, but he was also more relaxed than he'd been in weeks. He knew he had Lil to thank for that, and he knew, all other considerations aside, Lil was a damned nice woman. She was the only person other than Allie who accepted him the way he was.

Annoyed with himself for unconsciously linking the two in his mind, Delaney turned from that thought with an intense frown. In any case, he had accomplished all he had intended today. Now an even more difficult task lay before him. He was anxious to get it settled.

Looking briefly at the sun as it sank toward the horizon, Delaney gave an unconscious nod. By sunset tonight he'd know where he stood and where he'd go from there.

Her eyes intent on the road, Allie saw dust rising in the distance. It was the wagon! Delaney was coming home!

Glancing at the house behind her, Allie paused only a second longer before starting down the road at a run. Breathless, she slowed her pace as the wagon came more clearly into sight, and a smile stretched across her lips. It *was* Delaney! She had been so afraid.

Drawing herself to a temporary halt, Allie attempted to compose herself before continuing toward the approaching wagon at a fast walk.

Everything had been so terrible when Mother Case sent Delaney to town. James had been angry, and Papa Case's brow had been as black as thunder. She wasn't certain what had set off the trouble this time, and in truth, she didn't believe it was anything of particular consequence. It didn't have to be. James and Delaney were like oil and water. They'd never mix, not for long.

She didn't know why James hated Delaney so. Delaney and she had both come to the farm under the same conditions, but James was ever generous and kind to her, while he was hateful to Delaney. Of course, Delaney was just as hateful in return.

But this time had been worse than the others, because now Delaney was eighteen. He had turned eighteen a few months ago, and Allie had sensed he was making up his mind about something.

She knew what turning eighteen meant to Delaney. He was free of his contract. She also knew what it meant to James. He had expected Delaney to leave as soon as he was free, but Allie had known he wouldn't. He wasn't ready yet. Delaney had an ambition. He had worked hard at his studies and read the newspapers Miss Ferguson gave him from first word to last. Everybody else thought Delaney was odd, devoting so much time to book work, but she knew he wasn't. She was proud of him.

Delaney didn't know it, but she had an ambition, too. It wasn't as grand an ambition as his, but she worked just as hard at it. She didn't expect she'd ever be famous or rich. She didn't expect she'd ever even be pretty, but she did know she was smart. She was smarter by far than most of the girls her age in school, and her secret ambition was to study hard, so she wouldn't fall too far behind Delaney.

Delaney had smiled when he caught her reading the newspapers he had discarded in the barn, but he didn't know why she read them, or that she read every one. She didn't really understand all she read. Some of it was too complicated, and some of it sounded really foolish and trivial, considering all else that was going on in the country, but she understood a lot more about what was happening beyond the Case farm than Sarah and even James.

Allie frowned. James would not approve of her ambition because he did not approve of Delaney. Nothing Delaney could do would have made James think well of him, but it was an unde-clared and accepted fact that Delaney's help was now necessary on the farm. Because of Delaney, Papa Case had been able to cultivate more fields, and those fields had been producing well. More land planted meant more work, and Delaney had never spared himself in doing what was expected of him. The result was that Papa Case was faced with the prospect of allowing some of his truly fruitful fields to lie fallow if Delaney chose to leave and go his own way.

She had accepted the fact that Delaney would go his own way someday. She was just so glad he was not going yet.

Allie swallowed against a tightness in her throat she knew was not related to exertion. Smiling when she realized Delaney had seen her, she waved and started running toward him again. She was so glad he had come home.

One glimpse of Allie's slight pale-haired figure running to-ward the wagon, and tension knotted Delaney's stomach. Slap-ping the reins against the mare's back, he urged her to a faster pace, never taking his eyes off Allie as the distance between them narrowed. His heart was pounding like a drum. Something was wrong.

Delaney strained his eyes in an attempt to determine Allie's expression. Was she frightened? Anxious? He could make out no more than her slight figure, clothed in the familiar cotton dress, running toward him as she waved wildly. With the excep-tion of a few inches in height, it was a figure mostly unchanged from the child of ten Allie had been three years before. Her unusual silver-gold hair was longer now, flying out behind her as she ran; and as she drew closer, he could see that her delicate, fine-featured face was pulled into a grimace as she labored for breath.

Reining up sharply as she neared, he was about to jump to the ground when Allie startled him by smiling broadly. Surprised by the warmth of that smile, he waited until she came to an abrupt halt beside the wagon before reaching down to lift her up onto the seat beside him. She was grinning now, and he felt the sudden urge to wrap his hands about that skinny white neck and choke her.

"Allie Pierce, you scared the hell out of me running toward me like a maniac! I thought something was wrong!"

Halting his angry tirade as the smile vanished from Allie's lips, Delaney shook his head and picked up the reins. Using those seconds to restore his calm, Delaney turned back to Allie. Suddenly he was even more annoyed with himself for having wiped the sparkle from her dark eyes. He offered her a quick smile.

"All right, let's start again. What brought you out here on the run, Allie? I can't believe you're that happy to see me."

Allie flushed, momentarily averting her face, and Delaney's smile faded. Something *was* wrong, or at least had been wrong until she saw him. He had seen Allie behave like this a few times during the past three years, but never with this intensity. Gripping her small chin with his hand, he guided Allie's gaze back to his face.

"What happened, Allie?"

Allie shook her head and attempted to avert her face again, but he was having none of it. Realizing she could not evade his question, she shrugged.

"Nothing happened. Nothing bad, anyway. I wanted to talk to you before you got to the house. And I was glad to see you."

"So glad that you had to come running at me like the devil was at your heels?"

A wobbly smile broke across Allie's lips. "Yes."

Moved by the honesty of Allie's short reply, Delaney fell silent. Unconsciously sliding his arm around her narrow shoulders, he looked directly into her sober brown eyes.

"I wouldn't leave for good without telling you first. Don't you know that, Allie? Even if I didn't tell anybody else, I'd tell you."

Allie studied his face so earnestly that he could almost feel the touch of her serious dark eyes. She finally nodded. "Yes, I know that now."

His throat constricting as Allie leaned against his shoulder, Delaney lowered his head and rubbed his cheek against the warm pale silk of her hair.

"Allie, I always thought you were a smart kid."

She glanced up, embarrassed. "I guess you were wrong."

Relief removed the tension that had knotted his stomach, and

Delaney squeezed Allie's shoulder. "Now, what did you want to tell me that couldn't wait until I got home?"

Allie's smile slowly turned into a frown. "I . . . I wanted to tell you that you don't have to worry about James when you get back, Delaney, or Papa Case, either. Mother Case talked to both of them while you were gone."

"I figured she would."

"She reasoned with them, Delaney. You know she's the only one they listen to."

"I know."

"She can't make James like you, or make Papa Case feel the same way about you as she does, but it'll be better when you get back, you'll see. Even Sarah"—Allie grimaced unconsciously—"even Sarah got a firm talking-to, but I don't think she listened too much. She never does."

"You don't have to worry about me, Allie. I can take care of myself, and I can handle anything James and Papa Case dish out."

"I know you can, Delaney, but—"

"But . . . ?"

"But I want you to be happy."

Delaney again felt the touch of an emotion that was reserved for Allie alone. He covered it with a short laugh and a quick wink. "*You* make me happy—when you smile."

"Oh, Delaney." A full smile spread across her face and Allie shook her head. "I want you to be happy for yourself. I told James that he—"

Delaney stiffened. "I don't want you getting in the middle, between James and me, especially now."

"What do you mean, 'especially now'?"

"Especially now, when I have some things to talk about with Mr. and Mrs. Case." Delaney paused. "I've taken a position in town, Allie."

Allie's small face went still. "It's about your goal."

"It's the first step. I'm going to be working on the *Cass County News* three afternoons a week, whether the Cases approve or not."

Allie's eyes were suddenly suspiciously bright. "And you're going to be famous someday."

Somehow Allie's faith in him didn't make him smile this time.

"That part is still between you and me. I have to learn to walk before I can run."

"You'll do it, Delaney."

Delaney nodded. "We'll see, won't we, Allie?"

"They'll all see."

The thought that Allie believed in him almost more than he believed in himself touched Delaney deeply. The feeling was still with him when he turned the wagon into the yard.

"It's out of the question, Margaret. Three afternoons a week! Just who does the boy think he is? With the traveling time from here to town and back, that would leave most of the work for those three days to James and me. And how would he get to town, Margaret? Tell me that. Am I supposed to provide him with transportation, too?"

Margaret Case took a deep breath and stared at her husband's lined face. She had no heart for this conversation this evening. Supper was over and it would soon be dark, and she would have gone to bed if she hadn't felt it would alarm Jacob.

She had seen trouble in Delaney's face when he returned from town, and in Allie's, too, as she had ridden into the yard seated beside him in the wagon. It had merely been a matter of waiting until Delaney decided to speak. He had done that after supper, just before everyone had risen from the table.

The tension that had followed Delaney's quiet announcement had been so thick that she had realized it would be a mistake to discuss it as a group. She had sent the others off to do their chores, and she was now faced with Jacob's adamant disapproval. She was not up to it.

She had felt very weak today, increasingly weak over the past month. She had tried not to show it, but she was afraid the keen eyes of her family had noticed the paling of her skin, just as had she, and the fact that her clothes were beginning to hang on her frame. Allie had taken on a larger share of the chores in the kitchen and could not seem to do enough for her comfort.

Margaret felt love well in her heart for the child who had come to them in such an unusual way. Allie had been a true gift—solace for hearts saddened by loss and with love to spare. She knew she could not love her more if the child had been her own flesh and blood, and she wanted only the best, the very best for her.

Sadness touched Margaret's mind. Sarah, her own dear daughter, just was not capable of half the love this endearing child had to give, for Sarah loved herself best of all. It was obvious to Margaret that her fondness for Allie was shared by the other members of the family, with the exception of Sarah. Sarah was jealous of her and could not understand how Allie, dear plain little Allie, could inspire so much love.

How Margaret wished the same could be said for the boy who had come to their family with Allie. In truth, she could not truly understand her men's objections to Delaney. Was it that they felt threatened by his silent strength, or was it that they did not quite know what to expect of him?

In all candor, Margaret had to admit that she suffered doubts about the boy, as much as she truly loved him. She was uncertain where all his bitterness and his strictly controlled anger with fate would take him in the end.

"Margaret."

Snapped back to the present by her husband's anxious, softly spoken summons, Margaret attempted a smile. What was it he had asked her? She was so tired.

"Margaret, this work Delaney has taken on in town will put us all to a disadvantage. We cannot allow it."

"Jacob dear, you don't seem to realize that Delaney has already accepted the position."

Margaret saw her husband's stubborn flush. Inwardly, she despaired. Dear Jacob, as loving, generous, and considerate a husband as he was, could also be as obstinate as a mule. It was a side of him she had viewed infrequently until Delaney came to them. Since then she had fought long and hard against Jacob's inflexibility with regard to the boy, but now she was weary.

"Jacob dear, if we oppose him, we'll lose him."

A sound in the doorway told her that James had stepped into the room the moment before he spoke.

"It would be a small loss, Mama." Margaret's heavy eyelids closed briefly at the sight of her son's stiff, unyielding countenance. Not James, too. She did not have the strength to oppose them both.

"James, this discussion is between your mother and me."

James's fair face flushed. "Is it, Papa? I'm almost twenty years old. I'm an adult. I'll be taking over this farm one day, and I think it's about time I had some say in what goes on around here."

"James, dear, your opinions are of little use to us in this matter." Smiling in an attempt to soften her harsh statement, Margaret continued. "You cannot speak objectively about Delaney because you dislike him. You know it's true."

Concern touching his expression at his mother's weak voice, James nodded. "That's right, Mama. I don't like Delaney Marsh. I never have and I never will. He's not to be trusted. He's taken all of you in, and I have the feeling he's about to make us all pay."

"James is right, Margaret. This is my home, and I make the decisions. If Delaney doesn't agree with them, he's free to leave."

Margaret did not miss the satisfaction that flooded her son's face at his father's words. She closed her weary eyes briefly once more.

"Margaret!"

The anxiety in her husband's tone caused Margaret to open her eyes. "I'm fine, Jacob, but I would like you both to face the fact that you're being unfair."

"Unfair!" Jacob's face reddened at the obvious effort he made to restrain a more strident objection to her statement.

"Yes, unfair. The boy is asking us no favors. He says he will do all his work before he leaves for town or when he returns. If you were fair, you would give him a chance to prove himself."

"But, Margaret—"

"If he doesn't live up to his word . . ." Margaret's sentence drifted off as her gray brows drew into an unaccustomed frown. "There is another point, also, which I don't think you've taken into consideration. Allie loves Delaney dearly. If you force him to leave, she'll be desolate."

Noting that James's expression had changed, Margaret hesitated. James's fondness for the child grew greater with each passing day, but his antipathy for Delaney stood in the way of his allowing Allie to return his affection freely. She knew it was a point of deep contention between Delaney and himself.

"Margaret," Jacob said, "I think we've allowed our affection for Allie to influence us long enough in the boy's favor."

Nodding in agreement with his father's statement, James spoke again, his voice still firm, but greatly subdued. "I suppose the decision is up to you and Pa, Mama, but I want you to know that I think Marsh has had his way in this family long enough. I think it would be a mistake to give in to him again for anybody's sake."

Margaret turned back to her husband, after James left the room as unexpectedly as he had entered. She despised the quiver of weakness in her voice as she spoke.

"Jacob dear, is there no room for discussion in your decision about Delaney?"

She awaited her husband's response, knowing this exchange needed to be over soon. She could not take much more.

"Margaret dear."

Abruptly crouching by her side, Jacob raised his callused palm to her cheek. "Does it mean so much to you that we give this boy a chance? Isn't it time to allow him to go his own way?"

Not quite certain why she spoke the words, Margaret smiled into her husband's loving face. "Not yet, dear."

Holding her gaze in silence for long moments, Jacob abruptly slid his arms under and around her and slowly lifted her up into his arms. "I think it's time for us both to retire for the night, dear. We'll sleep on this and tell Delaney our decision in the morning."

Margaret shook her head in protest. "Put me down, Jacob. I can walk, and it's too early for you to go to bed. You can join me later."

His voice low, Jacob whispered into her ear, "Together, my dear wife. We'll lie together. I haven't held you in my arms often enough of late. And we can talk."

Emotion constricted Margaret's throat, as she nodded her head. "Yes, dear, we'll talk."

Smiling a good night to Allie, who was still working in the kitchen, and to Sarah as they passed her in the hall, Margaret closed her eyes to rest. Oh, yes, she would enjoy lying in Jacob's arms and resting. They would talk, and they would settle all this between them.

* * *

Allie's fair brows drew together in a frown as she watched Papa Case carry Mother Case upstairs. This conflict in her family was too much for Margaret, but none of it was Delaney's fault. Allie swallowed against the hard lump that blocked her throat.

She was not sure where Delaney had gone after he had made his short announcement to the family. She knew he was not in the room Papa Case had added to the back of the house shortly after their arrival. At least Sarah had gone upstairs. It was Allie's fervent hope that she would stay there.

The thought of Sarah stirred Allie to familiar annoyance. She had seen Papa Case's face and James's hard expression after Sarah had spoken out at the supper table with her usual careless disregard for others' feelings. Sarah's statement in support of Delaney had done him more harm than good, and Allie wondered if Sarah was truly too stupid to realize it.

Mother Case had told Delaney they would give him their decision tomorrow. She did not want to think about what would happen if they said no.

Refusing to face that possibility, Allie walked outside into the rapidly darkening yard. She would find Delaney and talk to him.

"Allie?"

Turning at the sound of her name, Allie saw James standing in the shadows nearby. She paused as he walked toward her. He smiled. She did not return his smile, and his faded.

"Are you angry with me, Allie?"

Allie averted her gaze and remained silent.

Waiting only a few seconds more, James spoke again. "Allie, I asked you if you're angry with me."

The eyes Allie lifted to meet James's sober expression were suddenly blazing. "Yes, I'm angry, James. I'm angry with you and Papa Case, but mostly with you. You're unfair."

James's expression tightened. "That's the second time somebody's called me unfair tonight. Why am I unfair, Allie?"

"You never give Delaney a chance—never—no matter what he wants to do. And you try to turn Papa Case against him."

"I don't have to turn Pa against him, Allie. Pa sees him the same way I do. I know it's senseless to try to make you see Marsh clearly for what he is. He has all of you—Mama, Sarah, and you—mesmerized into thinkin'—"

"Stop!" A sudden fury transfusing her, Allie shook her head. Her pale hair flew out to slap at her flushed cheeks, lending silent emphasis as she continued angrily, "It's not true!"

Breathing deeply against the rapid pounding of her heart, Allie continued flatly, "You're mean, and you're wrong about Delaney. You don't know him. You never even tried to get to know him. And if you don't like Delaney, you don't like me, because we're the same."

"No, you're not the same."

"We are." Allie raised her chin to finish simply, "I don't want to talk about it anymore, James."

Reaching out to grasp her arm, James prevented her escape. "Allie, it's up to Pa and me to do what we think's right for the family, and we both think—"

"Let me go, James."

"Allie." James's voice held a pained note that Allie refused to recognize.

"Let me *go*!"

Wrenching her arm free, Allie turned away and broke into a run, heading toward the barn. Turning back as she entered the darkening interior, she shot a heated glance over her shoulder. James was standing stiffly where she had left him. As she watched, he turned abruptly and strode out of sight.

Allie took a deep breath in an attempt to retain her tenuous control. It was James's fault, all of it. If Papa Case didn't let Delaney take the position on the newspaper . . .

Allie refused to allow her mind to finish that thought. She'd wait until tomorrow. Mother Case would talk to Papa Case, and everything would be all right.

Allie walked deeper into the barn, looking for a familiar shadow usually lurking there.

"Mischief?" she called. "Come on, little girl. Here, Mischief."

Within seconds a large striped cat was rubbing against her legs and a smile curved Allie's trembling lips. She scooped up the warm, purring animal and held her close.

"We know, don't we, Mischief? We know how good Delaney is."

Clutching the contented cat close, Allie walked to the empty rear stall and sat down on the hay in the corner. She rubbed her cheek against Mischief's smooth fur and whispered into the small silken ear, "James gave you to me, but he never pets you. Delaney pets you, and he talks to you, too, just as I do. Nobody understands Delaney but us. They're going to make him angry, and he's going to leave. We don't want him to leave, do we, Mischief? We don't ever want him to leave us."

Burying her face in Mischief's fur, Allie heard the cat's steady purring response, and she knew the sentiment came straight from the heart, just like her own.

Delaney heard the low sound the moment he walked into the barn. He paused to determine the direction from which it came, then started toward the back stall. He had been out walking, going over and over in his mind the events of the day. He realized full well the direction he would take from here was being determined inside the house right now. No, that was wrong. He was master of his own fate. All that Mr. and Mrs. Case could decide was the degree of bodily comforts that would attend him along the way. Their decision would not affect his determination to take the position Max Marshall had offered him.

The mumbling grew more distinct as he neared the rear of the barn, and Delaney recognized the high, soft pitch of Allie's voice. But she was not playing with Mischief. She was talking to the patient cat in a low, confidential tone, and he paused, uncertain if he should intrude.

"We don't care what they say, do we, Mischief? We don't care what James says, and we don't care if he never talks to us again. We don't like him anymore. And if James is mean to Delaney, we're going to tell him how we feel."

The bittersweet sadness that enveloped Delaney was too much to bear. He took the last few steps forward as Allie whipped her head around to meet his gaze.

"Allie, I told you not to get between James and me."

Jumping to her feet, Allie released Mischief and, protesting, took a few steps toward him.

"I didn't, Delaney. At least, I tried not to, but James asked me if I was angry. I didn't want to answer him, but he asked me again. Then I told him I was mad at him for saying all those mean things about you to Mother Case."

Delaney took a short breath. So that was the way things were going in the house. He should have expected it.

Allie moved to his side and Delaney slid his arm around her shoulder. She was looking up at him, those damned trusting eyes disturbed and upset. It never failed to amaze him how one look from her could tear him up inside.

Sitting down on a storage box nearby, he pulled her onto his knee. He controlled the smile that tugged at his lips. She was so small and light that he hardly felt her weight as she rested her arm on his shoulder, her delicate sober face only inches from his.

"Why doesn't James like you, Delaney? I told him that if he didn't like you, then he didn't like me, because we're both the same."

Delaney's discomfort with the tender emotions Allie raised inside him erupted in a short laugh. "I don't suppose James liked that very much."

"He said it wasn't true. He said we're not the same, but we are."

Delaney's smile slowly changed until it was colored a more somber hue. "I don't like agreeing with James, Allie, but he was right this time. We aren't the same."

Struck to the heart by his response, Allie stiffened, her small face twitching in an obvious effort to hide her distress.

Delaney forced a smile. "Allie, we're not alike at all. You're sweet and trusting. You're kind to everyone, and I'm anything but that." He laughed. "As a matter of fact, most people would say I'm—"

"I don't care what other people say. We are the same, Delaney, because you know my heart and I know yours."

Slipping her hand to his chest, Allie traced the outline of his medal, and Delaney's reaction was unexpected anger. She was linking him with the Lady again in her mind. He didn't want to think that was the only reason she—

Abruptly abandoning that thought, Delaney brushed her hand away. "Allie, I told you this medal means nothing to me."

"It does."

"No, it doesn't. You and I are nothing alike. James is more like you than I am. At least he believes."

"No, I'm not like him. I'm like you—not on the outside, but on the inside."

"Allie, nobody's like me on the inside. You don't know what goes on inside me."

"Yes, I do, Delaney." Allie nodded her head, her expression resolute. "Yes, I do."

Allie's confidence in him was unshakable, and incredulity touched Delaney's mind. He would never know how he had won this girl's absolute trust, but he was damned if he could find it in himself to disillusion her.

"Allie," Delaney continued softly, a despairing note in his voice, "if you do know what's inside me, you know how I feel about not wanting you to get into trouble for my sake. I'm going to work on that newspaper, Allie, no matter what Mr. Case decides tonight, and if I have to leave here, I want to be sure you'll be all right when I'm not around."

Allie glanced away from Delaney's intense gaze. She wanted to tell him she'd never be all right if he left, but she couldn't do that. She didn't want to get in the way. Instead, she turned back and met his eyes.

"I'll be all right, Delaney. I don't hate James. I'm just mad at him because he's so unfair."

"Allie." Delaney's low voice bore a strange note as he held her eyes with his. "The world isn't very often fair, and neither are the people in it."

Allie could do no more than nod.

Saddened more than he cared to admit at the unhappiness on Allie's face, Delaney felt his spirits sinking until he was struck with a sudden thought. Leaning to one side as he supported Allie's slender back with his hand, he took a small package from his pocket. The paper was crushed, and he was afraid that the contents were in like condition. He placed the package in Allie's small hand.

Her light brows moving into a confused frown, Allie glanced from the package to his face.

"Open it."

Allie unrolled the paper carefully until the ribbon became visible. Stopping abruptly, she looked up at Delaney and then back down at the ribbon. She removed it fully from the wrapping paper and smoothed it with her hand. It was remarkably un-wrinkled, and she looked up again and swallowed.

"It's pink, just like Elizabeth Morley's."

Delaney nodded. "It'll look better in your hair than it does in hers."

Allie lowered her gaze at the compliment, and Delaney had the feeling she didn't believe a word of it. He didn't know why. It was true. Allie had beautiful hair. He was about to tell her that when she looked up again and smiled.

"Thank you for the present, Delaney."

Although he was pleased to see Allie's smile, Delaney could not avoid the realization that sadness still lurked deep within those dark eyes.

"You're welcome. You can wear it to church on Sunday and make all the other girls jealous."

Slipping Allie off his knee, Delaney placed her on her feet and stood beside her. "You'd better go in the house now, Allie. It's getting dark, and Mrs. Case might need you. I have some chores to finish up here."

Allie nodded and turned toward the door. She had walked back out into the yard when Delaney realized she had not really reacted the way he had expected to his gift. Suddenly realizing she must have thought he had bought her the ribbon because he was going away, he was somehow more angry than he had been before. Turning, he walked back into the barn. What difference did it make, anyway? He'd do what he had to do, dammit! He wouldn't let anybody stand in his way.

Allie walked slowly across the yard, carrying the ribbon protectively in her hand. It was the second most precious gift she had ever been given, but she feared for the reason behind it. It would be a gift she always associated with pain if it meant Delaney was leaving.

Slowing to a stop as she neared the apple tree, Allie opened her hand and looked at the ribbon again. It was beautiful, just like Delaney.

"What have you got there?"

Stepping out of the shadows unexpectedly, Sarah approached her. As her eyes focused on Allie's hand, Sarah's smooth face twitched convulsively. "Where did you get that ribbon?"

Allie dropped her hand to her side, barely controlling the urge
to hide it behind her back. But she was not a child, and she
would not allow Sarah to intimidate her. "That's none of your
business, Sarah."

Standing a head taller than she, Sarah took a step closer and
looked down into Allie's face with unconcealed animosity. "Delaney gave it to you, didn't he?"

Recognizing the beginning of another of Sarah's tantrums,
Allie waited a moment before replying quietly, "I told you, it's
none of your business."

She was about to turn away when Sarah reached out unexpectedly and grabbed the ribbon from her hand. She gave a
short, tight laugh as Allie's mouth dropped open in surprise.

"None of my business? I'd say it's my business! What did you
have to do to get it? I'm sure Mama would like to know, and
you wouldn't dare tell her it's none of her business!"

"Give it back to me, Sarah."

Sarah took a short step back. The strange glitter in her eyes
grew brighter, and she laughed again. "Oh, no! I'm going to
show this to Mama, and I'm going to tell her I saw you sitting
on Delaney's lap with your arm around his neck, because I did.
And then I'm going to tell her—"

A sudden fury flooding her mind, Allie swallowed against the
knot of tears choking her throat. Sarah was vicious. Her heart
was as ugly as her face was beautiful and she was trying to make
everything as ugly as she was. Allie hated her.

"I said give it back to me, Sarah."

"No. I'm going to give it to Mama, and she'll burn it because—"

Abruptly unwilling to suffer another word of Sarah's viciousness, Allie lurched forward and snatched at the ribbon dangling
from Sarah's hand, but Sarah was too quick. With a quick, hard
shove, Sarah pushed her backwards unexpectedly and Allie fell,
striking her head on the ground with a resounding thud.

Disoriented, Allie opened her eyes and stared into the darkening twilight. The sound of Sarah's laughter brought her to her
feet. Her head still reeling, Allie hurled herself forward, her
small fists pounding at Sarah's sturdy frame even as she reached
up and pulled Sarah's dark, shining hair as hard as she could.
Momentary gratification assailed her as Sarah grunted with pain,

but Sarah was taller and much sturdier than she, and within moments Allie was staggering backwards under the force of a hard blow to her face.

Gasping, she felt the heat of tears sting her eyes. Her head was pounding, but she was determined. "Give it back to me, Sarah, or I'll—"

"You'll do what?" Sarah's laughter was shrill as she waved the ribbon tauntingly. "You'll call Delaney and make him take it from me? Wouldn't Papa love that! Papa would throw Delaney out for sure, and you don't want that, do you, Allie?"

"I don't have to call Delaney. I'll get it back myself."

"Oh, no, you won't." Sarah shook her head and drew her womanly form up to its full height. "You're no match for me in any way, Allie Pierce. You never were, and you never will be. Sooner or later you'll realize that." Sarah held the ribbon out, teasing her again as she snatched it back with a low laugh. "This is your first lesson."

Controlling with sheer force of will the sobs tearing at her insides, Allie warned in a low, shaky voice, "The ribbon is mine. Give it back to me."

Sarah's shrill laughter was suddenly cut short.

"Give it back to her, Sarah."

Twisting around at the sound of James's carefully controlled voice, Sarah stared at her brother. Her expression suddenly truly malevolent, she responded hotly. "No, I won't give it back to her! Do you know what it is, James? It's a pink ribbon. A present from Delaney! Do you know what she had to do to get it? Well, I'll tell you! I saw them in the barn. She was—"

"Shut up, Sarah! Shut your filthy, vicious mouth!"

"Me? Filthy and vicious? Oh, no! That sweet little innocent over there isn't as innocent as she seems! Delaney never gives me a second glance, but he gave *her* a present. Seems to me she learned more on the streets than we gave her credit for. But Delaney knows her better than all of us. No wonder he stands up for her and gives her presents and—"

"I said, shut up!" Striding forward, James snatched the ribbon from Sarah's hand. His voice low, he growled warningly in her direction, "Get back in the house! Now! And you'll keep your lies to yourself, if you know what's good for you. You want

Marsh to stay as much as Allie does. One word of all this hateful business and Pa will turn Marsh out on his ear.''

"Stay out of this, James!"

"If I don't, what will you do, Sarah? I'm bigger than you are, remember? You can't push me around like you did Allie. And you can't lie to Pa about me, either. He won't believe you.''

Raging frustration brought Sarah's face to twitching sobriety. His voice shaded with disgust, James ordered again, "Get back in the house and go to your room. It's all over, and you lost. And I'm warning you, if you give Allie any trouble about this ribbon, or about anything else, I'm going straight to Pa and tell him everything. You know you'll never see Delaney again if I do.''

"Bastard!"

James gave a short laugh. "Not me, Sarah. You have the wrong fellow. That name applies to Delaney Marsh better than it does to me."

Sarah stiffened further at that remark, but did not move until James barked, "Get back in the house. Now.''

Watching as Sarah walked rigidly into the house, Allie turned a fleeting glance toward the barn and released a low sigh of relief. She was exceedingly glad Delaney had heard none of this. She didn't want to burden him with her problems, especially now.

Looking back to James, Allie hesitated. Her gaze dropped to the pink ribbon he held in his hand.

"I'd like to have my ribbon, James.''

Allie stepped out of the shadows with her hand outstretched, but she drew to an abrupt halt at the sound of James's gasp. Closing the distance between them, James touched her throbbing cheek. She winced and attempted to turn away, but he held her head fast as he attempted to examine the welt. She winced again when he inadvertently touched the pounding lump on the back of her head where she had made sharp, jarring contact with the hard ground. James's lips moved into a straight, hard line.

"Sarah did this to you.''

It was a statement rather than a question, and Allie knew it was unnecessary to respond. James shook his head, his expression tightening with unspoken anger. He put the ribbon in her small hand.

"I guess you earned this."

Allie looked up at James, and he shook his head as he responded to her silent question.

"No, I don't believe a word of what Sarah said. She's spoiled and jealous, but nobody in this family seems to see that in her except me. I know that she and Marsh . . ."

Realizing Allie was again stiffening, James allowed that thought to drift away. He began again, resentment flickering across his face, "If Marsh bought the ribbon for you, then it's yours. If Sarah tries to take it away from you again, or if she gives you any more trouble, let me know."

As if he had read her mind, James shook his head. "No, I won't tell Pa. If I did, and Marsh was forced to leave, I know it would hurt you as much as Sarah. I'll handle it directly with Sarah, so don't let her take advantage of you."

"Sarah wouldn't have gotten the best of me, James." Her anger returning, Allie continued hotly, "She won't ever get the best of me."

Concern touched James's shadowed face. "Don't pit yourself against Sarah, Allie. You're no match for her."

Allie's lips tightened as James reiterated the statement Sarah had made only minutes before.

"Sarah's bigger than I am, and she's prettier, but she—"

"I didn't mean it that way, Allie." His rough hands cupping her face to hold her eyes in firm contact with his, James whispered gently, "You're no match for her because Sarah doesn't care who she hurts as long as she gets her way. That's the way she always has been and always will be, and you're too soft for that."

"I'm *not* soft."

"All right, then. You're not soft. You're kind."

"I—I'm not."

"Would you hurt Mama's feelings to get your way?"

Allie's response was immediate. "Never! I would never hurt Mother Case."

"Sarah would."

Allie averted her gaze, only to have James turn her chin back toward him with a firm hand.

"Promise me you'll tell me if Sarah gives you any more trouble tonight."

Allie paused, frowning. "I won't make a promise I can't keep, James, but . . . but I thank you for what you've done so far, and for wanting to help me. Especially after what I said."

James gave a short laugh. "That's the difference between you and me, Allie. You can get angry with me, but I can never get angry with you."

Allie sighed. "You're always kind to me, James. I don't know why."

James's eyes again touched the welt on Allie's cheek. "I guess when you compare me with Sarah, I'm not really so mean after all."

"Only with Delaney."

"And he doesn't deserve it?" Irritation again marked James's brow. "He was the cause of everything that happened to you tonight."

"No, Sarah was the cause."

James's mouth snapped tightly shut, and Allie knew she had accomplished nothing more than to make James angry with Delaney again.

"Thank you for helping me, James."

James nodded and pulled himself erect. His voice still touched with anger, he turned with her toward the house. "I meant what I said, Allie. If Sarah bothers you . . ."

The light from the kitchen shining in her face, Allie turned as they reached the door. "You *are* kind to me, James."

It was only after Allie had stepped out of sight that James realized she had not given him the promise he had requested. He shook his head, uncertain of his feelings.

Allie. Not child, not woman. It was taking her too long to grow up. He wanted . . .

Suddenly stunned at the direction his mind was taking, James turned back toward the darkening yard. His thoughts were as unclear, as much in the shadows, as the land around him, and he could not face them right now.

Having dallied as long as she could, Allie turned the knob and stepped into the silent room, knowing that Sarah was abed in the far corner.

With a careful step, Allie walked to her bed, then quickly stripped off her clothes and slipped into her nightgown. She pulled the pink ribbon out of the pocket of her apron and tucked it under her pillow. The bed creaked under her light weight as she lay down. Her head still ached terribly, and the wicked heat in the welt of her cheek had not yet abated. She only hoped there would be no visible mark in the morning. She did not want to cause Mother Case any more anxiety.

Allie closed her eyes and tried to summon a vision of the Lady, the kind face that listened to her prayers and sent them winging on their way to God's ear. She needed the Lady's strength this night.

"Don't think you've won."

The low threat emanating from the corner of the room froze Allie's thoughts and turned her head slowly toward the sound. Barely discernible in the darkness, Sarah raised herself on her elbow and leaned toward her menacingly.

"You're making a mistake if you think you've won." Sarah's low laugh grated on the silence of the room. "Delaney only bought you that ribbon because he feels sorry for you. The poor, plain little orphan girl who attached herself to him. That ribbon isn't going to make you any prettier, but you might as well enjoy it while you can."

Sarah's low tone changed, became sensuous. "All the boys want me, Allie. Amory Bishop, Charlie Knots, Bobbie Clark. But I just taunt them and laugh. I wouldn't let any one of them touch me. Do you know why? Because I'm saving myself for Delaney. He's the only fellow I want. I'm a woman now, and it won't be hard to make him want me back, because I know all the ways. Once I get him, he'll never look at you again. And when he leaves, I'll go with him."

Her voice becoming supremely confident, Sarah continued harshly, "So keep the ribbon, Allie. It's all you'll have to remind yourself of Delaney after he's gone."

The soft rustle of bedcovers followed Sarah's whispered words, signaling that she had finished speaking. Soon her light snoring told Allie she was asleep.

Allie stared unseeingly at the ceiling over her head. How could Sarah be so beautiful on the outside and so very ugly on the inside? Why didn't her meanness show? Allie had no doubt that what Sarah had said was true. All the boys did want her. But not Delaney. Delaney was too smart.

"Oh, Lady," she prayed softly. "I need your help, and Delaney needs it, too. Because we're the same inside, and I know nobody sees it but you."

Allie slid her hand under her pillow. She touched the smooth satin ribbon, clutched it tightly, then closed her eyes.

chapter

eight

DAMN IT ALL, he was exhausted!

Resting his elbows on the desk in front of him, Delaney covered his face with his hands. A few minutes later he glanced up at the clock on the wall. Midnight. He uttered a low groan. He had been up since four in the morning, and he would be back to work at the farm again a few short hours from now.

Taking a moment to rub his burning eyes, Delaney returned his attention to the copy in his hand and continued reading. A short grunt passed for a laugh as he read on. Max's editorial was really clever. The play on words he had used was just the right touch to sum up the ridiculous situation that had the town in an uproar.

It was a case of a mountain out of a molehill, all right. It seemed old Whitaker Snipes, on his usual Saturday night drunk, had staggered out of the Silver Dollar saloon carrying a bottle of whiskey. He had taken offense at a remark Sid Dearling made and had responded with a remark in kind, casting aspersions on Sid's parentage, which Sid found equally offensive. Blows were exchanged, and Whitaker had gotten the worst of the battle when he decided to use the bottle of whiskey with grievous intent.

But Brownie, Sid's old dog, was not about to let him get away with it. Seeing the danger to his master, Brownie had clamped his iron jaws on Whitaker's posterior and shaken him until the bottle crashed to the ground.

People said that Whitaker Snipes's bloodcurdling scream was still echoing in the hills around town.

But that was not the end of the story. Alma Snipes, the old biddy who doubtless had driven her husband to drink in the first place, appeared in town the next day, claiming that Brownie posed a threat to the community and should be destroyed.

From the resulting furor it was obvious that old Brownie had a lot more friends in town than Whitaker and Alma Snipes did. It had not gone over well when the sheriff went to Sid's house and arrested Brownie where he lay on the porch, innocently scratching at his fleas.

The issue of whether old Brownie should be destroyed was so hotly debated around town that it had overshadowed the news of the worsening situation in the country with regard to the slavery question, the fact that the long-disputed canal on the Isthmus of Suez had finally been started, and every other issue of true importance reported by the *Cass County News*. Delaney supposed that was the reason Max had written the editorial. If Max wanted to make the town sit back and laugh at itself, this editorial would do the trick.

Max's opening had set the tone for his commentary, and Delaney chuckled as he reread the first line: "To destroy, or not to destroy, that is the question. Whether 'tis nobler in the mind to suffer the stress and pain of outrageous incident . . ."

But Max's opening was met, and perhaps surpassed by his closing: "After heated debate, the consensus is that old Brownie did the town a favor—that he did not commit a crime. It is felt that the faithful, protective beast prevented a crime—a criminal assault intended by Whitaker Snipes. He did this quickly and efficiently by nipping a potentially serious situation in the buttocks and by bringing a colorful (if a bit torn and badly scratched) end to the story.

"Brownie, you are a hero! The kangaroo court of Cass County, a suitable legal body, considering the species against whom the charges were brought, finds in your favor. Not guilty!"

Delaney gave another short laugh as he dropped the page in front of him. He was finally done for the night, and damned glad of it. He glanced at the well-lit street outside, grateful for the full moon which would make the trip home easier.

Drawing himself to his feet, Delaney took his hat off the peg and walked out onto the board sidewalk, pulling the door closed behind him. The click of the lock echoed on the night air and he turned toward the spot where his horse was tied to the hitching post. A moment later he was mounted and riding out of town.

It was then that James entered his mind for the first time. A low snort escaping his lips, Delaney straightened his broad, stiff shoulders and flexed the muscles in his arms. He had never been this late in returning to the farm. James was probably all but certain he had absconded with the gelding and was on his way to the closest big city.

A muscle twitched in Delaney's cheek. It wasn't as if he hadn't been tempted.

He had been working three days a week at the *Cass County News* for a few months now, and in that short time he had gained some experience in almost every aspect of publishing the paper. Max Marshall had promised to let him begin writing short articles soon. It could not be soon enough for Delaney.

In order to get all this practical experience, however, he had to spend a great many hours in town and away from the farm. Unwilling to go back on his word, he had not allowed himself to fall behind in his chores, but working sixteen hours a day had not been easy.

Delaney raised his shoulders in a brief, unconscious shrug. He would have worked his fingers to the bone if necessary, just to show Mr. Case and James that they had been wrong about him.

And then there was Mrs. Case. Delaney knew it was because of her that he had been allowed to take the position on the newspaper, and he didn't want to let her down. Hell, not her, of all people, or Allie. His two allies.

Delaney frowned, his weary face drawing into deep lines. He hadn't had much time for Allie in the past few months, with his increased workload. Irritation crept over him. He knew Allie hadn't been neglected. Every time he had seen her lately, James was nearby.

His aggravation increasing with that thought, Delaney dug his heels into the gelding's sides, spurring him to a faster pace. He was annoyed with himself. He had wanted things to go that way, hadn't he? He had told Allie he wanted her to be friends with James so that when he decided to leave, he wouldn't have to worry about her. She seemed to have followed his suggestion to the letter, dammit.

Delaney realized that he was not being consistent. The truth was, he missed Allie, and he was more than annoyed with himself because of it.

Allie had been curious as the devil the first few weeks he had worked on the newspaper. She had waited for him to come home and had plied him with questions, and as much as he had protested her endless queries, he had enjoyed every minute of her interest. As the months passed and his working hours lengthened, he had begun coming home after she was in bed. He missed seeing her despite his fatigue.

His dark brows drawing into a familiar frown, Delaney recalled the situation at the breakfast table that morning. Mrs. Case had been paler and weaker than usual, and Mr. Case had seemed deeply concerned. Sarah, unconcerned about anyone but herself, was reciting an inconsequential tale about one of her many suitors. The last to be seated, Allie had been flushed and perspiring from her attempt to assume the majority of Mrs. Case's duties in the kitchen. The effort had not escaped him.

Nor had it escaped James. When everyone else had left the table, James walked over to Allie and, placing his hand on her shoulder, whispered something in her ear. Allie's smile flashed. In the face of the rush of puzzling feelings that assaulted him, Delaney had turned on his heel and walked outside.

His irritation had been tempered only slightly when Allie ran out into the yard prior to his departure for town and handed him a large piece of the spice cake she had baked for supper, wrapped in a cloth for his journey.

Delaney paused abruptly in his thoughts. He was not being honest with himself. The fact was, he resented the new intimacy that appeared to be developing between James and Allie. He more than resented it, and he could not afford to allow such intense feelings. It was strange. He had expected the bond between Allie and him to be a problem, but he had not expected *he* would be the one who would have difficulty severing it.

Engrossed in his warring feelings, Delaney frowned as the

final turn in the road brought the darkened farmhouse into view. A short time later, he had unsaddled the gelding, put him in the barn, and gone into the house. Overwhelmingly tired, he walked down the hallway toward his small room in the rear.

Lost in thought, Delaney pushed open the door and lit the table lamp. The flame flickered and grew brighter, and Delaney pushed the door shut behind him. He headed for the bed, but came to an abrupt halt as he stared into the flickering shadows. What the—

"Surprised, Delaney?" Sarah's low purr hung on the silence as she propped herself up on her elbow in his bed. Her seductive eyes were made brighter by the flickering lamplight reflected in her dark pupils.

Delaney jerked his head toward the door, and Sarah gave a low, husky laugh.

"Don't worry. Nobody knows I'm here. I even waited until the 'sweet innocent' was sleeping before I left. You're late. I've been waiting a long time, but I know it'll be worth it."

The silence between them grew strained as Delaney surveyed Sarah incredulously.

"It never ceases to amaze me that you're Margaret Case's daughter," he said at last.

Sarah's smile flickered. "I don't suppose you meant that as a compliment." Her eyes moved intently over his face for a few seconds longer. "Is it wrong to know what you want and to go after it? I would've thought you'd admire that quality in me. We're alike in that way, you know."

It was Delaney's turn to laugh, but the laughter was self-directed. He had denied a similar statement from Allie. He only wished he could truthfully deny this one as well.

"Are you boasting, Sarah? I wouldn't, if I were you."

"But you're not me, are you? You don't know what I think or what I've felt since the day you came here."

"You were a child when I first came."

"I was fourteen, and I wasn't a child. I knew what I wanted even then."

Gracefully swinging her legs over the side of the bed, Sarah slowly drew herself to her feet. She paused, allowing Delaney to take in the full effect of the long batiste nightgown that barely concealed her nakedness under the diaphanous folds. She took a short step forward, and the shadows of the dark erect crests of her full breasts were startlingly visible. Again he heard her low laughter.

"Like what you see, Delaney? It's yours for the taking."

Delaney shook his head, the hardening of his body contradicting his clear reply: "No, thank you."

Anger flickered in Sarah's light green eyes. "Afraid, Delaney?"

"No, I'm not afraid. I'm just too smart for you."

"Too smart? I don't think so. You aren't smart enough to know what you're missing."

"Oh, yes, I am."

Sarah closed the distance between them in a few steps. Her body brushed his lightly, and he could feel her warmth. She slid her arms around his neck and clung tenaciously, pressing her body close to his. Her breasts were warm against his chest, and he could feel himself swelling at the erotic stimulation. He was tired, but damn, he wasn't that tired.

"Sarah, you—"

Delaney's statement was cut abruptly short as Sarah raised herself on her toes and pressed her mouth firmly against his. Her kiss was hungry, aggressive, and he felt the rapid acceleration of his heart as he forced himself to remain unresponsive. Drawing away at last, Sarah circled his mouth with light, fleeting kisses, coaxing, taking advantage of a slight parting of his lips to slip her warm, moist tongue between them.

An unconscious groan escaped Delaney's lips as Sarah began rubbing her body erotically against his, increasing the pressure of her mouth until he accepted the full invasion of her tongue. She raked her long fingers through his hair, then slipped her hand between their bodies and opened the buttons of his shirt. Within seconds, she had exposed his chest, but she was not satisfied with that. She quickly unbuttoned her nightgown, and moments later her warm breasts were pressed hotly against him.

Somewhere in the back of his mind, Delaney heard her sharp intake of breath at the first meeting of their flesh, and his heart pounded anew. Excited to a heated frenzy, Sarah assaulted his lips and chin with sharp, sensuous bites before covering his lips with her open mouth to kiss him fully and deeply once more. Pulling back only when they were both breathless, she looked into his face, and Delaney suppressed his reaction to the power of her physical beauty. The knowledge that she was shallow, her beauty skin deep, had little effect on his body's spontaneous reaction to the sexual titillation.

His hands still clenched at his sides, Delaney barely suppressed his growing physical excitement, the urge to crush her body against his and sample all she offered him.

A low breathy laugh escaped Sarah's lips, her smile increasing her already incredible beauty.

"You want to hold me, don't you, Delaney? You want to take me in your arms and touch me. You want to feel me under you."

"Sarah . . ."

His voice was a pained whisper, almost unrecognizable to his own ears, and Sarah laughed again. Raising her hands, she stripped her gown off her shoulders, allowing it to fall to her waist. She turned slightly, allowing the shadows to play against the smooth flesh of her shoulders and breasts.

"All yours, Delaney. I've saved myself for you. Only you. I can give you everything you want. Tell me what you want, Delaney."

Delaney shook his head. She was wearing him down, and he knew damned well what would happen if she did. Hell, he couldn't hold on much longer.

"Take me, Delaney. Take me now."

Stepping forward quickly, Sarah locked her arms around his neck and kissed him hotly, her bare breasts scorching his chest. Despite himself, Delaney felt his arms closing around her, felt her smooth flesh under his hands, felt the swell of her feminine curves. Unable to withdraw from her, yet unwilling to take that final step, he hesitated.

Pushed into savage frustration, Sarah tore her mouth from his, her breathing ragged. Her eyes were hot pools of passion as they looked up into his face. "You're trying to show me who's master, aren't you? Well, you can be master. You can be anything you want with me. I'll show you. I'll prove to you how I feel."

Pressing her mouth against his once more, Sarah bit his lower lip painfully before releasing it to rain similar sharp bites on his chin and along the broad, tanned column of his throat. She kissed the hollows at its base, licking the salty flesh there, then laughed as he shuddered, a soft, wild sound, before trailing hot, searching kisses over the mat of fine hair covering his chest. Her smooth

hands spreading his shirt wide, she followed with feverish, sa-
lacious bites the fine line of dark hair as it dwindled downward.

Delaney gasped, his control all but gone as her tongue moved
wetly against his midriff. She was struggling with his belt when
a soft thumping overhead snapped his glance toward the ceiling.
The sound, apparently a branch falling on the roof, brought him
sharply back to his senses.

He must be crazy! The short hour of physical pleasure Sarah
offered was not worth the payment he would have to make if
they were found out. And he knew with a sixth sense that Sarah
would make sure the right people did find out. Well, he wouldn't
fall into her trap. No woman, especially Sarah, was worth sacrificing everything he had worked for during the last three years.
And no woman was worth sacrificing his future.

Sarah had succeeded in loosening his belt. Her fingers were
working open the closure of his trousers when Delaney clamped
his hands roughly on her wrists and pushed her an arm's length
from him. She struggled to close the distance between them, but
he rasped, "No, Sarah, your price is too high."

"Price! I want to give myself to you!"

"No, you don't."

"Nobody has to know, Delaney. I won't tell! We can—"

"You won't tell anybody because there'll be nothing to tell."
His voice growing harder as his control returned full measure,
Delaney shook his head. "Things wouldn't even have gone this
far if I hadn't been so tired."

Raising her flushed face to his, Sarah attempted to conceal
her fury. "Delaney, you want me, you know you do. I can give
you so much. Everything you see, and more. I'm beautiful, Delaney. My body is perfect and untouched. It has so much to
offer. *I* have so much to offer."

"Not enough, Sarah." His voice unexpectedly harsh, Delaney dropped his hands from her wrists and issued a concise
command. "Button your gown."

Sarah's mouth twitched revealingly as she responded in a single word: "No."

His patience beginning to wane, Delaney took a threatening
step forward. "You'll dress yourself, dammit, or I'll throw you
out into the hall just as you stand! You can try explaining that
to anybody who chances to see you!"

"Is that what you're afraid of, Delaney? Somebody seeing or hearing us? They won't. We—"

"They won't because there won't be anything to see or hear. Now get dressed, dammit!"

His eyes narrowing, Delaney watched as Sarah brought her fury under control. Slowly, sensuously, she drew her nightgown up to cover her shoulders. Her gleaming breasts peeked from the gaping bodice and she laughed as his eyes dropped toward them.

"You've deprived yourself of pleasure tonight for no good reason, Delaney. You could've had it all. I would have given you anything you wanted. You almost gave in, didn't you?" She nodded in silent confirmation of her own statement as her slender, graceful hands went to the buttons on her nightgown. "But you'll have another chance, I'll see to that. I'll give you plenty of time to think about what you've missed, and to wonder if Charles Knots or Bobbie Clark, or one of the other fellows got what you were afraid to take tonight."

Her gown secured at last, Sarah smoothed her long, dark hair back from her shoulders. Her small pink tongue flicked over her lower lip in a deliberately seductive movement.

"Next time, Delaney. Next time."

Slowly and sinuously, Sarah walked to the door and pulled it open. Raising her eyes to hold his for a moment longer, she gave a short laugh and stepped into the hallway, closing the door behind her.

Rigid, Delaney listened to Sarah's quiet steps as she moved down the hallway and beyond.

She was gone.

Releasing a low, shaky breath, Delaney was about to turn to his bed when he had a second thought. Shifting his weight, he gripped the dresser and pushed it across the floor until it blocked the door. He gave a short, self-conscious laugh. Hell, he wasn't going to take the chance of Sarah's coming back. Another few minutes and he would have had her pinned to that bed, and that damned conscienceless part of his anatomy would've been buried deep inside her, just as she wanted.

No, the price was too high. Nobody was going to get in the way of his ambitions, and nobody was going to make him do anything that would force him out of this house one minute sooner than he was ready to leave.

Suddenly exhausted, Delaney shot a glance toward the night sky outside his window. Damn! Was that dawn he saw streaking the darkness? He uttered a low groan and, not bothering to undress, flopped down on his bed.

He turned his head away from the window and closed his eyes. Sarah's sweet scent rose from the pillow, and he remembered her smooth white flesh. Then he remembered . . . He groaned again.

In his fatigued, dispirited state, the thought touched his mind for the first time in many years that maybe there was a higher power after all, for surely the sweet scent even now interfering with his sleep was payment extracted for his past sins. It was a hard penance indeed.

Allie wasn't certain what had awakened her, but her first instinct had been to glance toward Sarah's bed. It was empty.

She looked out the window of their room. It was a bright night. A million twinkling stars were visible in the endless dark blanket of the sky, but dawn was already beginning to lighten that blackness. Sarah had been gone a long time.

Allie turned away from the window and buried her face in the pillow. She did not want to think where Sarah had gone. The answers that crept into her mind caused her too much distress. She did not want to face them, and she had tried to avoid them by falling asleep, but she had found no escape there. Instead, she had remained awake, listening to the sounds of night.

A sound outside the bedroom door interrupted Allie's thoughts, snapping her head in its direction as it slowly opened and Sarah slipped into the gradually lightening shadows. She remained silent, but Sarah was too alert not to realize that she was awake.

Advancing slowly to the side of her bed, Sarah stood over her for long silent moments, her face glowing with triumph.

"Why aren't you asking me where I've been all this time, Allie? Could it possibly be because you don't want to know?"

Fascinated despite herself by the wildness in Sarah's brilliant eyes, Allie did not immediately reply.

''What's the matter, cat got your tongue? Or maybe you know the answer already.''

Realizing Sarah would not relent until she replied, Allie said, ''I don't know and I don't care where you were, Sarah. It's none of my business. Mother Case—''

Her eyes glittering maliciously, Sarah gave a harsh laugh. ''Mother Case! You don't give a damn about Mama right now and you know it. All you've been thinking about is Delaney, and you're wondering if I went visiting tonight. Well, I'm going to tell you. Yes, that's exactly what I did. You see, Delaney and I had a long talk before he left this afternoon, and we made plans. You know I'd never disappoint Delaney, don't you, Allie?''

Allie stiffened, pain stronger than any she had ever suffered twisting her stomach into tight, hurting knots. No, it wasn't true. Delaney would never do that. He had said he didn't even like Sarah.

Sarah did not wait for her reply.

''And Delaney didn't disappoint me, either.'' With a low, gloating laughter, Sarah turned away and went to her own bed, where she lay down and stretched gracefully.

''Delaney said I'm beautiful. All of me. He told me that he loves my body, and that he'll never get enough of me. He said—''

''I don't believe you! You weren't with Delaney! He wouldn't—''

''You're a fool, do you know that?'' Sarah's voice grew sharper. ''Do you really think any man would turn down what *I* have to offer? Never! And it was better than I ever thought it could be.''

''You're lying! I don't want to hear anymore.''

''You don't want to believe me, do you, Allie dear? You want to believe you've turned Delaney against me for good, just like you've turned my own brother against me, but you haven't. He wants me, Allie, and now that he's had me, he'll want me more. When Delaney leaves he's going to take me with him. I'm going to make sure he wants me so much that he won't be able to leave without me.''

''I don't believe you.''

''Yes, you do. You know you believe me.'' Laughing low in her throat, Sarah stretched languorously. ''I don't think I'll bother to bathe tonight. I like having Delaney's scent on me. It's easier to remember him that way.''

Allie stared in silence as Sarah finally turned her back and pulled the coverlet over her shoulders. She did not see the glow of victory slip from Sarah's face. She did not see the expression of seething jealousy and steadfast determination that replaced it before Sarah, with supreme control, closed her eyes to sleep.

Allie was still staring at her back minutes later when the low, even sound of Sarah's breathing reached her ears.

Allied closed her eyes against the burning ache inside her, against the sight of dawn creeping across the night sky. She didn't want to believe Sarah, but she could not truly believe that any man, even Delaney, could resist Sarah's beauty.

Willing herself to sleep, Allie attempted to dismiss the evil pictures that chased each other across her mind, and the excruciating sadness that overwhelmed her.

Oh, Delaney . . .

Delaney had been in a foul mood for the past week, and it wasn't improving. He lowered the pages to the desk and covered his eyes with his hand for a few silent moments. Damn it all, he had to get himself under control.

"What's wrong with you, boy? You're more damned irritable than a grizzly with a sore paw."

Delaney dropped his hand from eyes that were suddenly cold blue ice. "That's my business, isn't it?"

"The hell it is! I'd say it's my damned business, too, when I gotta sit here and suffer your moods."

Delaney's hands tightened into fists. "You're mistaken."

"No, you're the one who's mistaken, boy! Look here, don't you give me any of your threatenin' looks, because I won't put up with them. I want to get somethin' clear, right here and now. You aren't so big that I have to take any of your guff. And if you have somethin' to say, say it! There are only two of us in this here office, and it occurs to me that maybe that's the problem. I admit that we could use some more help, but there's no other help to be had that's worth hirin', if that's what's eatin' at you."

"No, that has nothing to do with it. I'm not afraid of hard work. I never have been."

Max squinted, his lined face screwing up into an expression of intense scrutiny. "No, maybe not, but I think you're stretchin' yourself pretty thin these days. Maybe I'm expectin' a little too much of you."

Delaney stiffened. "Have you ever given me anything I can't handle?"

"That isn't the problem."

"Then what is the problem?"

"That's what I asked you, boy."

Delaney's silent stare was his only response.

Max burst out in exasperation, "Is that all you've got to say?"

Silence once more.

Muttering low under his breath, Max stood up and covered the distance between their desks in a few short steps. Hands on his hips, he stood looking down at Delaney and shook his head. "You know, you're a hard one to figure. I took a chance, hirin' you. I didn't know you from Adam, except for the talk about you in town."

Delaney's eyes narrowed, but he made no response.

"Yeah, there sure as hell was plenty of that. Whether you know it or not, you've got a reputation as a surly brute with a bad history, and I'm thinkin' you earned that reputation."

"Maybe I did."

"That's what I figured. I also figured that someone with your background deserved a chance to make it in this line of work, if that's what he wanted. Hell, your pa was one fine newspaperman."

A long-subdued pride stirred deep inside Delaney.

"I figured you had a long way to go before you'd be fit to shine your father's boots, but I'm tellin' you now, straight and to the point, that you've got the makin's of bein' as good a journalist as your father was. Maybe even better."

Startled by Max Marshall's unexpected praise, Delaney did not reply.

"What's the matter, boy? You look as if somebody just kicked the chair out from under you. What were you expectin' me to say? You've done a damned good job, and you've worked like hell. You've got a sharp mind, and judgin' from the stuff you've already written, you've got a style all your own. You can organize your thoughts and put them down in a way to make people sit up and take notice. But more than that, you're more goddam determined than any fella I've seen around here in the past twenty years. I'm thinkin' that the life you led before you came here did a lot toward makin' you realize what you want and how you need to get it. And I think you're tough enough to do just exactly what you want, without lettin' anythin' get in your way.''

Pausing, Max shook his balding pate, his bushy gray brows furrowing. ''But you've got one drawback, boy. You're a damned nasty piece of work sometimes, and hard for people to swallow. Me included.''

Maintaining his silence a few moments longer, Delaney returned Max's stare. A small muscle twitched in his cheek. ''You trying to tell me something, Max?''

''I started out by askin' a question and didn't get an answer, so it looks as if I have to do the tellin', doesn't it? I'm going to lay some things out for you now, just so everythin' will be set and clear once and for all. I suppose you've been wonderin' why I've been pilin' so much work on you the past few months.''

''I haven't had the time to give it much thought.''

''Yeah, I figured that. Maybe that's part of the problem.''

Delaney stiffened, his pale eyes again cold. ''Well, if it is, it's my problem, not yours.''

''That's where you're wrong, but I don't expect to go over that ground again. Look, Delaney, take that chip off your shoulder and listen to me for a few minutes. You got shortchanged somewhere along the line, there isn't any doubt about that. You'd be workin' on a big-city newspaper right now if your pa was still alive, because you've got talent. You're quick and you're smart, and you've got instinct that doesn't come with book learnin'. I'm goin' to tell you somethin' else, too. It irks me that a man like your pa was beaten by big money and political influence just because he reported the truth.''

The sudden tension in Delaney's expression caused Max to shake his head emphatically. ''I know you don't want to talk about it, but your pa just bucked the wrong organization, and he paid the hard way. There's not a thing either one of us can do about it, but that doesn't make knowin' it easier to swallow.'' Max gave a short, hard laugh. ''Maybe that's a part of what's stuck in your craw, but I don't think that's what's botherin' you right now. Anyway, I think you deserve a chance. It's going to take a lot of hard work, and I'm not opposed to handin' it out if you're not opposed to takin' it.''

Delaney eyed the wizened face looking directly into his. "What are you trying to say, Max?''

"I'm tellin' you that if you object to the work you've been handlin' now, speak up. From the looks of you today, I'd say you've had just about as much as you can take, and if that's what's botherin' you, I admit that puts a crimp in my plans. I was thinkin' of expandin' your duties, takin' you out with me so you can see how I gather information. And then if you're up to it, I'm thinkin' of lettin' you start puttin' things together.''

"You know damned well I'm up to it.''

"I wouldn't say so from the looks of you today.''

"I told you—''

"You didn't tell me anything, boy. You're pulled as tight as a drum.''

"And I told you it's got nothing to do with work.''

"What does it have to do with, then? Play?'' Max's eyes intent on Delaney's face, caught the flicker in the light eyes returning his stare. His mouth suddenly dropping open, Max released a low grunt of disgust. "Oh, hell, not woman trouble!''

Delaney made no response, and Max shook his weary head as realization dawned full and clear. "Christ! That's what it is, all right.''

Taking a deep breath, Max turned and walked the few steps back to his desk. Sitting down, he contemplated Delaney's silence. "Well, my first impression of you was right, I can see that. You are a hard case, but even a hard case needs some softenin' sometimes.''

Pausing, Max turned to look through the window at a horizon streaked with gray and gold. He turned back toward Delaney.

"You're not much good to me today, Delaney. Get out of here and get yourself straightened out. I'm tired of your growlin' and your surly looks. When you come back on Thursday, I want you to be ready for the work that will be waitin' for you. There's goin' to be plenty of it.''

"Max, I don't need—''

"I know what you need boy. I'm not *that* old, you know. Take a walk around the corner to Lil's place, if that'll do the trick.''

Max didn't miss much. Irritation twitched at Delaney's lips.

"I don't like people telling me where to go or what to do on my own time."

The editor's bloodshot eyes narrowed further. "You aren't short on nerve, are you?" Watching as Delaney drew himself to his feet in silence, his expression black, Max eyed him just as blackly in return.

"I got a question to ask you, Delaney. Who's the boss in this establishment?"

Delaney stiffened. "You are."

"And what are you doin' here?"

"Working for you."

Max nodded. "You got that right. Try to remember it. Now, get the hell out of here and get yourself straightened out. I don't give a damn how you do it, and I don't care how much you don't like me tellin' you. Just get movin'."

Max made no effort to glance his way as Delaney turned, snatched his hat off the wall, and walked out of the office without another word.

The door slammed closed behind him, but not before Delaney heard Max's muttered reply, "A man of few words."

It occurred to Delaney as he reached the street, untied his horse's reins, and mounted, that maybe that was the problem. There had been too few words lately, and it was time he got things settled. Hell, it was long overdue.

It was unusually warm for so late in the year. That thought had crossed Margaret's mind several times during the afternoon while she sat on the porch and snapped the beans in the large bowl on her lap. The clanging of pans in the kitchen drew her mind to the young girl who was working there and to another young woman who wasn't.

Withdrawing a handkerchief from her apron pocket, Margaret blotted the perspiration from her fair brow and tried to take a deep breath. She was not successful. Why was it she could never seem to get enough air into her lungs these days? The attempt often left her breathless and light-headed, and she realized, not without considerable guilt, that her condition had not gone unnoticed by her family. She knew that was the reason Allie had suggested that she sit on the porch while she finished cleaning up the kitchen. Rather than argue with the girl's good intentions, she had complied.

Margaret's thoughts moved to Sarah, and familiar lines of worry appeared on her brow. Sarah had been extremely tense lately, and when she was not at her best, everyone suffered. The family tensions that had resulted from her strange mood the past week had been almost unbearable. How she wished it was easier to talk to Sarah, but the girl had long ago grown past the age where she confided in her mother.

In the hope of seeing an improvement in her daughter's disposition, Margaret had excused Sarah from her chores to ride out with Bobbie Clark when he arrived a few hours earlier. Bobbie's unexpected visit appeared to be just the medicine Sarah needed. The warmth of her reception had made Bobbie turn bright red with pleasure, and Sarah had not been satisfied until she had the poor boy so besotted that he could hardly talk.

Margaret shook her head in dismay. Sarah was incorrigible. She feared the girl was spoiled beyond redemption, and it was her fault. She had realized too late that, unlike her other children, Sarah took advantage of her love to the point where it had become detrimental to her character. Such was not the case with James, who was kind and thoughtful to everyone except Delaney, and dear Annie had been endlessly giving. As for Allie, love had made her bloom.

The problem with Sarah was that she had been an outstandingly beautiful baby and child, and now that she was mature, she was too lovely for her own good. She had always been fussed and petted over and had accepted the attention as her due. The result was that she expected too much without being willing to give in return. She only hoped that Sarah's demanding nature would not keep her from finding happiness. The fact that she could not always have what she wanted was a bitter pill for her to swallow, but Delaney seemed to be just the person to make her take that medicine.

Margaret's brow furrowed with anxiety. Sarah's infatuation with Delaney was only too obvious to her, and perhaps to the other members of the family as well. Margaret had spent many anxious hours contemplating the pressure Sarah's obsession put on the others in the household. It was to Delaney's credit that he was never more than polite to Sarah, most times not even extending her that courtesy. Well, Margaret could not blame him. She supposed a boy who had experienced so much hardship would have little patience for Sarah's pettishness. The sooner Sarah learned that Delaney was forever beyond her the better. Maybe then she would turn to Bobbie Clark with more honesty. He was, after all, a very personable young man.

A light step behind her turned Margaret from her thoughts. A smile broke across her pale face as Allie stepped out onto the porch.

"I've set a place for Bobbie at the table, too, just in case Sarah decides to ask him to stay for supper." Allie smiled as she lowered herself to a chair nearby, and Margaret's heart warmed. She had grown to love that smile, just as she had grown to love the child.

Reaching out, Margaret smoothed back a flyaway wisp of hair from Allie's perspiring cheek.

"Thank you, dear. I apologize for allowing Sarah to go off and leave you with all the work."

Allie's soft brown eyes were suddenly sober. "I don't mind. I'm truly glad to see Sarah doing something she likes *with* someone she likes, and Bobbie is nice. He makes Sarah laugh."

Aware of Sarah's viciousness toward the child who was speaking so generously, Margaret felt a flush of shame.

"It was a blessed day when Jacob and I went to the church meeting hall and found you. You've added immeasurably to our life, dear, and I thank the Lord every night for directing us to you."

Allie lowered her eyes, and Margaret realized the reason for Allie's silence: She had not included Delaney in her heartfelt declaration, and she knew Allie suffered for the omission.

"Allie, you know I love Delaney dearly. I could not help but love him for the concern he shows for you and me, but he worries me, dear."

Allie turned to her with a fearful expression, and Margaret shook her head in an attempt to banish it. "You don't have to worry, Allie. I give you my word that Delaney may remain here as long as he wants, as long as I have the strength to speak my mind. He's not in danger of being turned out."

Relief registered in Allie's eyes, but not in Margaret's.

"I worry about him in another way," Margaret went on. "There's a bitterness inside him, a relentlessness that drives him. He finds no peace, no matter how much he accomplishes. I fear he never will.'' Margaret lowered her voice to cushion the blow of her next words. ''I think you should prepare yourself for the possibility that Delaney may soon choose of his own free will to leave us.''

An unidentifiable emotion flickered momentarily in Allie's eyes, puzzling Margaret. She smiled reassuringly. ''Allie, surely you realized that?''

Allie did not respond, but her pale face grew even whiter, and Margaret was touched by concern.

''What's wrong, dear?''

Allie shook her head, but Margaret sensed there was more to her silence than Allie was prepared to admit.

''Allie.''

But Allie was no longer listening. She had looked up toward the rider who was approaching the house. She saw Allie's anxiety as she recognized Delaney's familiar broad-shouldered form. So that was it. Something was wrong between Allie and Delaney.

Remaining silent as Delaney continued his approach, Margaret concealed her disturbed feelings. She could not allow herself to become upset or to interfere. If she was patient, if she allowed them the opportunity, they would settle their differences. Delaney and Allie were too close to allow a misunderstanding to mar their friendship for any length of time. She only wished the situation between Sarah and Delaney could be as easily handled.

Watching Delaney as he approached, Margaret felt an almost maternal pride warm her heart. Delaney had grown since coming to them, both in height and breadth of stature. He was no longer a boy. He was a man. And he was handsome, probably the most handsome man she had ever seen. His features were perfectly proportioned, but that perfection did not diminish his manliness or his strength. There was a latent power and sexuality in those light, almost hypnotic eyes.

Margaret's pity for her own beautiful but besotted daughter deepened as she sensed for the first time the true depth of Sarah's despair.

Margaret had realized long before that despite the consideration and concern with which Delaney treated her, only Allie had been successful in penetrating the wall of ice with which the boy surrounded his emotions. Even now, as he approached, Delaney's glance was only cursory as it flicked over her to rest on

Allie's averted face. His jaw was hard with tension as he drew
his horse to a halt in front of them.

"Hello, Mrs. Case . . . Allie."

Delaney had never called her Mother Case, as did Allie, despite her request. She had no doubt that his reasons were diverse
and deep, and she was not offended by his formal manner of
address because it usually was accompanied by a spark of true
warmth in his light eyes. But there was no warmth there today.
Those incredible eyes were emotionless, intent on Allie as she
returned his greeting without directly meeting his gaze.

"You're back early, Delaney. We're not accustomed to seeing
you return before dark these days."

"Max let me off early today."

Delaney was dismounting, and Margaret noticed he had responded almost absentmindedly, his eyes still intent on Allie.
His words were clipped as he gripped his horse's reins.

"I'm going to rub Jack down now that I have a chance. He
could use some attention."

Allie made no comment at all as Margaret spoke into the
awkward silence.

"That's probably a good idea. Jacob and James are cutting
down some trees. They'll be back in about an hour. That should
give you time to do a really good job on him."

Delaney nodded and turned away, but Allie made no move to
follow. Margaret's lips twitched as she controlled her urge to
interfere. It pained her to see these two at odds when just a few
words could probably end any misunderstanding between them.
Delaney was just slipping out of sight in the barn when Margaret
could stand it no longer.

"Why don't you go and help Delaney, dear? I'll be fine here
by myself."

Allie's response was hesitant. "I . . . Delaney doesn't really
need my help, and I'd rather stay with you."

Margaret shrugged her frail shoulders. "Whatever you like,
dear."

It pained her deeply to see these two estranged, but there was
nothing she could do about it.

Barely controlling his irritation, Delaney walked Jack into the
barn. His chest heaving against the agitation growing stronger

every minute, he allowed the animal to lower his head for a mouthful of feed as he removed the saddle and blanket.

Dammit, Allie was still avoiding him! She'd been avoiding him for a week, and he feared that her unusual behavior coincided too closely with Sarah's nighttime visit to be a coincidence.

He had been confused at first. Allie had not actually ignored or been cold to him. She had merely managed to avoid any personal contact with him. It had been annoyingly easy for her to do so, considering his tight schedule, and he had originally intended just to ignore the whole thing. He had not expected that, as the days passed, his annoyance would turn to anger and then to a sense of loss so keen that he could no longer deny it.

Delaney took a deep breath and straightened his shoulders with determination. The girl had wormed herself into his emotional life, damn her, and now she would have to suffer the consequences. Sarah appeared to be nowhere around, and he supposed he would never have a better opportunity than the present to speak to Allie without being interrupted.

Quickly settling Jack with his feed, Delaney walked back to the door of the barn. He paused, only too aware that any other time Allie would have welcomed him home enthusiastically and followed him inside. But not this time. She was still sitting on the porch with Mrs. Case.

Delaney stepped into full view.

"You might want to come in here and look at Mischief, Allie. She's acting peculiar. She doesn't seem to be able to stand up."

Delaney sent a quick glance back into the barn. It occurred to him belatedly that Mischief might come running out at the sound of her name, but the patient cat was too engrossed in stalking invisible prey near the rear stall to respond. Relieved, he turned back to see Allie and Mrs. Case exchanging words. Allie drew herself to her feet, her reluctance obvious, despite the worried frown that marred her brow. She started toward him, and unwilling to watch her lagging step a moment longer, Delaney turned and walked back inside.

Anxiety gradually added haste to Allie's step. Mischief had been fine just a few hours ago. She couldn't imagine what could have happened to her.

It had been a terrible week. She had not been able to look at Delaney since that night when Sarah had come back to their room near dawn and told her she had been with him.

Allie attempted to swallow against the familiar ache in her throat. It had been bad enough the next morning, seeing the covert glances Sarah had sent in Delaney's direction. Delaney had not returned them, but Allie knew Sarah well enough to realize that the adoration in her gaze was not feigned. Delaney had left at noon to report for work in town, and she had not seen him again that day.

She had tried to convince herself that Sarah had lied about her visit to Delaney, but Sarah had sneaked out of their room again the following night and had not returned until nearly dawn. Unable to face Sarah on her return, Allie had pretended sleep. In truth, Allie had not slept a wink from that point on.

Sarah had sneaked out of their room in the middle of the night twice more in the time since, and Allie no longer had even the slightest doubt that everything Sarah said was true.

Allie blinked back the heavy warmth of tears. Her sense of betrayal was so keen that it was almost physical pain. She didn't want to look at Delaney. She didn't want to talk to Delaney. She wanted to stop thinking of Delaney, to pretend he did not even exist until that pain subsided. She had prayed to the Lady for help, but her prayers had gone unanswered.

Without the Lady, without Delaney, she was alone in her heart. So very alone.

Allie stepped through the doorway of the barn and into the shadows. Squinting into the darkened corner where Mischief usually lay, she was about to call her when a firm grip on her arm spun her abruptly to Delaney's tight, angry face. She attempted to pull free, but his hand tightened almost to the point of pain.

"Let me go."

Delaney gave a short laugh, but his clear, almost transparent eyes remained cold. "Well, you're speaking to me at last."

"You're hurting me. Let me go."

"No, I don't think I will. I'm waiting for you to tell me what's wrong."

Allie turned from his penetrating eyes. "Nothing's wrong. You said Mischief was sick."

"She's fine."

"But—"

"Allie, look at me."

Allie did not want to obey Delaney's command, spoken softly in a voice suddenly familiar and devoid of harshness. She did not want to turn back to face the searching gaze of those eyes that seemed to see right into her soul. She did not want him to know that she could not be happy for him if he really wanted Sarah.

Delaney's gentle, familiar hand was touching her chin, cupping it, turning her head to meet his eyes. She saw concern in those crystal depths and, startlingly, a pain that closely mirrored her own.

"Why won't you talk to me, Allie? I thought we were friends. Friends talk to each other about things that bother them. You used to like to talk to me." Delaney's gaze flickered, and he gave a short laugh. "I suppose James—"

"Oh, no." Allie shook her head in denial. "You know I would never listen to anything James said against you."

"Then what is it?"

Allie closed her eyes briefly, the only escape possible.

"Allie."

Allie's voice was a ragged whisper. "Sarah said—"

"I knew it!" Delaney's eyes turned to blue ice, and his lips tightened into a straight, hard line. A revealing tic in his cheek signaled his mounting anger. "What did she say?"

When Allie remained silent, Delaney sat on a storage box and drew her to him, frowning as he tilted up her chin and forced her to meet his eyes. "I asked you what she said."

"I . . . I can't repeat it."

Delaney's breath escaped in a low hiss. "That bitch!"

Allie's eyes widened at the epithet.

"Whatever she told you is a lie."

Allie took a short breath. "Sarah sneaked out of the room in the middle of the night. She was gone a long time, and when she came back she said she had been with you, in your room."

Delaney nodded with a low snort. "She came to my room, all right. That part was true. She was waiting for me when I came back from town, but I threw her out, Allie."

Fear thickened Allie's throat. She had never seen Delaney so furious. He was twitching with the restraint he was exercising, and his eyes, so cold only minutes before, were suddenly blazing.

"I threw her out, and I have to admit it was damned hard at the time to do it. But I'm glad I did. Sarah is a bitch."

"She sneaked out the next night, too, Delaney, and two more times since. She—"

"She might have sneaked out, Allie, but she didn't come to my room, not after that first night a week ago."

Allie was silent, and Delaney waited a few seconds before raising his hand to her white cheek and adding in a softer voice, "If I had been with Sarah the way she said I was, I'd admit it, Allie. I've always been honest with you. I wouldn't lie now and give Sarah an advantage over you. When I think how close I came." Halting, Delaney shook his head. "I've made a lot of mistakes, but that would've been one of the biggest mistakes of my life, in more ways than one."

Delaney paused again at Allie's silence. He slid his fingers into the fine silky hair at her temple and massaged her warm scalp unconsciously.

"You do believe me, don't you, Allie?"

Finally nodding, Allie sat down on Delaney's knee. His relief was obvious, and a small smile flickered across her lips.

As Allie slid her arm around his broad shoulders, her hand brushed the chain around his neck, affording her a moment of additional comfort in that bond they shared. Allie rested her forehead against his and closed her eyes briefly as Delaney's arm tightened around her waist.

"I'm sorry, Delaney."

Delaney's hand slipped up to tangle in the long, pale hair lying against her narrow back as she said, "I was silly for believing her. I should've known Sarah was lying. You told me you didn't even like her." Allie bit her lower lip, as she struggled to explain. "But Sarah was so . . ."

"Convincing?" Delaney's low laugh was devoid of mirth. "You don't know how convincing."

"And she's beautiful."

"Yes, she's beautiful." A small smile picked up the corners of Delaney's mouth. "But I prefer pale little girls with big eyes who weigh little more than a feather when they sit on my knee."

Slipping both arms around Delaney, Allie hugged him tight. Burying her face against his neck, she breathed deeply of his warm, familiar scent. Years had passed, but it was the same comforting scent she had breathed when she had lain on the floor of a rail car beside a somewhat frightening boy of fifteen and held his religious medal in her hand until she fell asleep. The solace it had given her then was magnified a thousandfold at this moment, and she was grateful to have Delaney with her, even if it was only for a little while longer.

Allie drew back at last, noting that Delaney's expression was suddenly sober. Hers was sober as well.

"I'll never doubt you again, Delaney."

"Never?" Delaney remained surprisingly serious. "Never is a long time, Allie."

"You'll always be my friend."

An unreadable expression passed across Delaney's face. Setting Allie lightly on her feet, he took her hand and started toward the door. It was Allie who broke the silence between them as she smiled up into his face.

"I'm glad you came home early tonight. Mother Case made something special for tonight. I was going to save you some anyway, but—"

"You were angry with me, but you were going to save me something special?"

"I wasn't really angry with you, Delaney. I was disappointed, and it hurt really bad, even to look at you."

As Allie walked into the yard with Delaney, she heard the rattle of an approaching wagon. She turned toward the sound, her smile vanishing as she met Sarah's frozen stare. Stepping to one side to allow the wagon to draw up in front of the house, Allie nodded in response to Bobbie Clark's greeting and heard Delaney offer a short hello as well.

"You're home early tonight, Delaney." Sarah approached them as soon as Bobbie had lifted her to the ground. "That's nice. Bobbie has agreed to stay for dinner. He—"

Sarah halted abruptly, her beautiful face suddenly whitening. Following her stare, Allie turned toward Delaney. She saw a fierce hatred in his eyes, the same hatred that held Sarah suddenly immobile.

"Delaney?"

His eyes snapped toward Allie as she spoke his name, and she released a tense breath as the ferocity there slipped away. Relieved, she felt Delaney's arm curl around her shoulder.

"I'll see you later, Allie. I'm going to rub Jack down."

Allie excused herself immediately after Delaney strode back
to the barn. Her shoulder still warm from Delaney's touch, she
walked into the kitchen and, with a steady hand, stirred the pot
simmering on the stove. All was right in the world again, and it
was right because of Delaney. When had it ever been different?

Witness to all that had taken place, Margaret remained seated
in the porch chair she had occupied for a greater part of the
afternoon.

Delaney had called Allie to the barn with an apparent subterfuge.
She had seen them both emerge a short time later, their differences
obviously settled. Anger had left Delaney's eyes, and joy had returned to Allie's sweet, immature face. It had occurred to her then
that there was no one who could bring Allie more happiness than
Delaney. And no one who could bring her more pain.

It had been inopportune for Sarah and Bobbie to return at that
moment, but it had brought only too clearly into focus the realization that the same could be said for her own beautiful
daughter.

But Sarah was now slipping her arm under Bobbie Clark's and
drawing him away, a smile on her lips. With a mother's insight,
she knew Sarah would not take Delaney's rejection lightly. Nor
would she accept it.

Suddenly tired, very tired, Margaret drew herself to her feet.
Swaying weakly, she grasped the arm of the chair for support.
She loved them all—Sarah, James, Allie, Delaney, and dear Jacob—but she feared she would not be present much longer to
soothe ragged feelings and act as a buffer between those in her
dear family who would cause each other pain.

Margaret raised her eyes to a vast expanse of blue sky unmarred by a single cloud. Afternoon was rapidly waning, but
the color was vibrant—so clear. She was touched by the thought
that if she strained, she might be able to see directly into the
eye of God. If she could, she would tell him she knew her time
was limited, but she needed a few more years. Just a few. She
would tell him she feared for the future happiness of the children
he had placed in her care. She would tell him that for a little
while longer, she was needed here.

1862

❋

AWAKENING

chapter

nine

MAMA HAD BEEN wrong.

A wry smile flicked across Allie's lips as she tied the apron around her narrow waist. Contrary to Mama's predictions, the passage of years and the onslaught of maturity had added little beauty to the face staring back at her from the mirror. Her skin was still milky white, the only spots of color the pale pink strip across her nose and under her eyes that had come from being outdoors without her hat the previous day. Her face was still too small, and her eyes—too large and too dark—appeared darker still in comparison with the silver-blond of her hair and her general lack of color. She was still thin, painfully so. Maturity had done little more than add a few inches in height and raise small mounds on her chest that Sarah had scathingly declared were not even worthy of the word "breasts."

Allie tucked a flyaway wisp of hair back into the pale coil she had wound so carefully into a bun only minutes before. The passage of time had also failed to improve the manage-ability of the colorless tresses that the frightened little orphan had despaired of six years before as she had made the long journey west. The young woman of sixteen still could not depend on the wayward strands to remain in place, even when tightly confined.

In retrospect, it amused her to think how patiently she had waited for the fulfillment of Mama's prophecy that she would one day be beautiful. An unconscious glance toward Sarah, asleep in the bed behind her, confirmed that it was Sarah who had grown more beautiful as the years passed, an improvement on physical perfection she had not thought possible. Her dark hair had grown thicker, more lustrous; her face, already faultless in every respect, had grown even lovelier. Time had sculpted her cheekbones almost exotically and added a flirtatious brightness to eyes already a glowing green. Stately. She was amused at her own modest description of Sarah's impressive womanly proportions, her full breasts, enticingly small waist, and a rear end that seemed to draw the attention of every male in sight. Allie had waited breathlessly for the time when she would begin to flower in just such a way.

Her silent amusement was touched with irony. She had flowered, but she had also come to terms with the realization that the mature blossom would never meet her youthful hopes. She was as she had always been—plain. She would never be any different.

Allie's wry smile flickered once more. Mama, unlike the father you said I resembled, and unlike you, I will never be beautiful.

Turning away from the mirror, Allie walked out of the bedroom. She shut the door quietly so as not to disturb Sarah, knowing there would be no end of complaint if she awoke the uncrowned princess of the family one minute before she was ready to be awakened.

Suddenly annoyed with herself, Allie slowly descended the stairs. She was being unfair to Sarah, and she disliked herself for it. The morning sky had not yet been touched by the new day's sun, and Sarah was not really late in arising, but she suspected today would probably be no different from any other day, with Allie getting up early and Sarah waiting until the last minute to arise, and usually arriving in the kitchen with one excuse or another when most of the work for breakfast was done.

Nearing the bottom of the staircase, Allie glanced toward the rear of the house and the room that had been added there to save Delaney from the freezing winter cold of the barn. She paused, hearing no sound coming from that direction. She supposed that meant Delaney had worked so late at the newspaper that he had stayed in town instead of coming home for a few short hours before returning again. She also knew that meant he would make up the lost time later in the day.

Allie worried about Delaney. He worked too hard. She had seen less and less of him as he had become more involved in his work at the newspaper, and she missed him terribly. She tried to tell herself that she should be pleased that Delaney's dreams were beginning to be realized, but she was continually at odds with her failure in that regard.

More upset by that failure than she cared to acknowledge, Allie walked toward the kitchen. The silence of the deserted room brought another realization to her mind. Ashamed of her selfish absorption in her own problems, Allie realized Mother Case was ill again. Her breathlessness had grown considerably more frightening over the past few years. Dr. Peters's most recent prescription seemed of little help in combating the affliction, which seemed to be at its worst during the late-night hours. She supposed Mother Case had suffered another severe attack during the night past, because nothing short of illness would have kept her from being the first into the kitchen in the morning.

Allie glanced up toward the second floor. No matter her concern, she would have to wait until someone came down before she could find out Mother Case's condition this morning. She could not take the chance of awakening either Mother or Papa Case after a difficult night.

A short time later the aroma of boiling coffee permeated the air, and Allie was busily kneading the dough for her special biscuits, the ones Mother Case enjoyed so much. She had already sliced the ham she had brought in from the smokehouse, and the eggs she had gathered yesterday were waiting for the sound of a step on the staircase before meeting the pan.

Brushing back a persistent wisp of hair with the back of her hand, Allie began rolling the dough. She hoped Mother Case was resting well now, and she hoped the aromas wafting upstairs from the kitchen would lift her spirits when she awakened. There was so little she could do for Mother Case, so very little in comparison with the generosity that had changed her life.

Everything she now had she owed to Mother Case and Delaney, and Allie had never lost sight of that. If it had not been for Mother Case, she might have been separated from Delaney all those years ago. She knew she would not have been able to bear being separated from the hard, bitter boy with no faith at all who had rescued her from total despair and given her back the faith her mother had bequeathed to her with all her love.

That hard, bitter boy of fifteen was now a man, and if she had trouble understanding his silences and his intensity of late, she still loved him. The statement made to him years before was burned into her heart. He would always be her friend.

"Allie."

Startled from her reverie by the unexpected voice, Allie turned toward James as he stepped into the kitchen.

"I didn't hear you come down, James. I—" Seeing James's strained expression, she took a short, nervous breath. "What's wrong, James?"

"I didn't mean to frighten you, Allie." James closed his hand reassuringly on her shoulder. His eyes flickered momentarily with an emotion other than concern as they studied her a moment longer. "Mama's not at all well this morning. Pa and I were up most of the night."

"You should have awakened me, James! I could've helped!"

"No, Allie, you couldn't have done anything more than we did for her, which was nothing at all except to try to make her more comfortable." James gave a short laugh, his face lined with exhaustion. "But I think she did a better job of comforting us than we did her."

The heat of tears heavy in her eyes, Allie saw James's expression twitch revealingly before he stepped closer and drew her against his chest. His voice was a hoarse whisper.

"Dr. Peters said he'd stop by today, Allie. Pa thinks if the doctor changes Mama's medicine, she might get some relief, but I don't know if any medicine will be of real help."

Realizing James held her as much for his own comfort as for her own, Allie wrapped her arms around him and returned his embrace. James's arms tightened. His hands caressed her back as he pulled her closer.

"Allie, we'd all be lost without you, especially me. Mama's right. You're the best thing that ever happened to this family. If she wasn't so sick right now, I'd—"

Halting in midsentence, James drew back. Flushed beneath his sun-reddened skin, he swallowed with obvious difficulty, and Allie noticed that his hand trembled as he raised it to her cheek.

"Mama's awake. Pa says you can bring up her breakfast, if you've no objection."

James's pain touched Allie deeply. He had tried to make her feel like a member of the family, and he was like a brother to her. She responded with a nod.

"Dr. Peters should be here in a few hours." James hesitated a moment, adding in a lower voice, "Mama says she isn't going to leave us yet, Allie."

Tears were again hot and heavy in Allie's eyes. She glanced away, but James drew her close once more.

"Don't worry, Allie. Mama always keeps her word."

James's voice broke, and he held her for only a few moments longer before releasing her and leaving the kitchen without another word. Allie turned back to the chore before her.

Delaney eyed with a frown the latest bulletin on the war to come across his desk at the *Cass County News*. So far, the county had remained relatively untouched by the harsh realities of the war between the states, except for the heated debates that sometimes erupted on the street. Earlier in the year the state legislature had passed resolutions that proclaimed the supremacy of the Union, and in a special session a few months later, the raising of ten regiments had been authorized.

Delaney's position on the *News* was now beginning to bring the realities of the war home to him in a way he had not fully expected. Frowning, he ran his eyes down the list of local men whose lives had most recently been sacrificed to principle. *Men*— Delaney's low snort expressed his skepticism about that word. Many of them had been little more than boys.

He had known many of the fellows named on this most recent list. He remembered Fred Bellows, who had not waited for the state to make a decisive move but had demonstrated his support of the Union by joining up. He remembered Willis Crane's smile when he was sent off by a cheering crowd. Delaney wondered how many of that crowd would meet the train to welcome Willis's body home.

Even James had not been deaf to the first call to arms in defense of the Union, but his patriotism had been tempered by Mrs. Case's quiet insistence that he was needed on the farm. Delaney had no doubt that when the heat of patriotic zeal had cooled, James had been glad he had not acted on impulse. After all, who would protect the family against Delaney Marsh if he left?

As for himself, the words "slavery" and "secession" had little bearing on the goals he had set for himself. He had relegated them to the specific portion of his mind that dealt with reporting the progress of the war to his readers accurately and in depth. He had also made certain to keep himself aloof from the emotional discussions that abounded.

The passage of six years since he had come to the Case household had wrought many physical changes in him, but inside he had changed little. He felt little sense of responsibility to a society that bowed to money and power and had so casually sacrificed his father's life and career. He was more determined than ever to one day be in a position where *he* would wield such power, so he would never be at its mercy again.

Delaney was only too aware of the manner in which he was regarded by most of the people in this small Michigan town, and he had made no attempts to change their opinion of him. In truth, he couldn't care less that most people thought him suspiciously uncommunicative, angry, arrogant, and hostile. Some still went out of their way to avoid him.

His association with Lil and her like was general knowledge around town and frowned upon by most, although the subject had never been addressed in the Case household. It was apparent, however, that most of the "nice" girls in the area were kept out of his way. He was secretly amused, for he had not the slightest interest in them.

The town merely tolerated him, and he knew it. He also knew his success in any endeavor would always be overshadowed by his prison-boy reputation. In truth, he cared very little what the townspeople thought of him. He was only passing through.

Delaney glanced at Max, seated at his desk a few feet away, realizing that the editor was one of the few exceptions. Delaney's respect for Max Marshall had increased with each passing year. He had worked hard for Max, but Max had rewarded him in an invaluable way.

His hard expression softening momentarily, Delaney noted that Max had again forgotten to shave and that his hair was longer than was either fashionable or tidy. As a matter of fact, Max actually looked seedy, but Delaney knew the brain inside that grizzled head was nowhere near following suit. Three years of working side by side with the crusty fellow had given Delaney a healthy respect for the knowledge stored behind those blood-shot eyes and that dour expression, and he had been more than flattered when, unknown to most in town, Max had turned over the editorial page to him a year before.

Delaney was conscious that their positions on the newspaper had slowly reversed themselves during the past three years, and he knew the gradual changes had not come about without Max's deliberate intention. Now it was Delaney who made most of the major decisions about coverage of the news, with Max oversee-ing. Max had not yet given him a completely free hand, but Delaney's ideas were always explored and considered, and often were implemented. Max had trained him very well.

A familiar nagging realization again assailed Delaney. Max had trained him so well, in fact, that he had learned just about all he could here. It was time to move on.

Running his hand roughly through his hair, Delaney massaged the tension at the back of his neck. He had come to that realiza-tion several weeks before but he had not yet acted upon it. The reason for his hesitation eluded him.

A wagon traveled past the window, catching Delaney's eye. The flashing glimpse brought him upright in his chair. Getting to his feet so quickly that his chair fell to the floor behind him, Delaney ignored the crashing sound and Max's protest. He strode to the window as the wagon drew to a halt in front of the general store a short way up the street. Allie. There was no way he could have mistaken that hair.

Delaney was again assailed by a peculiar restlessness he had begun to experience whenever he thought of Allie lately. She had taken to wearing her hair up since she turned sixteen. He didn't like it that way. He missed seeing it hanging long and unbound against her shoulders or flying out behind her when she ran.

"Delaney!"

Delaney turned with a frown at the gruff summons that broke into his thoughts.

"Dammit, man, are you deaf? I called you three times!"

Delaney turned back to the window, his eyes on James as the younger Case stepped to the ground and swung Allie down beside him. A familiar knot twisted inside his stomach as James smiled into Allie's face, his hands lingering on her waist.

"Delaney, dammit!"

"What do you want, Max?"

"What do I want!"

"That was my question."

"I'd like to have your attention while I discuss this piece you did about Adam McDonald."

Delaney turned to face Max's obvious annoyance. He didn't have the slightest desire to talk about the piece he had written about Widow McDonald's only son, who had died a hero. He doubted the widow found much consolation in that fact, and he had stated as much in the article. If he did not miss his guess, Max took exception to that comment, but he was not in a mood to discuss it.

Delaney snatched his hat off the peg on the wall and placed it on his head. "I'm going out. I'll be back in a little while."

Leaving Max's sputtering protests behind him, Delaney strode down the street toward the empty Case wagon. Ahead of him, James stepped into the drugstore. He was alone. Quickening his step, Delaney turned into the general store. He glanced around the dim interior and saw Allie by the rear counter. Her back was toward him, but she turned abruptly as he neared, a smile on her lips.

"I thought I recognized your step."

"Did you." It was a statement rather than a question, and Delaney did not expect a response. His annoyance dissipated. Allie's smile still had the power to light him up inside like no other. He brushed a wisp of hair from her cheek and saw her flush, knowing she was berating herself for being untidy. She would never understand the appeal of those little wisps and the way they seemed to call his hand to her cheek. She did not know how often he had been grateful to them for giving him an excuse to touch her.

Allie's smile dimmed. "Mother Case is feeling poorly, Delaney. The doctor came out this morning and left a different prescription. James asked me to come to town with him while he had it filled, and Mother Case insisted. She said we needed some things from the store, and I needed some time to myself." Her voice dropped a notch lower and she turned a fleeting glance toward the counter to make certain she would not be overheard as she continued. "I didn't want to leave her, but I thought if I did, Sarah would be forced to spend some time with her."

Delaney knew that Sarah's attitude of late had not endeared her to anyone. Caught up in her own concerns, she appeared to be completely insensitive to her mother's severely deteriorated condition. But Delaney was not in a mood to think about Sarah right now. He wanted—no, he needed—to have Allie to himself for a little while.

Delaney took the list from her hand and gave it a quick appraisal. Sending a glance toward the waiting clerk, he set it down on the counter.

"It'll take Elmer at least a half hour to fill this order. There's no point in waiting here. Come on."

To his annoyance, Allie held back. "James will be expecting me to be here when he comes back."

"There's only one person in town slower than Elmer, Allie, and that's Joe Stoeller when he's filling a prescription." Delaney ignored Elmer's annoyed snort, as he directed, "When James comes back, tell him Allie and I went for a walk."

Curving his arm around Allie's shoulders, Delaney turned her toward the door. Her momentary resistance stirred his annoyance anew.

On the sidewalk outside the door, Allie turned to him disapprovingly. "Why do you go out of your way to make people dislike you, Delaney? You were insulting to Elmer, and you know James is going to be angry when he comes back." Her earnest reproof trailing to a halt, Allie paused with a frustrated shake of her head. "You don't care what people think of you or what they say behind your back, but I do!"

Allie's candid statement touched him more than he wanted to

admit, as Delaney took her arm and urged her down the street
at a rapid pace.

"Delaney, you're walking too fast."

"Not fast enough."

"I don't want—"

"Come on."

He was all but dragging her as they turned the corner and
walked past the livery stable and out into the field behind it.
Against her protests, Delaney pulled Allie up the sharp incline
of Tillman Hill. Just over the crest and out of sight of the town,
he came to a sudden halt and released her. Without a word of
explanation, he sat down on the grassy slope.

Hands on her narrow hips, Allie looked down at him in an
unspoken bid for an explanation. Instead, Delaney curved his
arm around the back of her knees, and pulled her down beside
him.

"Delaney!"

"Mother Case was right. You need some time away from
everything, and so do I. This is the perfect place, isn't it?"

"Delaney, she didn't mean you had to practically drag me
through town!"

Conflicting emotions battled with Delaney. He was annoyed
with Allie's resistance, touched and warmed by her concern.
And he was angry at her and at himself for the sense of urgency
that had driven him to drag her off so he could have her to
himself for a little while.

But Allie was angry, too. Delaney marveled at the change that
came over her small, almost angelic countenance when she was determined to make him sit up and take notice of what she was
saying. Her cheeks were pink, her delicate nostrils were quivering, and her dark eyes were snapping. But most appealing of
all was the way she unconsciously pursed her lips as she glared
unflinchingly at him.

"Delaney—"

"You never answered my question."

"What question?"

"I asked you if you thought this was the perfect place to get
away and relax for a few minutes."

"It's very pretty."

"Then just lie back and enjoy it for a little while. Besides, I want to talk to you."

Following his own suggestion, Delaney flipped his hat to the ground beside him and lay back against the thick mat of grass beneath him. Ignoring the impatient sound that issued from Allie's throat, he looked up at the sky over his head. He couldn't remember the last time he had lain back and just stared at the sky. The only notice he had taken of it in the past few years was in judging the weather in which he could expect to be riding or working that day. He'd been too busy to do anything but work. He had sacrificed all to driving ambition and now he—

"You wanted to talk to me?" Allie's tone was clipped. She was still angry.

"I've missed talking to you, Allie."

Allie continued to sit stiffly, looking down into his face.

"Dammit, Allie!"

Catching her off balance, Delaney pushed Allie to her back and then leaned over her, his palms resting on the ground on either side of her shoulders.

"I remember when I didn't have to talk you into spending time with me. You were always cuddling up next to me."

"I've grown up a little since then."

"And you're too old to waste time talking to me?"

Allie's tight expression finally faded. A reluctant smile touched her lips.

"Delaney." Her voice held a futile note. "You know I'll never be too grown up to spend time talking to you."

Then she glanced at the incredible blue of the sky. "You're right, it is beautiful here. It's sunny and quiet, and it smells like flowers. You can't even smell the livery stable up here."

"I remember when you didn't object to the smell of horses or cows, when you preferred to sleep in the barn rather than in the house because—"

"Because you were there." Allie gave a small laugh. "I'd still prefer you to Sarah as a roommate."

Delaney wasn't amused by Allie's statement. She wasn't as grown up as she thought. Living with Sarah had educated her to certain facts of life, but it was obvious she didn't apply them to herself. It bothered him even more to remember that James seemed only too willing to fill in that void in her education.

Delaney avoided that disturbing thought. "You said Mrs. Case is doing poorly today."

Pain flickered in Allie's eyes. "She had a very bad night, and when I took breakfast up to her she looked . . . she looked like—"

"Allie." Delaney silently cursed his stupidity. He should have realized why Allie was out of sorts. "You know how ill she is."

Allie nodded, tears welling in her eyes. "I know."

Delaney touched Allie's cheek, then trailed his fingers to the corner of her mouth. Her lower lip was trembling, and he ran his fingertip lightly across it. She turned her head away.

"That tickles."

It had not been his intention to tickle her, and staring down at Allie, Delaney was suddenly uncertain just exactly what his intention was.

He was so damned confused. It seemed he had spent most of the past six years being confused about Allie. Everything else had been so easy. He had done his work on the farm and on the newspaper, and had allowed no personal feelings to touch him. He had even held himself aloof from Mrs. Case's illness, realizing that he could not forestall the inevitable. He had used the shield he had developed as a child on the streets both to protect himself and to allow him the single-mindedness necessary to fulfill his ambitions.

That shield had never protected him from Allie. She had managed to creep behind it, to snuggle deep inside him, and to find a home there. She had trusted him when no one else thought him worthy of trust. She had loved him without reservation. She called him her best friend.

Friend.

Cupping Allie's cheek with his hand, he slid his fingers into the pale wisps at her hairline. He frowned in annoyance at the restriction imposed by her tightly coiled hair.

"I don't like your hair bound. I like it better hanging loose."

Allie appeared startled and a little hurt by his comment. She gave a small shrug. "I'm too old to wear my hair down."

"Too old? Who told you that?"

"No one *told* me. No one had to tell me. Sarah started wearing her hair up at sixteen, although she still wears it down sometimes."

"Sarah is different. Besides, I couldn't care less how Sarah wears her hair. She could shave her head for all the difference it would make to me."

A smile tugged at the corner of Allie's mouth. "She'd be beautiful even then."

"I told you, I couldn't care less."

"Anyway, my hair stays neater this way, most of the time. James says he likes it."

James again.

Delaney slid his fingers into Allie's hair. He had tossed the first pin into the grass before she realized what he was doing. Her protest was instantaneous. When he pulled the second pin free, Allie slapped angrily at his hands.

"What are you doing? I'll never find those pins! Delaney, stop!"

Ignoring her, Delaney was not satisfied until Allie's hair was free at last. With great deliberation, he tossed the last pin over his shoulder and met Allie's heated glare.

"If James likes your hair pinned up, tell *him* to buy you more pins."

Furious, Allie struggled to sit up, but he would not allow it. He had never seen her so angry, and he was suddenly disgusted with his own high-handedness. Damn it all, what had gotten into him?

"Allie, I'm sorry."

"Let me up!"

"Allie, listen to me. I said I'm sorry."

"I said, *Let me up*!"

Dammit, dammit, dammit!

Restraining her as she attempted to pull herself up, Delaney waited until her struggles had finally subsided before releasing her enough to slide his hand into her unbound hair. The silky strands were warm against his palm, distracting, and he frowned.

"You can wear your hair any way you like it. I'll buy you new pins to replace the ones I threw away."

"I don't want new pins. I want the old ones. And I want you to let me go."

Allie was perfectly still at last, and Delaney released her slowly, with caution. She glared at him, her small face set in angry lines.

"What's the matter with you, Delaney? Why are you so angry

with me? What difference does it make if I wear my hair up or down, or if I cut it all off, for that matter?''

Yes, what did it matter how Allie wore her hair, except that Allie was growing up and slipping away from him, and he didn't like it? But even that didn't make sense, because he would be leaving soon. Delaney shook his head, more confused than ever.

"I suppose I don't want you to change."

Now it was Allie's turn to be confused. "Everybody changes, Delaney. You've changed. You've gotten older. You're bigger and more handsome than you ever were."

Delaney frowned at Allie's unconscious compliment, realizing she would never believe him if he paid her a compliment in return, no matter how heartfelt.

"But I don't tell you how to wear *your* hair."

Delaney gave a short laugh. "Maybe you should."

Allie shook her head. "No, it's not my place."

Delaney's smile slowly froze. "Just as it's not my place to tell you how to wear yours. Is that what you're trying to tell me?"

"Yes."

Delaney took a deep breath. Allie was growing up, all right.

"You're right, and I was wrong. I'm sorry. Can we forget the whole thing if I get you some new pins?"

"No, I want you to help me find the old ones."

Delaney was beginning to get annoyed. They were wasting time arguing, something Allie and he seldom did. Time was slipping away and he didn't want to waste what was left in searching for hairpins.

"To hell with the hairpins. I told you I'll buy you new ones when we get back to the store."

"Delaney—"

In a swift, unexpected movement, Delaney seized Allie's wrists and pinned them to the ground beside her head. He brought his face closer to hers. The dark pupils of her eyes widened at his whisper, "And if I say I won't let you up?"

"Bastard! Take your hands off her!"

Delaney's head jerked up at the sound of James's voice. Hesitating only a moment, he stood and extended a hand toward Allie.

"Don't touch her, Marsh!"

Ignoring James's warning, Delaney grasped Allie's hand and

drew her to her feet. He was turning back to James when a blinding pain exploded against his jaw, sending him staggering backwards. He hit the ground with jarring impact, the sound of Allie's sharp cry echoing in his ears as he fought the wave of blackness that threatened to overwhelm him. He felt a light touch on his cheek, heard Allie's voice close to his ear, only to have it suddenly withdrawn.

Still reeling, he sat up, his uncertain gaze fixing on Allie's frightened face as she pulled herself free of James's hold and ran to his side.

"Delaney, are you all right?"

Delaney slowly rose to his feet. He did not bother to respond to Allie's shaken question. He would show her he was all right. He'd beat her puny protector to a bloody pulp!

"Delaney, no! Please!"

The panic in Allie's plea halted Delaney. "It was a misunderstanding, Delaney." She darted a pleading glance toward James. "Tell him it was a misunderstanding, James!"

His eyes raking Allie's disheveled appearance, James covered the steps between them and took her by the arm. "It was no misunderstanding, Marsh, except on your part! And I'm telling you now: Touch Allie again and you won't live to see a new day!"

Fury pushed the last trace of confusion from Delaney's mind. He wiped the blood from the corner of his mouth with the back of his arm.

"Whatever you thought you saw, you were wrong, Case. You should know Allie better than to think—"

"Allie? The only problem with Allie is that she's too innocent! She should've known what you had in mind when you dragged her out of town and up here to this deserted hill. The rest of the town did! You didn't give a damn for her good name. You left tongues wagging up and down Main Street. She would never listen to a word I said against you. Even now, after you proved I was right, she's standing up for you!"

"James, please listen to me." Her face white, Allie shook her head. "Delaney wasn't hurting me! He only wanted—"

"I know what he wanted!" Shaking with rage, James paused to take a deep breath. "Come on, Allie. We're leaving."

"Allie's not going anywhere with you." His head completely

clear at last, Delaney took a warning step forward, ignoring Allie's grip on his arm. "Get out of here, Case. Get out of here before I show you how lucky you were to get in that first punch."

"No!" Releasing Delaney's arm to squeeze between the two men, Allie held them apart. "James, you're wrong. You didn't see what you thought you saw."

"Don't tell me what I saw, Allie!"

"I told you to get out of here, Case. I won't tell you again."

"When I walk away from here, I'm taking Allie with me."

"Oh, no, you're not. You're laboring under a misconception, Case. Your family didn't get ownership papers when they took Allie in. She doesn't *belong* to you."

"Bastard! Are you trying to tell me she belongs to you? Never! She's too good for you!"

Delaney nodded. "Maybe, but she's too good for you, too."

"At least I wouldn't try to take her innocence out in the open, on the ground, like an animal. But you wouldn't know how to treat a decent woman, would you, Marsh? Cheap trollops don't teach a man how to treat a good woman."

Overcome by rage, Delaney pushed Allie from between them.

"Delaney! I . . . I'm going with James."

Delaney threw an incredulous glance toward Allie. "You don't believe this bastard? You know I'd never—"

"I know." Allie was holding his arm. She loosened her grip and rubbed his arm in silent commiseration. "But I also know neither of you is willing to listen to a word of good sense right now."

"I don't want you to go back with him, Allie."

"I came to town with James, Delaney. Mother Case is waiting for us, so I'll return with him as planned. You have to go back to the newspaper. When you come home tonight everything will be straightened out."

"Everything will be straightened out, all right!" James said angrily.

"James, please . . ."

"Let's go, Allie."

Allie was turning away, and Delaney shook his head in disbelief. "Allie?"

"I'll see you later, Delaney."

Biting her lip, Allie turned at James's urging and walked to the crest of the hill. James spoke to her, and she anxiously pushed her hair back from her face. Delaney closed his eyes briefly, disgusted with himself and his stupidity. When he opened his eyes again, Allie and James had disappeared over the rise.

Delaney wiped the blood from his mouth again and shook his head. Christ, he felt rotten. He hadn't wanted to hurt Allie, to make her cry. Not Allie.

For a few short moments, Delaney stared down at the grassy slope beneath his feet. Hairpins. Allie and he had been arguing about hairpins. Where in hell were they, anyway?

Realizing that searching for them was futile, Delaney snatched up his hat and started up the slope with a slow step. He'd buy her new ones, just as he had said.

Damn that bastard James!

Delaney reached the crest of the hill just as James and Allie turned onto Main Street and out of sight. The taste of blood was strong in his mouth, and he wiped at the corner of his lips one more time before starting down the hill. His step slow, he walked past the livery, noting Mosley Rourke's disapproving glare followed him. He had been renting a horse from Rourke for the past two and a half years, since James had made it clear that using the gelding was putting a hardship on the family. He had never bothered to exchange even the time of day with Rourke, and it was obvious what the fellow was thinking. Well, let him think whatever he wanted.

Delaney walked onto Main Street just as the wagon carrying Allie and James turned out of sight on the road out of town. Just as well. He walked past the *News* office and on to the general store. Elmer Winthrop observed his entrance with obvious distaste. His small eyes darted to the corner of Delaney's mouth with satisfaction.

"I did like you said and told James you and the Pierce girl went for a walk. Too bad he caught up with you, huh?"

Elmer's arrogance wilted under the heat of Delaney's silent gaze, and he twitched nervously. "What can I do for you?"

"Hairpins."

His surprise obvious, Elmer turned to the shelf behind him and, after a fraction of a moment, put the hairpins down on the counter.

"Anything else?"

"No."

Slapping down a coin, Delaney waited only long enough for change before snatching up the small package and walking out of the store. He was striding back toward the *News* office when a familiar figure emerged through the doorway of the dressmaker's shop.

"I'd say good day, but it doesn't look like you've had such a good day so far." Lil gave him a brief smile. "You look like hell, Delaney."

Delaney's attempt at a smile resulted in a pained wince.

"Looks like you're right, Lil."

"Come home with me for a few minutes, boy. Mama Lil can cure all ills." Delaney hesitated and she slipped her arm through his. "Might as well, Delaney. You've got the whole town buzzin' already."

Delaney looked down into Lil's pleasant smile. She made him feel good. With a small shrug, he fell into step beside her.

Delaney was keenly aware of the curious eyes that followed Lil's and his progress down the street and around the corner toward her rooms. Obviously aware of the onlookers, Lil played her role to the hilt, sending coy glances to him from under the brim of her ridiculous hat and swaying boldly as they walked. It was only after they had climbed the familiar wooden staircase to her rooms and the door had closed behind them that she released an annoyed breath.

"Well, do you think we put on a good enough show for the nosy bastards, darlin'?"

Watching as Lil carefully removed her hat and placed it on the dresser, Delaney gave a short nod. "I suppose. But the truth is, Lil, I don't know what the hell I'm doing here."

Lil gave a small laugh. "You're makin' up for havin' badly neglected your friend Lil these past few months, that's what you're doin'. And while you're sittin' here talkin' and doin' whatever else comes into your mind, I'm goin' to take care of that cut on your mouth. What the hell did that fella do, anyway? Did he knock out a tooth?"

Annoyed, Delaney did not bother to respond. Dammit! He still didn't know how Allie had managed to stop him from giving James what he had coming.

Turning to the washstand, Lil allowed Delaney his silence as she poured water into the basin and picked up a towel. At his side again, she instructed huskily, "Sit down and make yourself to home. You've been here often enough not to wait on invitation."

Wincing as Lil pressed the moistened cloth against his mouth, Delaney stayed her hand. "I can do it, Lil. This isn't the first time I've had a split lip, and I don't expect it to be the last."

Resisting his attempt to take the cloth from her hand, Lil shook her head. "It was all so unnecessary, darlin'. You didn't have to rile up the whole town by draggin' that sweet young thing through the streets and out of sight on that deserted hill when Lil was waitin' to accommodate you any time you wanted."

"It wasn't like that, Lil."

"Wasn't it?"

"No."

Lil's light eyes searched his face. "Then why didn't you beat that fella to a pulp for hittin' you? I saw him and the girl when they came back. He didn't have a mark on him."

Delaney shook his head. "I don't really know. Allie was crying and I didn't want to upset her any more, and . . . well, it doesn't matter much. I won't be around here much longer, anyway."

Lil's hand stilled. Her expression blank, she dropped the cloth back into the basin. "You expect to be leavin'?"

"Soon, Lil." A sense of commitment finally settling inside him as he spoke the words aloud for the first time, Delaney attempted a smile. "I haven't said anything to anyone else about it, yet."

"The girl and you came to the Case farm together. That's why you dragged her up there, isn't it, to tell her you made up your mind. She's the first person you wanted to tell."

"I promised her."

Lil turned away abruptly. She replaced the basin on the washstand and turned back toward him with a smile.

"I suppose I should be happy that you told me before you told anybody else, but I'm not." Covering the distance between them in a few short steps, Lil pressed herself flush against Delaney's length. She wound her arms around his neck and pressed closer still. "I'd much rather you told me you was goin' to make this town your permanent home."

"You never really expected that, did you, Lil?"

"No, I guess not."

Lil was pressing light kisses against his chin and neck when Delaney carefully dislodged her arms from his neck. There was a strange sadness inside him.

"No, Lil, not now."

Delaney did not expect the tears that sprang into Lil's light eyes.

"Lil . . ."

"Hell, boy, I knew you was slippin' away from me when you stopped visitin' me except to talk these past months. But I knew you wasn't spendin' time with any of the other girls, so I figured I'd give you some time to work out whatever was botherin' you."

The sadness inside Delaney expanded into a deadening ache. He hadn't made a conscious decision about any of this today, but somehow seeing Allie so unexpectedly with James . . .

"Lil, you know I appreciate everything you've done."

"I don't need gratitude, Delaney. It was my pleasure."

"And mine."

Lil's hand slipped up to caress his cheek.

"Sure you wouldn't like one last time?"

"Lil . . ."

"I figured I'd offer."

Lil's womanly heat was still tight against him, but it somehow stimulated nothing more than a friendly warmth inside him.

Friend.

A vision of Allie's face suddenly supplanted Lil's vibrantly painted features, and Delaney stepped back. He had some unfinished business to settle, and now that he had said what he had to say to Lil, he was just wasting time.

"Dammit, Lil, I—"

"I can see you got a lot on your mind, darlin', and I'm not about to get in your way. Just remember, I'm here for you any time you want me. I always will be, so get yourself along, now."

Sliding her arm under his, Lil stepped to his side as she walked with him to the door. "Your mouth's still a little puffy, but the bleedin' is stopped, and you spent enough time in here to keep tongues waggin' for another week, at least. What's this town goin' to talk about after you leave?''

Hesitating only a moment at the door, Delaney pressed a light kiss against Lil's full lips.

"You're one in a million, Lil."

Lil's smile widened. "That I am."

Delaney rapidly descended the wooden staircase, the woman standing in the upstairs doorway behind him already replaced in his mind by the vivid picture of a small, pale face and disturbing dark eyes. He did not look back to see a tear slip down Lil's cheek as she slowly turned and closed the door behind her.

Allie's eyes closed briefly. Her mind was still reeling from the rapid progression of events that had run so suddenly out of control on the sun-drenched rise of Tillman Hill. The wagon rattled noisily along the road and Allie raised her eyes to the farmhouse, which had come clearly into view with the last turn. Anxiety choked her as she glanced covertly at James's stiff expression.

The long ride from town had been a terrible ordeal. She had employed every conceivable line of reasoning in an attempt to convince James that he had jumped to the wrong conclusion when he saw Delaney and her together, but she had been unsuccessful. The realization that her continued efforts only served to incite James to greater anger had finally silenced her. But the silence that had reigned for the last few miles had been so heavy and uncomfortable that it had only increased the strain.

Panic overwhelmed Allie. She could not allow James to speak to Papa Case in his present frame of mind. She had to convince him that Delaney would never hurt her. Why couldn't he understand that, in hurting her, Delaney would only be hurting himself because Delaney and she were part of each other?

Instinct had sealed her lips to that approach with James. He had never understood the bond between Delaney and herself, and in his present state of agitation she knew he would be more hostile than ever to any mention of that unspoken bond. But she could not let him tell Papa Case what he thought he had seen. She could not fail Delaney.

A new panic assailing her as James drew the wagon to a halt in front of the house, Allie watched as he stepped down and rounded the wagon to lift her to the ground. Her hands closed over his in a last appeal as her feet touched the ground.

"James, please, won't you believe me? Delaney and I were having a foolish argument, and he was angry."

"Allie, I don't intend to discuss this with you any further. Go into the house."

"I won't go, James."

James's pale blue eyes met hers and Allie despaired at the anger there.

"James, don't be angry with me, please."

James's heated gaze flicked measuringly over her face for long seconds before he spoke again. "Is that what you think, Allie? That I'm angry with you?" His color high, James gave a short laugh. "I'm angry with myself for having allowed this whole thing to go as far as it did."

"You misunderstood, James. Delaney—"

Suddenly seizing her shoulders, James gave her a hard shake. "What will it take to make you see what Marsh really is, Allie, to see what he intended today up on that hill?"

"We were arguing, James."

"That wasn't anger I saw on his face. It was . . . ." James shook his head. A muscle twitched in his cheek. "I always knew I was wasting my time trying to talk some sense into you about Marsh. Like a fool, I kept trying until it was almost too late. Well, the time for talk is past, Allie. If you're too blind to protect yourself against Marsh, I'm going to do it for you. And if you hate me for it, I'm sorry."

"James—"

"Go into the house, Allie."

Dropping his hands from her shoulders, his expression resolute, James did not wait for her response. Turning, he strode toward the barn and the shadowed form of his father just inside the entrance.

Her breath catching on a sob, Allie turned toward the house. A sense of foreboding forming a hard lump in her throat, she quickened her step and walked into the silence of the kitchen. Somehow she knew that silence would not be of long duration.

"Get your things together, Delaney."

Allowing the kitchen door to close behind him, Delaney appraised Jacob Case's stiff expression. The room was unnaturally bright in contrast with the twilight from which he had emerged, and Delaney squinted against the glare. James stood a few steps to his father's right, and there was no need to ask for an explanation of the short command. James had obviously done his work well.

Delaney met Mr. Case's gaze. "I don't suppose it would do any good for me to tell you what really happened on Tillman Hill today."

"Pa knows what happened there, Marsh! What's more, he knows what *almost* happened, and he's no more willing than I am to wait around and let you have a second chance."

Ignoring James's heated interjection, Delaney turned back to his father. "Mr. Case—"

"You're wasting your breath, Delaney." His voice low, Jacob Case frowned. "If circumstances were different, we'd sit here and talk this whole thing out, but your presence in this household is too heavy a burden for this family to bear any longer."

Stiffening, Delaney shook his head. "You've always gotten your money's worth out of me. I've never put my work off onto anybody, no matter how much time I spent at the newspaper."

"I'm not arguing that point, Delaney. You've worked hard and long on this farm, and you fulfilled every stipulation of your contract with us and more." His expression suddenly weary, Mr. Case shook his head. "If you think a little harder, you'll realize what I'm trying to say. The fact is, boy, you never fit in here. Allie was one of us from the beginning, but you were a point of friction that's only gotten worse with the years. It's time to rid ourselves of that friction once and for all."

"That's not fair, Papa!" Stepping into the kitchen, Sarah continued, her beautiful face flushed with anger, "James never gave Delaney a chance to be a part of the family. He smiled and fussed over his little pet, Allie, from the day she came, but all he ever did was pick on Delaney. And now he's telling lies about him! I don't believe a word he said! He's just jealous because Delaney's a better man than he is and can get any girl he wants! He's jealous because he wants—"

"That's enough!"

"No, I'm not going to let you throw Delaney off the farm! If you'd open your eyes, you'd see everything I'm saying is the truth! Delaney doesn't want any part of that skinny little—''

"Sarah!"

Startled into momentary silence as her father took a threatening step forward, Sarah raised her chin defiantly. "Mama won't let you do it. I'm going to tell her right now."

"I've already discussed this with your mother, Sarah. She thinks it's time for Delaney to leave, too."

"I'm going to ask her!"

"Sarah!" Jacob Case's expression was suddenly menacing. "You will not take one step toward your mother's room or excite her in any way. She is ill, and it is expressly because of her poor health that we must settle this once and for all."

"If *Allie* asked you to let Delaney stay, you'd listen to her!"

"Allie has asked me, but she had the good sense not to place the burden of this decision on your mother's frail shoulders, as you are wont to do. Now, go to your room!"

"No, I—"

"I said go to your room!"

His massive form quaking with barely suppressed fury, Jacob Case took another step toward his belligerent daughter. The threat in his flushed face succeeded in driving Sarah another step backwards, but she turned toward Delaney with a final word of defiance. "Don't worry, Delaney. I don't believe anything James said. And even if they make you leave here, we'll see each other again."

"Sarah!"

Turning on her heel, Sarah fled into the darkness of the hall. Waiting until her step sounded on the floor above them, Jacob turned back to Delaney.

"I don't think I have to say any more, Delaney. It should be as obvious to you as it is to me that you can no longer live here as a part of this family. I'm sorry. Now that the time has come to make a choice, I find I truly have no choice to make."

Nodding, Delaney turned toward his room. He had expected it would eventually come to this. He only had one true regret.

Mr. Case's voice halted Delaney.

"Before you leave, Mrs. Case would like to see you."

Not bothering to respond, Delaney continued on down the hallway.

* * *

His dark brows pulled into a hard frown, Delaney paused outside Mrs. Case's bedroom door, aware that James had followed and had paused a few steps behind him. He sent a contemptuous sneer in James's direction, experiencing immeasurable satisfaction as a new flood of angry color washed James's freckled face.

The bastard. Dogging Delaney's heels, James had waited silently outside the bedroom door as he packed his few belongings. He had followed him to the porch and watched as Delaney had deposited his things outside the kitchen door. He had then followed a few steps behind as he had ascended the steps to the second floor to see the bedridden Mrs. Case.

Delaney gave a short, bitter snort. He was wise to James's strategy. James was making very sure he made no attempt to see or talk to Allie. If he did, James would deliberately provoke him into a fight so that he might prove to the others just how right he was about a "prison boy" never changing his stripes. But if that was his intention, James was going to fail miserably. Delaney had no intention of giving James that satisfaction.

It occurred to Delaney that he could have deprived James of the final victory of having him ousted from the Case farm. It would have been so easy to stop the whole scene in the kitchen with the announcement that he was leaving Cass County, but he did not regret adhering to his promise to tell Allie first. She had earned that right.

Delaney's light rap on Mrs. Case's door was met with a weak response that tore at a spot deep inside him. Mrs. Case did not deserve the fate that had been allotted her. Two steps inside the door Delaney halted in his tracks. With great deliberation he hardened himself against the deterioration evident in the shadowed lines of her familiar face.

A sound to one side of the darkened room made Delaney turn at the moment Allie stepped into the ring of light from the lamp. Her relief in seeing him was obvious in the moment before she looked back to Mrs. Case, her eyes visibly moistening.

"Allie."

Mrs. Case's low whisper brought Allie immediately to her side. Mrs. Case patted her small hand. "Allie, this is not a happy night for any of us. Although Papa Case and I are agreed that it's time for Delaney to leave us, we are not happy with that decision.''

''Mother Case, you know it isn't true—what James said. He was mistaken.''

''Dear, leave us now. Delaney and I want to talk. And please tell James not to worry. Delaney won't stay long.''

His gaze on Allie as she left the room, Delaney was called back to attention by Mrs. Case's soft sigh.

''It is my one regret in life that Sarah, for all her beauty, has not discovered the secret of making herself loved, as that sweet child has.''

At Mrs. Case's summons, Delaney moved to her bedside.

''Closer, Delaney. Pull the chair up beside the bed so I can see you better. We may not have a chance to talk again and there are things that must be said.'' Mrs. Case gave a short laugh. ''I don't mean to mislead you with that statement, dear. I don't intend to die just yet, despite the fears my family seems to have for me. I think I have one or two more rallies left inside me. Rather, it's my thought that you probably won't be staying in Cass County much longer.''

The glimmer of surprise in Delaney's light eyes did not go unnoted by Mrs. Case.

''Delaney, dear, I've never forgotten our conversation that first day in the church hall. You have an ambition. Although you've never defined that ambition to me, I've seen you work diligently toward it year after year, and it seems to me the time has come for you to strike out on your own.''

''You don't miss much, Mrs. Case.''

''No, I don't, Delaney. I've devoted my life to the people I love, and I worry for their future in these uncertain times. It is precisely for that reason that I allowed Papa Case to ask you to leave.''

Delaney's frown brought a look of concern to Margaret Case's face. ''Whether you believe it or not, Delaney, I love you, too, and my concern for you is as deep as the concern I feel for the other members of my family.''

Delaney chose not to respond.

''You are a very kind boy, Delaney. I seem to contradict myself, and you don't wish to call that contradiction to my attention. But you see, dear, what I've just said isn't a contradiction.

It is truth, a sad truth, which I feel I must speak to you, whether I am right or wrong.''

Mrs. Case took Delaney's broad hand in hers and gripped it with surprising strength as she continued. ''Delaney, I love you as a son, but I know you only too well. You were an angry and bitter boy. You maintained your guard, refusing to allow love to temper those harsh feelings, and your bitterness and anger have not dissipated now that you are a man. That bitterness is like a sore deep inside you. It robs you of joy, and it will rob those who love you of joy as well. Allie has always loved you without reservation, and she has suffered at the lack of feeling you evidence for those around you, as well as the criticism it calls down upon you. She is totally devoted to you, Delaney, and while you remain here she will be true to that devotion.''

Pausing to take a pained breath, Mrs. Case gripped Delaney's hand tighter, her faded eyes intent on his. ''Over the years, Jacob and James often voiced their concern over Allie's devotion to you, but I saw what that devotion brought to Allie. She was a child, and it brought her security when she felt most alone, and love when she felt most abandoned. She needed you, Delaney, and to your everlasting credit, whatever your true feelings were, you were there for her.''

Mrs. Case attempted a smile. ''But Allie is a child no longer. And, my dear, I hope you will forgive me when I say this, but the devotion she feels for you is now as great a hindrance to her future as it once was a necessity for her survival. It's time for you to set her free to make a life of her own, Delaney. You have your ambition to give you what you need in life. Allie needs more. She needs security and she needs love, but she will never be free to seek them while she is bound to you.''

The protest that rose within Delaney brought with it a hot flush of color, but the concern in Margaret Case's pale countenance tempered his reply.

''I'm just starting to realize that none of us gave Allie enough credit, Mrs. Case, including me. Allie has said many times that no one understands the bond between the two of us. I thought you understood it, but I guess I was wrong.''

The tears that glazed Mrs. Case's dull eyes caused Delaney a moment's regret for his outspokenness.

"No, Delaney, don't regret your words. I don't regret mine, and I hope I am wrong when I say I think it is beyond your ability to truly love. Bitterness is too consuming, and you seem to have devoted all the passion remaining within you to achieving your goal in life."

Mrs. Case's smile appealed for understanding. "Delaney dear, I am trying to set you free. It's my thought that you hesitate to leave for Allie's sake, because of her attachment to you. I know you never needed Allie. It was Allie who needed you. She was the first to admit that."

Mrs. Case paused again. "She doesn't need you anymore, Delaney. Whether you realize it or not, in the past few years the situation has slowly reversed itself. Allie has come to feel responsible for you, for your hard ways and the general distrust within you that turns people against you. She agonizes over the fact that others do not value you in the same way she does, because she very much wants you to be happy. Delaney, my dear adopted son, I know in my heart there is only one thing that will make you happy, and that is to achieve the status you wish to attain in life. For that reason, not because of the story James brought to us about the scene on Tillman Hill, Jacob and I are telling you to go."

Mrs. Case momentarily lowered her eyes.

"If I am to be totally honest, Delaney, I must say that our concern for Sarah also colors the decision Jacob and I have made today. Despite Sarah's fervent wish, she can never be the woman for you. She would need more from you than you would ever be willing to give. You have seen that from the beginning, but my very spoiled daughter has deluded herself into believing that her beauty and her obvious feminine attributes will bring you around. It is my hope that when you finally choose a woman, Delaney, you will choose one who will be satisfied with the part of you that you are willing to share, for only then will you both be happy. And I do wish you happiness, Delaney."

Neither rejecting nor accepting Mrs. Case's words, Delaney started to stand up.

"Not yet, Delaney, please. I have a final request to make of you." Mrs. Case did not wait for a response she knew would not come. "I know I ask a lot, but I want you to leave directly from here, without making an attempt to talk to Allie."

Delaney maintained his silence.

"Delaney, whether he was wrong or right about what he thought he saw, James believes he must protect Allie from you. His feelings are presently running at too high a pitch to allow peaceful settlement of the dispute between you. I'll talk to Allie after you leave, and I'll explain the reason you couldn't talk to her yourself."

"You're asking too much, Mrs. Case."

"If you care for Allie, you will spare her, Delaney."

Mrs. Case was beginning to tremble. Her fine lips were turning a pale blue, and Delaney felt his resentment crumble and die inside him. He could not cause this woman any further distress.

"All right." Delaney drew himself to his feet, his brows knitting in a frown as Mrs. Case made a gallant attempt to control her quaking. He paused with the realization that this woman had spoken as she had for the good of those she loved, that she had never been anything but kind to him, with little affection shown by him in return, and that he would probably never see her again.

"Thank you for everything, Mother Case."

A tear slipped into the gray hair at Margaret Case's temple.

" 'Mother Case.' I had despaired of hearing you call me by that name." Margaret took another uneven breath. "My dear Delaney, you are welcome."

"Good-bye."

"My very dear boy." Tears flowing freely, Mrs. Case motioned Delaney closer, then drew his head down and pressed her lips against his cheek. "Good-bye."

Delaney straightened up and turned toward the door. Within seconds he was in the hallway. Sparing only a brief glance for Allie, who stood with James at her side, he descended the stairs and walked out of the house.

Delaney sat on the edge of his rumpled bed and pulled on his boots. He was still angry. Mosley Rourke's glance had been too knowing when he turned in his horse at the livery the night before and said he wouldn't be needing it on a regular basis anymore. The memory of all that had gone unsaid behind those watery eyes still rankled.

Standing up, Delaney cast an appraising glance around the

room he had rented in Mrs. Porter's rooming house. The furnishings were Spartan—a double bed covered with a handmade quilt, a mirrored dresser, and a night table supporting a single lamp—but they would have been more than adequate if he had intended to stay long. He did not.

Delaney stretched his powerful frame and took a deep breath. He didn't need to look in the mirror to see that lines of weariness marked his face or that his frown was so intense that his dark brows looked like a single slash over the clear ice of his eyes. He was exhausted. In the last twenty-four hours he had worked around the clock, had taken one major step in his life, and had made the decision to take another. The long ride back to town the previous night had been difficult. When he arrived at the boardinghouse door, he had been too tired to react to Mrs. Porter's raised brow and sniff of disapproval. He might have been amused by the speed with which word of the incident on Tillman Hill had spread if he had been in a better mood. As it was, he had dragged himself upstairs and fallen, fully clothed, onto the bed. But he had slept very badly. Unfinished business had tormented him.

That unfinished business was Allie. He could not seem to forget the expression on her face as he walked past her and out of the house without a word. He also could not forget the spark of triumph in James's eye as he stood beside her.

His frown tightening, Delaney pulled open the bedroom door and strode into the hallway and down the narrow staircase. He did not bother to respond to Mrs. Porter's inquisitive glance as he walked past the breakfast table where her other boarders were noisily consuming their morning meal. He wasn't hungry.

Out on the street at last, he paused to scan the passersby as the morning sun touched his shoulders. The town was just coming to life in the light of early morning. On the farm, Allie would already have been up for hours, working in the kitchen. He could almost see the slender curve of her neck as she turned toward him, could almost smell the fresh scent of her skin as she brushed past. The memory of the dilated pupils of her eyes as he had leaned over her on Tillman Hill, the sweet taste of her breath when her lips had been only inches from his, had plagued him more than he cared to remember during the long hours of the night past. Confused emotions warred within him. The only thing of which he was certain was that his sense of loss was profound, and that he despised the weakness within him that allowed those feelings.

Unable to banish the image of Allie's pale face from his mind despite his fervent attempts, Delaney was suddenly furious. Mrs. Case's words had rung over and again in his mind through the restless night. When he had finally forced himself to face them, he had recognized the truth in some of the things she said. Allie was no longer the child who had sought him out for the consolation of the medal he wore around his neck. She was a grown, very capable woman. She was well loved in the Case household, and she didn't need him to protect her anymore.

So why couldn't he let go?

The deadening ache inside him that accompanied thoughts of Allie expanded and Delaney speeded up his pace. Damn Allie for worming herself inside him, for tying him up in knots when he should feel free to leave and pursue his dream! He had never wanted to take responsibility for her. She had forced it upon him with her trust. If it had not been for her, he would have walked away from the Case farm a long time ago without a backward glance. He would be in Chicago now, instead of in Cass County, tormenting himself.

The *News* office came into view, and Delaney forced aside Allie's persistent image. She had brought on herself whatever misery she now felt at his leaving, and he knew the same was true for himself. He had made a mistake by getting so deeply involved years ago. He had known it then, and he knew it now. It was time he corrected his mistake.

Pushing open the office door with a determined thrust a few minutes later, Delaney was relieved to see Max already at work. A few long strides brought him up in front of the editor's desk.

"I'm leaving, Max."

Silent for a moment as he raised his head and stared at Delaney's tight expression, Max nodded. "I can't say I'm surprised. I know you've been thinkin' about leavin' for a while, and I don't need to ask what brought on this sudden decision. The story's all over town about Tillman Hill and you draggin' yourself back into town late last night and takin' a room at Mrs. Porter's. Got thrown off the Case farm, huh?"

Delaney made no reply and Max shook his head.

"Still a man of few words. Well, I think there are a few things we should discuss before you leave."

Delaney's reply was touched with impatience. "What's on your mind, Max?"

"I could tell you were gettin' restless these past months, and I knew why. You've learned just about all you can on this paper. You know that and I know that, and it got me to thinkin'. If you're not above acceptin' my opinion, I want to tell you that you turned into a damned good newspaperman. You're sharp, you're quick, you know a real story when you see one, and you write like a pro. You've lived up to your pa's blood every step of the way."

Pausing, Max frowned, his gaze becoming more intent as he drew himself to his feet and walked around the desk to stand directly in front of Delaney.

"But I'm not into throwing bouquets, so along with the good you have to hear the bad. You haven't changed at all in another area. You're still a cold bastard. Nothin' touches you, and because of it, most people would like to see things go wrong for you. About the only ones who don't seem to resent you are the young ladies who prance past the window in a steady line when you're workin' at your desk."

At Delaney's raised brow, Max shook his head. "Don't give me that look. You saw them as well as I did, and it's to your credit that you ignored them. They would've been trouble for a fella like you. You played it smart stickin' with Lil."

"Come to the point, Max."

"The fact is, I think of you as my protégé, boy. I'm proud of the work I've done in makin' you the newspaperman you are, and I don't care who knows it. Another fact is, I've still got some influence with the people in Chicago I mentioned a long time back. One of them is an editor on the *Chicago Tribune*. If you agree, I'll write to him and find out what he can do to help you get started. It shouldn't take more than a few weeks, and while we're waitin' for a reply, I can look around for somebody to replace you here."

Delaney remained silent, staring into Max's face.

"Hell, don't look right through me with them eyes! There's nothin' to see but what I already told you. Now, if you're too big to accept my help . . ."

Undecided, Delaney maintained his silence. Now that he had been forced to sever his tie with the Case family, he was anxious to get away from this town and everybody in it. But he'd be damned if he'd let anybody force him to leave even one minute before he was ready.

"No, I'm not too big to accept your help, Max."

"Good."

"But I'll be leaving at the end of the month, whether you get a response to your letter or not."

Max paused. "I guess that's fair enough." He paused again. "There's just one more thing I've got to say, and it's this: You have a great gift. I don't think I ever saw a natural talent like yours before, but you're your own worst enemy, boy, and there's nobody who's going to defeat you but yourself."

Delaney could feel the heat of anger again rising. "My short-comings are my own business."

"That's for sure, boy."

"And in case you haven't noticed, I'm not a boy anymore, Max."

Max gave a short laugh. "I noticed."

Delaney turned to his desk. Seating himself, he picked up the nearest page of copy and started to read.

chapter

ten

ALLIE STIRRED THE pot bubbling on the stove in front of her with unseeing eyes. A week had passed since Delaney had turned so coldly away from her and walked down the stairs and out of her life, and the ache inside her had grown to encompass her body as well as her mind. Mother Case's soft explanation had been little consolation. Allie had been unable to believe Delaney could leave without talking to her. But he had.

It was strange. She had known Delaney would leave someday, and she thought she had prepared herself for that eventuality. She was now a grown woman who had accepted the major burden of work in the house. She was no longer the little girl who had turned to Delaney because she was lost in so many ways.

Allie took a shaky breath. She had seldom mentioned the Lady to Delaney in recent years, but she had always thought that as long as she remained close to the Lady, she would be close to Mama and to Delaney as well. The presence of the medal glinting around Delaney's neck and the knowledge that it was hers to share whenever she needed it had confirmed the bond of love between Delaney and her. In all these years she had never doubted that love.

She doubted it now.

A fierce pain stabbing her anew, Allie blinked back the tears that stung her eyes. She wanted to feel Delaney's arms around her again. She wanted to hear his deep voice in her ear, telling her he was not leaving, that he never would. She wanted to feel his hand caress her cheek, to see his clear eyes look into hers with that strange intensity she had seen there of late. She wanted to experience the stirrings within her that intensity evoked, the unexplained force that drew Delaney closer to her than he had ever been.

But Delaney had walked away.

Allie brushed a persistent wisp of pale hair from her forehead. It had been a difficult week. Papa Case and James had been concerned about Mother Case's illness and the necessity of keeping a strict eye on Sarah until her resentment over Delaney's departure had cooled. Mother Case's gradual recovery and Papa Case's decision to allow Bobbie Clark to visit Sarah so she might be diverted from her willfulness had relieved some of the tension in the last few days, but the emptiness inside Allie had not abated. It occurred to her that within this household, which she had considered her home only a short time before, she now felt more alone, more abandoned, than ever.

"Allie, are you still angry at me?"

James's voice penetrated the silence of the kitchen, and Allie glanced over her shoulder and then back to the bubbling stew. Her light brows furrowed in a frown.

"James, I don't feel like talking now."

He took a step closer. She could feel his warmth radiating through the thin material of her dress as his hands closed on her shoulders.

"You haven't felt like talking to me since the day Marsh walked out of this house. It's been a week, Allie. When are you going to try to understand?"

The mention of Delaney's name returned a familiar thickness to Allie's throat as she turned to meet James fully. Momentary regret touched her mind at the lines of strain obvious on his fair face, the unnatural pallor beneath his sun-reddened skin as she responded.

"I don't want to talk about Delaney."

"Neither do I, but I think we have to. Allie, you can't ignore me for the rest of your life."

"I haven't been ignoring you. I've been busy with Mother Case."

"She's almost better now."

"She still needs me."

"So do I, Allie."

Allie remained silent at James's low-voiced declaration. She saw his mouth twitch in controlled anger.

"Does that surprise you? It shouldn't, but then, you never did spare much time to think about me when Delaney was around."

"I told you I don't want to talk about Delaney. You've finally won. He's gone and he isn't coming back."

"Is that what really bothers you, Allie—that Marsh is gone? Or does it hurt to face the fact that, for all his professed concern for you, Marsh turned his back on you without a word and walked away?"

"Don't you say anything against Delaney!"

"Why? Because he's your friend? That's what you've told yourself all these years. And all these years I told you he was just using you, that he didn't care about anybody but himself."

A hot flush flooding her face, Allie made an attempt to shake herself free of James's grip. Her temper flared when he held her fast. "Let me go, James. You don't understand. You'll never understand how it is between Delaney and me."

"I understand how he would have liked it to be!"

Allie clapped her hands over her ears in an effort to block out James's words. "I won't listen to you! Delaney is a part of me. He and I are the same inside. He feels what I feel, and he never would have left without talking to me if you hadn't made Mother Case so sick with all your talk that he was afraid of hurting her. It's your fault he's gone, James, and I'll never forgive you for it!"

His fair skin paling noticeably, James shook his head. "Don't say that, Allie. I did what I had to do. You don't understand what was really happening on that hill."

"You're the one who doesn't understand."

"I understand enough, Allie." Making an obvious effort to control his emotions, James drew Allie's hands away from her ears. "Marsh was bound to leave someday. You know that. You also know that if you were really important to him, no one would have stood in the way of his talking to you before he left this house.''

"He was afraid for Mother Case. She told me she asked him to leave without talking to me so there wouldn't be any more trouble.''

"He's still in town, Allie. Why hasn't he tried to see you?''

Allie's heart leaped. "He hasn't left town yet?''

James's angular face tightened. "He's still working at the newspaper. Max Marshall told Elmer that Marsh is leaving at the end of the month—something about him waiting for a letter from Chicago.''

"No matter where he is, I know he misses me, James. Just as I miss him. He's sick inside, just as I am because he's gone.''

"Delaney Marsh doesn't care enough about anybody to miss them!''

"He cares about me!''

"Is that why you're so worried about him, Allie? Because you think he cares about you? What about me? I care about you.''

"It isn't the same.''

"That's right, it *isn't* the same. I can't relegate you to the back of my mind, as Marsh does, and give you second place in my life. You come first with me, Allie. You have for more years than I want to admit.''

James slipped his arms around her and pulled her closer. A change came over his expression as he raised his hand to cup her cheek, holding her immobile with the intensity of his gaze.

"It was hard waiting for you to grow up, Allie, but I did. And I swore to myself that I'd never let Marsh take advantage of your trust in him.''

Allie shook her head. "James, you're my brother.''

"I'm not your brother, Allie. After the first few years you spent here, I stopped fooling myself that I wanted to be your brother.''

"Is that why you did it, James? You knew how close Delaney and I are and how much Delaney dislikes you. Is that why you said what you did about Delaney and me? So Papa Case would run him off?''

"No, Allie.''

"Delaney never said anything bad about you to me, James.

He told me he wanted me to have you for a friend. And even if he had spoken against you, I would've made up my own mind."

"Allie, the way I feel about you has nothing to do with what I saw on that hill."

"But you didn't see anything!"

"Allie . . ." James closed his eyes briefly in obvious frustration. "Allie, we have to put this thing to rest once and for all between us." Holding her gaze intently with his, he continued softly, "I did what I had to do, but if it hurt you, I'm sorry. I'm asking you to forgive me."

Unable to remain unaffected by James's pain, Allie shook her head. "It isn't as easy as that, James."

"It is. All you have to do is forgive me."

"How can I when you're responsible for Delaney's leaving without speaking to me?"

"Marsh is still in town, Allie. If he wants to talk to you, he will. You and I both know that. The rest is up to him. In the meantime, I'm asking you to believe I did what I felt was right."

His hard expression suddenly crumbling, James slid his arms around her and drew her into a gentle embrace. His voice cracked as he whispered against the moist skin of her temple, "Allie, I don't want you to be angry with me."

"James . . ."

"I need to know you forgive me."

"Oh, James . . ." Touched by the pain in James's voice, Allie drew back and raised a hand to his cheek. "So much has happened in the past week. You were wrong about what you thought you saw on Tillman Hill, but maybe I was wrong in some ways, too. There's been too much anger in this house, and I regret the way I contributed to it. If you need to hear the words, I'll say them. I forgive you, James."

The moistness in James's eyes brought a similar moistness to her own, blurring her vision as James lowered his head to brush her mouth with his. The unfamiliar intimacy snapped Allie's head up.

"I waited a long time for you to grow up, Allie."

The intensity of James's gaze said far more than his words in the few moments before he turned and walked out of the kitchen.

James's steps sounded on the staircase before Allie became fully aware of the implications of his sober statement. Life had taken a step forward that could not be retraced, and she knew with an inborn certainty that things would never be the same between James and her.

Allie turned back to the stove and the boiling pot. That last thought faded from her mind, and a faint smile touched her lips. Delaney hadn't left town—not yet. She would see him again. She knew in her heart she would.

James climbed the staircase to his room, breathing deeply in an attempt to rein in his emotions. Allie had forgiven him, and although he felt she should have thanked him instead, he knew she would never see it that way. Innocent, trusting, loving— Allie was all of those things, and he would make sure all her love was his alone.

A sense of unrest drew James's light brows into a frown. Only one person stood between Allie and him: Delaney Marsh. And despite his firm declarations of a few minutes before, he was uncertain what Marsh's next move would be.

James squared his shoulders with an unconscious sense of purpose. There was only one thing of which he was truly sure: If Marsh tried to touch Allie again, he would regret it.

A few doors down, Sarah waited for the sound of James's door closing behind him. A broad smile covered her lips. Her world had all but come to an end when Delaney had ridden away from the farm forever. Now things were beginning to look better!

Leaning back against the door to her room, Sarah raised her brilliant green eyes to the ceiling. In her mind she reviewed the tender scene she had overheard between her brother and Allie, her pleasure growing. Oh, she would not have interrupted James's moment of restrained passion for the world!

She hadn't needed to eavesdrop to find out that Delaney was still in town. Bobbie had told her that. Inadvertently, her devoted suitor had also kept her informed on Delaney's activities and his expected departure. Sarah's smile broadened. She had Bobbie so securely wrapped around her finger that he would do just about anything to please her.

The brilliance of her smile fading, Sarah acknowledged a distasteful thought: If Delaney had never come into her life, she might have ended up on the Clark farm, cooking Bobbie's food, bearing his children, and growing old and bored under his devoted eye. That would not happen now.

Turning to the mirror, Sarah stared at the image reflected therein, her sense of purpose growing. No, her beauty was never intended to be wasted on someone as ordinary as Bobbie Clark. She had known from the first that Delaney was meant for her. She had known it because Delaney and she were so much alike. Delaney cared little for anything except the direction in which life was taking him. He was determined not to waste his life on a small farm, never seeing any more of the world than the far horizon. He was going to go to Chicago and be successful, and she had known from the first that, no matter the direction he chose to take, Delaney's path would be hers as well.

Sarah could not withhold a satisfied smile as her mind treated her to images of the splendid couple they would make when they took Chicago by storm.

Oh, yes, she had James to thank for removing a serious impediment to the life Delaney and she would spend together. And she was determined that Delaney and she *would* have a life together. Pa and James watched her too closely now, but she would find a way to get to Delaney before he left. Away from the farm and the possibility of Pa's discovering them, Delaney would be unable to resist all she offered him, and she would make certain that once he'd had her he would never want to let her go.

A low laugh escaped her throat as Sarah indulged herself in the erotic pictures that flooded her mind. She would find a way to go to Delaney. It was only a matter of time.

chapter

eleven

ALLIE NERVOUSLY SMOOTHED her upswept hair. She cast a last glance toward the mirror in her room. Her lips tightening, she realized she had made a mistake the moment her gaze touched the image of the beautiful woman who stood a short distance behind her.

Sarah's low laughter rent the silence that had reigned between them as they dressed.

"I must admit, there are times when even I feel sorry for you, Allie dear." Sarah raised a graceful hand to pat a shining dark curl into place. She turned so Allie might view the perfect cameo of her face in the glass. "Why do you even try? You're no match for me. All your fussing this last hour hasn't accomplished much, has it? You're still pale and plain. But you mustn't worry, dear. James has a weakness for you. For some strange reason, he doesn't seem to see any other woman when you're around. But then, it isn't James you're interested in, is it?"

Allie was determined not to be drawn into a game she could not win.

"You look lovely, Sarah." It was a truth that cut deeply as Allie studied the brilliant green dress Sarah wore. It comple-

mented her coloring exquisitely and revealed her womanly figure
to perfection, and she was certain Sarah would draw even more
than her usual share of gasps when she entered the Farmers'
Meeting Hall for the Harvest Dance later that evening.

Allie did her best to restrain a grimace. Sarah had spent the
greater part of the past week working on that dress while Allie
shouldered her chores. It was her own intercession that had interfered with Mother Case's reprimand, but Mother Case's health
was still fragile despite the tremendous gains she had made in
the past few weeks. It had seemed kinder to allow Sarah to go
her own way than to put Mother Case through the stress of pressing her to do her share of the work.

But that was then and now was now. Standing beside Sarah's
glorious reflection in a redone version of her old blue batiste dress,
Allie found her generosity of little consolation. She looked terrible.
The strain of the past weeks had made itself only too apparent in
the thinning of her normally slight frame, causing her dress to sag
unbecomingly. The newly redone neckline, which she had cut lower
and trimmed with white lace to imitate the more mature styles of
Sarah's dresses, had not turned out as she had planned. It served
only to reveal the pathetic lack of curves in that particular area of
her anatomy. To make matters worse, the fitful nights, during which
Delaney's image had haunted her, had left their mark on her countenance. There were shadows under her great dark eyes, and the
contours of her cheek were sharper. Sarah was right. She was pale,
colorless, and thin. Plain.

The thought entered Allie's mind that if she and Delaney were
indeed two parts of a whole, as she believed, they were the
reverse sides of that whole. For Delaney possessed a physical
beauty she would never have. He was a pleasure to her eyes as
he was balm to her heart. She missed him and ached at being
separated from him.

Delaney had made no attempt to contact her in the few weeks since
he had left the farm. She had accompanied the family into town on
two occasions during that time, but James had remained close at her
side, and she had not had as much as a glimpse of Delaney. If she
had not been kept up to date on Delaney's activities by Sarah's malicious tongue, she would have thought he had left town.

But Sarah had seen Delaney. She had made it her business to

see him, if only for a few minutes, and she had treated Allie to
a detailed description of the exchange between them, assuming
that Allie was foolish enough to believe all she said.

Allie was not that foolish. She chose to believe that Delaney had
good reason for keeping his distance from her. She also clung to the
hope that she would see him tonight at the Harvest Dance.

With a low sigh, Allie acknowledged that her preoccupation
with Delaney had grown until thoughts of him had taken prec-
edence over all other aspects of her life. She had given little
thought to the growing warmth of James's regard. For the most
part she had been successful in avoiding his tender touch and
the gentle brush of his lips, and she had deafened her ears to
the promise in his voice when he spoke of the future. It was
Delaney's image that was present in her mind, waking or sleeping. It was Delaney's touch for which she yearned, the sound of
his voice she desired to hear. It was Delaney she wanted close
to her. It was Delaney, the other part of herself, the intimate
core of her, whom she missed to the point of pain.

She would see him tonight. She knew she would. He would
come to the Harvest Dance, even though he had never attended
the yearly function in the past. He would seek her out, and he
would explain to her why he had neglected her these past weeks.

And he would say good-bye. The end of the month, when
Delaney was expected to leave, was only a few days away.

Unable to bear that last thought, Allie turned toward the door,
unaware that Sarah followed her with her gaze.

"Daydreaming again, Allie? It's no use, you know. You hope
to see Delaney tonight, but James will keep you under his watchful eye the entire evening so you'll have no opportunity to slip
away. I, on the other hand, am very good at slipping away. And
I intend to make good use of my skill. You see, I'm not weak
like you, Allie. I go after what I want. I want Delaney, and I'm
going to get him." Turning so Allie might get a full view of her
magnificence, Sarah raised one perfect brow. "Do you have any
doubt I'll succeed?"

Turning without response, Allie pulled open the door and
stepped into the hall. Sarah's low laughter accompanied the
sound of the door clicking closed behind her.

* * *

"James dear, don't upset yourself."

"This is a mistake, Mama, and you know it. We shouldn't be going to this dance."

Casting a quick glance toward the hallway beyond her bedroom door, Margaret Case lowered her voice so the animated exchange between her son and her would not be heard.

"We've gone to the dance every year since we settled here, James. It's a tradition that means a lot to your father. My health is quite improved, and there is no reason for this to be the first year the Case family is not present."

"I'm not arguing about your health, Mama. You've been much better these past two weeks; you're just about back to your usual self."

Margaret nodded. She was almost her old self, but no one knew the magnitude of the effort she expended to appear that way. She knew her health had taken a sharp decline and that she would soon be unable to fool everyone as she did now. She had resigned herself to that truth. In the time left to her she was determined to give all the happiness she could to those she loved. She cherished a fervent wish to see her children settled before she was taken home. In the meantime, she would not deprive Jacob of the joy of celebrating another successful harvest with his neighbors. It was to be her gift to him—a gift he would remember, always.

"Yes, I'm almost my old self, and I know the reason for your concern. James, Delaney never attended the annual Harvest Dance in the past. What makes you believe he'll come tonight?"

The tensing of James's facial muscles was more revealing than words, and Margaret raised her hand to her son's cheek.

"James dear, you mustn't worry that Allie will—"

"He's all she thinks about, Mama, and he doesn't deserve her! She'll never believe me, but I know what would've happened if I hadn't shown up in time on Tillman Hill. I saw his face, the bastard!"

"James!"

James gave a short laugh. "No, I'm not sinking to his level, Mama—although sometimes I think Allie would appreciate me more if I did." He gave a short shake of his head. "I could never treat her the way Marsh did. I love her."

Margaret's faded eyes misted.

"James dear, you must face the fact that Allie doesn't love

you, not in the way you love her. You know who she loves, even if she doesn't realize it yet.''

"Yes, I know." James's expression tightened further. "But Marsh will be leaving soon. I just want to keep Allie out of his way until then. I don't like the idea of giving him an opportunity to see her tonight.''

"James, there are certain things you must put in the hands of a higher power.''

"No.''

"James!''

"I won't, Mama. If you insist on going to that dance tonight, I'll go, but before Marsh gets near Allie, he'll have to get past me.''

Margaret dropped her hands to her sides, her brow knotting with despair. "James, I don't want to see anyone hurt.'

"I don't care. Marsh will be leaving Cass County soon, and when he's gone, Allie will turn to me. It may take a while, but I'll wait as long as I must for it to happen.''

"You're letting yourself in for a lot of heartache, James.''

"I don't have any other choice.''

"If that's the way you see it, dear.''

Taking a moment to smooth her son's dark jacket and adjust his tie, Margaret swallowed against the lump in her throat. James was an honest, good-looking young man, with his fair hair and boyish face. He would make a good husband and a good father someday, and she was very proud of him. But looking at him through Allie's eyes, she knew he faded into insignificance when compared with Delaney's dark, vibrant appeal, and the male magnetism he exuded without any effort at all. But James had so much more to offer her darling Allie than Delaney did. She could only hope Allie would recognize that before it was too late.

Slipping her arm under James's, Margaret offered softly, "It's time to go, dear. Your father will have finished hitching up the team and will be impatient to leave.''

Turning, Margaret urged her son toward the door. Yes, James had so much more to offer. He could give Allie security, devotion, and love without reservation. Dear, angry Delaney, his emotions so deeply scarred from childhood, was not capable of that depth of emotion. She so dearly wanted Allie to be safe and secure when she was gone.

Emerging into the hallway just as Allie's fair head disappeared around the bend in the staircase, Margaret felt the rush of emotion that touched James at the sight of her. Her heart ached for her son. But this would work out for the best. She knew it would, and Allie would remain in the bosom of their family forever.

The lights from the Farmers' Meeting Hall at the far end of the town blinked brightly in the darkness of the clear fall night, calling him, but Delaney's determination remained firm. Turning, he seated himself at his desk.

Ignoring the affair about to commence in the well-lit hall, he had walked to the *News* office earlier in the evening, silently acknowledging that this was the final test. He had no doubt the entire Case family was in attendance. He knew the importance Jacob Case put upon the dance. He had heard that Margaret Case had again rallied from her illness, and he knew that as long as she had the strength to pull herself to her feet, she would be at her husband's side. Now an hour later and countless aborted attempts to work behind him, he was still determined to maintain his resolve. Picking up another sheet of copy, he attempted to concentrate on the words as music echoed on the mild evening air.

The last three weeks had been hell. Had he not given Max a promise to remain until the end of the month, he would have packed his belongings and left the first time Allie came to town with the family. It was then that he had first realized several things about himself.

The first realization was that he despised the sight of Allie seated at James's side. The second was that he despised the weakness within him that allowed his mind to taunt him with images of James's hands on Allie's waist as he lifted her from the wagon, of his proprietary stance beside her, and—most cutting of all—of Allie's eyes turned up to James with unspoken confidence as they had so often looked into his.

Pushing back his chair, Delaney returned to the window to stare in the direction of the hall. The third realization, which had been the most difficult to accept, was that the love Allie had given him so freely had made him vulnerable. It was a defect in the wall he had so carefully erected around his emotions, and it was a hindrance to the future he had mapped out for himself so long ago. By avoiding Allie since he had left the farm, he had strengthened that part of himself, and he had no intention of allowing himself to weaken by seeing her tonight.

He could not afford to say goodbye.

Keeping that thought foremost in his mind, Delaney turned back to his desk. He gave a low, disgusted snort. It would be a long time before the new man, Bart Malone, would be able to give Max the help he needed. The fellow was one step up from an idiot, but Max had been desperate. Time was running out. Delaney was due to leave in a few days whether the response from Chicago came or not.

His frown tightening, Delaney marked the sheet before him with a bold stroke. Bart would spend a full day tomorrow correcting his mistakes, but he supposed he should be grateful to Bart for keeping him occupied with work, especially tonight.

A new burst of music from the far end of town brought a lilting melody to Delaney's ears, but he forced his mind back to the article before him with rigid control. A familiar face supplanted the printed words, and dark eyes spoke silent volumes. Callous to their mute appeal, Delaney continued reading.

Allie took a sharp breath, her small hand clutching James's shoulder tightly as his dancing became more vigorous. Mistaking her gasp for delight, James smiled, increasing his whirling revolutions.

The large hall was beginning to spin around her in dizzying circles when Allie raised her voice above the deafening din of boisterous music, dancing feet, and raucous calls.

"James, you're making me dizzy!"

Responding immediately to her appeal, James slowed his step, amusement obvious in his face.

"Last year you couldn't get enough dancing, especially the waltz."

"Last year you allowed me to keep my feet on the floor. Tonight I'm not dancing. I'm flying!"

Slowing to a complete stop, James drew Allie off the floor, his hand firm at her waist as her step faltered. Waiting only until they had succeeded in escaping the crush of spectators around the dance floor, James slipped his arm around her waist and led her toward the door. He smiled at Allie's curious glance.

"You need some time to pull yourself together. And we need some privacy."

The tone of James's voice drew Allie's light brows into a frown as he urged her through the doorway into the yard. Allie didn't want to be alone with him. She wasn't ready.

They were walking in silence when James drew her into the shadows of a nearby tree. He attempted to take her into his arms, but Allie resisted with a soft plea.

"James, please."

"Please what?" James's anger was sudden and unexpected. "Please hold me closer, James? Please kiss me? Please love me? Those are all the things I've wanted to hear for a long time."

"No, James. I . . . I'm not ready."

"Don't say no, Allie." The anger suddenly vanishing from his voice, James caressed her shoulder with familiar gentleness. "You'll never be ready if you keep chasing me away. Is it really so distasteful to be in my arms?"

Allie swallowed, mesmerized by the intensity mixed with pain in James's shadowed face. She did not want to be responsible for the anguish she saw there.

"No, James. It isn't distasteful. I like being with you. I like talking with you, and I like dancing with you if you aren't making me dizzy. I like it when you put your arm around me and smile, but . . ."

"But kissing you is another matter."

James's stiff lips curved into a patient smile. "You're not used to kissing me, Allie, that's all. But you'll grow to like it as much as I do." Lowering his head unexpectedly, James brushed her lips with his.

"Was that so bad?"

"James—"

"How about this?" James touched his mouth to hers once more, his kiss lingering. "Answer me, Allie."

Allie avoided his eyes.

"It . . . it was pleasant, James."

The brief silence that followed was broken by James's coaxing whisper. "Allie, look at me. Come on, look at me."

The plea in his voice more than she could bear. Allie met his gaze. The love so openly displayed in his familiar face choked her with regret.

"Allie, this is all so new to you. You aren't accustomed to having a man show how much he wants you. And I do want you, darling. I want you more than I've ever wanted anyone or anything in my life."

His tenderness touching a spot deep inside her, Allie did not resist when James drew her closer. She closed her eyes as his lips touched her temple, her cheek, the corner of her mouth.

"You don't feel the same way about me. I know that. I know your loyalty to Marsh stands in my way right now, and although I can't understand that, I can accept it because it's only a temporary impediment. But I want to declare myself to you tonight, Allie. I want to tell you that I love you, that I've loved you since the day you came out of that chicken coop all scratched and bleeding and I slid my fingers into your hair to find the wounds there. You were such a brave little girl, with so much love inside you.

"That's what I'm offering you tonight, Allie—all the love I've stored up for you over the years. I'm offering you myself." James paused, his light brows drawing into a small frown. "I'm not big and handsome like some others. But I'll always be here for you, Allie. I'll take care of you and cherish you and love you. I'm offering you all that I am—all that I'll ever be. I want you to marry me, Allie."

Unable to react to James's unexpected declaration, Allie remained motionless as he lowered his mouth to hers. She did not resist as he slipped his arms around her, drawing her close. She felt the touch of his lips, the trembling that shook his frame, even as her mind echoed with shock at the depth of the love James had revealed to her. It was a love she did not share.

Desperately wishing that she did, Allie allowed James's hungry kiss.

He was separating himself from her when she saw the hope in his eyes. Oh, James . . .

He paused as he drew back. "Your face is an open book, Allie."

"It is?"

"Yes. And I don't want you to suffer because the loving is all on my side right now."

"James, I don't want to hurt you."

"You won't, Allie, because you're going to grow to love me just as much as I love you."

Allie did not respond and James drew her close once more. He brushed her lips lightly with his.

"How did that kiss make you feel, Allie?"

Allie hesitated, her dark eyes intent on his face. A shaft of moonlight penetrated the branches above their heads, illuminating her countenance, and James's love for her swelled anew at the innocence he saw there.

"Answer me, Allie."

Allie searched her heart for a truth that would not sting. "Your kiss is like you, James. It's soft and gentle and caring. I want you to care for me because I care for you, but—"

James pressed a hand across Allie's lips, halting the conclusion of her statement. "Allie, listen to what you said. You said you want me to care for you because you care for me. We can build on those words, Allie, until you feel the same way I do. And I promise, you'll never be sorry."

Tears welled in Allie's throat. She did not deserve James's love, not when she couldn't return it. But he had always given her more than she had given him back. She still could not understand why.

"Allie? James?" Mother Case stood in the doorway behind them with Jacob at her side, anxiety apparent in her expression. Her gaze searched the shadows where they stood unseen, relief lifting the planes of her face the moment they stepped into view. Her smile was apologetic.

"I'm sorry, dears. I was concerned. I thought perhaps . . . Well, now I know I needn't have worried. I'm sorry if I disturbed you." Turning, Margaret took her husband's arm. "Jacob, next time you must make certain an old fool doesn't intrude on young people's privacy."

Waiting only until his parents had moved out of sight, James slipped his arm around Allie's waist. He brushed a wisp of hair from Allie's cheek with a tender smile. "Come on, Allie. It's time to go inside. You can think about what I've said, or not think about it, whatever you want. But I promise you, Allie, you're going to love me one day with your whole heart."

Turning at James's urging, Allie looked toward the hall where the vigorous dancing continued. Still in the circle of James's protective arm moments later, she joined the cheerful crowd.

She would not think about anything James had said now. Not tonight.

Dancing couples whirled around her, but Allie was uncertain how much longer she could continue to force her feet to move and make her smile shine. Refusing to allow her gaze to return to the hall entrance where it had lingered in frustrated hope the entire evening, Allie acknowledged for the first time that Delaney might not come. Her spirits plummeted even as she forced a new brightness to her smile and looked up at the badly concealed despair in her partner's eyes.

Poor Bobbie. If there was one person at the dance who was more unhappy than she, it was Bobbie Clark. He cast a glance at the couple dancing beside them, his heart in his eyes as his gaze touched on Sarah's animated face. She had all but ignored Bobbie the entire evening as she danced with the other young bachelors who had swarmed around her the moment she entered the hall. It was difficult for Allie to comprehend that Sarah was enjoying Bobbie's despair.

There was no understanding Sarah. Bobbie was a good-looking fellow, with heavy dark hair, dark eyes, and a well-built physique. His family had one of the best farms in the county, and he adored Sarah. He only had one shortcoming: He was not Delaney.

Allie's forced smile tightened. Sarah would never get Delaney. She was a fool for believing she would.

Allie squeezed Bobbie's hand sympathetically. Having succeeded in drawing back his attention, she offered encouragingly, "Don't worry, Bobbie. Sarah is beautiful and she enjoys attention, but I know she thinks more highly of you than any of the other fellows here tonight."

Allie was comfortable with that statement because it was true. Delaney had not come to the dance—not even to say good-bye.

"Do you think so, Allie?"

"It's the absolute truth."

Bobbie gave a short laugh. "She has a strange way of showing it."

Slipping his arm companionably around her waist as the music drew to a close, Bobbie leaned toward Allie. "If I could only get Sarah alone for a few minutes, I'd talk to her and find out what's wrong tonight. But it doesn't look like there's much chance of that.'' Giving a small shrug, he forced a smile. ''Before James catches up with us, would you like to join me for some punch? I think we've both worked up a pretty good thirst.''

At her nod, Bobbie took Allie's hand and drew her toward the buffet. She felt him stiffen as the crowd separated to reveal they were heading directly toward Sarah and her current partner. Sarah waved a graceful greeting to Bobbie as they approached, her smile devastating. She detached herself from Jeremy Bellows as they drew abreast and slid her hand under Bobbie's arm with a coy glance.

''Bobbie Clark, you've been neglecting me.''

Realizing she had been all but forgotten as Bobbie stared into Sarah's beautiful face, Allie felt a new distaste for Sarah expand within her. Bobbie was stammering a response when Sarah raised a slender, caressing finger to his cheek.

''I would truly enjoy a bit more punch, Bobbie, but I have no desire to wait on that long line. Do you think you could get some for me?''

Casting an apologetic glance toward Allie, Bobbie responded politely, ''I . . . Allie and I were just heading in that direction. I'd be happy to get a cup for you, too.''

''Dear boy.''

Waiting until Bobbie had attached himself to the end of the refreshment line, Sarah turned her back on her former partner in rude dismissal. Her softly spoken words were meant for Allie alone.

''Did you enjoy yourself outside with James, Allie dear?'' Sarah laughed at Allie's startled expression. ''James is such a fool for you. I suppose you realize how fortunate a plain girl like you is to have someone like James take a shine to her. If you play your cards right, you just may end up with the Case kitchen as your own.'' Sarah gave an expansive sigh and lifted her graceful shoulders. ''As for me, I don't expect to spend much time in the kitchen. I don't think Delaney will want his woman slaving over a stove.''

Allie's stiffening did not go unnoticed.

''You didn't really think I'd given up my plan, did you? I think I've played my part well tonight. Everyone will think I disappeared with Bobbie or Jeremy or one of the other fellows when I finally decide to slip out. But you know where I'll be, don't you, dear? You won't warn anyone because you know I'll make a scene, and a scene could be dangerous for Mama. You also know I'll do exactly as I choose in any case, so you must try to console my parents as well as yourself if I don't come back. It may be a very long night.''

Allie gritted her teeth against Sarah's maliciousness. From the other side of the hall, James began making his way toward her as Sarah continued in a low undertone, ''Oh, here comes James. Dear James. He's such a comfort, isn't he?''

Her eyes blurred with tears as James reached her side, Allie tried unsuccessfully to avoid his glance.

''What did Sarah say to you, Allie?''

Sarah had already turned toward another fellow who had appeared at her elbow, and Allie shook her head. ''Nothing, James. She didn't say anything.''

''Allie . . .''

''Please excuse me, James.'' Allie managed a smile. ''I'll only be a few minutes. The convenience isn't far.'' Not caring whether he saw through her attempt to avoid him, Allie made her way through the crowded room. She needed desperately to get away, for a short time, at least.

Stepping outside the rear door of the hall, Allie walked slowly along the path to the convenience, grateful to be alone. She could not force her smile a moment longer. Nor could she continue to pretend—

A heavy hand clamped across Allie's mouth, muffling her startled scream as she was suddenly pulled into the heavy foliage that bordered the path. Unable to make out the shadowed figure holding her prisoner in the darkness, Allie fought and squirmed for release, flailing her arms in a vain attempt to strike at her unknown captor.

''Stop fighting! Allie, dammit, it's me.''

The low growl of a familiar voice brought Allie suddenly stock still. The confining hands fell away and she took an involuntary step back. A shaft of silver moonlight fell on her face, illuminating it, and Allie heard the shadowed figure's low epithet.

''Delaney, is it you?''

A step forward brought him into the limited light, and happiness soared to life inside her. A relieved gasp escaping her, Allie threw herself against Delaney's chest, straining on tiptoe to encircle his neck with her arms as she held him close with all her strength. Her heart pounding she breathed in his familiar scent and rubbed her cheek against his neck, her happiness pouring from her lips in a low, almost unintelligible stream.

"I knew you couldn't leave without saying good-bye! Everyone said you would, but I didn't believe it for a minute. When you didn't try to see me, I knew there had to be a good reason. I ached without you, Delaney. The ache wouldn't stop, no matter what I tried."

A low, bitter sound escaped Delaney's lips. "Is that what you were trying to do when you were outside with James a little while ago—trying to forget me?"

"Delaney, I—"

Dislodging her arms from around his neck, Delaney held her an arm's distance from him. His eyes were blazing. "I've been standing here for the last hour, telling myself what a fool I am. I had everything under control. I wasn't thinking about you all the time anymore. I was actually able to put you out of my mind while I worked, and I wasn't getting up to look out the window every half-hour to see if I could catch a glimpse of you on the street. Then tonight came and it started all over again. I knew it would be so damned easy to see you."

Delaney's expression hardened. "But I didn't want to see you. Damn it all, you've made a cripple out of me! I don't feel whole without you, and I don't like that feeling."

The emotion in Delaney's voice brought a strange new warmth to life inside Allie. She could feel his trembling, his frustration and anger, and for some reason that warmth grew. She felt a deep, inexplicable yearning to assuage Delaney's anguish. She wanted to hold him in her arms, to feel his strength, and to lend him her own. She wanted to give him peace, to give him love. She wanted—

"Allie, are you listening to me?" A new fury suffused Delaney's tone. "Was James that convincing when he kissed you? What did he say? Did he tell you to forget me, that you didn't need anybody because you had him? Did you believe him?"

"Oh, Delaney, you know I wouldn't listen even if he said those things. You're part of me, just as I'm part of you."

A muscle twitched in Delaney's cheek, and Allie noted the tense spasm. Her eyes lingered on the clear eyes, which pinned

her with their gaze, the sharp planes of his cheek, the full mouth
that twitched with anger.

The silence between them lengthened as Delaney's grip on
her arms tightened almost to the point of pain. "Did you enjoy
James's kiss, Allie?"

"I . . . I don't know."

A low, unidentifiable sound echoed in Delaney's throat, and
Allie attempted to explain her confused feelings. "James asked
me the same thing, and I told him his kiss was pleasant. It was
gentle and caring, just as he is. He told me I would grow to like
it more if I—"

"Will you let me kiss you, Allie?"

The warmth inside Allie began to blossom. "Do you want to
kiss me?"

"Yes."

Allie's heart fluttered within her breast. "I want you to kiss
me, too."

Delaney's lips touched hers, and Allie leaned full into his
arms, melding to his strength. The joy of all that was Delaney
swept over her, filled her, and an incredible exhilaration came
alive inside her. His mouth sought a greater intimacy, and she
allowed it willingly. She reveled in the taste of him, straining
closer. She felt his fingers in her hair, caressing her scalp as his
tongue sent shivers of joy streaking to the core of her being.

His breathing ragged, Delaney tore his mouth from hers to
press hungry kisses against her eyes, her ears, the column of her
throat. He was consuming her, and she was quaking, drowning
in the desire to be absorbed into him totally, to join with his
body as she had joined with his spirit so long ago.

Breathless, his familiar, loved face racked with a torment
echoing deep inside her as well, Delaney drew back. His chest
heaving, he swallowed in an obvious attempt at control. "You're
shaking, Allie. Are you afraid of me?"

"No. I could never be afraid of you, Delaney."

"Allie . . ."

Glancing up, Delaney appeared suddenly conscious of the hall
nearby and the people milling around it. He looked back down
into her face.

"Allie, there are too many people here. I want to be alone
with you. Will you come with me?"

Giving the only answer her heart would allow, Allie nodded.
Delaney's clear eyes held hers for a long moment in silence
before he slid his palm down the length of her arm and gripped
her hand tightly with his. Within moments they were moving
through the semidarkness of the heavy foliage. Allie followed
Delaney blindly. She knew she always would.

Covering the ground with a rapid pace that all but lifted Allie from
her feet, Delaney moved deftly through the trees. A sense of urgency
drumming at his mind, he held tight to her hand. He had come too
close to losing her. He had only just begun to realize the supreme
price he would have paid for that loss.

Allie was a part of him. He had never been more aware of his
helplessness against his feelings for Allie than he had earlier in the
evening when he realized he couldn't stay away from her any longer.

At that moment he had decided to leave on the morning train.
Within a short half-hour he had packed his belongings and tied
up all the loose ends of his life—except one.

A familiar tightening within him signaled the return of the
harsh image of Allie in James's arms. James kissing her, tasting
her mouth. James taking what was his. His Allie.

The blind fury that had suffused him had driven him to step
forward just as Margaret Case appeared in the doorway of the
hall. Her frailty had been obvious, and Delaney had been unwilling to shock her with an unexpected appearance just then.
Instead, he had lingered in the foliage in the hope of getting
Allie to himself. He had all but given up that hope when Allie
had finally made her way down the path toward him. But his
anger had fallen victim to a stronger emotion once he held Allie
in his arms.

Delaney drew to a halt at the edge of a small clearing. He
quickly perused the dense woods surrounding them before drawing Allie forward into the silver moonlight that lit the leafy
bower. The silence of the secluded spot was broken only by the
sound of their rapid breathing, but Delaney knew his breathlessness was not due solely to their hasty flight.

Cupping Allie's face with his hands, Delaney looked down at
her in silence. The shimmering moonlight imparted an ethereal
glow to the pale silk of her hair, deepened the darkness of her
eyes, glistened on her lips. He noted the new hollows in her

cheeks. Allie was thinner than she had been when he had last seen her, but the effect was a further enhancement of her delicate bone structure and the unusual loveliness that was hers alone. Allie was beautiful, although he knew she would never believe it was true. She was a precious gift he had almost squandered.

He knew he did not deserve her, but he surrendered to the selfishness that made him take this precious gift to his heart. His only consolation was that in her innocent way, Allie wanted him, too. She did not know the true scope of desire, but he would teach her all the glittering facets, and then he would sate them one by one—if it took a lifetime.

A compulsive shudder shook Delaney as he acknowledged for the first time the consequences of losing Allie. For he knew that Allie was his soul. Without her, he was lost.

His heart filled to bursting, Delaney pressed his mouth to Allie's. It was incredibly sweet—open, accepting, loving. Suddenly past rational thought Delaney devoured her lips, his fingers tightening in her hair to hold her fast to his ravaging mouth. The clinging warmth of Allie's arms moved to his shoulders as he tasted her fluttering eyelids, pressed heated kisses against the delicate pulse throbbing so wildly at her temple. Wild with the aching desire consuming him, Delaney spread moist, eager kisses along the line of her brow, the delicate curve of her ear. His heated murmurs caused Allie to tremble anew and all thought of Allie's inexperience was stripped from his mind by the passion that drove him. Accepting her loving response, demanding more, Delaney raised her with him on the radiant wings of a passion so supreme that he was lost in its beauty.

The lace-trimmed bodice fell away under Delaney's impatient hands, and a new tenderness suffused him as the small, virginal mounds of her breasts were revealed to him for the first time. He covered the roseate tips lovingly with his lips, suckled them gently, a thrill moving down his spine at Allie's ecstatic gasp.

His hunger for Allie was voracious, the need within him swelling with each moment he held her in his arms, and Delaney could bear the impediment of clothing between them no longer.

His fingers were working at the closing of her skirt when he noted Allie's sudden stiffening. The warm flush that covered her face was visible even in the limited light of the small clearing.

A pain stronger than any he had ever experienced drew Delaney's loving ministrations to a halt as she averted her eyes from his.

Delaney took a deep, hard breath.

"Allie, do you want me to stop?"

Allie's eyes snapped back to his, her short protest simultaneous with a vigorous shake of her head. "No."

But there were tears in her eyes that could not be denied.

"Then what is wrong? Tell me, Allie."

"I—I don't want you to be disappointed. I'm not beautiful to look at, Delaney."

Profound relief flooded through Delaney as he touched Allie's warm cheek with a trembling hand. "You *are* beautiful, and you're all I ever wanted. Let me prove it to you, darling."

Undressing her carefully, gently, Delaney followed the fall of fabric from Allie's body with his lips. He caressed her warm, sweet flesh as it was uncovered to his gaze, worshiping it with the love he cherished within him for the fragile child-woman in his arms.

Allie was quaking under his touch as Delaney lifted his lips from her heated flesh. Compassion momentarily overwhelming the hunger that drove him, he scooped her up into his arms, carried her to a mossy pallet nearby, and laid her gently upon it.

A low gasp escaping him as his·body met Allie's fully for the first time, Delaney looked down into her passion-flushed face. Her heart raced beneath his own as he slowly drew the pins from her hair and set the pale strands free.

"This is the way I imagined it, Allie, in all those dreams I pushed to the back of my mind. This is the way I wanted it to be. I can't deny it any longer. I've always loved you. I always will."

Poised above her, Delaney paused a moment longer. A tender smile flicked across his lips at the fear that shone momentarily in her dark eyes, knowing it would soon be replaced by a light of another kind. Suddenly driving deep within her, Delaney exulted at Allie's stifled cry even as he regretted her temporary pain. Held fast and still as Allie's moist warmth closed around him, Delaney cupped her face with his palms, his clear eyes consuming even as he was consumed.

"You're mine now, Allie. You'll never belong to anyone else the way you belong to me."

Brushing her lips with loving kisses, Delaney began a slow movement within her and Allie fought to suppress the low ecstatic sounds escaping her throat. Clutching him tighter, joy overwhelming her discomfort, Allie closed her eyes, disbelieving the beauty that swelled with each penetrating thrust.

She had not known she could feel like this. She had not known that in joining her body with his, Delaney would transform it into a vessel of love that would fill them both. She had not known that together they would soar high above this dim, still night in each other's arms until their vessel of love, filled to overflowing, would erupt in a flood of brilliance so complete that she would be encompassed by its splendor. She had not known that their joy complete, they would lie in each other's arms, never wishing to be free.

She had not known.

In the stillness that followed, grateful for the gift of love Delaney had given her, Allie clutched him closer still. She broke the silence with a soft whisper that echoed within her heart.

"I love you, Delaney. I'll love you always, all my life."

Margaret fought the quaking that had beset her as she continued to stare into the darkness outside the Farmers' Meeting Hall. She had not realized this evening would prove to be such a trial; she had not anticipated Allie's disappearance, James's barely controlled fury, or Sarah's rage.

Looking back over her shoulder, Margaret surveyed the couples within the hall, dancing past the door with endless enthusiasm. Her tension mounted. The music would soon draw to an end, and she had no intention of revealing to the other families that Allie had disappeared with Delaney Marsh.

Margaret knew without doubt this scandalous turn of events had not come through Allie's thoughtlessness. This flaunting of convention and disregard for public opinion was Delaney's work, and she was furious with him for taking advantage of Allie's love by compromising her in this way. He would be leaving soon, but Allie's reputation would be stained forever. She did not deserve such callous treatment. Margaret knew she had been right all along. She had known Delaney was incapable of making Allie happy, and she was determined he would not ruin Allie's life.

James returned from another search of the woods, and Margaret motioned him toward her, then took his arm and lowered her voice so Sarah would not overhear.

"William Sears is certain it was Delaney he saw near the rear exit earlier?"

James paled, and fury twitched at his lips. "He's certain, Mama. Where else would Allie be? You know she wouldn't wander off by herself. I've checked the rooming house, the *News* office, and his 'friend' Lil's rooms. He's nowhere to be found. So he must be with Allie."

"James, you mustn't upset yourself."

James gave his mother a short, hard look. "I asked Allie to marry me tonight, Mama."

Closing her eyes, Margaret found herself frighteningly short of breath. She was struggling against light-headedness when Jacob took her arm.

"Margaret, you mustn't stand here any longer. James and I will find Allie. Go inside. Just sit down, smile, and pretend all is well, and try to relax. I'll tell Sarah to stay with you."

Margaret shook her head. "No, dear. My daughter's company right now would be the final straw. I'm not up to another of her tirades."

Jacob cast a disgusted glance at his daughter, who was pacing back and forth in obvious agitation. He silently cursed Sarah's supreme selfishness. He was only too aware that she had even managed to repulse Bobbie Clark's well-intended efforts as she allowed her jealousy to consume her. He turned back to his wife as she spoke again.

"I have stopped berating myself for my failure with Sarah, Jacob. I did my best for her, and I would not have known how to raise her in any other way. If she has not turned out as we wished her to, I can only think it was beyond our power to change her. In any case, I prefer to remain here. I have a feeling there will be need of a peacemaker this night."

"This is partly my fault, Margaret. Allie was always too trusting of Delaney. As much as I dislike admitting it, I should have listened to James from the beginning. He saw through Marsh as none of us did."

"Jacob, we are jumping to unfair conclusions. Delaney may have spirited Allie away so he could talk to her alone. He—"

"Margaret, stop defending him! His actions tonight are inexcusable, and he will suffer the consequences."

"Jacob . . ." Her heart beginning an uneven tempo that made breathing even more difficult, Margaret said softly, "Please, no scenes. I just want to take Allie home where her innocence will not be exploited again."

"Margaret—"

"Please, Jacob, tell James the same. He is so upset, and I wouldn't want him to do anything he would regret."

With a callused hand Jacob brushed a tear from Margaret's cheek, and she flushed. She had not realized she had lost control to that extent.

"All right, dear. I'll tell James. I'll also tell him that Delaney Marsh is never to set foot on our farm again."

"Thank you, Jacob."

Turning away, Margaret strained her eyes into the wooded land shrouded by darkness. She bit her lip to hold back the tears, truly uncertain how this night would end.

His face buried in the long silken strands glowing a molten silver in the moonlight, Delaney held Allie close. He was reluctant to separate from her. Her pale arms loosely encircled his neck, and he lifted his head to trail his lips over her smooth flesh before easing away from her.

Allie's low murmur of protest accompanied their separation, and the well of joy within him that was Allie came to life once more. Covering her parted lips with his own, he drank deeply from that well. Drawing back, his heart again pounding, he realized his thirst for Allie would never truly be quenched. He accepted that now, just as he accepted the years that lay before them, during which he would return to that well time and again, with love.

Delaney trailed his fingertips lightly against her cheek. He loved Allie's skin. He loved its scent, its taste, the remarkable color, so white, so clear that it glowed with an almost jewellike sheen. He loved the way her light brows arched over those incredibly dark eyes, the way the thick gold-tipped lashes curled so tightly. He loved the short, straight line of her nose, the contours of her cheek. And he loved her mouth. It was a mouth that smiled often, that filled his heart with its laughter, that often spoke wisdom beyond its years. And it was a mouth that accepted his and murmured words of love that touched him in a way no other could.

He drank again from that font of love, deeply, drawing back as Allie uttered a low sound of discomfort. Frowning, he separated himself from her, his eyes moving to the spot between her breasts where she rubbed a small bruise. The medal suspended from his neck, hanging between them, glittered in the silver light, marking the source of the problem.

"So, the Lady is making her presence felt. Do you think she's voicing her disapproval?"

Too late, Delaney realized his comment was unwise. Regretting his careless words, he watched Allie's brow pull into a frown as she took the medal into her hand. Pausing only a moment, Allie then raised her eyes to his, her frown slipping away.

"No, I don't think so. The Lady sent you to me and held us together. She—"

"No, Allie." Delaney didn't want to share this moment with the Lady. It was theirs—Allie's and his alone. He didn't want Allie to confuse her feelings for him with mixed-up beliefs in which he had no faith. He wanted Allie to believe in *him*.

"The Lady didn't bring us together. *I* brought us together when I took your hand that morning in the church hall and didn't let it go. *I* kept us together when I decided nothing James or anybody else would do could drive me from the Case farm until I was ready to leave you. *I* brought you with me tonight and made you a part of me, and *I* am the one who's going to keep you with me. I told you, I don't believe in the Lady or anything connected with her."

Allie was silent for a moment before she whispered, "I believe in her, Delaney."

His dark brow still tightly furrowed, he held her sober gaze. Making a sudden decision, he sat up and drew her up beside him. Then he slipped off the medal and placed it around Allie's neck, carefully extricating the strands of hair trapped by the chain until it lay unrestricted against her skin.

"Then you should wear the medal, Allie, not me. It's yours now, a gift from me."

Allie's hand closed around it as she shook her head. "It's yours. It's always been yours."

"No, it's always been yours."

"I can't accept it."

Recognizing Allie's distress, Delaney attempted a smile.

"I wore the medal because it was my only tie to the past, and the only thing that belonged to me alone. It was the only thing I really owned. Right now it's the only thing I have to give you. I want you to have it."

Delaney touched the chain with his fingertip. It was warm from his flesh and he felt a familiar heat suffuse him as Allie released the medal and allowed it to lie against her skin. It lay between her small breasts as he trailed his finger to a swollen pink crest. When his burgeoning desire became more than he could bear, he lowered his head to kiss one tempting bud and then the other, drawing back sharply as his emotions began to rise out of control.

Drawing himself to his feet, Delaney drew Allie up beside him. She was so small, so slight, to carry all his hopes and dreams.

"We have to go back now, Allie. You've been gone a long time. I think the family suspects you're with me by now. They'll be waiting for you to return."

Allie flushed. "I almost forgot. Mother Case will be worried."

"After tonight, they won't have to worry about you anymore."

Allie turned and started dressing. Sensing her discomfort, Delaney turned her to face him.

"What's wrong, Allie?"

"I'm worried about Mother Case. She . . . she thinks that you—"

"I know what she thinks, but she's wrong. I love you, Allie. I've loved you since the day you crawled up beside me in that rail car. You're the only reason I've stayed here this long, and now that I'm leaving, I'm going to take you with me. I don't have much to offer you, but I will someday. I'll be able to offer you the world. The only trouble is you'll have to take me along with it."

"I don't want the world, Delaney. I only want you."

Allie's whispered response touching him to the heart, Delaney pulled her close against him, belatedly realizing as her arms closed around him that she was making a quick departure extremely difficult to accomplish.

Delaney separated himself from her with a small groan. "Get

dressed, Allie. We have to go. Just remember, whatever Mrs. Case or anyone else says, I'll take care of you. And we're leaving tomorrow.''

Allie's dark eyes perused his face. He could feel their touch just as he could feel her indecision and her fear.

''I love you, Allie.''

The smile that touched her lips swelled inside him as Allie started to dress.

Within a few minutes they were moving back along the same path they had traveled a short time before. Allie's small hand in his, Delaney lent her his strength as she lent him her love. They were part of each other.

Allie stumbled again. Her lurching pitch forward was cushioned by Delaney's steadying arm as he cast her a concerned glance. She offered him an embarrassed smile as they continued along the wooded path.

Angry with herself for the quaking that made her unnaturally clumsy, Allie heard the sound of music drawing closer. They would soon emerge from the shadows at the rear of the hall. She would have to face everyone, and she despised her trepidation.

Abruptly, they were there. Pausing before stepping out into the open, Delaney turned to Allie once more. He slid his hands into her hair and drew her up to meet his mouth, his kiss deepening as his arms slipped around her, crushing her tight against the firm wall of his body. Allie's heart sang as she gave herself up to the wonder of him. Oh, Delaney, she thought, I've never loved anyone the way I love you.

Just as suddenly she was separated from Delaney's warmth. Bereft and alone, she looked up at him in mute appeal.

''Only for a little while, Allie.''

They emerged from the shadows and Allie was suddenly unable to move, as James turned in their direction. Taking up a protective stance beside her, Delaney waited as James walked forward, the remainder of the family trailing behind him.

James's gaze raked her disheveled appearance, and Allie's hand sprang to her unbound hair. She had lost the pins, but somehow had not given her hair any thought until now. Her face flushing, Allie dropped her gaze, missing the hatred in James's accusing glance as he looked toward Delaney.

"There was no protecting her from you, was there?" James said angrily. "You were determined to get what you wanted and you didn't let anything, not even Allie's innocence, stand in the way."

The malevolence in James's voice brought a protest from Allie's lips. "No, James, you're wrong. I went with Delaney willingly. He . . . we—"

"You don't have to say anything, Allie. Get away from him— over here, by me."

"Don't move, Allie."

Delaney stepped in front of her. Casting James a warning look, he turned to Mrs. Case. "I'm sorry to upset you, Mrs. Case, but Allie is leaving tomorrow, with me."

"No!"

The single gasping word that escaped Mrs. Case's lips appeared to sap her strength, and she swayed weakly.

"Margaret, please, let me take you back to the wagon." His face deeply flushed, Jacob flashed an accusing glance toward Allie. "If she wants to leave with him, let her."

"No, she can't, Jacob. She's too young. She doesn't understand what's in store for her." Turning toward Allie, Margaret appealed softly, "Allie dear, I only want what's best for you. I won't be here much longer and I—"

"Margaret, please . . ."

But Margaret continued in a weakening voice, "I want to know you will be safe and cared for when I'm gone, Allie. You must come home with us."

"Delaney loves me, Mother Case." Finding her voice, Allie resisted the urge to run to Mrs. Case's side, to support her frail limbs with her strong arms, to lend her strength. Instead, she continued quietly, "We're going to Chicago, and we'll be together—always."

"No, Allie. No." Turning to Delaney, Mrs. Case pressed her plea. "Delaney, have you no heart? Don't you realize this child believes in you, is trusting you with her life? You want her now, but when you're in the city and busy with your career, you won't have time for her. You'll be meeting new people, going new places, and she'll be in your way. What will she do then? She'll be neglected and alone. She'll never be alone with us, and she'll never be neglected. You want her now, Delaney, but that will change, because you don't need her. You don't need anyone."

"You're wrong, Mrs. Case. I love Allie and I'll take care of her."

"With what? How will you take care of her? If you really love her, you'll leave her behind. If you still feel the same way after a few months, you can come back for her."

"I'm taking her with me."

"No, you aren't!" Moving forward, James attempted to grab Allie's wrist, only to have Delaney take another threatening step forward.

"Leave her alone, Case! You never wanted to believe it, but Allie belongs to me. She always has, and I'm taking her with me."

Squaring his stance, James shook his head. "No, you aren't."

"This has gone far enough!" Handicapped by the need to support his wife, Jacob growled, "Get out of here, Marsh. You never belonged here in the first place. Go to the city. It will be home to you like Cass County never was. But leave Allie here. This is her home."

"Allie's home is with me."

"No, it isn't." Catching Delaney unawares, James grasped Allie's arm and pulled her behind him. Allie was struggling against his unyielding grip when James suddenly staggered backwards under Delaney's blow. Abruptly released, Allie watched with horror as Delaney and James met, fists swinging, to fall back among the trees bordering the clearing.

The unexpected violence held Allie immobile until the sound of a rasping breath turned her toward Margaret Case. With a low cry, Allie rushed to her side as the frail woman collapsed in her husband's arms. Her lined face a ghastly white, Margaret struggled for breath as tears streamed freely down Allie's face.

"Mother Case, please . . . please don't be frightened. James and Delaney will stop fighting." Looking up to see James at her side, she continued, "See, they've stopped already. They don't want to see you ill, either of them." Allie raised her eyes in a soft plea. "Tell her, James. Tell her you won't fight with Delaney anymore."

James held his mother's arm encouragingly, but his expression was unyielding as he responded to Allie's impassioned appeal. "I won't let you leave with Marsh while there's a breath left in my body, Allie."

Allie turned back to Margaret, her fear growing as the shuddering woman strained to breathe. She saw the harsh blue color that lined Mother Case's lips, as she spoke, "Come . . . come back with us, Allie."

Mrs. Case's rasping plea grated on the unnatural silence and Allie looked up at Delaney. His demeanor did not soften as he demanded, "Let's go, Allie."

The ice in Delaney's clear eyes startled her. He was unaffected by Mother Case's pain. Didn't he see she was dying?

"Allie . . ."

"I can't leave her now, Delaney."

The slow stiffening of Delaney's frame was more revealing than words, but Allie shook her head.

"Delaney, can't you see Mother Case is ill? I just want to stay a few more days, until she's a little better."

"No, Allie. You're coming with me now, and we're leaving tomorrow."

"Delaney, I can't!" Rising to her feet, Allie took a step toward Delaney, only to have Mother Case's low gasp turn her back. "I can't."

Delaney's face was grim.

Speaking soft words of encouragement to the prostrate woman, Allie did not notice when James left to get the wagon. Crouched at Mother Case's side, she did not hear it approach, but drew herself to her feet and stepped back automatically as Jacob gently lifted his wife into his arms. Allie walked to the wagon behind him as he laid his wife tenderly on a blanket in the rear. James touched her arm, but she turned back to Delaney with another low plea.

"Delaney, please understand. I must go with her now."

"Think carefully of the choice you're making, Allie." Delaney's voice was cold, lifeless. "I'm leaving on the morning train. I won't be here when you come back."

James lifted her onto the wagon bed and Mother Case's trembling hand reached for hers. Her faded eyes closed as she labored for breath, and a low sob escaped Allie's throat. James swung a silent Sarah onto the front seat beside her father before climbing into the rear to support his mother's quaking frame.

The wagon lurched forward and Allie saw Delaney's face the moment before he turned, his back rigidly erect, and walked back toward town.

* * *

"I don't need her," Delaney murmured. "I don't need anyone."

His heels clicked on the board sidewalk, but Delaney did not hear the echo on the nearly deserted street as he continued walking in a long, even stride that belied his inner turmoil.

Delaney shook his head in an attempt to clear his mind. It had all happened so quickly. Allie had been in his arms a few minutes before, telling him that she loved him and would be with him the rest of his life, but that joy had been fleeting. Reality had returned when Allie turned her back on him.

Even now he could not quite believe it. He had always been so sure she loved him, if not with the physical passion she had shown tonight, at least with her full, innocent heart. He had been certain that when the time came to choose, she would choose him over all others. It was now obvious that she was just like everyone else, another person who had let him down.

Delaney's frown deepened. James's pleas, Jacob Case's warnings, and Sarah's maliciousness had had no effect on Allie's faith in him, but the doubts Mrs. Case had put in her mind had turned the trick. Why couldn't Allie see that for all the sincerity with which Mrs. Case spoke, her love for James influenced her heavily against him? Why didn't she realize that Mrs. Case would never see anyone but James in Allie's future? Why didn't she understand that once she went back with the Case family, they would see to it that she never left them again?

The answer to those questions was simple: Allie did not see because she did not choose to see.

Delaney attempted to ignore the pain of that realization. He was sure of only one thing now: He was leaving tomorrow morning, with or without Allie.

Suddenly slowing to a halt, Delaney gave a short, harsh laugh. His steps had taken him automatically to the door of the *News* office. A wounded animal returning home.

Not enjoying the analogy his mind had conjured, Delaney pushed open the door and strode to Max's desk. He was through with being a fool. He had thought the hard lessons he had learned on the streets so long ago would never be forgotten. He had not realized that love could replace common sense and render him vulnerable once more. And he had forgotten that life was fickle, that time and circumstance altered all, and that the only protection against pain was to be sufficient within oneself. He would not forget those hard-learned lessons again.

Delaney jerked open the desk drawer and took out the bottle Max "consulted" several times a day. He held it up to the light. The amber liquid stood at the three-quarter mark, and he gave a short, satisfied nod of his head. Turning, he walked out of the office and pulled the door shut behind him.

Stepping into his room a few minutes later, Delaney paused as the light from the hallway behind him touched on the small, cheap suitcase he had packed earlier. Not much to show for twenty-one years of life.

Delaney pushed the door closed behind him, and made a silent vow: He would have much more to show for the *next* twenty-one years.

Walking the few steps to his nightstand, Delaney turned up the lamp. He flopped down on the bed, the thought occurring to him that he had been right all those years ago when he had taken that little pale-haired girl's hand in his own in silent commitment. He had sensed he would regret it one day.

Pulling the cork from the bottle, Delaney raised it to his lips and drank deeply. The burning heat that scalded right down to the pit of his stomach was a welcome relief from the ache that had lodged itself there. He took another, determined to shorten the long night ahead of him and to drive a familiar image from his mind any way he could.

The ride from town had been endless. Allie raised her gaze from Mother Case's ashen face, grateful that she appeared to be sleeping. She looked into James's stiff expression where he continued to cushion his mother against the wagon's sway.

"She's going to be all right, isn't she, James?"

James did not answer.

She tried again. "James, I'm sorry that everyone was upset about Delaney and me, and I—"

"I don't want to talk about Delaney and you." James looked at his mother. Satisfied that she did not appear to hear them, he looked back to Allie, his expression grim. "As far as I'm concerned, it's over and done. Marsh will be leaving tomorrow and

I'm going to do my best to forget he ever existed. I suggest you do the same.''

Allie shook her head. ''Delaney won't leave without me, James. He was angry, but he loves me.''

''Marsh doesn't love anyone but himself. What does he have to do to make you see him for what he really is?''

''James, please, I don't want to argue. I just wanted to tell you I never meant to hurt anyone, not you or Mother Case. I'm sorry things happened the way they did. I didn't intend it that way, and neither did Delaney.''

James held Allie's gaze, finally shaking his head in apparent disbelief. ''You still don't realize what happened, do you, Allie? Delaney took what he wanted from you, and when the going got a little rough, he backed off and walked away. He's leaving without you.''

''No. He was angry, but he'll think everything over tonight and he'll wait for me. He couldn't leave without me, not now. He loves me, James, and I love him.''

Regretting the pain that flickered across James's face, Allie reached out to him, but James shook off her touch.

''Save your comfort for yourself. You're going to need it more than I do after the morning train leaves tomorrow.''

Allie turned away from James's hard-eyed expression, biting back tears. She wished so desperately things could be different, but she had learned a long time ago that wishing did not make things so.

Her eyes intent on Mother Case's pale face, she did not notice that Sarah had subtly shifted her position on the front seat so she might listen to the exchange between James and Allie. She did not see the fresh surge of jealousy that altered Sarah's beautiful face into a vicious mask. She did not see the new determination in the set of her shoulders as Sarah faced forward once more.

chapter

twelve

THE SILENT TABLEAU in Margaret's bedroom was one of exhaustion and temporary relief. It had been a long and terrifying night. Mother Case, laboring for each breath through the endless hours before dawn, had finally found some relief, but the price she had paid was written in her pallor, in the deep lines in her face, in the marked deterioration from which Allie knew instinctively there was no return.

The realization that Mother Case had looked into the eyes of death but had managed to face it down once more filled Allie with pain at the part she had played in this close encounter.

Allie noted Jacob Case's exhaustion and sorrow as he sat on the opposite side of the bed, holding his wife's hand. Behind her, where he had stood most of the night, James lent his mother the solace of his presence in silence. Sarah had been noticeably absent during the long vigil. Claiming exhaustion after the first hour, she had retired to her room and had not been seen since.

But Mother Case had not appeared to note her daughter's absence. It was Allie to whom she had looked during the moments when her agony had abated enough to allow her lucidity, and it had pained Allie to realize the extent of Mother Case's concern for her.

Allie desperately wished she might talk to Mother Case, convince her that her fears were unfounded. Had circumstances been different, had not this violent attack occurred, she was certain she could have made Mother Case understand that Delaney's coldness did not extend to the place in his heart where he had declared Allie alone abided. When Mother Case was well enough to listen, she was determined to try again. She was just as determined that when she left with Delaney, it would be with Mother Case's blessing.

Raising her gaze to the window beside the bed, Allie was startled to see dawn beginning to streak the horizon. A momentary anxiety flicked across her mind, but she shrugged it away. Delaney was probably watching the coming of dawn just as she was, and he was probably regretting the harsh words between them just as much as she. She wished with all the strength within her that she were lying in his arms or standing beside him on the railroad platform awaiting the train as they had planned.

A touch on her arm interrupted Allie's thoughts, turning her toward James's pale face. She saw deep sorrow and acceptance of the inevitable there, and she suddenly wished she could put her arms around him and offer him consolation. Realizing that would be unwise, Allie attempted an encouraging smile. James did not return her smile, but his expression evinced a concern for her that did not waver.

"Allie, Mama seems to be resting. It's almost dawn. Why don't you lie down for a while? Pa and I will watch over Mama while you rest. If she wakes up and looks for you, we'll call."

Seeing the wisdom of James's suggestion, Allie nodded wearily and crossed the hall to the room she shared with Sarah. Desperately hoping the girl was sleeping, Allie pushed open the door and looked toward Sarah's bed. The bed was empty and the coverlet had not been disturbed!

Her heart pounding, a new, growing anxiety taking shape in her mind, Allie opened the wardrobe. She swallowed at the sight of her own few articles of clothing lying in a wrinkled heap on the floor. The rest of the cabinet was bare.

Unwilling to allow her suspicions full realization, Allie quickly left the room. She had run to the staircase when the door to Mrs. Case's room opened. James stepped into the hall and took her arm.

"What's the matter, Allie?"

"Sarah . . . she's not in bed."

James shook his head, not quite comprehending her concern. "Maybe she's in the kitchen."

"Her bed hasn't been slept in, James, and her clothes are gone."

His tired face suddenly flooding with color, James pulled Allie aside and descended the staircase without a word. Unable to move, Allie was still standing where he had left her a few minutes later when she heard James returning. Her gaze clung to his as he reached her side.

"The gelding is gone and so is Sarah."

Allie closed her eyes, knowing full well where Sarah had gone. Jealousy and contempt at her own weakness overwhelmed her. Sarah had been right all along. She had proved herself stronger than Allie, and had proved her love for Delaney took second place to no other. Fool that she was, Allie had allowed her own guilt and her concern for Mother Case to force her to turn her back on Delaney, if only temporarily. Sarah had taken the opportunity to step into the breach.

James's arms closed around her, drawing her close. Allie did not realize she was crying until James separated himself from her and wiped her tears from her face with a gentle touch. He was about to speak when the sound of a horse approaching in the yard below drew her attention. Within moments Allie was running down the staircase, hardly aware that James was behind her. She wanted so desperately for the rider to be Delaney. She needed to feel his arms around her, to feel his mouth on hers. She needed . . .

Reaching the front door with a gasping breath, Allie pushed it open.

It was not Delaney.

Reining the gelding to a halt in front of the porch, Sarah dismounted without a word. Her eyes strangely haunted, she attempted to walk past Allie and James without speaking. Not allowing her silent dismissal, James grasped his sister tightly by the shoulder.

"Where have you been, Sarah?"

No response.

Fury assuming control, James shook her roughly. "I asked you where you've been!"

Green eyes wide, Sarah returned his stare for a silent moment before jerking herself free of her brother's hold and running past him into the house. The sound of her footsteps on the stairs and the slamming of her bedroom door were her only response.

A new quaking besetting her shaking limbs, Allie did not hear James's softly spoken appeal. Suddenly unwilling to reenter the house, she turned and walked blindly into the yard. A deadening ache began inside her.

Why was it suddenly so clear to her that she had failed Delaney? Why had she not been able to view events through his eyes before this, to see that despite her avowal of love only a short time before that dreadful scene in town, she had turned her back on him? Why had she not seen that Mother Case had used her ill health unfairly to keep her from leaving? Why had she not seen that in allowing that to happen, she had sacrificed Delaney to salve her own conscience, when the only true guilt she should have felt was in failing him? Why had she not realized that in attempting to force Delaney to remain until she was ready to leave, she had proved to the hardened and penniless boy of fifteen who was still alive inside Delaney that her love was conditional, and that, as such, it was a luxury he could not afford. Why had she made Delaney believe that she, who had loved him all her life, did not love him enough.

It was Sarah, for all her faults, who loved Delaney enough to sacrifice all to be with him. Allie knew Delaney saw that now, and she knew he would not forget it.

In the distance a train whistle sounded, and a sob rose in Allie's throat. The echoing sound signaled the approach of the morning train. With a sudden, devastating insight, Allie knew it also signaled, with mournful finality, a last farewell.

Standing on the railroad platform, Delaney looked at the distant horizon, at the streaks of gray beginning to stripe the sky with morning. His breath was visible on the chill air as he squinted against the brightening light, the pain in his head throbbing anew.

Silently berating his own stupidity, he recalled his patient attention to that bottle of rye the night before. He gave a short, self-deprecating laugh as he remembered his surprise at the soft knock on his door when he was deeply under the influence of the whiskey an hour or so later. Certain that it was Allie, that she had relented and come to him, he had stumbled to the door, cursing his clumsiness and the stupidity that had allowed Allie to find him in such a condition. His heart had been pounding so hard that he was breathless when he opened the door. But it was not Allie.

His sense of loss as keen as it had been at that moment the night before, Delaney closed his eyes. Furious with the caprice of fate that had brought him a woman he despised instead of the only woman he wanted, he had finally allowed Sarah inside. Delaney gave another short laugh. And he had given Sarah something to remember him by.

Dismissing the memory, Delaney touched the corner of the note protruding from his jacket pocket. Insisting that his friend on the *Tribune* would come through, Max had slipped the note into Delaney's pocket before he said good-bye and told him to present it to his friend in person. Delaney supposed he would. He had nothing to lose.

His gaze dropped to the suitcase at his feet. A note and a suitcase. He was traveling light, much lighter than he had hoped.

The sound of a whistle in the distance announced the train's approach, and Delaney's heart began a nervous hammering in his chest. He would soon sever all ties with this place, but it would not be a painless separation. He would bleed. He would bleed for the rest of his life.

A light step behind him—a light, feminine touch on his arm and Delaney's heart leaped. He turned, but the joyful words that sprang to his lips went unspoken as he saw Lil's familiar smile.

"I'm sorry, Delaney. I'm thinkin' you're a bit disappointed it's me." Lil gave a small shrug, her light eyes suspiciously bright as her smile broadened. "If I could change myself into someone else for you, darlin', I sure enough would, but we are who we are, and I suppose we have to make the best of it."

Smoothing the shoulder of his new dark jacket, Lil appraised the open-necked white shirt beneath, the well-fitted trousers. She touched the brim of his hat with a little snap, her voice a low purr. "You look delicious, darlin', and I don't mind sayin' I wish with all my might that I was makin' this trip with you."

Delaney smiled, stroking Lil's shoulder with friendly familiarity. "I'm happy to see you, Lil."

Lil cocked her head, studying his face for a few short moments. "Well, maybe you are and maybe you aren't, but the fact is, I wasn't about to let you leave with nobody here to see you off. Hell, that isn't civilized—and it certainly isn't lovin'."

Delaney's smile dimmed. "No, I suppose it isn't."

The train whistled into sight, and Delaney squeezed Lil's shoulder as he looked into her face. He was suddenly grateful to have known this woman who had always given more than she had received from him. He pressed a light kiss against her lips.

"Thanks for everything, Lil."

A tear slipped down her cheek, and Lil tossed her flaming curls with annoyance as she brushed it away. She curved her small hand around his neck with a flirtatious smile. "That isn't the proper way to say good-bye, boy. Hasn't anybody ever taught you anythin'?"

Drawing his mouth down to hers, Lil pressed her lips against his in a deep, lingering kiss, releasing him with obvious regret as the train steamed into the station. She waited until he had picked up his suitcase before taking his hand once more.

"I'm thinkin' you're a fella I'm never goin' to forget, Delaney Marsh, so don't you go forgettin' old Lil, either. And if ever you need anythin', you know where to find me. I'm not about to move very far."

Lil drew back as the conductor called, "All aboard." She smiled as Delaney looked down at the neat roll of bills she had pressed into his hand.

"I can't take this from you, Lil."

"Yes, you can, and you will. Consider it a loan, and if you ever get rich enough, you can even pay me back with interest. Now get on that train and wave good-bye to me proper, Delaney Marsh."

Delaney took the few short steps up to the train. He stood on the platform between the cars as the train whistled once more and lurched forward.

Lil was waving vigorously, tears streaming down her face, but Delaney's last frantic glance searched the platform, the train yard, the street beyond. He swallowed at the realization that the petite, pale-haired figure he sought would not come racing around the corner of the station at the last moment, wanting to be scooped up into his arms and carried away with him. Her slender arms would not cling to his neck. Her dark eyes would not look up into his with love.

Lil's smiling face was no longer distinguishable in the distance, but she was still waving. Delaney waved back, then turned abruptly and entered the car. He found a seat and sat down, determined not to look back. He made himself a promise: From this moment on, he would only look forward.

There was very little behind him worth remembering.

Unable to run any longer, Allie dropped to her knees in the rapidly brightening field. Tears streamed down her cheeks as she struggled to catch her breath, but she gave little thought to her physical discomfort.

The shrill echoes of the train whistle were fading into the distance, and she strained to hear the last, plaintive cry. The medal Delaney had placed around her neck slipped outside her dress to hang in her line of vision, and a small sob escaped Allie's throat. Sitting back on the ground, she clutched the pendant in her hand as tightly as the pain clutched her heart.

When her breathing returned to normal, Allie rose to her feet. She was so empty without Delaney. There was a void inside her she knew would never be filled by anyone else. So she would wait. As long as it took, she'd wait.

That thought affording her little consolation, Allie turned back to the house. In the meantime, Mother Case needed her.

chapter

thirteen

"I TELL YOU, aside from being the longest telegraphic dispatch ever carried in a newspaper in the Northwest and a real milestone, it's great news! Do you realize what it means? This victory offsets Burnside's December defeat at Fredericksburg. It also means a Federal flanking movement in the West is in progress!"

Delaney considered Peter Mulrooney's statement as he faced him across the desk in his small, cluttered office. In the three months he had been working at the *Tribune* under the wing of this veteran newspaperman to whom Max had directed him, he had witnessed the highs and lows typical of his personality and of his boundless enthusiasm for his work. Pete Mulrooney was a staunch Federalist who would defend the cause with his mouth or his fists if it came to a showdown, despite his being past the prime of youth and having a bad leg.

Delaney looked down at the four-column report of the Battle of Stones River—or Murfreesboro, as it was known to some. It was a masterful piece by one of the *Tribune*'s best correspondents, Albert Holmes Bodman, describing Rosecrans's victory over Bragg in vivid detail. But Delaney felt little emotion other than admiration for a job well done.

He glanced up into Pete Mulrooney's flushed face. "It's an excellent job of reporting."

Pete Mulrooney's lined, jowled face, remarkably similar to Max's with its drooping lines and air of seedy dissipation, sagged with disappointment. As with Max, appearances were deceiving. Mulrooney was a top-notch newspaperman and he missed very little with those bleary, bloodshot eyes. His only problem was that he expected everyone to share his enthusiasm. Delaney did not.

"Dammit, boy, what do you have in your veins? Ice? You act like a newspaperman when it comes to putting words on paper, but that's where it all ends."

Delaney frowned. "Do you have some complaints about my work?"

Mulrooney paused, slowly drawing himself to his feet behind his paper-strewn desk. It occurred to Delaney, not for the first time, that all resemblance to Max Marshall came to an end as soon as Mulrooney stood up, for Pete Mulrooney was massive. Well over six feet, he stood eye-to-eye with Delaney only because his carriage was careless and stooped. His excess in height was carried to weight as well, and Delaney figured he weighed close to three hundred pounds. But little remained of what had undoubtedly been an impressive physique at one time. Instead, once broad shoulders were now rounded in a clerical-worker's curve, and a well-muscled chest had deteriorated into a paunch, the result of too many days behind a desk and, as Mulrooney was the first to admit, too many nights at Murphy's Bar.

But the brown eyes that pinned him from beneath bushy gray brows were astute and piercing, holding him fast.

"About your work? No, I guess I can't complain about your professionalism. You're all Max claimed you to be in his letters, and I'm damned glad I hired you, especially with the shortage of help we've had here since the war." Mulrooney's eyes narrowed into slits, and Delaney felt his hackles rise.

"If it still bothers you that I'm not wearing a uniform and lying in a ditch somewhere fighting for the Union, that's your problem, Mulrooney. When you hired me, I explained the goals I've set for myself. Nothing has changed since then, and my reasons for feeling the way I do are nobody's business but my own.''

''And I told you when I hired you that this paper is staunchly pro-Union and pro-Lincoln, that we won't harbor any Confederate sympathizers in our midst.''

Delaney paused, then gave a short laugh. ''Is that what you're thinking?'' He laughed again. ''You couldn't be more wrong. If I were to get personally involved in this conflict, I'd be wearing Union blue, not Confederate gray. I don't approve of slavery. I think every man should have the right to control his own destiny. That's what I intend to do, control my own destiny.'' Delaney held Mulrooney's gaze fast with his. ''But if you're uncomfortable with my outlook, I can look for another position.''

Refraining from an immediate response, Mulrooney considered Delaney in silence, his wild brows meeting over his hawklike nose. He shook his head. ''You're a cold bastard, aren't you?''

''What are you trying to say?''

''I'm trying to figure you out. I want to be honest with you, Marsh. You've got something special to bring to this kind of work. I sensed it the first time I saw you, and I saw it in the first article you wrote for me. You haven't let me down with anything you've done in the past three months, but the fact is, there's something missing. It's as if you have no feeling, as if nothing touches you.''

''That's my business.''

''Not when it's carried over into your work.''

''I thought you said you were satisfied with my work.''

''As far as it goes.''

''Meaning?''

''Meaning there's more to reporting than stating the facts. A good reporter brings a sense of the moment to his readers. He goes farther, searches deeper. He gets to the heart of things instead of being satisfied with straight-line reporting. You're intelligent and perceptive, Marsh, so I know you know what I'm trying to say.''

''You're trying to tell me I have no heart.''

Mulrooney considered Delaney's statement. He nodded. ''I suppose you're right.''

Delaney gave a shrug. ''It took you three months to realize

it?'' His lips twisted in a hard smile. "I've heard that before. But the truth is, I don't see why my personality should have any bearing on my work. I'm not a columnist. I'm a reporter, and I report events as I see them."

"I suppose that's the problem—your viewpoint. It's frigid. I get the feeling you'd be just as comfortable writing for the *Times* as for the *Tribune*."

Delancy gave a short laugh. "You're saying that I would have no problem working for the pro-Confederate *Times* when I just told you how I feel about slavery?"

"I'd say you're capable of subjugating your personal feelings to that extent."

Delaney shrugged. "Maybe you're right."

"That's a hell of a note!"

"But the fact is, I'd rather be working on a paper where that wouldn't be necessary."

"You have some saving grace, anyway."

Delaney's small smile faded. "What's the point of all this, Mulrooney?"

Taking a deep breath, Mulrooney shook his head. "I don't really know, Marsh. I suppose I'm just feeling you out, in a way. You've been working here three months, and I don't feel that I know you any better now than I did when you first walked in that door. You keep to yourself and don't say much, except for things that pertain to your work. From what I've been hearing, you don't even have much of an eye for the ladies, judging from the way you've been ignoring the ones who have taken to frequenting the post office downstairs when you're due to pass by."

Immediately defensive, Delaney stiffened.

Mulrooney raised his eyebrows, realizing he had touched a nerve. "I'm trying to help you, Marsh."

"I don't need your help with my personal life."

"Personal life, professional life—I'm trying to tell you that you have to let some of that ice inside you thaw if you're going to make it to where you want to be. You've got great potential, boy, but you have to bring something more to this work. You have to bring heart and soul to it."

"Soul? What if I told you I don't have a soul?"

Momentarily startled, Mulrooney gave a short laugh. "Well,

then I'd tell you that you'd better go out and find one." Suddenly serious, Mulrooney frowned. "Look, Marsh, I don't know much about your background except for your professional experience on the *Cass County News*, and I don't care to know. I suspect you haven't exactly led a sheltered life, but whatever happened to you, boy, put it aside and start out fresh, because all that talent you've got inside you isn't going to amount to much unless you cut it loose."

Delaney's clear eyes grew colder. "It's as loose as it's ever going to be."

"That's a real pity."

Delaney gave a short, hard laugh. "You're trying to tell me I'll never be another Albert Holmes Bodman."

"You could be."

Delaney's smile dropped away. "I'm satisfied to be Delaney Marsh."

The tired lines of Mulrooney's face sagged as he turned and walked back behind his desk. He lowered his massive frame into the chair with a suddenness that caused it to squeak loudly in protest. He picked up a slip of paper from the pile in front of him and held it out toward Delaney.

"I want you to go out to Camp Douglas, south of the city. Thirty-eight hundred Confederate prisoners have arrived for internment in the barracks there. There'll be a lot of concern about this whole thing from nearby residents, politicians, the city administration. I'm thinking a lot of our readers would like to know just what those prisoners are like—what they're thinking. I'll be expecting a pretty comprehensive piece when you're done."

"You'll get it."

Delaney attempted to take the paper from Mulrooney's hand, but Mulrooney held it fast.

"Did you hear a single word of what I said before, Marsh?"

A small muscle twitched in Delaney's cheek. "I heard you."

Mulrooney gave a brief nod. "I'll be expecting that piece for the morning paper."

"You'll get it."

Turning without another word, Delaney pulled open the office door. He barely acknowledged the faces that turned toward him as he zigzagged through the maze of desks in the city room.

On the street a few minutes later, he adjusted his jacket against the bite of winter cold and ignored the coquettish glance of a slender, dark-haired woman as she paused in front of the post office to give him a short wave. He did not spare a glance for the heavy pedestrian traffic or the solid bank of three-story buildings that housed some of the city's major newspapers. After three months, he was inured to being a part of that section of Clark Street between Randolph and Lake that was known as Newspaper Row.

If he had been in a better mood, he would have laughed at the conversation that had just been concluded in Mulrooney's office. The Emancipation Proclamation had become effective on January 1, but three million Negroes were still slaves. General Grant had begun a sanguinary struggle to open the Mississippi. The capital of the United States was threatened, and some people thought the South was capable of breaking the Federal blockade. There was even danger that the Confederates and their Copperhead supporters would carry the war into Illinois and Indiana.

And Peter Mulrooney's main concern this morning was that Delaney Marsh had no heart.

Delaney took a deep breath in an attempt to draw his anger under control. He slowed his step, the thought occurring to him that he was not as emotionless as Mulrooney seemed to think. But that big Irishman was a deal more insightful than he had expected. Or was it, perhaps, that the emptiness inside him was more visible than he realized?

Delaney dismissed that thought. He was an old hand at disguising his emotions. The only person he could not fool was himself. Despite his determination not to look back, his mind continued to betray him. In countless dreams, Allie spoke to him, laughed with him, appealed to him, and returned his loving. He knew that his determination to dispel those memories had made him harder and more bitter than ever. But if he had failed so far to escape thoughts of Allie, he was now all the more determined to succeed.

Slowing down, Delaney reached into his pocket for the paper Mulrooney had handed him. The barracks south of Chicago. He surveyed the street for a carriage. Spotting one vacant, he raised his hand in summons, not realizing he had caught the attention of two young women passing by. He did not notice the appreciation with which they studied his well-dressed figure, the line of his strong profile. He did not hear the gasps of admiration that escaped their lips as he turned in their direction to rake the street with his clear-eyed gaze. Instead, he entered the vehicle, barking the address to the driver in a tone that set the carriage off at a brisk pace.

He had two thoughts on his mind. First, he was determined to do a job on this assignment that would make Mulrooney eat his words. Second, he meant to make this the first day that he would truly begin to put the past behind him.

The frigid January temperature had penetrated the small upstairs room where Allie sat beside Mother Case's bed. Allie could not seem to stop shaking. She glanced toward the window, looking at the stark winter landscape. Trees void of leaves now wore a cover of snow frozen to their branches by plummeting overnight temperatures. In the fields, exhausted furrows, barren of summer's plenty, stretched to the horizon in a network of low, rolling mounds covered by a blanket of unblemished white. The scene glistened with a pristine beauty in the afternoon sun, but the beauty was cold and frozen, just like her heart.

Drawing her gaze back to the room around her, Allie was intensely aware of the stale air and the silence. She had grown accustomed to both in the last few months, having spent the major portion of her day sitting beside Mother Case's bed. But she had experienced a new discomfort in the closeness of late.

Clutching her heavy shawl around her shoulders, Allie swallowed against the queasiness that rose to her throat. She was grateful that Mrs. Case was sleeping and could not view her distress. She was determined not to allow it to progress to a more advanced state.

In an effort to take her mind from her physical discomfort, Allie looked toward the woman lying almost hidden beneath the heavy comforters. The vigil at Mother Case's bedside would not be of much longer duration. The doctor had not needed to speak the words on his last visit. Everyone knew Mother Case would not last much longer.

Allie's eyes touched Mother Case once more, and the well of sorrow within her deepened. The dear woman was so still. Always slight, she was now no more than a shadow against the spotless bed linens, her sweet face gray and lifeless. Allie listened with sudden anxiety for the sound of her breathing. She released a relieved breath when she heard the shallow sound, not quite understanding the complexities of a sickness that forced the victim to labor pitifully to breathe at one moment while allowing her to do so with unexpected ease the next.

Her mind on Mother Case's deterioration, Allie gave no thought to the changes that had taken place in her own appearance in the months since Delaney's departure. In truth, she had given scant attention to her reflection as she had absentmindedly braided her hair each morning and twisted the coils around her head. She had paid little notice to the shadows beneath her eyes, which bespoke a sorrow not entirely related to the sickroom. She had not noticed the marked thinning of her already slight frame or the complete absence of color in her cheeks. Instead, she had occupied her time in going over in her mind, time and again, the events that had led her to this point in her life. Her regrets were overwhelming.

Swallowing against the bile rising in her throat, Allie gripped the medal suspended around her neck—Delaney's medal— needing its comfort. She knew her time in this house was limited. Although she was uncertain where she would go, she did not expect to remain after Mother Case was gone. She was certain she would not be wanted or needed in a place where hatred and resentment of her abounded.

The hatred was on Sarah's part. Sarah had changed little since Delaney's departure, except that her abhorrence of Allie seemed to have intensified. That was evident from the venom in her unrelenting gaze and the fact that she had spoken hardly a word to Allie since Delaney left.

But the truth was, Sarah had spoken hardly a word to anyone since that morning. Shocking everyone, she had seemed to withdraw into herself, spending most of her time in her room. She had steadfastly refused to see any of her suitors, including Bobbie Clark, who was genuinely distressed. He had not skipped a single week in stopping by.

Always difficult, Sarah had surpassed herself in her dealings with the family. Her mother's dire state of health affecting her little, she had refused to pull her fair share of work in the house until Papa Case had stepped in with a threat she could not ignore. In silent protest, she had kept even more closely to her room and had maintained her unyielding silence. This behavior was so uncharacteristic of Sarah, with her need for attention, that it had caused everyone deep concern.

But as Mother Case's illness had progressed to the critical stage, concern for Sarah's reclusiveness had ceased. Allie could not understand Sarah's resentment of her own mother or her refusal to spend time with Margaret despite the knowledge that her mother was dying. Allie was aware that her thoughts were of small consequence in the final outcome of things, but she also knew that neither Jacob nor James would ever forgive Sarah.

Closing her eyes as yet another wave of nausea all but overwhelmed her, Allie clutched the medal tighter, desperately fighting the chills that shook her.

"You need some fresh air, Allie. Then you'll feel better."

Allie jumped at the thin, unexpected voice that rose from beneath the comforters. Determined not to reveal the full extent of her physical discomfort, Allie rose carefully to her feet and took the few steps to the bed with a smile on her lips.

"I didn't realize you were awake, Mother Case." Reaching out, Allie stroked back a silver strand that clung to Margaret's gray cheek. "It's almost suppertime; I'll get you something to eat if you're hungry."

"I'm not concerned with food right now, dear." Her faded eyes assessing Allie's face, Mrs. Case attempted a smile. "My dear Allie, you look terrible."

At Allie's startled expression, Mother Case's smile softened. "I'm the one who's ill, Allie. Only I have the excuse to look poorly. I don't like to think you've been neglecting your own health to take care of me."

"I'm all right." Allie pulled her shawl closer, tears filling her eyes. "I'm chilled today, that's all." Making an attempt to change the subject, Allie looked toward the window. "Have you looked outside, Mother Case? The fields are several feet deep in snow, and the surface is frozen solid."

"And you haven't had a breath of fresh air for a week." Allie protested, but Mrs. Case reached for her hand, taking it with a small shake of her head. "There's no use denying it, Allie. I haven't been so ill that I haven't seen you sitting by my bed day after day. You've kept good watch over me. You've been a good daughter to me, Allie, better than the child of my own flesh.''

"Mother Case, Sarah is unhappy."

"Sarah wanted Delaney, and he's gone. He wouldn't take her with him, and I credit him for his intelligence, even if I am angry with him for—"

"Please."

In deference to Allie's appeal, Margaret halted her words. She suddenly gasped. An expression of panic flickered across her face, only to disappear as quickly as it had come.

"Are you all right, Mother Case?"

"It was just a twinge." Margaret paused, holding Allie's gaze in the brief silence. "And then again, maybe it was the Lord's prodding finger."

"Please, Mother Case."

"Allie, you must try to understand that I know I'm dying. I've known for a long time that it will not be long before I'm called home. I can only think that the Lord has not seen fit to make his final summons in consideration of my many prayers. Do you know what I prayed for, Allie?"

Allie shook her head.

"I prayed that God would not call me home until I was able to see my children settled and happy in their lives. But time is growing short, Allie."

"Mother Case, it will be a long time before Sarah accepts that she cannot have the man she wants."

"I'm not talking about Sarah. She has made her own unhappiness with her disregard for the unhappiness she has caused others. She will never be happy until she realizes she cannot always take from life, that there comes a time when she must give. The children I am concerned about are James and you, Allie."

Allie averted her head, but Mrs. Case continued.

"James loves you, Allie. He told me he asked you to be his wife."

Allie could not meet her eyes. "That was before."

"Before you went off with Delaney? I know that. I also know it has had no effect on James's love for you. He's told me that himself, several times these past few months. He said he considers everything that happened his fault. He—"

"I can't marry James, Mother Case, even if he does still want me. I don't expect to stay here on the farm after you no longer need me. I'm going away."

"Away!" Surprise flushed Margaret's face a pale red. "Not to Delaney! You'll never be happy with him. We both love him, but we must be honest with ourselves. He doesn't possess the capacity for true happiness. He's too bitter and angry."

Allie closed her eyes against Mrs. Case's words, opening them a moment later when she again had herself under control. "No, I'm not going to Delaney. I failed him and he'll never trust me again."

"Dear, you must realize that it's for the best. You must not berate yourself for whatever happened that night between Delaney and you, and you must never think of leaving us. If it were possible, I would strike that night from your mind as thoroughly as I have struck it from mine."

"Mother Case—"

"James loves you, Allie. That will never change. He still wants you to be his wife. My dear, it is my fervent wish that I might see that union accomplished before I must leave you."

Margaret's voice was beginning to weaken. Her lengthy speech had taken its toll, and a slight quaking began to shake her frail limbs as she grasped Allie's hand more tightly.

"Allie, dear, I don't have much longer. Please think about what I've said. James—"

"I'm leaving here, Mother Case! I can't marry James, and if he knew, he wouldn't want me!"

Margaret's gaze was suddenly intense. "If he knew what, Allie?"

"If he knew I'm going to have Delaney's child."

The flash of pain on Mother Case's face intensified her own, and Allie drew herself abruptly to her feet. She took a short step in retreat even as Margaret raised her hand toward her.

"I'm going downstairs now. I'll send Papa Case up so you won't be alone."

"Allie."

Turning from the sympathy in Mother Case's voice, Allie walked rapidly to the door. In the hall, her pace accelerated almost to a run. She reached the base of the staircase breathless, panic overwhelming her as she paused once more. Dropping her shawl on a nearby chair, she snatched her coat from the peg on the wall as she turned toward the kitchen and called, "Papa Case, Mother Case is alone. I'm going out for a while."

James followed his father into the hall, his expression concerned as Jacob started up the stairs. Allie could not face James.

"Is something wrong, Allie?"

"No. I . . . I need some fresh air."

"It's freezing outside."

"I'll be all right."

Clutching her coat closed, Allie slipped her shawl over her head and turned toward the door. She had closed the door behind her before James could utter another word of protest.

A gust of bitter cold cut through her cloth coat as Allie walked across the yard. Her quaking increased, but she leaned into the blast and lengthened her step. She needed this, to have her mind forcibly removed from the anxieties that had left her no peace, and the prospect of being alone when she needed someone most.

Her stiff hand moving inside her coat, Allie touched the medal that rested against her breast. No, she would not be completely alone.

Drawing her coat more firmly around her, Allie trudged on through the snow. She did not hear Jacob step out of his wife's room and call his son upstairs. She did not see James enter his mother's room and close the door behind him a few moments later.

She did not hear Margaret Case's quivering voice as she whispered, "James, take my hand. I have something to tell you."

Delaney adjusted the collar of his coat up around his throat and hunched his shoulders against the penetrating cold. The wind was bitter and piercing as it whistled through the corridors between the rows of barracks at Camp Douglas. Belatedly he realized that he had chosen this new coat more with an eye to impress than with the thought of keeping warm, and he was suffering the consequences.

He perused the blank faces of the men standing behind the hastily erected fences of the prison. Far less adequately dressed than he, many of them stamped their feet and rubbed their hands in an effort to keep warm, but it was not those men who held his eye. It was the others who drew his gaze, those who were motionless and silent. Their Confederate gray uniforms looked faded and worn, and it bothered him that their vacant expressions seemed familiar. Where had he seen those empty stares before?

Realization hit Delaney with the force of a blow, and he was suddenly staggered. How could he have forgotten? He had seen that same look on cold winter nights in the streets and alleyways of New York, on the faces of the children with whom he had shared warm doorways or empty packing crates. It reflected a state of mind that exceeded despair, a loss of hope so profound that it scarred the heart.

Delaney's step faltered under the debilitating effect of again being witness to the cruel annihilation of the human spirit. He had suffered rigors such as these a long time ago. He had survived them, and the experience had made him strong. He had made only one mistake in the time since, and it had almost been his undoing.

Mulrooney had said he had no heart. Mrs. Case had said he needed no one.

Steadily, deliberately, Delaney walked up to the fence, toward one of the stone-faced men there. He had worn that expression himself a long time ago. He would never wear it again.

Allie wasn't cold anymore. The gusts of wind that had battered her when she emerged from the house had abated. The late afternoon sun had slipped from behind a snow-laden cloud and was now shedding its brilliance on the frostbitten landscape and turning it into a glittering, jewel-bedecked panorama that was breathtaking. It was so beautiful. This dazzling resplendence was a parting gift to her, a memory she would not allow to fade. When she was far away from here, she would try to always remember this day.

Allie was not quite certain how far she had walked. She was not cold, but she could not seem to control the shudders that racked her. Perhaps she didn't feel cold because her hands and feet were so numb, but whatever the reason, she could not make herself go back yet. Mother Case had been right. She needed this time away from the sickroom to clear her mind of the cobwebs of sorrow and despair that had made logical thought impossible.

At the sound of the crunch of footsteps in the snow behind her, Allie turned stiffly toward James's approach. He wore a heavy jacket and boots, but no hat, and his fair hair glinted in the sun. His was a comforting image, but she didn't want company right now. She just wanted to be alone.

James halted as he drew within a few feet of her. His face was pinched, and his light brows furrowed in a frown. "Allie, it's cold. You've been out here too long."

"I'm not ready to go back inside yet, James."

The lines of James's face tightened into unexpected anger. "When will you be ready? When you're chilled to the bone? When you've succeeded in getting yourself sick? Are you trying to punish yourself? Is that what you want?"

Startled, Allie shook her head. She clutched her shawl tighter as it threatened to slide off her head. "What I'm doing out here is my concern, James. You're not my keeper. I can take care of myself."

Grasping her hand, James held it up to her face, forcing her to look at it. It was surprisingly colorless, almost blue.

"Is this how you take care of yourself? The circulation has almost stopped in your hands, and if I don't miss my guess, your feet are in the same condition. Do you know what it's like when frost touches the bone, Allie? It's dangerous, and it's painful."
His stiff expression suddenly breaking, James pulled her close, wrapping his arms around her as he whispered unevenly into her ear, "I don't want you to suffer any more pain, Allie. You've suffered enough. You deserve to know the same kind of love you've given to others. Let me take care of you."

A sudden realization touched Allie's mind, and she stiffened. Suddenly struggling to be free of James's arms, she pulled back. Her pale face flooded with color.

"She told you, didn't she?" Allie shook her head in disbelief. "Why? I didn't want anyone to know."

Anguish that matched her own was reflected in James's attempted smile. "You can't hide the truth forever, Allie. It's going to be obvious in a few months."

"I'll be gone before then."

"No."

The tight knot of tears that choked her throat made response difficult, but Allie persisted in the attempt. "You . . . you know

Mother Case won't last much longer, James. When she's gone, I'm going, too. I'll find a place where I can work, where no one knows me, and I'll—''

"No. You'll stay here."

"I won't bring shame down on this house, James! I won't let everyone whisper how foolish your family was to take orphans from the streets into your home just so they could dishonor you."

"You're going to stay here and have your baby, Allie. And no one will talk, because you're going to marry me. The baby will be mine."

Allie took a sharp step backwards. "No, James. The baby is Delaney's. It will always be his. I won't take that from him."

"Is that who you're worrying about, Delaney Marsh?" James's fair-skinned face was incredulous. "How can you be such a fool? Marsh took what he wanted from you and he's put you behind him. You still cling to the hope that he'll come back, don't you? Well, he won't! You're a part of his past now, and he won't give you another minute's thought. He doesn't deserve you, and he doesn't deserve the child you're carrying."

"You're wrong, James. Delaney loves me. It's my fault we're apart. I let him down."

"Marsh is incapable of truly loving you, Allie. You can say I'm prejudiced against him, and maybe it's true, but Mama isn't, and she's told you the same thing."

"Mother Case is wrong."

His gaze stricken, James fell silent. Then, exasperated, he shook his head. "You're shuddering, Allie. We shouldn't be having this conversation here."

"Yes, we should, James. We're alone here, and there's no chance of our being overheard. I don't want to upset you or anyone else when I tell you that I can't marry you. There are so many reasons." At James's attempted protest, Allie shook her head. "You should marry someone more deserving of you, James."

"I don't want anyone else, Allie."

"You deserve someone who will love you more than anyone else in the world. I'm not that person."

"You could be."

"No. My mind and heart are too filled with Delaney. Can't you see that? Delaney didn't leave me; I left him—turned my back on him. And while I still carry the guilt for betraying our love, I can never marry anyone else."

"Allie, the guilt isn't yours."

"It is."

"Allie." Sliding his arms around her once more, James held her close. "None of this makes any difference to me. I love you. I'll always love you. I know it's useless to say anything else right now, but I want you to know that." Releasing her, James stepped back and took her hand. "Will you come back in the house with me now, Allie? It's too cold out here."

With a low, resigned sigh, Allie nodded her head. James was right. She was behaving like a fool. It was cold, and she could not afford to get sick. Good health was necessary for her plans for the future.

Allowing James to draw her supportively against his side, Allie walked back to the house. It occurred to her that the reasons for loving were unfathomable. Surely she had never done anything to deserve James's deep devotion, and she suddenly wished, with all the fervor within her, that she could return that love and be the wife he truly deserved. But there was only one man in her heart, and while he remained there, she could not give herself to another.

Her thoughts thus engaged, Allie stepped into the house with James close behind her. The warm air touched her face and she felt an unexpected relief. She had been colder than she thought, and she supposed she owed James yet another debt for saving her from herself. Drawing her shawl from her head, she was about to express that thought when Sarah suddenly stepped forward from a darkened corner, pinning her with the malevolence of her gaze.

"I heard Mama talking to James. I didn't believe it at first, but it's true, isn't it? You *are* going to have Delaney's child."

Backing up against James's chest, Allie raised her chin defensively. "Yes, it's true."

Sarah's wild laughter brought a heated flush to Allie's face. The shrill sound was still echoing when Sarah brought it to an abrupt halt with a tight smile. "And James still wants to marry you. How very noble of him, and how fortunate for you."

"I won't be marrying James."

"Oh, yes, you will!" Rage turning her smile into a contorted mask, Sarah took a threatening step forward. "You will marry him, damn you! I will not have anyone suspect the truth! I will not have anyone know Delaney Marsh fathered your child as well as mine!"

A sudden silence followed Allie's gasp. Staggered, she was hardly conscious of the hand James raised to her arm in support.

"Yes, it's true, you stupid fool! What did you think happened that night I went to Delaney? Did you think he turned me away when I went to his room? You'd like to believe that, but he didn't. I knew once he was away from this house he would act differently, and I was right. He let me into his room, and I thought I had won. Oh, but I didn't give Delaney credit for being the true bastard that he is. Damn him, he took everything I gave him—myself and all my love—and when he was done, he threw it back in my face! He said he was traveling light and had no intention of taking anyone with him. He told me he had given me something to remember him by and he hoped it was enough, because that was all I was ever going to get from him!"

Unable to speak, unwilling to believe Sarah's virulent tirade, Allie leaned back against James's chest. His supporting hand gripped her tighter as Sarah's wild laughter sounded once more and she then continued, "I suppose it is rather humorous in a way. And so generous of Delaney—to leave us both something to remember him by."

"No, it isn't true. You're lying!" Managing to choke words past the obstruction in her throat, Allie shook her head. "Delaney didn't. He couldn't. He loved me. He said he loved and wanted only me!"

"Fool! Why do you suppose I've stayed in my room these past months, hardly spending any time with my own dying mother? The early stages of pregnancy aren't easy, are they, Allie dear? Why do you think I've refused to see any of my beaux? Because I couldn't stand the thought of someone touching me after Delaney humiliated me! But that's over now. The child you have in your belly has forced it to be over."

Taking another step closer as Allie reeled under the shock of her revelations, Sarah hissed into Allie's white face, "I will not let Delaney Marsh demean me further by allowing anyone to know he fathered both our children on the same night! I am special! I always have been! I am more woman than you will ever be, and I will not allow anyone to consider that there is any similarity between us at all! So you *will* marry James, if you know what's good for you!'' Sarah shot a short glance to her brother's stiff face. ''And you'll take care of her, won't you, James? You'll pretend to be the loving husband and father because you know you're no match for Delaney Marsh—you never were and you never will be—and this is the only way you would ever have gotten her.''

James responded in a low, controlled voice, ''If I were you, Sarah, I would devote a little more thought to what you're going to do and a little less to Allie's plight. At least Allie has me. Who do you have?''

''Stupid James! I have Bobbie, that's who! He's more of a fool for me than you are for Allie! It won't take much to convince him that Delaney took advantage of me. He'll be only too happy to save me from disgrace by marrying me and claiming the child as his, especially when I tell him I love him.''

''He'll never believe you, not after all this.''

Sarah's small laugh brought a heated color to James's face. ''Oh, yes, he will.''

Finally regaining her voice, Allie shook her head in an unconscious effort to negate the horror of reality. ''It isn't true, Sarah. You're lying. You're not pregnant. Delancy couldn't—''

''Look at me, damn you!'' Pulling off her oversized apron, Sarah gave a low, disgusted snarl. ''You've faded to skin and bones, but Delaney's seed is blooming full and well inside me. Damn you, I said look!''

Allie's gaze fell to Sarah's waist. Her throat tightened convulsively, slowly choking the air from her lungs. It was there, obvious to the eye, the thickening of Sarah's waist, and the small, high protrusion of her stomach, previously hidden by her voluminous aprons. Oh, God, it was true!

''I love you, Allie,'' Delaney had said. ''I've never loved anyone but you. I'll always love you.''

Lies! Nothing but lies! The words had slipped so easily from Delaney's lips and taken root in her heart. But they had meant nothing! Only a few hours later he had taken Sarah in the same way and joined her body with his own. With that act, he had tarnished the beauty they had shared. Delaney had defiled her, made her unclean, because he had never loved her the way she loved him.

Everything he had said had been lies. Lies. Lies. Lies.

The word drummed over and over in Allie's brain, a deadening litany of despair. Fragmented images deluged her mind, touching her with a new anguish. Their numbing assault was more than she could bear, supplanting time and space, removing the reality of the darkened house, the seething hatred of the woman standing before her, the truth her whirling mind could not accept. Darkness and oblivion hovered at the edges of fading reality. Abruptly they overwhelmed her, and Allie slipped into the merciful void of unconsciousness.

Delaney adjusted the lamp on his desk, but the script on the sheets of paper in front of him was still blurred. Sitting back in his chair, he rubbed his tired eyes. Allowing himself a few minutes' respite, he gazed around the limited confines of his rented room, considering the faded wallpaper, the worn oilcloth on the floor, the sparse furnishings—a bed, a dresser, a night table, and the desk at which he sat. It was a far cry from the home he hoped one day to own, but it was a beginning.

Unwilling to allow his thoughts to stray further, Delaney turned back to the report with which he had struggled for the greater part of the night. Despite himself, the plight of the Confederates in Camp Douglas had touched a raw spot inside him. Destiny and circumstance had taken the course of their lives out of their hands, and they had suffered the consequences. Somehow, he could not help but relate their circumstances to his own.

Fate had thrown Allie and him together. He had not wanted responsibility for anyone to enter his life. It had, and with it had come love. But fate had interfered once more, turning Allie from him. His shock, anger, and pain had been profound at that moment outside the Farmers' Meeting Hall when Allie had left his side. He had been certain that nothing and no one could accomplish that after the love they had shared. Why hadn't Allie been able to see that Mrs. Case would use any weapon at her disposal to keep her from leaving? Why hadn't she trusted him enough to consign the ailing woman to her family's care and take his hand?

The answer was simple. She had not loved him enough.

But in the silence of the night, Delaney could not deny that he wanted Allie still, that the spot inside him that had been Allie's alone was now a cold, aching void that numbed him.

Suddenly angry with himself for slipping into a familiar trap, Delaney gave the sheaves lying on the desk in front of him a last dismissive glance. Pushing back his chair, he drew himself to his feet. He was too tired to work now, and too tired to think. Tomorrow he would be contemptuous of this fleeting weakness. And then he would force himself to go on.

chapter

fourteen

So MUCH HAD happened in the last month.

Allie was trembling, but not from the cold. She glanced briefly out the window of her room, her mind registering the fact that a fresh snowfall the night before had refreshed the white blanket that had covered the ground since the beginning of the year. Not a single track marred the rolling field of white that met the horizon. It was breathtakingly beautiful.

A sound in the hallway below drew Allie's mind from its wanderings, and she was suddenly grateful there was no witness to her shaken state. She was grateful Sarah was gone, even though the circumstances of her departure could have been more pleasant.

A frown creased Allie's fair brow. Within three days of the confrontation between Sarah, James, and herself a month before, Sarah had run off and married Bobbie Clark. Neither family had been present at the wedding, which had taken place in the next county, and since Sarah's condition was obvious, it was the general opinion around town that Bobbie had done the right thing in taking responsibility for his actions.

James had commented that Bobbie had accepted with grace

the few ribald comments around town about his hasty marriage, and she was certain Bobbie had told no one, not even his family, that the child Sarah carried was not his. She did not think Bobbie realized how Sarah had manipulated him, and, in truth, she hoped he never would. He had appeared happy when Sarah and he had stopped by shortly after their marriage, and Allie was grateful that Sarah had made her peace with her mother, even if they had seen her seldom since.

The sound of male voices raised in hearty conversation drew Allie from her meandering thoughts, and she turned to the mirror to check the new blue gown that James had insisted she buy. It fit smoothly against the slender lines of her body, minimizing her weight loss of the last few months. The shade softened her stark lack of color, and the blue ribbons secured in her upswept hair lent an air of festivity to her appearance. She was glad that her waist was still slender, and that except for the slight increase in the size of her breasts, there was no outward sign of her pregnancy.

She was exceedingly grateful for James's sake, because today was their wedding day.

The male voices below drew closer. They were coming upstairs, and Allie's heart began an accelerated beating.

As she had many times during the past month, she told herself she should be grateful for Sarah's malicious revelation of her pregnancy. The shock had forced her to face some important facts.

The first was that Delaney would never come back. Whatever course their lives might have taken if she had remained at his side that night outside the Farmers' Meeting Hall, the pattern for the future had been set by the events that followed.

The second harsh reality was that Delaney was guilty of the true betrayal. He had made love to Sarah only hours after declaring his love for Allie, only hours after they had consummated the beautiful emotion they shared with an act of love more binding for her than a spoken vow. In doing so, he had reduced that emotion to the level of physical lust and had forced her to face the reality that their views of love and fidelity were so diverse that although she loved him still, the disparity separated them more effectively than the miles between them ever could. It was a disparity that would keep them apart forever.

The third reality, and the one that had brought her to this day, was that her own feelings were no longer of paramount importance. Her first responsibility was to her child. She could not make her child suffer the insecurities of her own childhood simply because of her pride. James would make an excellent husband and father. And she was determined she would make him a good wife.

An unexpected flutter of movement inside her momentarily took Allie's breath. Her hand moved to her stomach in the realization that the child within her had made itself felt for the first time. She wanted to share her incredulity and joy with someone. Tears filled her eyes, for she knew that person would not be Delaney.

The voices in the hallway drew closer, and she felt a moment of panic. There was one thing left to do. One final cord to sever.

Reaching inside the high neckline of her dress with trembling fingers, Allie touched the chain hanging around her neck. Every nerve in her body screaming in protest, she slipped it off. For a few seconds, she held the medal in her hand. It was warm, comforting, against her palm, and she clutched it tight with regret.

With great determination, Allie turned and walked to the dresser behind her. Pulling open the top drawer, she placed the medal on top of the neatly arranged undergarments folded there and pushed the drawer closed.

Disturbingly numb, Allie turned at the knock at the door. Moving forward unsteadily, she opened the door to meet James with a shaky smile. She stared in silence at his fair, freshly shaven face, the pale dusting of freckles across the bridge of his nose. His light hair was carefully slicked into neatness, and he wore a dark jacket and trousers purchased for the occasion. He looked very handsome, and she knew she was exceedingly fortunate to have this man love her. She hoped to be worthy of him.

"You look beautiful, Allie."

"Oh, James." Allie shook her head. "I don't."

"You do." His voice emphatic, James hesitated only a moment before touching his lips to hers. "Even if you don't believe me, it's true." Raising his hand, James cupped her cheek, a world of love flowing from his eyes as his voice dropped to a whisper. "You'll never regret this day, Allie."

Allie covered his hand with hers. "It's your regrets I worry about, James."

"Never, Allie. This is the happiest day of my life." Slipping his hand around hers, James drew it down to his side as he urged her into the hallway toward the slender gentleman awaiting them by Mother Case's bedroom door.

Allie swallowed past the lump in her throat and forced a smile. "Hello, Reverend Whittier."

"My dear, you are a beautiful bride. The Lord will bless your generosity in consenting to this hasty marriage in order that dear Margaret might still be with us to witness it."

Unable to respond, Allie followed James as he entered his mother's room. Leaning over the bed to kiss her gray cheek, Allie was struck by the joy in her dim eyes.

Mother Case raised her hand, and Allie held it tightly, realizing the silent woman was too debilitated to speak. James's arm circled her waist. She turned to him, hardly able to control her quaking at his low whisper.

"I love you, Allie."

Unable to risk words, Allie nodded in response.

"Are you ready, children?" the minister asked.

"We are."

His voice deep and resonant, the Reverend Mr. Whittier started the ceremony, but Allie did not hear the words. Echoes of countless tears resounding in her mind, she was too busy saying goodbye.

chapter

fifteen

THE BRIGHT SUN warm on his bare head, Delaney walked rapidly along Clark Street. It had been a long, cold winter, and spring was extremely welcome. That was as obvious on the smiling faces of pedestrians passing by as it had been in the *Tribune* office yesterday, where the lighthearted atmosphere had not quite fit the news from the front.

Spring had brought about no improvement in the Union's efforts in the war. General Hooker had replaced Burnside at the head of the Army of the Potomac in April and had set off confidently in another Union attempt to take Richmond. Hooker's confidence had suffered a blow when his army was put to flight by Lee's much smaller forces at Chancellorsville. As things now stood, Richmond looked as far away as ever.

The outlook to the west was just as bleak. There, Grant appeared to be making little headway in the swamps and wilderness areas near the Mississippi as he applied pressure to Vicksburg.

In the city, the news since the turn of the year had been both good and bad. Chicago had replaced Cincinnati as the pork-packing center of the United States, and residents were jubilant at the growth of the economy. The city had received a new charter granting the municipality additional powers. Earlier in the year, Wilbur Storey, the editor of the *Chicago Times* who had become the Union's most vehement opponent, was censured by the federal government. The order to shut down the presses caused a riot, and President Lincoln revoked the order, but the bad feelings had not yet come to rest.

Delaney's face softened into a smile. He was grateful his own bad feelings had finally been laid to rest. He was well aware that his decision of the night before, arrived at after months of fighting a long-standing inner battle, was the reason behind the feeling of peace with which he had awakened.

A new enthusiasm quickened Delaney's step as he approached the Clark Street post office and the offices of the *Tribune* directly overhead. He glanced up toward the window facing the street, wondering if Pete Mulrooney's bloodshot eyes had followed his approach. He would not be surprised if they had. Mulrooney was a hard taskmaster and had overseen Delaney's work with unrelenting diligence. Of late, he was certain something was brewing behind that scowl. He supposed Mulrooney would let him know what it was when he was good and ready.

Nodding briefly to the young woman posed so artfully in the doorway of the post office, her fashionably coiffed brown hair contrasting well with her green walking ensemble, Delaney felt a glimmer of recognition flash across his mind. He had seen her in much the same spot on several occasions this week. The woman's heavy-lidded glance answered the question his mind had posed, and he absentmindedly thought he probably should be flattered to be so pursued. He wasn't.

Delaney pulled open the street door and started up the stairs to the *Tribune* office. As Mulrooney had commented several months before, he hadn't been much interested in women since arriving in Chicago, aside from the physical comfort they provided. He had told himself he was too busy to allow a woman a place in his life.

Pushing open the door of the *Tribune*'s noisy city room, Delaney nodded toward the reporters who turned his way. A feeling of mutual respect existed between him and his co-workers, but he had not gotten close to any of them. Since joining the staff seven months before, he had steadfastly devoted himself to the advancement of his career. He had taken time for little else.

Pausing at Mulrooney's office, Delaney knocked briefly. After catching the editor's eye through the window, he entered and pulled the door shut behind him.

"What are you doing here, Marsh? You're supposed to be out covering the Sanitary Commission meeting. You know how strongly I feel about that organization. There's a real need for the services of a nonpartisan group to overlook the suffering that comes about as a part of an extended war, and since it looks as if this war's going to be extended for a few more years—"

"I took care of it."

"What do you mean, you took care of it?"

"Just what I said." Reaching into his coat pocket, Delaney withdrew some folded sheets of paper. "I interviewed the principals on the committee yesterday, and I've already written the story. That should beat all the other dailies into print. You can send somebody to do a short report on the meeting."

Delaney threw the papers onto the desk, but Mulrooney gave them only a brief glance. "We can talk about that later. I've got something else I want to discuss with you. Sit down."

Delaney's nerve endings were prickling. "No, I'll stand."

"Suit yourself."

Mulrooney drew his full bulk to his feet. He walked to the window facing the street, his deep voice rumbling over his shoulder as he spoke. "We've had a few talks about your work since you started working for the *Tribune*, Marsh."

Delaney nodded, his expression tightening. The silence caused Mulrooney to turn in his direction.

"You were good when you came here. I told you then I saw great promise in you. I also told you that you were a cold bastard and it showed in your work."

Delaney did not respond.

Taking a few steps forward, Mulrooney rested his large palms on his desk to look up into Delaney's cautious expression. "How much do you know about Albert Holmes Bodman?"

Mulrooney's question was unexpected, and Delaney took a moment to gather his thoughts.

"Not much," he said, finally. "I know he's the *Tribune*'s top war correspondent. I've never met him, but I hear he's young, sharp, intelligent, and dedicated to his work. I also hear he's quiet and a bit of a recluse. On the other hand, he's supposed to be a damned good poker player and a man who knows where to invest his money and when. I've heard some of the other men call him 'the cotton broker.' They say that he's made a lot of money, that everything he does is legal and aboveboard, and that it doesn't interfere with the performance of his job. Of course, that's all speculation. I don't know if there's any truth in it."

"I'd say there is. Bodman is investing his money in real estate. He'll probably be a very wealthy man someday. But I'm not thinking about someday. I'm thinking about now and about the job he's doing for us. In a few short words, he's the best there is."

Delaney nodded, still uncertain of the point Mulrooney was trying to make.

"We received a wire from Bodman last night," the editor went on. "He wants to take a short leave in a few months. He's with Grant at Vicksburg, and he says it's his personal opinion the rebs are finished there, although they don't know it yet. As soon as Vicksburg surrenders, he wants to come back north for a few weeks."

"So . . . ?"

"We'll be sending him back to whatever spot is the hottest after that. I'd like to send you along with him."

Delaney was taken totally by surprise by the editor's statement.

Mulrooney's stare intensified at Delaney's silence. "You're good, Marsh, but you have a lot to learn. I've told you that before. The truth is, you aren't going to learn it covering the Sanitary Commission meetings and dodging the pretty ladies waiting for you in the doorway downstairs."

The thought that he had been right about Mulrooney not missing much occurred to him as Delaney met Mulrooney's fixed gaze. "You're thinking Bodman can teach it to me?"

"I don't know. But I do know if you haven't learned what you need by the time you come back from working with him, you never will. I'm offering you the chance of a lifetime, Marsh. I think you're up to the challenge, but neither you nor I will ever know unless you try."

The slow smile that curved Delaney's lips was touched with irony. "I suppose you came to this decision last night, after you got the wire from Bodman."

Mulrooney looked annoyed with his response. "What difference does it make when I made the decision to offer you this spot?"

"It doesn't. It's just that I came to a decision last night, too. I came in here this morning to tell you I wanted to take a few days off."

The editor's annoyance increased. "What in hell does one have to do with the other?"

"I expect to be going back to Michigan for a day or so, and when I return, I'll be bringing somebody back with me."

An extended silence ensued. It was broken at last by Mulrooney's incredulous tone. "Well, I'll be goddamned. A woman."

Delaney did not reply.

"You're going to pass up the chance of a lifetime because you don't want to leave a woman?"

Again Delaney did not respond. He did not feel the need to tell Mulrooney that after seven months, it had finally become clear to him that he already *had* passed up the chance of a lifetime. He had also admitted to himself that he had been a stupid, jealous fool who had allowed pride to stand in the way of following his heart. Most important of all, he had finally acknowledged to himself that Allie was a part of him, that she always would be, and that his life was empty without her.

Neither did he feel a need to tell Mulrooney that he was determined to do whatever he must to bring Allie back with him.

The new assignment was out of the question. He would not go.

"Marsh, answer me, dammit!"

"I'm sorry."

After a few minutes more of silence, Mulrooney lowered himself into his chair. He picked up the carefully written article Delaney had put on his desk. He did not look up as he spoke.

"Bodman probably won't be coming up this way for a while, yet. Think it over. I'll talk to you again when you get back."

Grateful for the abrupt end to the conversation, Delaney nodded and turned and within moments was weaving his way through the city room toward the doorway.

In his mind, Allie was already in his arms.

* * *

The landscape flashing past the windows of the rapidly moving train was almost obscured by darkness, but Delaney sensed a vague familiarity in the gradually lightening shadows. The rhythmic clicking of the rails was strangely soothing. The sway of the car and the screeching whistle that echoed in the darkness brought back memories of another time.

He remembered another view, seen through the open doors of a boxcar filled with orphans as it rattled through the countryside. Orchards filled with apples, fields of pumpkins—"mushmillons"— spread out before the eyes of youngsters traveling toward an unknown destination. He remembered the sounds in the darkness within the car as day slowly faded into night. He remembered the congestion, the lack of air, the small bodies curled in sleep surrounding him on the floor. He had been immune to the discomfort and to the plight of the others. He had not considered himself a part of that group of needy children. He had not been a child, despite his young age. He had been old beyond his years, a prison boy hardened by circumstance and determined never to suffer at the will of society again.

A smile touched Delaney's lips as another memory returned. A small, pale-haired girl crawled between the sleeping children, inching her way toward him. A child, pathetically thin, she continued to approach, her dark eyes apprehensive but determined. She hesitated a short distance from him as he feigned sleep, then reached for the chain around his neck. He grasped her hand, and her dark eyes snapped wide open with fear. They looked directly into his.

The memory changed—Allie, a woman, was in his arms, lying close to him. The taste of her fresh on his lips, her warm body scent taunted him as she lay flush against his flesh. His hands tangled in the pale silk of her hair as he lowered his mouth to hers again, drinking deeply of the joy she gave him. He had not believed such joy possible. He felt that he had never been truly alive before that moment, that he could not get enough of her, that he would never let her go. He had told her he loved her, that he would always love her. He wanted to love and care for her all the days of his life.

It all had changed so quickly. He had been struck to the heart when Allie unexpectedly left his side. It had been too soon after their lovemaking for him to share her with anyone. He had been filled with bitterness and disbelief when she put a different kind of love ahead of her love for him.

He had turned and walked away, certain almost until the last moment that Allie would never let him leave without her. But she had. The bitterness that had always been so much a part of his life had then returned full measure.

But that angry young man had finally overcome the hostile prison boy inside him. He had finally come to his senses. He had acknowledged that after seven long months of separation, Allie was as much a part of him as she always had been. He knew that no matter how hard he denied it, it would always be so.

He had also acknowledged that life had no joy without her.

The shadowed sky was gradually lightening. It would be almost dawn when the train reached the Cass County station. His heart drumming, Delaney ran a nervous hand through his hair and adjusted his position in the seat. He could almost feel Allie in his arms, could almost taste her mouth. The echo of her soft voice reverberated in his mind, and he longed for her with such intensity that it was almost pain.

Their separation would soon come to an end, but it could not be soon enough.

Allie turned in bed and adjusted her position. She was unusually restless. Glancing toward the window, she searched the night sky for the first trace of dawn. She saw it in the subdued glow that began to raise the darkness. She heard it in the first chirping sounds from the tree beyond her window. She felt it in the sudden movement of the child within her.

James's warm hand curled around her distended abdomen, and she was again grateful that her appearance was deceiving, that her pregnancy did not appear as advanced as it was. Her misleading appearance had allowed no speculation about the baby she carried being other than James's child. For James's sake, she wished it were true.

His gentle lips brushed her ear with a whisper. "Is anything wrong, Allie?"

Allie shook her head, meeting James's concerned expression with a small smile. "No. I can't seem to sleep, that's all."

James pulled her closer, fitting her into the curve of his body, and the seldom-dormant ache inside Allie stirred to life anew. She fought to silence the voice within her, which cried out Delaney's name. She sought to concentrate on James's voice as he whispered loving words in her ear. She wished with all her heart that she could love James as he loved her, that she could cast Delaney from her heart forever.

Delaney was already standing on the boarding step when the train pulled into the station. Not waiting for it to come to a full halt, he leaped onto the platform and headed toward Mosley Rourke's livery stable at a pace just short of a run.

Grateful that the train had arrived ahead of schedule, bringing him into the station just before dawn, Delaney carefully avoided being seen. He turned into a familiar alley that led to the rear door of the livery. He was determined word of his return would not reach the farm ahead of him. It was his intention to catch Allie alone somewhere before the family was aware of his presence. He wanted to speak to her without being interrupted and without the pressure of interference. He intended to take her back with him on the noon train. It would not do to prolong the agony. They had been apart too long.

Working at the feed bin, Rourke did not see him enter through the rear door of the stable. Delaney nearly laughed at the shock so clearly displayed on the man's heavily stubbled face when he turned with a start at the sound of Delaney's step.

"Delaney Marsh! I thought you was gone for good."

"Wishful thinking on most people's part. I want to rent a horse for the day."

"Well . . . all right. Sandy's available. It'll seem like old times, you and him travelin' the road to the Case farm again. That is where you're goin', ain't it?"

Neglecting to respond, Delaney walked toward Sandy's stall. He had no time for Rourke's probing questions. Nor did he have the patience for his notoriously slow pace in serving his customers.

Delaney acknowledged Sandy's friendly nudge with a low word of greeting before swinging a saddle blanket onto the animal's back. Rourke was right behind him as he set the saddle in place.

"How long you been gone now, Marsh? What is it, seven, eight months?"

"About that."

"Sure been a lot of changes around here durin' that time."

It did not take more than a nod to encourage Rourke to continue.

"Yes, sir, a lot of changes. Don't know if you heard. Mrs. Case died a few months ago. The family was real upset. Jacob ain't the same man he used to be."

Delaney's hands stilled momentarily as he adjusted the saddle. So she was dead. Sorrow mixed with relief within him. He regretted not having made his peace with Margaret Case before she died, but Allie would have no reason to remain on the farm now. Even if Mrs. Case had been alive, she could have made little objection to Allie's leaving. Whether it had been his intention or not, he had done exactly as she had suggested. He had given himself time to get established in his new job before returning for Allie. He had also given himself time to realize how much he loved her.

His spirits rising, Delaney tightened the cinch tight under the gelding's stomach. He waited for the sly animal to let out his breath so he could pull it tighter. He smiled. He would never fall for that trick again.

"Yes, sir, things are a bit different this spring at the Case farm, now that Sarah's gone."

Surprise made Delaney turn toward Rourke. Satisfaction lit Rourke's rheumy eyes. "Oh, didn't know that either, huh? Sarah went and married Bobbie Clark. Run off, they did, and got married in the next county a little while before her mama died. I expect she did the family a favor, what with Bobbie and her expectin' a little one so soon. As big as a house she is now, that girl. Bets are she'll have that baby before another month is done."

Resisting the urge to express his reaction to Sarah's departure with a low "good riddance," Delaney flipped down the stirrups and adjusted their length. It looked as if the only person left on the farm who might give him trouble was James. Well, he was prepared to make short work of any interference from him.

"I'm thinkin' Mrs. Case was right happy to see all of her children married before she died. Everybody had to give that little girl credit for givin' up a proper weddin' so's she could get married at that poor lady's bedside. Everybody knew it probably meant more to the poor woman to see that orphan marryin' James than it would have meant to see her own daughter married. After all, the girl was always . . ."

Rourke's voice droned on, but disbelief held Delaney immobile. He couldn't mean Allie had married James! She wouldn't! Delaney turned to Rourke once more. "James is married?"

"Guess you didn't know that, either, huh? You shouldn't be as surprised as you seem, rememberin' how fightin' mad James was when you dragged that sweet young thing up to Tillman Hill."

Delaney shook his head. Allie didn't love James. She loved him. She had said she would always love him—for the rest of her life.

Rourke gave a short laugh. "That James. He didn't waste no time at all gettin' his bride in a family way. If I don't miss my guess, she'll be presenting him with a little James, Jr., in another six months or so. And you never did see a happier daddy-to-be."

Delaney turned from Rourke's pleased expression without comment. It was a mistake, all of it! It had to be.

Mounting up, Delaney pressed his horse forward, only to be halted by Rourke's restraining hand on the bridle. The smile had dropped from his craggy face.

"It don't make no difference if you don't like my conversation, but I take my money in advance, Marsh, like I always did."

Reaching into his pocket, Delaney slapped some money into Rourke's hand. He did not bother to acknowledge Rourke's low grunt of satisfaction as he urged his mount forward.

Allie's image was bright before his mind as he turned the gelding onto the back road out of town.

The bedroom door closed behind James. Waiting until his footsteps sounded on the stairs, Allie released a low sigh, threw back the covers, and rose to her feet. She frowned at the image reflected back at her from the dresser mirror and deliberately turned her back.

The mirror's unfortunate position forced a daily viewing of her swollen shape each morning on arising. It was an image that had grown increasingly distasteful to her eyes as her body had thinned and her belly had grown greater. She was out of proportion, a wisp of flesh and bone not worthy to be called a woman except for her expanding stomach. And yet James loved her.

Tears rising to her throat, Allie pulled her nightgown off over her head and reached for the newly enlarged shift lying on the chair beside the bed. She turned to the wardrobe behind her and then removed a blue gingham dress, one of two she had recently sewn to accommodate her expanding size. She had left the remainder of her clothes in the room she had formerly shared with Sarah.

She missed that room. She missed its femininity, its coziness. She was not fully at home in this room to which she had moved on the night of her wedding to James. But it was difficult to be at ease under the unusual circumstances that found her sharing James's bed, lying nightly in his arms as he whispered his love to her, although their marriage had never been consummated.

Anxiety and no little guilt assailed Allie once more. She knew if James were to follow his inclinations, her circumstances would be far different. She also knew he loved her too deeply to press himself on her until she was truly ready to receive him. She knew he would wait for her to turn to him with love in her heart, no matter how long it took, and that realization was her everlasting torment.

It was not as if she did not love James. She did, but her love did not bear the passionate intensity of his love for her. She feared it never would.

And it was not as if she indulged herself with thoughts of Delaney. Those memories, which she had once thought to cherish her life long, now only caused her distress. She did not even allow herself to think of the child growing within her. She was in a strange limbo, not truly lover, not truly wife, not truly mother. The strangest part of all was her realization that while James was her torment, he was also her consolation. She was uncertain what she would have done without him.

Taking only a short moment longer to complete her dressing, Allie returned to the mirror. With practiced fingers she rolled the long pale strands streaming over her shoulders into a loose knot and fastened it atop her head. James liked her hair that way and it was little enough to please a man who gave her so much.

Guilt stirring anew, Allie made her way downstairs to the kitchen after a glance toward Papa Case's bedroom door revealed he had not yet arisen. She knew he had lost the incentive to begin his day without Mother Case beside him, and she worried for his state of mind.

Pausing in the hallway, Allie turned on impulse toward the front door. Slipping outside, she glanced around the yard, her mind registering the beauty of the spring dawn making its way across the sky. Hearing sounds of movement nearby, Allie started across the yard, halting as James rounded the corner of the barn and turned toward her.

His expression registering concern, he quickened his step. His eyes assessed her anxiously even as he spoke. "What's the matter, Allie?"

Confusion, regret, and a great humility choked Allie's throat with tears. It took her a few moments to overcome them.

"Allie?"

"I'm fine, James. I just wanted—" Closing the distance between then, Allie slipped her arms around James's waist. She leaned full against him, holding him close. The child within her registered its protest, and she attempted to pull back, but James's arms closed around her, allowing her only limited withdrawal as he looked down into her face.

"You just wanted what, Allie?"

A familiar pain twisted within Allie at the renewed hope in James's eyes. She cursed herself for her awkwardness, knowing she had sought James for a purpose and knowing she must follow through.

Her voice low, quaking, Allie managed a small whisper.

"I can't start another day, James, without saying some things that have gone unsaid too long. I hope you'll forgive me if they're not exactly what you want to hear, but they come from the heart."

James's short nod urging her on, Allie fixed her gaze on the blue eyes filled with love looking into hers as she continued, "For a long time I thought I knew what love truly was. I felt it in my heart and let it become a part of me. But that love was not returned full measure. I recognize that now, and I've accepted it. The only trouble is, I haven't been able to stop that loving, James.''

James's fair face paled and Allie shook her head in the hope of assuaging the pain there. ''I haven't been able to stop the loving, but there's been something else growing within me these past months, aside from the child I'm carrying. It's been growing greater each day. It's my love for you, James. I don't know where it's taking me. I only know that I feel good in your arms, that I feel consolation in the sound of your voice, and that I want to make you happy. I want that desperately, but I'm so confused, James. I'm not certain where one love ends and the other begins.'' Allie paused. She shook her head as she struggled for the words, which came with so much difficulty.

''Oh, James, I guess I'm asking you to be patient with me for a little while longer.''

''You don't have to ask, Allie. I told you once I'll always be here when you need me. I didn't qualify that promise.''

A deep hurt burning inside her, Allie nodded. ''I suppose that's the difference I couldn't see. Your love has no qualifications.''

''It never will, Allie.''

Allie's voice was low, choked. ''I don't know why you love me, James.''

''Someday you will, because you'll love me just as much as I love you.''

Allie nodded again, unable to speak as James lowered his face to hers. ''Kiss me now, Allie. And remember—I decided a long time ago that I would wait as long as necessary. Nothing has changed that decision, and nothing ever will.''

James's lips touched hers, and Allie gave her mouth to him. She slipped her arms around his neck and closed her eyes, willing away the image that threatened to invade this moment and come between them. She made herself a promise not to allow it to return.

James drew back from her at last. Allie offered him a tremulous smile as he touched a trembling hand to her cheek and whispered, ''We have a lot to look forward to, darling, and it'll be worth the wait.''

Allowing James to draw her to his side, Allie walked with

him back to the house. Pausing as he brushed her mouth once more with his, she turned toward the door. She wanted so desperately to believe him.

Concealed behind the barn, Delaney shook his head in disbelief. It couldn't be true.

Closing his eyes against the image of Allie in James's arms, her swollen body tight against his, Delaney choked back the grief threatening to explode within him. He turned toward the rear pasture where he had left his horse. The sky was rapidly lightening, but he was unable to see anything but the image that haunted him. How he wished he could forget the silhouette he had seen etched against the brightening morning sky. How he wished Allie had not been so beautiful. He would never forget the outline of her small features raised to James, her slender form frighteningly fragile despite the curve of her abdomen.

He didn't want it to be James's child that filled Allie! He didn't want it to be James's arms that held her! He didn't want it to be James who would be beside her the rest of her life while he was left with only memories and broken dreams!

When he had reached the pasture, Sandy moved toward him and Delaney attempted to assume control of his riotous emotions.

This cruel twist of fate was beyond him. Why had he been given the consolation of Allie's love? Why had he been allowed to learn to trust in it, only to have it all snatched from him when he finally had the courage to admit his need? Why had fate created this void within him, which would never be filled? Why had he been so brutally forced to acknowledge that even Allie, for all her beauty, her sweet honesty and innocence, could not be trusted to love him forever?

The low, pained sound that escaped Delaney's throat was overwhelmed by the sound of creaking leather and Sandy's restless shifting as he mounted.

There was no such thing as love. Allie's love had been a temporary respite. How could he have believed in it even for a moment? How could he have believed his childish dreams could ever become reality?

The truth was that ''love'' was a flexible emotion, shaped to fit circumstance. Seeing Allie in James's arms was proof of that truth.

Delaney spurred his horse forward in an attempt to escape the relentless image so clear in his mind's eyes. He needed to face the fact that Allie had given herself to James as she had given herself to him. He had seen her offer her lips to James willingly, her arms clinging to his neck. He did not want to remember that those same arms had held him close as Allie had lain in his embrace. He did not want to recall the magic of her sweet flesh pressed against his, of her moist warmth enclosing him, holding him fast within her. He did not want to believe that he would forever be denied the supreme elation of knowing Allie was his.

Suddenly furious with his thoughts, Delaney took a deep, hard breath. He would not torment himself. He had relearned a very hard lesson. It was one he would not forget again. He didn't need love. He didn't need anyone, least of all a slender, fragile child-woman who had been more cruel than all the rest because she had made him believe.

The screech of a train whistle sounded in the distance, and Delaney stiffened in the saddle. It was the maintenance train returning to Chicago. It would pause for a few minutes around the next curve to take on water.

Making an abrupt decision, Delaney spurred his horse sharply forward. He leaned low over the saddle as the animal broke into a gallop, pressing him to the fullest.

He reined up beside the train a short time later, just as it prepared to depart. He dismounted and caught the hand rails as the car lurched into motion. He took the few steps up to the platform between the two cars as the foreman of the work gang inside the car started toward him. Delaney withdrew a roll of bills from his pocket.

Not bothering to assess the foreman's slow smile as he pressed the bills into his hand or the fellow's silent return to his men, Delaney watched as Sandy grew smaller in the distance. The horse had already turned toward the road to town. Within an hour he would be back in Rourke's livery stable where he had been raised. Delaney supposed the animal needed the security of a home, just as Allie had chosen a secure life with James over the uncertainty of a new life with him.

Allie had shaped her "love" to fit the circumstances.
He guessed he couldn't really blame her. But he did.

Mosley Rourke lifted his battered hat and scratched his balding pate as James Case drove his wagon up the main street of
town at a casual pace. Rourke was still watching when James
reined up in front of Bosley's general store and started up the
few steps toward the door.

Walking through that same doorway a few minutes later,
Rourke strolled up to the counter. He nodded at Elmer Winthrop
behind the counter and smiled as James turned in his direction.

"Well, now, James, I haven't seen you in a dog's age. How're
you doin'? And how's the missus?"

James's narrow face creased in a smile. "Real well, Mosley,
on both counts."

"That's real fine." Rourke's puzzlement grew as he assessed
James's pleased expression. Everybody knew James doted on his
bride. It seemed nothin' had changed between them. He tried
another tack. "I was kinda disappointed to see you comin' in
alone today. It ain't often enough that we see your little bride in
town these days."

A sound at the doorway made James turn around. His smile
broadened and Rourke turned to see Allie Case enter the store.
James stepped forward and took her hand as she approached.

"That was fast," James said. "Mosley was just asking about
you. Wasn't the drugstore open?"

"No. The out-to-lunch sign is up."

Rourke smiled and tipped his hat. It was no wonder that James
was so wrapped up in this little girl. Hell, she was prettier and
more dainty looking every time he saw her, in spite of her expanding middle. And there was no doubting the warmth between
these two. His puzzlement grew.

"How's your pa doin', James?"

James's smile dimmed. "Not as well as we'd like. The doctor
prescribed a tonic. That's why I dropped Allie off at the drugstore on the way in. We're hoping it'll get him back to feeling
his old self."

Rourke nodded. He liked the Case family. They'd been mighty
kind to him, especially Margaret, when his Mary was doin'
poorly some years back. He'd never forget their thoughtfulness.

"I hope so, too. Tell him I was askin' about him, James."
Rourke turned to smile at Allie Case. "Pleased to see you again,
ma'am."

Rourke turned at the young woman's nod and walked toward
the door. He was heading back to the livery a few minutes later,
his wiry brows in a tight frown. He couldn't figure the whole
thing out. Delaney Marsh hadn't said where he was going yesterday, but he had taken the back road out of town so there was
no other place he could have gone but to the Case farm.

Old Sandy had come walking up the back alley all by himself
a few hours later and put himself back in his stall just as nice as
could be, but Rourke hadn't seen hide nor hair of Marsh.

The strangest part was that nobody else had mentioned seeing
Marsh come to town or leave. The strangeness of it all had made
Rourke feel a need for caution that overcame his usual tendency
to gossip. He knew there was bad blood between James and
Marsh, and he had seen the look on Marsh's face when he men-
tioned that James had taken Allie as his bride.

Rourke had expected there to be some trouble at the Case
farm. He had been waiting for somebody to say something but
nobody had.

Now, seeing James and his bride together, looking just as
happy as could be, it seemed as if Marsh had never stepped foot
back in town!

Shaking his head as he entered the stable, Rourke stared for
a moment in the direction of Sandy's stall.

Damned if he knew what had happened to Marsh!

Still puzzling, Rourke began tossing hay into the nearest stall.
Well, it didn't matter much to him anyway. He had never liked
Marsh. The fella was a troublemaker from the start, and if he
had met up with some kind of foul play, well, he had only gotten
what he had coming.

Nodding as he came to a firm decision, Rourke tossed another
forkful of hay into the stall.

Nobody seemed to know Marsh had been back in town, and
if James didn't want anybody to know, well, they'd never hear
it from his lips. As far as he was concerned, Delaney Marsh had
never returned to Cass County.

Hell, nobody had missed him, anyway.

chapter

sixteen

ANOTHER PAIN GRIPPED her, and Allie strained to remain calm. She tried to take a deeper breath to relieve the contractions that were all but tearing her apart, but the simple effort was beyond her. It was as if she had lost control over her muscles and reflexes had assumed control of her body.

Allie was tempted to laugh. That was exactly what was happening, wasn't it?

The pain was fading, rounding the curve of the circle that would bring it back in all too short a time. During the few moments' rest in between, Allie attempted to empty her mind and breathe deeply as she fixed her eye on the green fields visible through the bedroom window.

Summer had worked its magic on the land that had been frozen and white through most of the long winter months. Now the fields were brimming with life and the trees, which had been stark and bare, were verdant and heavily laden. It was going to be a bountiful harvest this year, and Allie was glad. James had worked so hard.

The pains had started in the dark hours of the morning, but they were so light that she had been uncertain if her time had indeed come. James had been certain, though. She had told him not to go for Dr. Peters so soon, but he had set out for town at daybreak.

He had returned a short time later, Dr. Peters riding behind. James had stayed at her side up until an hour ago when Dr. Peters forced him from the room because the pains had become more intense. She had not protested, because the lines of strain on James's face had revealed only too clearly the stress he suffered.

Pain again. Determined not to cry out, she nodded at the sound of Dr. Peters's voice.

"It won't be much longer, Allie."

She attempted a smile that proved no more than a grimace as Dr. Peters wiped the perspiration from her brow. It was so hot. Her white shift was soaked with perspiration that was as much a result of the midsummer heat as of impending birth. It stuck to her skin, outlining the swollen contours of her body as she went through the final stages of birthing. She raised a hand to her hair in a tentative attempt to lift the damp, heavy strands from her scalp, but the effort was useless. She knew she looked terrible. She had looked terrible for more months than she cared to remember, but James still loved her.

He had taught her much about love.

The door to the room opened and James entered. He walked immediately to her side. His face was pale under his sunburn, and the freckles, which had come in abundance with the summer, stood out darkly on his cheekbones. His blond hair was bleached a lighter color still, and the lines at the corners of his eyes had deepened from his perpetual squint against the brightness of the long days. He was thinner than he had been during the winter, for all his sinewy strength. He looked healthy, virile, and very worried, and Allie felt a love for him that was warm and deep within her.

"James, I asked you to wait outside," the doctor said. "You have no place in this room right now. Allie will be very busy soon, and I don't want you in the way."

James cast a glance toward Dr. Peters's impatient frown, then turned back toward Allie. "Do you want me to leave, Allie? If you'll be more comfortable without me here, I will."

"No, James. I don't want you to leave."

Dr. Peters snorted with exasperation. "James, you did your part in this whole affair nine months ago. Allie doesn't need your help now."

Allie flushed, but James gave her hand an encouraging squeeze. She was glad Dr. Peters did not suspect the child was not James's, even though he did realize the baby was conceived before they were married. But the thought gave her little consolation. The fact was, this child was *not* James's. It was Delaney's, and she was now more intensely aware than ever that it should be Delaney who was with her now, holding her hand.

Sarah had given birth to a baby boy only two days before, a son who would not bear Delaney's name, just as Allie's own child would not bear the name of its true father.

Another deep, shattering pain made Allie gasp. But this pain was different, without end, and a sudden panic assailed her. Her baby was near to being born! What kind of mother would she be, married to one man while her mind and heart strayed to another? How would she teach this child to love when she was no longer certain what love really was? How could she guide this child to a full and happy life when she had made such a terrible mess of her own?

Fear, pain, and anguish deluged Allie, threatening to overwhelm her troubled mind. Her heart began a rapid, uneven pounding and her panic swelled. Her body tensed, fighting the spasms that drew her closer to the moment of birth, resisting the birth with all her strength.

"Allie, what's wrong?" Dr. Peters's low voice was laced with concern, and Allie felt James's hand tighten on hers. But all consolation had fled from her mind with the realization that her moment had come, and with the realization that despite the concern and love surrounding her, she was alone in her heart.

"Allie . . ."

She turned to face James's tense gaze, but she was powerless to speak.

"Allie, breathe deeply." Dr. Peters's voice held an edge of concern. "Don't panic, dear. It'll all be over soon."

The doctor's low words of assurance had little effect on Allie as a peculiar breathlessness assailed her. Familiar, almost translucent eyes returned to haunt her, and Allie fought their silent appeal. She could not allow the memory of Delaney's love to console her now. Nor could she allow James's love to carry her through the birth of another man's child. She was alone. Suddenly overwhelmed by her insecurity and torment, Allie was uncertain she had the will to endure.

The pain intensified and Allie's body became more rigid.

"Allie, stop this! You're hurting yourself!" Dr. Peters demanded.

But she was powerless against the emotions that ruled her mind, powerless against a vision of a long life in which she and her child would have no true place. Far better to succumb to the pain, far better to yield to the darkness hovering over her, far better to sink into the dark abyss where anguish could never find her again.

Her world of despair was so complete that Allie was not aware of the moment when James slipped away from her side. She did not see him walk to the dresser and open the drawer. She did not witness his distress as he withdrew the silver medal and returned to her side.

Her breathing shallow, her consciousness fading, Allie heard a low whisper in her ear, but she could not make out the words above the voices screaming in her mind and the endless pain holding her immobile in its throes. She did not realize James had pried open her tight fist and placed something in her hand until she felt the familiar shape of the medal against her palm.

Allie's hand closed around it. She felt its strength and love transfuse her. She heard her mother's voice whisper to her consolingly. She saw a love untainted by bitterness in Delaney's eyes. She saw the Lady's sweet face.

A stronger pain gripped her, but a new peace began to replace her fear. She was no longer alone in her heart. The memory of love had returned to dwell there and it made her strong. The promise of love had found its place, and it gave her hope.

She gripped the medal tighter, turning to flash a brief, grateful smile toward James. She saw understanding in his eyes.

Another wrenching spasm—a breathtaking thrust—deep, tearing pain, then it was over.

And there was life.

It was evening. Allie had awakened an hour before and she was strangely unwilling to yield again to sleep, despite her exhaustion. Dr. Peters had returned to town, leaving behind a few instructions, which James had listened to with sober attention. Allie had listened, too, for she had no intention of allowing James and Papa Case to do her work for long. She was young, she was strong. She would soon be on her feet.

But for now, Allie was content to lie abed with her baby in her arms. Love welled within her as she adjusted the lightweight coverlet in which her daughter was wrapped. She was so beautiful.

A step sounded at the door, and Allie raised her eyes to James as he entered the room and came to sit beside her on the bed. He pressed a light kiss against her lips and reached out a freckled hand to stroke the baby's cheek.

"She looks like you, Allie. I'm glad."

Taking only a moment to consider her daughter's fair skin, dark eyes, and the silvery gold down that covered her head, Allie looked back at James.

"Would you feel differently if she didn't, James?"

James frowned at her question, finally raising her chin with his hand so he held her gaze firmly with his.

"I love her because she's a part of you, Allie. She's my daughter now, and no matter who she resembles, I'll always love her. But I admit to being pleased she looks like you. I like the idea of having two Allies instead of one."

"No, James. Allie and little Margaret."

James's eyes grew suddenly moist, and his voice was husky with emotion when he finally spoke. "Thank you, Allie. Pa will be very happy to know his grandchild bears my mother's name."

Allie's smile dimmed. "Do you think he'll really come to think of her as his grandchild, James?"

"Pa already thinks of little Margaret as his grandchild. Don't ever doubt that he loves her. And don't ever doubt that I love you both."

Allie nodded, her eyes on James's face as his expression flickered momentarily and he continued in a new, deeper tone. "Margaret was my daughter even before she was born, Allie. I watched her grow inside you, I felt her move, and I shared your anticipation. She's as much mine as she would be if my own blood ran in her veins. I have only one thing to ask of you,

Allie.'' James paused, his brow tightening in a frown. "I want you to promise me that you'll never tell anyone she's not mine.''

"I would never do anything to embarrass you, James. I'm your wife, now.''

"Promise me, Allie.''

Tears flooded Allie's eyes.

"I promise.''

Nodding, James remained silent a moment longer before lowering his head to press another kiss against her lips. This one lingered. It was a kiss filled with love and promise, and Allie returned it full measure.

James finally drew himself to his feet. His smile was tremulous.

"Try to get some rest now, Allie. I'll be back in a little while.''

Watching as James closed the door behind him, Allie lowered her daughter to the bed beside her. She studied the small, perfect face, the fine lips which smiled briefly. There was no trace of Delaney in her daughter's light coloring and small features, but James had not noticed the firmness of Margaret's wee chin, or the determination in her searching, unseeing gaze and tiny frown.

Much had changed for Allie in the past few hours. A strange metamorphosis had occurred at the moment of her child's birth. No longer in limbo, she had come to life as an adult, a mother, and a woman.

An adult, she accepted the painful reality that Delaney would never return to claim his daughter. As a mother, she realized that her first responsibility was to her helpless infant. Truly a woman at last, she knew where her duty lay, and to whom. She also knew that if passion did not play a part in the life ahead of her, a deep, abiding love and gratitude would.

That would be enough. It would have to be.

In those hours since her child's birth, Allie had also recognized the mistakes she had made in attempting to come to terms with the direction her life had taken.

Delaney's familiar image appeared again in her mind, his handsome face sober, his translucent eyes seeming to see into her soul. Allie smiled. She had tried desperately to expel him from her heart in an attempt to deny a basic truth. Delaney would always be a part of her and she would always love him.

That would never change. Her mistake had been in attempting to forget him. She now knew that was impossible. But whether he had failed her or she had failed him was no longer of consequence. The time had come to put memories behind her and make a permanent place in her heart as well for the man who would share all her tomorrows.

Turning on her side, Allie drew her child close. With her free hand she clutched the medal she wore around her neck, her eyes closing briefly at the bittersweet memories that ensued. She prayed that she would have the courage to put her past behind her, that she would be a good mother to her child and a good wife to James.

Then she added a final, silent prayer. She asked the Lady to forgive Delaney because he no longer wore her medal. She asked the Lady to send her prayers for him into God's ear, to protect him, even from himself, for deep in her heart, Allie knew Delaney needed the Lady much more than ever before.

Still holding the medal, Allie allowed her eyes to dwell on her sleeping daughter's face. Quiet settled within her heart.

She hoped she would see Delaney again someday. Maybe by then she would be able to forgive him.

The intense heat of summer had been unabating, and the city of Chicago sweltered under its assault, but Delaney was all but oblivious of its rigors. He glanced at the man who walked at his side through the busy rail terminal.

Albert Holmes Bodman, the *Tribune*'s dynamic, irrepressible representative in the "Bohemian Brigade" of war correspondents, was not the kind of man one would have come to expect from reading his articles. The physical differences between Delaney and Bodman could not have been more extreme. Delaney's classically handsome features, his unusual translucent eyes and his naturally muscular stature were in direct contrast with the short, plump, sleepy-eyed Bodman. But Delaney was aware that Bodman, although at times solemn and aloof, was a brilliant correspondent and businessman from whom he had much to learn.

Vicksburg had surrendered to Grant's siege on July 4, in line with Bodman's expectations. Bodman had returned to Chicago for a few weeks as planned. He was now returning to the front, and Delaney was going with him.

Delaney had not bothered to respond to Mulrooney's grunt of satisfaction when he had accepted the opportunity to work with Bodman. He had known the entire issue hinged on Bodman's approval. Surprisingly, a chord of mutual respect was struck between Bodman and himself upon their meeting. The result was that they would soon board the train that would take them on the first leg of their journey to the continuing war on the western front.

Bodman made a few brief comments about the noise and congestion in the terminal, the confusion that accompanied the arrival and departure of trains in wartime, and the fact that he would be glad to be back at work again.

Delaney nodded without replying. The congestion and noise did not bother him, nor did the confusion. Very little touched him these days. Very little had touched him since early spring when he had returned to this same terminal from Cass County.

They approached the train, and Bodman began a discourse on the progress of the war as he saw it and the eventual course it would take. He was still talking as they took the few steps up onto the rail car and entered to find their seats.

His comments precise, detailed, and to the point, Bodman continued speaking as they settled themselves in the car, but Delaney had considerable difficulty concentrating on his words. Despite himself, his mind wandered to a time years before when a group of orphans trailed through a train station like this. The focus of that memory was inescapable—Allie. It was always Allie. Delaney attempted to dismiss the image of her dark eyes filled with love and the echoes of her soft voice whispering his name.

The whistle screeched and the train began its first quaking rumbles forward. It moved slowly onto the open track just as an unexpected sound of flapping wings at the window caused Delaney to turn toward a bird fluttering at the glass. Flying down, it settled on the track beside the car, seemingly inured to the turmoil around it.

It was a dove.

His throat tightening, Delaney watched as the bird cocked its head in his direction. It remained motionless for the long space of a moment as it appeared to study him with its dark, unblinking eyes.

The car suddenly jerked as it picked up speed. Startled, the bird took wing, flying directly up into the sun. Delaney leaned closer to the window following its flight steadily upward until it disappeared from sight in the cloudless expanse of blue sky above him.

Beside him, Bodman was still talking. Delaney nodded, hearing little that the man said.

He was too busy remembering.

1870

RENDEZVOUS

chapter

seventeen

MORNING SUN FILTERED through the closed blinds of the bed-room, playing against Delaney's eyelids as he resisted awaken-ing. Finally surrendering to the persistent light, he stretched the long length of his body, frowning in momentary discomfort as something pricked the skin of his back. A moment's search of the mattress beneath him revealed the source of his annoyance. A hairpin.

Holding the slender object between his fingers, Delaney frowned at the resurgence of an unexpected memory—a sunny hillside, warm grass beneath him, and a slight fair-haired girl lying beside him, struggling furiously as he freed her long, pale hair from confinement. Delaney's frown deepened as he firmly dismissed the intrusive image from his mind. He had severed all ties with that portion of his past several years ago when he heard about Max Marshall's death. That part of his life was over, and he had determined it would be forgotten.

With the aid of long practice, Delaney forced his mind back to the present and the article in his hand. A faint smile slowly erased his frown. Sybil's hairpins were distinctive, doubtless or-dered specifically to match the raven sheen of her hair, and he remembered the inborn sensuality with which she had slowly removed them the night before and allowed those heavy tresses to fall to her smooth ivory shoulders. He also remembered, almost too distinctly, the heated gaze she had gradually raised to him as she stood naked before him in this room and beckoned him toward her. There was nothing shy about Sybil. She was an intelligent, beautiful woman born of wealthy parents, who had always had everything she ever wanted. Now she wanted Delaney, and she was determined to have him on her own terms.

Delaney's smile hardened. Sybil was extremely lovely, worldly, cultured, and she was a willing and eager mistress. But he had had many mistresses before her. He would have many more after her. He had told her as much the first night he had taken her to his bed six months ago, and last night he had repeated that warning. Sybil had laughed and he knew she had paid little heed to his words.

He shrugged. Whatever she chose to believe, marriage was not in his plans. He had been honest with Sybil, and if she refused to take his admonition seriously, that was her problem.

Delaney drew himself slowly to his feet, stretching his naked muscular frame to its full height as his gaze skimmed the masculine furnishings of the master bedroom. He had selected the pieces carefully. There was not a touch of femininity here, or anywhere else in his eight-room home on Wabash Avenue at Peck Court, one of Chicago's better neighborhoods. He had also chosen the furnishings with an eye to reflecting the status he had attained with the hard work, clever investing, and courage of a man who had everything to gain and nothing to lose.

Taking the few short steps to the massive wardrobe in the corner of the room, Delaney pulled open the door and surveyed the custom-tailored suits inside. With a low grunt of satisfaction, he remembered he had come to this city with only the clothes he wore on his back, a deep ache inside him, and a fierce, driving determination to succeed. Now, eight years, a war, and what felt to be a lifetime later, he had achieved most of the goals he had set for himself. He had also established the pattern he intended to follow for the rest of his life.

Selecting a blue serge suit that he knew complemented his dark coloring and minimized the breadth of his impressive physique, Delaney withdrew it and threw it onto the rumpled bed.

In a few hours he would interview Otis Davidson II, one of Chicago's wealthiest men and head of the city's most powerful family. Today he wanted to deemphasize his physical stature and to impress with his intelligence and shrewdness. The fact that Davidson was also Sybil's father was of little consequence. It would be a difficult interview at best, since the Davidson family concern owned a major part of the slums known as Conley's Patch and Healy Slough. A sector of ramshackle wooden buildings that comprised a neighborhood of cheap saloons, pawn shops, brothels, and disreputable boardinghouses that were no more than tinderboxes during rainless months, these slums were a disgrace to the city, a point he had been hammering home to the readers of the *Tribune* during the past few weeks.

But in truth, his interest in the slums was twofold. His articles on Otis Davidson's properties provided an excellent opportunity for a covert investigation into a prostitution ring rumored to have formed in that area of the city, one that held young immigrant women slaves in the establishments where they worked. The death of three such women had already been reported, but the payment of bribes to men in high places had slowed police investigation to a halt.

A familiar anger tightened Delaney's handsome features as hard memories invaded his mind. As a child he had become all too familiar with the corrupting power of money. He would not stand silently by while defenseless people suffered at the hands of evil men.

Delaney took a shirt from the wardrobe. The expensive fabric slipped across the rippling muscles of his back as he pulled it on, but he was used to the caress of fine material against his skin. A brief twinge in his chest tightened his frown and he unconsciously touched a ragged white scar marking his taut flesh. He was scarred in many ways by his past, but he supposed he should be grateful for this mark. It had been the catalyst of change.

Delaney automatically continued the motions of dressing, his mind moving far from the opulent room in which he stood. He remembered his earliest personal experience with war and the strange coldness with which he had viewed the death and misery surrounding him during the first six months of his apprenticeship under Al Bodman. At the outset, Bodman had respected his analytical ability to report the progress of the conflict between the states, but he had also realized that the tragedies unfolding daily before Delaney's eyes rarely touched him. Bodman was puzzled by his reaction, and, in truth, Delaney was puzzled as well. But the numbness, the distance between his inner self and the chaos of war, had come to an abrupt end the instant a Confederate shell struck his chest.

Closing his light eyes briefly, Delaney relived the pain and shock of that moment, as well as his startling realization, in the brief second before he drifted into unconsciousness, that he might not survive.

He remembered clearly the tricks his mind had played as he floated in the netherworld between life and death. The vision of Allie's face hovering above him as he struggled for each painful breath was still amazingly vivid after all this time. He remembered the concern in her face, the love in her eyes, the sweet sound of her voice as she spoke words of consolation he could not quite understand. He remembered her expression as she clutched the medal of the Lady in her hand.

And he remembered his rage. He had not wanted Allie to pray for him! He had wanted only to forget her!

Driving Allie's persistent pale-haired image from his mind during the weeks of inactivity while he recuperated had been a slow process. Now, in retrospect, he was only too aware it was that vision and the anger and perverse longing it had stirred in him that had given him the strength to survive.

In the end, the long weeks in a hospital bed, surrounded by men who were similarly wounded, had effected a change that made him the man he was today. Several years later he had finally admitted to himself that he owed this change, the empathy he eventually developed for suffering people, to Allie. For in his desperate attempt to oust her from his thoughts, to expunge the mental anguish that made his physical distress acute, he had finally lowered the barriers between himself and the wounded men around him. No longer aloof, he had become one of them, able to see the world through their eyes as he never had before. The view added a new dimension to his life.

Delaney's frown darkened as he fastened his trousers and reached for his vest. His outlook on the tragedy of war from that point on was no longer dispassionate. The difference in him was immediately discernible in his reporting, and a short time after his return to the western front, the *Tribune* gave him full status as an independent correspondent.

But that promotion did not come about until he had learned well all the lessons Al Bodman had to teach him; and he was the first to admit that he owed his present success as much to Bodman's financial genius as to the man's superior talent as a correspondent.

A hard smile returned to Delaney's lips as he tied his cravat with a practiced hand. The war had been over for five years. In those years he had amassed a considerable sum in the bank, enough to make him financially secure beyond his most ambitious expectations. He would become wealthier still through his investments, but wealth in itself was not the source of his greatest satisfaction.

Delaney slipped his jacket on and adjusted it across his shoulders. He turned, scrutinizing his appearance in the dresser mirror. Financial independence was a luxury his father had neither known nor sought, but if his father had realized its importance, he would not have suffered a wealthy man's revenge.

Delaney's smile turned into a grimace. He had not yet achieved the status his father had once enjoyed in their profession, but he was already acknowledged as one of the best newspapermen in Chicago. He would continue to do his job as well as he could— but there was one major difference between his father and himself. Delaney had secured for himself a financial position that would allow no man the power to bring him to his knees.

Picking up his brush, Delaney gave his dark hair a few strokes that put it neatly into place. His final appraisal was not meant to take into account the changes years and seasoning had made in his appearance. For that reason he paid scant attention to the lines of maturity at the outside corners of his peculiarly light eyes—lines that intensified the power of their acute perusal and made his potent, knowing gaze a formidable weapon whenever he confronted an opponent. He neither realized nor cared that the impressive firmness of his jaw was a weapon of silent intimidation or that the smile that touched his mature, handsome face was often his most effective weapon, for all its rarity.

He accepted without vanity the awareness that the promise of youth had been totally fulfilled in the impressive stature of the man he had become and that the age of thirty would find his erect, broad frame well muscled and lean, fit, and free of the excess weight that afflicted so many of the members of his profession.

"Formidable" and "intimidating" were the words most frequently used to describe him by men who opposed the reforms that were the aim of his work on the *Tribune*. "Breathtaking" was the word most commonly used by women. Aware of all three descriptions, he gave little heed to them, except to the extent that they allowed him to accomplish the objectives he had set for himself.

Turning from the mirror, Delaney left his bedroom. He was strikingly handsome and well dressed, the epitome of the respectable, successful Chicago businessman. It was only the flash of relentlessness in those clear, penetrating eyes, the frequent frigidity there, that hinted at the last remains of the prison boy hidden beneath.

When he reached the foot of the staircase a few moments later, Delaney turned to the short, gray-haired woman rounding the corner of the hallway.

"I won't bother with breakfast today, Olga. I expect to be home at the usual time."

Not waiting for his housekeeper's response, Delaney pulled open the front door and descended the steps to the quiet tree-lined street. Oblivious to the spring sun that warmed his shoulders as he walked rapidly toward the intersection, he raised his hand, hailing a passing hack. He gave an elegant Terrace Row address to the heavily mustached driver and settled onto the velour seat.

Relaxing for the first time since awakening, Delaney reached into his pocket and retrieved the slender article he had dropped into it a few minutes before. He stared at the gleaming hairpin, a smile moving across his lips. The Davidson family was one of Chicago's wealthiest. It was socially prominent and extremely influential. Otis Davidson II, if he had known the truth, would not have approved of his daughter's liaison with a man of common origins, and Delaney sometimes wondered how big a part that fact played in the attraction Sybil held for him. Sybil was a challenge, and challenge was the major impetus of his existence.

Delaney's smile faded. He was victorious in meeting most

challenges these days. He made certain of it. He had determined
long ago that he had lost often enough.

Allie withdrew a shirt from the laundry basket at her feet. She
raised her face to the cloudless blue of the sky as she clipped
the garment to the clothesline, luxuriating in the bright morning
sunlight that warmed her skin. A brisk spring breeze pressed the
soft cotton of her dress against her body, outlining a slenderness
unaltered by womanhood and whipping free a few locks from
the pale, shimmering mass of hair so carefully secured atop her
head. Experiencing a familiar annoyance, she brushed the errant
strands back from a face refined to incredible delicacy by maturity, and from deep, dark eyes and small features set to perfection there.

Abandoning the futile attempt to confine the wayward locks,
Allie returned to the business at hand. Her chore almost complete, she paused again, breathing deeply, taking in the sweet
scent of freshly turned earth and budding trees. The familiar
fragrance brought to mind the morning after she had arrived at
the Case farm as a child, when she had stepped out of the house
almost disbelieving the beauty and redolence that abounded in
the raw, unspoiled beauty of her new home.

Allowing her eyes to wander over the sun-washed, rolling land,
the farmhouse that had welcomed her home, the cows that moved
leisurely in the corral behind the barn, and the chicken coops
on the small rise in the rear, she was aware that nothing, and
everything, had changed since that morning.

A flicker of movement on the porch behind her alerted Allie
to the advance of a small striped cat. Bittersweet memories swept
her mind as the purring feline continued its approach. Whiskers
was several generations removed from Mischief, who had been
gone for a few years. She had never known the stroking caress
of the little girl Allie had once been, or the surprisingly gentle
touch of the silent prison boy who had also been her friend.

Allie withdrew the last garment from the laundry basket, her
fingers moving quickly to pin it to the line. Those times were
long gone, and she had come to terms with the past and with
life's natural, sometimes painful progression.

Papa Case was gone. Life had held little joy for him after
Mother Case's death, and Allie was certain that he had held on

only long enough to help James take a firm hold on the farm. When it was financially secure and he felt his work was done, Papa Case had left them silently, without pain, to join his beloved Margaret.

Allie was glad he had not lingered to witness the poor run of luck that had plunged the farm heavily into debt shortly thereafter. She was also glad he was not present to see the pleasure Sarah seemed to take in her brother's dire financial status. But then, Sarah had never quite forgiven Allie for bearing Delaney's child, or James for accepting that child as his own.

And then there was Sarah's son, Jeremy. He was a truly handsome boy, with the dark hair and sturdy build of his father. Allie had often thought that it was fortunate for Bobbie's sake that the boy's resemblance to Delaney stopped there, that the boy's green eyes and handsome features were young replicas of Sarah's, for there had never been a hint of suspicion in the mind of the townsfolk that Jeremy Clark was other than Bobbie's son. But for all the care Sarah took in guarding the secret of Jeremy's paternity from others, she took great pleasure in flaunting the true circumstances of his conception to Allie.

For that reason, James had limited contact with Sarah and Bobbie over the years, and for all the affection Allie felt for her brother-in-law and her beautiful, guiltless nephew, she had to admit to relief.

And then there was little Margaret. A fierce, protective love flared to life within Allie at the thought of her darling child. She would be forever grateful that James had been strong and loving enough to completely accept another man's child as his own. Allie's throat tightened, and she swallowed against a warm rush of emotion. She supposed James's capacity for giving love was the reason her own love for him had grown steadily over the years. Totally different in character and scope from the compelling, all-consuming love she had felt for Delaney, it was nonetheless powerful and true.

Turning at the sound of a step behind her, Allie met James's sober expression with a smile. His sandy hair was now lightly touched with gray, and his freckled face was faintly lined, but he had the sinewy build of a hardworking farmer in his prime. He was a good, kind, loving man, and Allie was proud to be his wife. She knew she would never regret or betray the vows she had spoken to him.

But James did not return her smile. Instead, his expression remaining solemn, he searched her face intently in an uncharacteristic silence that raised a sudden apprehension within her. Allie's heart began a rapid, erratic pounding as he finally spoke in a low, uneven tone.

"I've come to a decision, Allie. I think you should leave at the end of the week."

The library of Otis Davidson's Terrace Row home reverberated with silent tension as Delaney held the older man's gaze unflinchingly. Impervious to the anger reflected in Davidson's tight expression and to the symbols of old money discreetly displayed in the extensive collection of leather-bound volumes filling the shelves behind the great mahogany desk, in the painting on the side wall, which bore the signature of an old master, and in the manner of the man himself, Delaney pressed his point relentlessly.

"Chicago is the Gem City of the Prairie, the Garden City, the Queen City. Thirteen major railroads service it, and it is the fastest growing city in the country. Doesn't it bother you that, despite your family's wealth and social prominence, your contribution to this city includes one of its seediest, most disreputable slums?"

"Mr. Marsh . . ." Mr. Davidson paused in an obvious attempt to temper his response. The lines of his narrow, mustached face tightened further and his lips twitched revealingly as he drew himself more rigidly erect. "I admit to nothing more than considerable surprise at the ignorance with which you have approached this interview."

Delaney had all he could do not to laugh aloud. He had succeeded in getting the superior old bastard too furious for his usual double-talk. Making certain not to allow a trace of his satisfaction at that thought to become visible, Delaney responded with a raised brow.

"Ignorance? You're mistaken, Mr. Davidson. You may rest assured that I am aware of the extent of your holdings in Healy Slough and Conley's Patch. I can describe each and every street to you—the dilapidated houses, the sagging porches and staircases that put life and limb at risk, and the filth that has accumulated there and continues to grow. I've walked those streets—been in those houses. Can you say the same?''

''That section of town is only a portion of my holdings in this city, and if you've done your research as well as you say, Mr. Marsh, you're well aware of that fact.''

''I'm aware that you're a wealthy man, Mr. Davidson. I'm also aware that you profit almost as much from those slums as you do from other properties you own and that you don't return a penny of your profits in improvements that are desperately needed.''

''How I run my business is not the concern of you or your newspaper, Mr. Marsh!''

''That's where you're wrong. You're profiting from the poverty and misery of those who are less fortunate than you. You're robbing the poor even as you deprive them of hope as well, and that is my business.''

''How dare you!'' A heated flush transfused Otis Davidson's face, and he took a step forward. The nostrils of his aquiline nose flared briefly with rage. ''How dare you attempt to tell me how to manage my affairs! I admit to no culpability whatever for the condition of those two areas. They're my holdings, but I am not to blame for the irresponsibility of the scum that chooses to live there!''

''That 'scum' pays you good rent.''

''That 'scum' makes its own filth and would return that area to the same condition of disrepair within weeks of any improvements I might implement!''

Delaney's dark brows rose in an exaggerated expression of surprise. ''Is that so? On what basis have you come to that conclusion, Mr. Davidson? According to my investigations, it's been years since you have financed as much as a single nailhead in repair of your holdings there.''

His narrow chest heaving beneath the expensive fabric of his well-tailored jacket, Otis Davidson clamped his mouth tightly closed as he retreated to the chair behind his mahogany desk. When he spoke again his voice was cold and dismissive.

''This interview has come to an end, Mr. Marsh. I can see no point in continuing this discussion further. My business affairs are not the concern of the *Tribune* or you.''

"Wrong again, Mr. Davidson. The *Tribune* has a deep interest in the welfare of the residents of Chicago, even those poor immigrants who have nowhere to go but the dilapidated housing you offer."

"Slums *they* have created!"

"Slums you perpetuate with greed and a lack of concern for the people who have come to this country seeking a better life. You take their money and steal their hope."

"Out! Out of my house, and don't come back!" Livid, Otis Davidson rose and rounded the corner of his desk with a rapid, angry step that brought him face to face with the taller man. "And you may tell your newspaper editor that I'll respond with a libel suit to any unfavorable comments he might publish about the manner in which I conduct my business. Is that understood?"

Delaney smiled for the first time. "Libel can be claimed only if the statements made are untrue, Mr. Davidson. But I can see I've upset you, and I think it's probably best that I leave now. I'll contact you again in the near future so we might continue this interview."

Davidson's cold stare was his silent response.

Delaney turned to the door, aware that Otis Davidson followed close behind. He drew the door open, immediately spotting a beautiful, startled young woman standing in the hallway nearby. Walking toward her with an innocuous smile, he took her hand in greeting.

"It's a pleasure to see you again, Miss Davidson. My name is Delaney Marsh. We met at the charity concert last May. I've been interviewing your father, but he has run out of time. Perhaps you and I will meet again when I return to finish the interview." Turning back to the seething gentleman, Delaney smiled more broadly. "Good-bye, Mr. Davidson. I'll contact you soon."

"You'll be wasting your time and mine, Mr. Marsh."

"We'll see."

Aware of the intense stares that followed him, Delaney accepted his hat from the maid at the door. The door clicked closed behind him as he started down the front steps, satisfied with the first in a series of interviews he was determined to conduct with Otis Davidson II.

"Arrogant, insufferable—"

Sybil turned to face her irate father. The beauty of her patrician brow was compromised by a frown. "Father, I've never seen you so furious. What happened?"

"Insolent, irritating—"

"Father . . ."

"That man came here today on the pretense of conducting an interview regarding the Davidson family's contribution to Chicago's growth. He then proceeded to attack me and my policies with regard to the immigrant problem in this city. The man has more gall than—"

"Delaney Marsh is a respected journalist, Father. He was honored for his work as a correspondent during the war."

"I don't give a damn who he is or what he's done! He's not getting in this house again! And I don't want to hear any more about him."

Turning on his heel, Davidson walked back into the library and slammed the door behind him.

The pale floral print of her gown enhancing the beauty of her vibrant coloring and classic features, Sybil remained where her father left her. She suddenly gave a short laugh. Raising her left hand to smooth the upward sweep of hair at the nape of her neck, she slowly uncurled her right, which Delaney had taken so politely in greeting. One of her own hairpins lay in her palm.

Arrogant, insufferable, possessed of tremendous gall—yes, Delaney was all those things. He was also handsome, intelligent, quick-witted, and daring, and every inch of her cried out to be loved by him. She had never met a man like Delaney Marsh before, not in the boring social circle in which her father would have her travel. She had kept her association with Delaney a secret from her father to eliminate the possibility of his interference until she was more certain of Delaney's devotion. But she was now unsure as to the prudence of that decision. Judging from her knowledge of her father and the depth of his anger, she suspected that Delaney had deliberately provoked him.

Delaney was up to something, and it irked her that he had not even mentioned his impending interview with her father when she was with him the night before. But then, that was just another of Delaney's attempts to put distance between them, and she'd be damned if she would let him succeed.

A small smile played around her perfect lips as Sybil raised her chin and took a deep, firm breath. But these problems were all temporary. In the end she would let neither her father's anger nor Delaney's reticence interfere with her plans. She was well aware of her attributes, both physical and material. She was all a man could ever want in a woman, and she would make sure Delaney realized it.

And whatever his game was now, damn him, she would not let Delaney Marsh get away!

Twilight had tempered the brightness of day, casting the familiar kitchen of the Case farmhouse into shadows. Allie's gaze strayed to a point outside the window despite the seriousness of the conversation that had caused James's sun-reddened brow to wrinkle into a frown. Taking a short step forward, he followed the line of her gaze. He saw Margaret standing in the doorway of the barn, a small black and white kitten in her arms. Her face was veiled by a fall of pale hair across her cheek, but it was obvious by the motions of her head and her gentle stroking of the feline's fur that she was deep into a one-sided conversation with the purring animal. James's heart softened. There were times when the depth of love he felt for Margaret astounded him.

Turning his attention back to Allie, James was aware that for all intents and purposes she had forgotten his existence. A possessive love welling inside him, he took a step closer and drew Allie's slender frame back against his chest. A sweet fragrance rose from the pale silk of her hair, so similar in color to her daughter's, but the fragrance was Allie's alone. It intoxicated him and he pulled her closer still.

"Oh, James, I'm sorry. My mind was wandering. What were you saying?"

Taking advantage of the opportunity her soft apology offered as she turned to him, James claimed her parted lips. The joy he experienced in Allie had not abated in the years they had been together. He knew it never would, but realizing it was not time to indulge the emotion that always lay so close to the surface when Allie was near, James drew back.

Allie glanced again toward the window.

"She's such a frail little thing, isn't she, James?"

"Allie, you of all people should realize appearances are deceiving."

"But Margaret—"

Allie's response went unfinished as Margaret lowered the kitten to the ground and gave it a gentle shove to start it back into the barn. James felt Allie tense as the child started toward the house, walking with a pained, ragged limp. Margaret's lurching gait worsened as she continued her approach, and James felt Allie's shudder.

Abruptly halting, Margaret glanced over her shoulder toward the barn. Two little furry heads appeared in the doorway behind her, and after a few seconds' hesitation, she turned laboriously back in the direction from which she had come. The child was obviously determined to return the kittens to the safety of their mother's care before she came inside, and James was grateful for the few additional moments of privacy she would allow them.

"You don't have any choice, Allie. Dr. Lindstrom is due to arrive at the clinic next week."

Avoiding his eye, Allie bit her lip with obvious anxiety, and James fought to subdue the protective feelings rising within him.

"I . . . I don't know if I want to take the risk, James. Margaret's so young."

"You don't really mean that, Allie. Margaret's hip is deteriorating rapidly. Do you want to wait until she's completely crippled?"

"We don't have the money right now, James."

Resurgence of an old guilt rose to color James's face. "You left Margaret in my care that day. It's my fault she was injured. If an operation can help her, I'll get the money."

Allie shook her head in vehement denial. "It wasn't your fault. It was an accident. You had no way of knowing Margaret would find her way into that stall."

"I should have watched her."

"James, she was so young and you thought she was asleep."

James nodded. "And because of my mistake Margaret will soon be completely crippled."

Allie glanced away, and James realized she struggled to suppress tears. But he would not relent.

"Allie, if you put this consultation off, it may be too late. Dr. Peters has no idea how long Dr. Lindstrom will remain in Chicago before he continues his tour. He's already made arrangements for you to stay at the home of an acquaintance who owns a boardinghouse in the city.''

''I—I don't think this is the right time, James.''

''Allie, I'd go with you if I could, but you know I can't afford to hire someone to take care of the farm. Dr. Peters says you'll be safe with his friends. They've even consented to accompany you to the doctor if—''

Allie took a step closer, her faltering words halting his plea as she spoke in a hoarse whisper. ''James, I'm afraid Dr. Lindstrom won't be able to help Margaret.''

Drawing her closer, James swallowed against the voicing of a fear he had been determined to suppress. Still refusing to allow it credence, James forced a smile. ''He will, Allie, you'll see. When you bring Margaret home, she'll be well and perfect again.''

Holding Allie until her quaking subsided, James did not speak again. Further words were beyond him.

chapter

eighteen

"YOU'RE A DAMNED fool, Marsh!" Pete Mulrooney's bellow echoed within the confines of his office.

From the corner of his eye, Delaney saw several heads pop up in the city room and turn in their direction. Pushing the door closed behind him, he shook his head. "Mulrooney, you'll never change."

"I don't expect to change. I'm the boss here, so if there's any changing to be done, it's going to be on your part. And I'll tell you again, you're making a mistake the way you're handling Otis Davidson. You're underestimating his influence in this city."

Delaney paused, his light eyes surveying the massive proportions of the man standing in front of him. He had been right when he had said Peter Mulrooney would never change, and he supposed he was glad he wouldn't. Almost eight years had passed since he had first met this veteran journalist and editor. Mulrooney was now grayer, a little more stooped, and incalculable pounds heavier than he had been, but the changes were all superficial. Inside, Mulrooney was still a fair, keenly intelligent, surprisingly sensitive man despite his deceiving appearance and his current state of agitation. Delaney was only too aware that

Mulrooney's sensitivity was responsible for allowing him to develop to his present level of journalistic ability. But Mulrooney was still committed to his convictions and willing to defend them to the death.

He was also a damned good friend.

"Calm down, Mulrooney. You know it never works to pull rank with me."

Mulrooney shook his large, untidy head. "You're right, I should know better. I keep forgetting who I'm talking to. After all, you're Delaney Marsh, veteran war correspondent, entrepreneur, and spiffy man-about-town. But you still work for me, dammit!"

Delaney could not suppress a laugh, which drew a startled expression to Mulrooney's face. "Well, that's the final damned straw!" the editor bellowed.

Realizing he was doing little to lessen his friend's agitation, Delaney sat down in the nearest chair and looked up into Mulrooney's angry face. "All right, talk."

Suspicious, Mulrooney squinted in Delaney's direction for a few silent moments before lowering himself into his chair. When he spoke again his voice was more subdued. "You're asking for trouble, Marsh."

"I'm only following through on the assignment you gave me."

"No, you aren't and you know it. In the event you've forgotten, I'll reiterate the editorial policies of the *Tribune*. We're the enemy of monopolies and tax thieves in national and state politics, and we're the champion of the people. We do not support woman suffrage—"

"A mistake in policy—"

"We speak for tariff and revenue reforms on the national level, and we support the reappointment of David Wells as special revenue commissioner. On a local level, especially now that we've moved into one of Chicago's largest fireproof buildings, we have embarked on a project to awaken the people of this city to the fact that the Queen of the Prairie is in reality a sprawling tinderbox awaiting a spark! This is an important project, Marsh! The wooden construction used in this city puts thousands of lives at risk every summer when the dry season is upon us. The prairie winds make every brushfire a threat."

Pausing, Mulrooney drew back his head, tucking his neck into his rounded shoulders, and Delaney was reminded of a watchful turtle pulling cautiously back into its shell. He was tempted again to laugh, but he did not.

"All this does have a familiar ring to it, doesn't it, Marsh?" the editor continued. "It should, because it's the same speech I gave you several weeks ago when I handed you this project. Fireproofing! That was the reason you were to interview Otis Davidson! A man of his stature could lend considerable credence to the cause. If he will agree to begin fireproofing his properties, the lambs of this city will soon follow behind him. We want to make Chicago impervious to fire! We want to make this city safer for its inhabitants. You were supposed to court the man, dammit, not alienate him!"

Delaney shook his head, his temper starting to rise. "I never had any intention of courting Otis Davidson, Mulrooney. That man doesn't care about the inhabitants of this city—except for those few who are on his social level, and he's not about to spend a single cent that won't benefit him directly. But he's too slick to come right out and say that. In order to get the truth out of him, you have to get past his condescension and platitudes, and the only way to do that is to make him angry."

"Well, you've accomplished that, all right. We've received a warning from his lawyers."

"Is that right? So I've succeeded in getting him to take me seriously."

Mulrooney's eyes narrowing. "You may be an arrogant bastard, Delaney Marsh, but I know you too well to accept this whole thing at face value. You're up to something."

"I'm just following your orders."

"Marsh . . ."

"I'm trying to make Chicago safer for some of its inhabitants—namely a particular group of immigrants who are being taken advantage of and whose lives are in danger."

Mulrooney's attention was immediately riveted. "You're talking about those murders in Healy Slough and Conley's Patch."

"That's right."

"What information do you have on them? The police appear to be stymied."

"By the power of money."

"Whose money?"

"That's what I intend to find out."

"You're not implying that this money is Otis Davidson's—"

Delaney shook his head. "No, I'm not. Davidson is a lot of things, but he's not involved in prostitution."

"Prostitution!" Mulrooney shook his shaggy head. "But if Davidson's not involved, why—"

"Most of my articles so far have been concerned with fire hazards in Conley's Patch and Healy Slough. Everybody knows that Davidson owns most of the property there. Certain people will be less suspicious about my spending so much time in that vicinity if I keep writing about Davidson's neglect of his holdings, and if I keep demanding that he make improvements. It will also be easier for me to get the people down there to talk to me if they believe I'm on their side, especially if I'm willing to buck Davidson's big money for them. So I'm killing two birds with one stone—taking care of the assignment you gave me while I investigate the murders."

Mulrooney shook his head. "You're a crafty bastard, Marsh."

"I thought you said I was an arrogant bastard."

"You're that, too. But if you're not careful, you're going to find yourself up against someone who will give you a little more trouble than you can handle."

A smiled played over Delaney's lips. "Does that mean I have your approval for this investigation—boss?"

Mulrooney's eyes narrowed. "Damned arrogant, too." After a moment, he slowly nodded. "Yes, you have my approval, if it means anything to you. I'll run interference between Davidson and you for a while, but be careful. I'm not about to lose the investment I have in you."

An unaccustomed warmth touched Delaney as he drew himself to his feet. Mulrooney's concern wasn't all professional, and he knew it. "Don't worry, you won't."

"And keep me informed."

"I will."

Delaney covered the distance between himself and the doorway without another word. He stepped out of the office and pulled the door closed behind him, not bothering to look back. He didn't have to turn around to know Mulrooney's eyes followed him through the glass panel, that he was shaking his head and mumbling.

* * *

The sun beat warmly upon her shoulders, but Allie was immune to its tranquilizing rays. She glanced to her side, noting the manner in which Margaret's head turned from left to right, her bonnet bobbing as she followed the morning activities at the train station.

Allie turned toward James as he emerged onto the platform where she and Margaret waited. He held two tickets in his clenched fist, and Allie's heart leaped.

After sending a reassuring glance into her tense face, James leaned toward his daughter. "I have the tickets right in my hand, Margaret. You and Mama are almost on your way to Chicago. Are you excited?"

Her heart constricting in her chest, Allie watched Margaret's fair brow tighten. "I—I don't think I want to go, Papa."

Allie saw the pain in James's eyes as he raised Margaret's small chin with the tip of his finger. "Oh, yes, you do, honey. Mama and I already explained to you that this doctor Mama is taking you to is a very famous man. He's helped a lot of people who have problems like yours, or worse. Because of him, most of those people can walk normally again, and he's going to do the same for you."

Margaret flashed Allie a quick plea for understanding. "But I want you to come with us, Papa."

"I can't, Margaret. You know I have to finish putting in the crops. And I can't leave old Bessie and Jack, Whiskers and the kittens, and all the rest of the animals with no one to take care of them. But I'll be thinking about you and Mama while you're gone, and I'll be waiting for you to come walking off that train, good as new."

Unable to bear James's reassurances any longer, Allie shook her head. "James, I think it's best if Margaret realizes that Dr. Lindstrom might not be able to—"

"There is no such possibility." His fair skin coloring, James kept the vehemence of his statement carefully controlled. "The doctor will help Margaret and she'll walk perfectly again."

Allie watched in silence as James crouched down and took Margaret into his arms. He held her close, and Allie heard his hoarse whisper. "Papa will miss you, darling—both you and

Mama, so you must be good and listen to the doctor and Mama so you can come home all the faster. Do you promise?''

Margaret's response was a muffled ''I promise,'' and Allie saw tears marking her daughter's pale cheeks as James released her.

Hearing the whistle of a train in the distance, they turned in the direction of the dark cloud of smoke drawing ever closer along the tracks. James straightened up and turned to Allie. Without speaking, he took her into his arms, and she leaned full and hard into his strength and goodness. She gave him her mouth, allowing him full possession, realizing with a startling stab of fear that the time had truly come for parting. She did not want to leave him.

The ground-shaking thunder of the train's engine was deafening as it drew into the station. James released her with reluctance, reaching down to grip the hand Margaret raised to his. A few minutes later they were inside the railway car seeking their seats, and Allie fought the assault of memory as the familiar smell of old leather, mildew, and ash met her nostrils. She closed her eyes briefly, seeking to cast aside memories she had thought long buried.

''Mama, over here!''

Fixing a smile on her lips, Allie closed the distance between Margaret and herself as James carefully stored their suitcase. The conductor's warning call from the platform outside the car reached them over the sounds of the wheezing engine and the whistle's screech, and Allie gave James a look filled with apprehension. His response was to take her in his arms once more. The love and concern in his eyes was almost more than she could bear.

''I asked Dr. Peters to guarantee the clinic the money for an operation.''

''But how? You know we can't—''

''Margaret is all that matters right now, Allie. Let me know when the doctor decides to operate.''

''But, James—''

The conductor's appearance inside the car and the lurch of the train as it started into motion raised a sudden panic inside Allie. She clutched James more tightly, breathing in the soft whisper of his words against her lips.

"I love you, Allie. Come home to me soon, both of you."

Tearing himself abruptly from her arms, James was gone. His fair hair glinting in the bright sunlight where he stood on the platform a few moments later, he raised his hand in farewell as the train pulled out of the station.

Seating herself beside Margaret, Allie leaned toward the window, her eyes unmoving from James's gradually diminishing figure. All too soon it slipped from sight, and Allie was suddenly aware of the small tear-streaked face looking up to hers. She forced a smile and held Margaret's hand.

"No more tears, Margaret. This is going to be a great adventure for us. You're going to meet a wonderful doctor, and he's going to fix your hip so you'll never limp again. We're going to do it together, you and I, and we'll take care of each other. Now, let me see you smile, darling."

Hours later, Allie stared unseeingly into the darkened landscape flashing past the window, her mind far from the rail car in which she and her daughter traveled. The rhythmic clicking of the tracks beneath her, the car's jolting sway, the screeching whistle, and the conductor's droning calls returned her to the child she had once been. She recalled her fear of the uncertain future as she had traveled in a darkened car similar to this. She remembered that she had been lost and alone, and without hope—until Delaney.

Raising her hand to her throat, Allie unconsciously fingered the outline of the chain and medal concealed beneath the cotton fabric of her dress. Her mind reverted inevitably to the hard, sullen boy who had given her back the gift of faith.

Clutching the medal tightly, Allie was unable to suppress the memory of the man that boy had become, and the solemnity of the moment when he had placed the chain around her neck. She remembered the love she had felt for him, the beauty, the fulfillment of the intimate moments they shared. She remembered the commitment she had read into the act that had joined their bodies . . .

Unable to bear the pain of the memories that followed, Allie closed her eyes to the shadowed landscape, her fingers whitening around the silver disk, but she was allowed no respite from their assault. The image she had sought to banish from her mind emerged bright and clear, translucent eyes appearing to see into her soul. She saw again, burning in their crystal depths, the love she had once believed was so firm and true. It seared her.

A small movement at her side brought Allie back to the present. She turned toward Margaret's sleeping form and leaned closer to pull the blanket up more firmly around her. Love for her small pale-haired child welled within her. No matter the course her life had taken after that night, this child had been conceived in love, for she had loved Delaney deeply. She supposed a part of her would always love him, and a part of her would always be grateful that Margaret was Delaney's child.

But Allie was intensely aware that the small, frightened girl who had traveled these rails to an unknown destiny so many years ago no longer existed. She was now a woman, a wife, and a mother. The past was dead. There was only the future, toward which this train raced through the long, sleepless hours of night.

chapter

nineteen

"REALLY, SYBIL, DO you think this is wise?"

Sybil Davidson's response was a flirtatious, heavy-lidded glance that left no question as to the reason for her unexpected appearance on Dearborn Street, a short distance from the *Tribune* building. She stepped up beside Delaney and tucked her hand under his arm. She assumed his pace as he continued walking, pressing herself tightly to his side. She felt Delaney's muscled thigh brush against her skirt as his elbow lightly touched the full outer curve of her breast, and her smile broadened. She thoroughly enjoyed the calculated seduction she practiced, which had been successful in drawing Delaney to her despite his early reservations. She knew she needed to keep him intrigued and challenged to maintain his interest, and she worked diligently at doing just that. She also knew her audacity in appearing unexpectedly and openly attaching herself to his arm amused him despite his comment.

"Delaney you're a cad. How dare you seduce me with your gaze in full daylight, right here in view of passing traffic?"

Delaney's knowing glance was a silent refutation. "Who's seducing whom, Sybil? I'd say it's more than coincidence that you decided to take a casual stroll along Dearborn Street at noon when I usually emerge from the office for my midday meal. The only problem is, I'm going into the building today, not coming out.''

"Well, that's fine with me. I'll go inside with you."

"Oh, no, you won't!"

"Delaney, darling, we have to talk!"

"Oh, is talking what you had in mind for this afternoon, Sybil?"

Sybil cast Delaney a confident, knowing glance. She looked her alluring best in her forest-green walking-out suit, and she knew it. The tight, narrow waist of the garment made the most of her womanly curves, and the modified bustle was just flirtatious enough to draw attention. Her fashionable Rembrandt hat, ornamented with fluttering ostrich feathers, was cocked jauntily to one side, calling attention to the soft blue of her eyes. She knew Delaney appreciated every aspect of her appearance, and that realization increased her temerity.

"Well, I thought we'd talk . . . among other things."

Delaney's low, husky laugh shot a thrill up Sybil's spine.

"You're a temptation, Sybil."

"Where shall we go?"

"I'm going upstairs to work."

"You're being tedious, Delaney. I'm very serious when I say I must speak with you. Father was very angry after your interview with him several days ago. You know, of course, you handled him all wrong. If you had mentioned your interview to me, I could've helped you to—"

"I don't need your help." Delaney's gaze was as cool as his voice. "And I don't want it."

Anger tightened Sybil's lips. "Father is determined not to speak to you again. As a matter of fact, if he has his way, he'll—"

"I'm not worried about your father."

"Well, perhaps you should be!"

Realizing she was pushing too hard, Sybil swallowed her words and attempted another tack. "Delaney, don't look at me that way. You make me quite upset. If you don't want my help—"

"Your interference—"

"Whatever you choose to call my desire to help you in dealing

with my difficult father, I'll certainly let you struggle on alone.
I would much prefer that the two of you get along well, but—''

"What possible difference could it make to you if your father
and I get along or not?''

Delaney was obviously baiting her, waiting to spring on her
response, but Sybil was not about to accommodate him. Realizing their conversation was drawing stares, Sybil managed a
coy smile as they drew up alongside the entrance to the *Tribune*
building.

"I repeat, you're a cad, Delaney Marsh, and I can see this
particular conversation has come to an end. And since part of
my reason for being here today has been accomplished, only the
other part remains.'' Pausing, Sybil gave Delaney a slow wink.

Delaney considered Sybil's statement for long, silent moments, the ice in his gaze melting slowly. "I have to take care
of a few things for the late edition.''

"I'm free this afternoon, and I really don't mind waiting,
darling, provided the reward is suitable.''

Another pause. Appearing suddenly to have made a decision,
Delaney nodded. "It shouldn't take long, and then I'll be free
for a few hours.''

"Only a few hours?'' Sybil held his gaze, sliding her small,
pink tongue tantalizingly along her bottom lip. "I was hoping
we might spend the rest of the day together. As a matter of fact,
I've come up with some rather clever innovations in the ways
we might—''

Contrary to her expectations, Delaney did not smile. "You'll
do anything to get your way, won't you, Sybil?''

Deciding to brazen it out, Sybil fluttered her heavy fringe of
lashes as she responded softly, "Anything.''

The smile that finally touched Delaney's lips was cool. "So
will I.''

Drawing open the door, Delaney ushered Sybil inside.

The monotonous click of the rails continued in rhythm with
the car's jolting sway as the sun-drenched prairie flowed past the
train window. Civilization was beginning to make inroads into
the panorama stretching out before her eyes when an unexpected
sense of anticipation began to temper Allie's anxiety. She glanced
toward the seat beside her where Margaret gazed intently out

the window, realizing her mixed feelings were influenced by the excitement in her daughter's expression as their journey neared its end.

"Mama, look! I think I can see Chicago! It's a big city, isn't it?" Apprehension flickered momentarily in her daughter's dark eyes as she continued, "But Papa said the place we're going to stay is nice and cozy. Papa said that the time will pass so quickly that I'll have to think really hard to remember it."

Allie nodded. Margaret's attention had already returned to the passing landscape, and she did not really expect a response. But Chicago was not as close as Margaret thought. Judging from the conversations she had overheard, they had at least another hour's traveling time.

Restless, Allie glanced around her. The car had been nearly empty when Margaret and she had boarded, but almost every seat was now filled. Her eyes lightly scanning the passengers, Allie noted that there were only a few other children in the car, and each of them appeared to be part of a large family. The other passengers looked like businessmen and frequent travelers, judging from their bored expressions. One short, slim fellow with a bright face and quick smile seemed to be a drummer, for he kept his sample case within reach when he engaged a fellow passenger in conversation. Allie guessed that he was a frequent traveler on this line for he had spoken quite knowledgeably to his seatmate about the area through which they were passing.

Her gaze returning to the passing landscape, Allie heard the familiar voice of the drummer as he engaged another passenger in conversation. He had an enthusiastic voice that distracted her mind, and she was grateful for the diversion. Smiling despite herself, Allie realized her eavesdropping was allowing her an insight into the problems the city of Chicago faced because of its rapid growth. Poor construction was one problem. Some of the larger buildings had been slapped together so quickly that bricks often fell into the streets from the facades, injuring pedestrians. Inadequate housing was another, and many immigrants were forced to live in slums. And then there was—

The drummer's monologue ended with an unexpected gasp, and Allie glanced in his direction. The fellow had pulled himself upright in his seat and was staring out the window toward the

curve of track ahead of them. He was tense, his expression incredulous.

"What the hell . . . ? Look! There's a train coming around
the curve!" His voice cracking, the fellow crouched forward to
stare more intently before exclaiming, "It's on the same track
we're on! It's coming straight at us!"

The screech of the train's whistle was simultaneous with the
grinding of braking wheels that threw passengers forward in their
seats, knocking others to the floor into a melee of dislodged
packages, tangled limbs, and cries of pain. Thrown into the aisle,
Allie scrambled to reach Margaret even as realization turned to
terror in her mind. The train's shrieking whistle again rent the
air only to be echoed by a helpless response from the approaching train in the few seconds before the world exploded in a
jolting, tumbling crash of tearing metal, agonized screams, and
then . . . merciful darkness.

The light tapping of Sybil's foot again interrupted his concentration, and Delaney, totally disgusted, slid a weary hand over
his eyes and attempted to maintain his control. Sybil and he had
entered the office an hour before, and the few details, which
should have taken no more than fifteen minutes to finish, had
become a monumental task because of the burden of her presence. He had been a fool to think that Sybil would conduct
herself in a mature manner and allow him to work in peace, but
he was fully aware that he had no one to blame for his aggravation but himself.

Casting a glance around the city room, Delaney noted that
Sybil's presence had finally been accepted for the most part and
the curious whispers and craning of necks had stopped. The
admiring glances had also ceased, at least temporarily. He should
have anticipated that his appearance with Sybil Davidson on his
arm would cause a stir, but he had expected a more professional
attitude from his contemporaries. His mistake apparently had
been in neglecting to take into consideration that his co-workers
were mainly male and only human. Sybil was a beautiful woman
who made the most of her physical assets. Her clothes were
expensive and eye-catching and her proportions were perfect.
She turned heads on the street, and had nearly snapped necks in
this office.

He suspected the impact of Sybil's presence was not entirely due to her physical appearance, however. The fact that she was immediately recognized as Otis Davidson's only daughter, and that the bad blood between that snobbish boor and Delaney himself was well known, probably had played a large part in the attention paid to her entrance.

Delaney was surprised at Sybil's desire to bring their association into the open at such an unpropitious time, but the consequences mattered very little to him, since he would not be the one to suffer them. As for Sybil, he had no doubt that there was method to her madness. There usually was. But he also had hidden motives for associating with her, and he was too smart to fall into any of her traps. He would have been a fool to refuse her lascivious invitation, wouldn't he?

Wrong.

Sybil made that realization only too obvious to him the moment she entered the busy *Tribune* office, disrupting it with her flirtatious glances and coy remarks and playing the gaping young men against one another as they fought for a better view or another smile. When attention to her began to wane, she became bored and took to annoying demonstrations of her boredom, ranging from subtle yawns and drumming fingers to tapping toes, which were about to drive him crazy.

It was also obvious that Mulrooney was not pleased.

Casting a glance toward the glowering editor's office, he saw Mulrooney rise to his feet. It was apparent from his expression that he did not intend to wait a minute longer for Delaney to finish the piece he needed for the next edition. Opening the door of his office with a jerk that set the glass panel to wobbling, Mulrooney started heavily in Delaney's direction, only to be stopped as a copyboy pushed a slip of paper into his hands. Taking only a moment to read the message, he continued on toward Delaney's desk. "You have the damnedest luck, Marsh."

Delaney drew himself to his feet as Mulrooney thrust the slip of paper into his hand. His gaze dropped to the printed lines as the agitated editor continued, disapproval apparent in his tone. "It looks like you're going to be spared my opinion of your judgment in bringing a visitor into the office when there's work to be done. This wire says there's been a train wreck just outside the city—a bad one. It's your baby, and I want comprehensive coverage, Marsh. I want to know the reason two trains were moving at full speed in opposite directions on the same track. I want to know the extent of the damage, the number of casualties—deaths and injuries. I want to know the kind of response received from emergency services. I want human interest stories. I want to hear about the heroes and the villains, and I want to be able to feel the pain, Delaney. I'll send some other men later on, but I'm depending on you to coordinate the effort and get me the story first. Now get moving before every hack in the city is gone!''

Reaching for his hat, Delaney had taken his first step toward the door when an exasperated protest sounded behind him.

"Delaney, you aren't going! What about me!"

Realizing he had forgotten all about Sybil, Delaney turned to frown into her incredulous expression.

"Another time, Sybil. Scott . . . ?'' A red-haired young man a short distance away turned at Delaney's summons. "Would you see to it that Miss Davidson gets home?"

"Delaney!"

"I'm sorry, Sybil.''

Sybil's astonished gasp sounded behind him as Delaney slipped the wire into his pocket, jammed his hat onto his head, and started for the door. It occurred to him as his footsteps echoed his speedy descent down the staircase that in leaving Sybil behind he experienced no regret at all.

He hadn't seen anything like this since the war.

Frowning into the choking black smoke spiraling upward from several burning rail cars, Delaney strained to see as he picked his way through the wreckage of the colliding trains. Only two cars were still upright. The others were strewn like broken matches along the tracks. Wounded and dead passengers were scattered amid the debris, impeding the progress of fire fighters. Several more ambulances arrived, but their number was still pitifully inadequate. Confusion abounded, further hindering the rescue process as fires continued out of control and the cries of the wounded grew louder.

An apparent switching error had caused the two trains traveling at top speed to meet head on with enough impact to wreak almost total devastation. A fire had erupted in one of the cars

and strong prairie winds had quickly spread the blaze, compli-
cating the rescue efforts. The situation was so dire that after
arriving at the scene, Delaney had taken only the time to record
a quick summary of the situation before sending his notes back
to the *Tribune* with a copy boy. He had then jammed his pencil
and notebook into his pocket and joined the rescue effort. In the
time since, Delaney's fedora had gone the way of his stiff collar
and cravat and his jacket had disappeared across the chest of a
badly injured man in his total absorption in aiding the wounded.

His eyes smarting from the smoke emanating from a nearby
car, Delaney helped lift another wounded man into the rear of a
heavily loaded volunteer wagon before turning to survey the accident scene once more. A long line of injured passengers lay
sprawled and bleeding along the tracks, waiting to be trans-
ported to the nearest hospital, while others wandered dazedly in
search of their loved ones. The rescue attempt had not even
touched some of the cars farther along the track, although vol-
unteers and professionals were working at maximum effort.

Turning at the sound of a muffled cry, which was almost indistinguishable in the pandemonium around him, Delaney
strained to see through the gritty, unnatural twilight. A small
figure near an overturned car staggered into his line of vision,
and he moved immediately toward it. He was within a few feet
of the child when he jerked to a halt and a low gasp escaped his
throat. That pale hair and slender outline, the way she moved
her head . . . No, it could not be!

The girl staggered again, and Delaney ran toward her, catching her as she lurched weakly forward. The small, soot-stained
face she turned dazedly up to his froze the name on his lips.

Allie!

"Mama! Mama . . ."

The girl's ragged whimper snapped him out of his bemused
state, and Delaney shook his head in an attempt to clear his
mind. No, it was impossible. This girl was a child, near the age
Allie had been when he first saw her. She was the exact image
of Allie, with her pale flowing hair and small pointed face. Even
her great dark eyes were the same, and she was of a delicate stature
so similar to Allie's that his heart ached as his arms closed around
her and he attempted to carry her away from the wreckage.

"No!" Suddenly struggling, the child fought his protective

embrace, squirming and crying in desperate appeal. "Mama . . . she's hurt!"

Unable to restrain the frantic child any longer, Delaney lowered her to the ground, supporting her until she regained her balance. Not waiting to see if he followed, the child scrambled back in the direction from which she had come and within moments was kneeling beside the partly concealed body of a woman. Darting him a frightened glance, she began struggling with a huge metal panel that lay across the upper body of the woman.

Signaling the child back, Delaney took one corner of the heavy panel and strained to raise it. He noted that it rested partly on the dislodged passenger seat that lay beside the woman, sparing her most of its crushing weight. Grunting, his muscles straining, Delaney felt the metal sheet begin to move at last, and with a final powerful thrust he pushed it aside. The woman's face was turned away from him, allowing him a view of pale hair, the like of which he had seen only once before. Shaking, almost unable to breathe past the obstruction that had formed in his throat, Delaney carefully turned the woman's face toward him.

Dazed disbelief reverberated in Delaney's mind as he stared for an incredulous moment into Allie's blood-streaked face.

A low gasp, not quite a sob, not quite a groan, sounded in his throat as he strained to see her more clearly. His trembling hand moved against her throat, seeking a pulse, and he closed his eyes briefly, breathing freely once more only after he felt life fluttering beneath his fingertips.

The child at his side began sobbing, and Delaney turned in sudden realization that she was Allie's daughter.

"You . . . your mother will be all right. Don't cry. I need you to help me rescue her."

His plea brought the child's gaze to his face, and Delaney was impaled by eyes so similar to Allie's that they stabbed him with pain. Near panic, Delaney glanced around. Realizing there was no help to be found, he worked carefully, with trembling hands, to remove Allie from the remaining debris. When she was totally free but still unconscious, he examined her cautiously. The blood from the gash on her forehead was beginning to clot, and he saw no immediate danger there. He was more concerned with the peculiar angle of her arm and shoulder, but a closer examination did not reveal any broken bones. The pronounced swelling of her right ankle and his subsequent examination led him to believe the same was not true there. A quick check revealed no other visible injuries, and realizing he had to take the risk of moving her, Delaney slid his arms under Allie's slender frame and slowly lifted her.

Bittersweet joy tempered the panic that threatened to overwhelm him as Delaney started forward. Clutching Allie as tightly as he dared, he strained his eyes into the dusky turmoil around him, a part of his mind aware that the child who clung silently to his side was limping painfully.

Suddenly aware that Allie's breathing was becoming more shallow, that she was going cold in his arms, Delaney was swept with a wild, overwhelming fear. Reacting violently to it, he increased his pace almost to a run, as he tried to convince himself that fate could not be so cruel. He could not have found Allie again simply to lose her!

chapter

twenty

A PINPOINT OF light appeared in the darkness. It grew gradually larger, beckoning her forward, but Allie's struggle to reach
its flickering glow was fraught with pain. Her body ached, and
the pounding agony in her head was a burden she could not
escape. It impaled her with each stabbing thrust, weakening her.

A rumble of voices reached her from beyond the dark tunnel
that imprisoned her. Her mind separated a child's sob and a
familiar male voice from the muddled sound, filling her with
anxiety.

The anguished sobs grew louder, and Allie despaired. She
knew that sound. She recognized its pain. With an excruciating
effort, she began moving toward the light. Her breath quickened
as the glowing circle widened to reveal strange faces, concerned
frowns.

"Doctor, the patient seems to be regaining consciousness."

A practiced hand touched her brow, and an unfamiliar voice
spoke words she did not quite comprehend. She felt a small,
anxious hand slip into hers, and she heard a halting, whispered
appeal. Margaret.

There was movement beside her, and a gasp escaped Allie's

throat as clear, translucent eyes met her gaze. It was a familiar dream, an image that haunted her, but she knew she would be free of it if she could summon the courage to dismiss it once and for all.

Margaret's sobs grew louder, bewildering her. Dream or reality, she was unsure, but she could not ignore her daughter's appeal.

With an effort that exhausted the last reservoirs of her strength, Allie willed her hand closed. She experienced a brief elation as her fingers curled around the small hand clutching hers, holding it fast. The sobbing ceased, and she squeezed harder, holding tightly to Margaret's hand in unspoken promise until the light faded away.

Relief softened the tired lines of Dr. Willis's face as he turned toward Delaney with a weary smile. "It's my guess that this young woman has just taken her first step toward recovery."

Standing beside the bed in the guest room of his house, where he had kept vigil since he placed Allie there almost twenty-four hours before, Delaney gave a short nod. His stiff muscles ached with fatigue and the stress of the hours past, and he was not satisfied with the doctor's comment.

"How much longer do you think it'll be before she'll be totally conscious?"

"I'm a physician, Mr. Marsh, not a prophet. This woman has had a very close call. Her body suffered a severe shock, which she very nearly did not survive. The laceration on her forehead is superficial, but she is severely concussed. Her shoulder is seriously traumatized, her ankle is broken. In addition to that, she's badly bruised and in considerable pain. The only positive statement I can make at this time is that although it's difficult to ascertain internal problems, I believe there is no serious injury. Her response to her daughter shows she's in control of her faculties and that she is strong-willed enough to battle the trauma she has suffered. My belief is that, from this point on, rest will cure far better than any medicine I might administer."

Pausing, the aging doctor sighed briefly. "I must say I'm pleased to be able to speak these words to you. She's a lovely young woman, and there's been enough tragedy already in the wake of the accident."

Aware of the older man's fatigue, Delaney did not press him further. Watching as Dr. Willis dropped a few things back into his bag and reached for his coat, Delaney turned to the nurse who stood watchfully a few steps away.

"Miss Hatcher, I'm going to see Dr. Willis out now. When I return, you can put Margaret to bed."

"I want to stay with my mother!"

Turning to study the child who still clung tightly to her mother's hand, Delaney frowned. She was the image of Allie, and she obviously possessed her mother's courage as well. Concealed as Allie had been beneath the wreckage, she might have gone unnoticed until it was too late had the girl not had the presence of mind to seek help. He would be forever grateful to the child for that, but gratitude was the only emotion he could manage. She was Allie's daughter, but somehow he could not seem to forgive her for being James's child as well.

"Your room is nearby if your mother should need you."

"Mama always needs me. She—"

Dr. Willis interrupted with a gentle smile. "Your mother needs rest and quiet now more than she needs your company, dear." Noting that the girl's stubborn expression had not softened, he continued in a kindly tone, "It will be far better if you get some rest now. You may spend all day tomorrow with your mother if Mr. Marsh agrees. She will need you to help her when she finally awakens. Your mother would agree, I'm sure."

Turning back to the bed without response, Margaret buried her face against her mother's arm. Dr. Willis moved toward the door. When it closed behind Delaney and him, he shrugged. "You really can't blame the child, can you? She's had a terrible fright, and she doesn't want to let her mother out of her sight. I suggest you tread lightly."

"It was not my intention to beat the child into submission, Doctor."

"Appearances would make it seem otherwise." Dr. William Willis's bushy gray brows drew together in a frown as he walked down the stairs beside Delaney. "There it is again. If looks could kill . . ." He shook his head. "Well, I suppose we're all tired and could use some sleep. Miss Hatcher is an excellent nurse, and there's no need for you to remain by Mrs. Case's bedside through the night. I gave Margaret some good advice just now. I'll give the same to you. Get some rest, and when Mrs. Case needs you, you'll be there for her.''

At the front door Delaney extended his hand toward the stooped physician as he prepared to leave. ''Thank you, Dr. Willis.''

''You've thanked me several times, Mr. Marsh, and you've not argued with a word of my advice. So why is it I get the feeling that the moment I leave this house you'll do exactly as you see fit?''

''You may rest assured Mrs. Case's treatment will follow the exact guidelines you detailed.''

''And the rest of my advice be damned.''

Not bothering to respond, Delaney drew open the door. ''Will you stop by in the morning?''

''On my way to the hospital. Every retired physician in the city has been called out for this emergency. If there's any difficulty during the night, remember, I live only a few houses down the street.'' At the dark knitting of Delaney's brow, Dr. Willis added hastily, ''I said *if* there's a problem. I don't anticipate there will be.''

A short nod was the only reply he received. Dr. Willis studied Delaney briefly with a narrowed gaze before turning to make a stiff descent down the front steps.

Waiting until the doctor stepped onto the sidewalk, Delaney closed the front door and started rapidly back up the staircase.

Two steps into the sickroom and Delaney knew he would receive no further argument from Margaret that night. Still seated at her mother's side, her head resting on the bed, the child was asleep.

Lifting Margaret in his arms, Delaney signaled the nurse to follow as he carried her to the bedroom at the end of the hall. He laid her carefully on the bed, then gestured to the young nurse to follow him outside again. Closing the door behind them, he spoke in a whisper. ''Take care not to awaken her when you prepare her for bed. She's exhausted and not reasonable at this point. You may have difficulty handling her. I think you'll be comfortable sleeping on the chaise longue beside her. There are extra blankets in the wardrobe.''

Confusion touched the young nurse's round face. ''I had expected to care for Mrs. Case.''

"I'll stay with Mrs. Case tonight. The child may need you if she awakens during the night."

Not awaiting the young nurse's response, Delaney turned and strode back up the hall, relieved to hear the click of the bedroom door behind him.

Delaney approached the bed and looked down into Allie's face. The disbelief with which he had first viewed her amid the wreckage of the train was undiminished. Incredibly relieved to be alone with her at last, he needed time just to look at her, to allow his thoughts to filter free of the myriad emotions that had assailed him since he found her unconscious. The only clear-cut thought that had emerged through his shock and fear was the realization that he had been wrong to think he no longer cared.

Delaney strained his muddled memory in an attempt to recall the progression of events after discovering Allie and lifting her into his arms. He remembered his panic, his dash to the closest carriage, Margaret clinging to her mother's skirt as he dragged her along beside him. He could not remember the argument he had used to persuade the reluctant driver to take them immediately back to the city, but he recalled his anxiety upon their arrival at the hospital when he learned that it was filled to the limit and there was no room for Allie. It was then that he had remembered Dr. Willis.

The frantic drive to his home was a nightmare, but Dr. Willis had been at Allie's bedside within minutes. The next few hours passed in a blur, and he lived a lifetime as he waited for Allie to awaken from her unnatural sleep.

During that time he thought very little about the child who clung so tenaciously to her mother's bedside. He felt nothing for her beyond a mild sense of relief when Dr. Willis examined her, found her miraculously uninjured, and concluded that her limp was due to a hip problem that was not related to the wreck.

Allie's whimper brought Delaney's thoughtful meanderings to an abrupt halt. She moved in her sleep, and Delaney stepped closer to her bedside and crouched beside her. A multitude of memories flooded his mind as he stroked her cheek. It was strange how the years of separation seemed to slip away now that she was here, close to him again. He had never been able to strike from his mind the texture and fragrance of Allie's skin, the purity of feature that was exclusively hers. Gently brushing a few pale strands of hair away from the dressing on her forehead, he reaffirmed in his mind that there was no match for the pale silk of her hair, in color or texture, just as he knew there was no match for Allie in any way at all.

He sought the physical changes that years had wrought, but he could find few differences. Maturity had touched Allie lightly. She was still slight, her frame as delicate as that of the child he had held in his arms years earlier. The planes of her cheeks were more clearly defined by the years in a way that simply added to the grace of their line, and the light brows and the fan of lashes, which lay on her skin, subtly complimented her fragile appeal. The years had refined Allie's delicacy, and the pallor, the "lack of color" Allie had despised, had become the gossamer luster of a rare, unconventional beauty. It was a beauty that would go unacknowledged by some, but which he had seen in her from the first moment of their meeting. It had torn at his heart years ago, and it tore at it still.

Allie's breast rose and fell in a gentle natural sleep as Delaney trailed his hand along the rise of her cheek, the line of her jaw, the slender column of her neck. His fingertips rested lightly on the spot where the narrow lace edging on the oversized sleeping garment Miss Hatcher had furnished met Allie's throat. He paused in his caress when the glimmer of silver around her neck met his eye. He stiffened.

His heart began a rapid pounding as he turned the lace down with trembling fingers, then jerked back from contact with the familiar chain as if he had been burned.

Drawing himself to his feet, Delaney took a step back, self-anger transfusing his mind. What was the matter with him? Allie was no longer a child. She was a grown woman, married to another man and mother of another man's child. She had changed, and so had he. It made little difference that she still wore the medal he had given her. That was part of a past that was irrevocably lost.

Jerking spasmodically in her sleep, Allie gave a low gasp. As if in the throes of a frightening dream, she moved once more, but the effort seemed to cause her pain and she trembled visibly.

Fear replacing the anger that had filled his mind only seconds before, Delaney crouched at her side. Uttering soft words of consolation, he drew her close, curving his arms as tightly around her as he dared. Leaning toward her, he pressed his cheek to hers, allowing the warmth of his presence to still her unconscious fears.

The past was dead and gone, but the memory lingered, and he could not deny that Allie had touched him in a way no other woman ever had—or ever would. She was with him now, and he would take care of her until she was well. He owed her that.

Allie's tormented shaking had ceased, but Delaney did not draw away. A smile touched his lips as he again stroked her cheek. Allie had always felt safe in his arms. Much had changed between them, but that had not.

Her lips twitching with suppressed anger, Sybil strummed her fingers impatiently on the velour seat beside her. Through the carriage window she looked at the early morning streets as her lumbering conveyance made its way at an unbearably slow pace along Wabash Avenue. She had risen at an ungodly hour with the specific purpose of speaking to Delaney at home before he left for the office. She had no intention of confronting him anywhere near the *Tribune* building where he had embarrassed her so dreadfully three days before.

Her tender sensibilities still outraged, Sybil fumed with renewed heat as she recalled the way Delaney had turned his back and abruptly dismissed her from his mind at the first mention of the train wreck. And then he had turned her over to that popeyed, red-haired adolescent to be delivered home like some unwanted baggage! As if that was not enough, Delaney had left her to stew in her own fury for three days, during which he had not even attempted to apologize!

Her anger and disappointment at Delaney's boorishness and the cancellation of the lovely afternoon she had intended they would spend together had finally begun to fade as she dressed for Harriman Bain's party the previous night. She began to mellow, recalling that she had always forgiven Delaney his minor transgression, and thinking that things would change after she managed to maneuver him into marriage. The rumor that reached her ears during the party, however, was the last straw. She'd be damned if she'd be dropped for some unknown woman he had picked up at the train wreck and taken home with him! It was humiliating!

With a furious sweep of her hand, Sybil smoothed her raven locks and adjusted the guinea fowl plume on her stylish Windsor hat. Delaney was a fool! Didn't he realize whom he was tossing aside for some common wench? Sybil gave a short, angry nod. Well, if he didn't, she intended to make sure he did!

All but twitching as the carriage turned onto Peck Court, Sybil drew herself stiffly erect. She was well aware she looked lovely in her striking royal blue wool gown and matching wrap, that the shade deepened the azure hue of her eyes and complemented her vibrant coloring. She knew she far surpassed the other women on her social level in natural beauty, good taste, and cultivated grace, and she was certain she would outshine the cheap trollop Delaney had taken to his bed. She was also determined to dispense with the woman once and for all!

The shadow of a smile touched the outer corners of her lips as Sybil added a well-considered postscript to that thought. She would then forgive Delaney—but when the time was right, she would make him pay.

The carriage drew to a halt before the stone facade of Delaney's home, and Sybil made a last-minute check of her appearance as her driver opened the door. With a short admonition for him to wait for her, she stepped down onto the sidewalk and stalked toward Delaney's door. Olga responded to her sharp knock. The old dowd's startled expression might have amused her under other circumstances, but her agitation allowed no reaction but annoyance.

"Is Mr. Marsh at home, Olga?"

"Yes, he is, Miss Davidson, but he—"

"You needn't tell him I'm here. I'll let myself up."

Brushing past the flustered woman, Sybil walked directly to the staircase and climbed to the second floor. She was familiar with the location of Delaney's bedroom, and she intended to become even more familiar with it, as well as with the remainder of Delaney's adequate but entirely unappealing bachelor residence. She had already formulated in her mind the changes she would make in the decor after they were married. She would turn it into a showplace.

But first things first.

Stepping onto the second floor landing, Sybil headed for the master bedroom at the end of the hall, only to be startled as a door on her left opened unexpectedly.

"What are you doing here, Sybil?"

Stepping stiffly into the hallway, Delaney pulled the door closed behind him. Sybil was startled by his appearance. He did not look at all like a man who was enjoying a three-day romp with a woman of questionable virtue. Quite the contrary. He had never looked more intense. He was casually clad in an open-necked shirt and trousers tailored to the exact measurements of his impressive lower portion, and Sybil's heart gave a little leap at the sheer masculinity he exuded. His handsome face was sober and a bit drawn, with shadows apparent underneath his clear eyes. A shock of black hair hung forward on his forehead, as if he had run his fingers through it with an anxious hand. Jealousy surged anew within Sybil at the thought that it might not have been Delaney's hand that had caused the disarray.

"I've come to see you, Delaney." Forcing a smile, Sybil attempted to close the gap between them, but Delaney held her back with his arm.

"I'm not in the mood for visitors. If I were, I would have extended an invitation, Sybil. I did not extend one to you."

"Oh, did you not!" Enraged, Sybil glanced at the doorway through which Delaney had just emerged. "If rumor is correct, it wasn't necessary to extend an invitation to the guest you're hiding in that room. It's my guess that *she* usually extends the invitations—especially to men! Really, Delaney, I'm disappointed in you! You needn't have resorted to a common woman you found at the train wreck for company. I'm certain I could do as much for you as she—and much, much more."

"Keep your voice down, Sybil."

Glancing again toward the doorway behind him, Sybil felt a slow flush rising to her cheeks. "Why? Does your ladybird resent being awakened early? That's unfortunate, because it's time she was pushed out of the nest!"

"And who's going to do the pushing, Sybil? You?"

"If necessary!" Sybil turned toward the door, but Delaney grabbed her arm roughly. Almost lifting her off her feet with the strength of his grip, he turned her forcibly toward the staircase and started down, dragging her behind him. Halting at the front door where Olga still stood, openly staring, Delaney glared heatedly into Sybil's flushed face.

"I think it's time for me to make myself perfectly clear to you, Sybil. The situation is as follows. This is my house. I invite those whom I choose to invite into it, and I invite those whom I choose to invite into my bed as well. The lady in the room upstairs is here at my invitation, and you are not. She will stay as long as I wish her to stay, whereas you are leaving—right now!"

"You're making a mistake, Delaney." Jerking her arm in an attempt to free herself from his grasp, Sybil was tight-lipped with fury as he threw open the front door. "You'll regret your treatment of me."

Delaney's response was a brief, infuriating laugh that did not touch his eyes as he moved her out onto the doorstep with a firm, unyielding thrust. "Perhaps I will, but I doubt it very sincerely. Good-bye, Sybil."

Humiliation, rage, and an almost overwhelming desire to cry robbing her of words as Delaney closed the door in her face, Sybil whirled to face the street. Raising her chin, she made no effort to look around for witnesses to her debasement as she descended the front steps at a carefully controlled pace. Walking directly to the carriage that awaited her, she didn't bother to assess her driver's expression as she ordered imperiously in a slightly quaking voice, "Take me home, Barnes."

Holding herself rigidly erect, the stain of humiliation still coloring her face, Sybil vowed her revenge.

Delaney turned away from the door, his anger apparent as he met his housekeeper's apprehensive gaze.

"I'm sorry, Mr. Marsh," Olga said. "I wasn't expectin'—I mean, the lady pushed right past me!"

Ignoring the woman's halting apology, Delaney responded in an ominously low voice. "Miss Davidson is no longer welcome in this house. If she appears unexpectedly again as she did today, you have my permission to tell her so and close the door in her face. Under no circumstances will I suffer her entrance. Is that understood?"

"Yes, sir."

Turning away from his housekeeper, Delaney started back up the staircase. He took a deep, steadying breath in an effort to control his anger at Sybil's denigrating remarks about Allie, and her supreme presumption in entering his house and attempting to eject one of his guests. It would never have occurred to Sybil that a man could prefer another woman to her. He had been amused by her antics for a short time when he first met her, and his amusement and her considerable expertise in more intimate matters had kept him pleasantly entertained. But he was tired of her conceit, her snobbishness, and her maneuvering. Most of all, he was tired of her. He was fairly certain he had gotten that message across to her. He hoped he had.

Dismissing Sybil Davidson from his mind as easily as he had closed the door behind her, Delaney experienced the return of the anxiety that had been his constant companion since Allie had reentered his life. After three days, Allie still had not regained full consciousness. It was too long. That thought had prompted him to summon Dr. Philip Selby, a renowned specialist in head injuries, the previous day. After a brief visit, Dr. Selby confirmed Dr. Willis's assessment of Allie's condition. She was mending slowly and would regain full consciousness when the pressure of her concussion lessened enough to allow it.

It could not be soon enough.

His dark brow knitting in a frown, Delaney took the last three steps to the second floor and stood staring at the closed door of Allie's room. The house was quiet. Margaret had not yet awakened, and Miss Hatcher, who had been on duty through the night, had gone home. The day nurse had not yet arrived. He had planned it that way so that he could spend some time with Allie alone. He had had little opportunity for such a luxury since the night he brought her home.

Frowning more darkly, Delaney started toward the door, remembering the peace he had made with the past during that first silent night when he held Allie in his arms. He remembered how difficult it had been to release her when he heard footsteps approach the room the next morning.

Circumstances had seemed to slip beyond his control after that. Margaret, bright, tenacious child that she was, had returned to her mother's side immediately upon awakening, and it had been difficult to persuade her to leave the room even for meals.

Delaney paused outside Allie's door. The whole situation had turned into a nightmare from which he could not seem to awaken. Unwilling to return to work while Allie's condition remained uncertain, he had not left the house in three days. Messages from Mulrooney had become stronger and more frequent until he had finally appeased the angry editor by sending him an article about the accident. It had since received critical acclaim and would doubtless advance his career immensely. All his other projects in connection with the *Tribune* had come to a temporary halt, and at the present time he neither knew nor cared when he would resume them.

Delaney pushed open the door and entered Allie's room. He looked at the bed where she lay, still unmoving. A familiar ache coming to life inside him, he swallowed against the lump that formed in his throat. There was very little outside this room that meant anything to him anymore, most especially the presumptuous witch he had unceremoniously dumped on his doorstep only a few minutes before.

Slowly, Delaney walked to Allie's bedside and stood looking down at her. She lay so still that she hardly appeared to be breathing at all. How long would this agony of suspense continue? How much more of it could he bear? He felt a perverse desire to shout, to startle Allie awake from her unnatural sleep, to shake her until she shouted back, her dark eyes snapping with anger and life. The great, painful emotion building inside him for the past three days was screaming for release, and Delaney clenched his fists tightly closed as he strained to maintain control.

Unable to restrain the words escaping his tight lips in a low hiss, Delaney spoke with a passion that came from the depths of his soul: "Wake up, Allie, damn you! Wake up *now*!"

In startling response to his command, Allie opened her eyes.

A gasp escaped Allie's throat as an angry translucent gaze met hers, and she closed her eyes again. She was still dreaming.

"Allie!"

But the voice was too clear, too intense to be a phantom sound, and she forced her eyes open once more. The vision that had tormented her dreams was closer. She could feel its breath against her face, could smell its sweet scent. It was so clear that she almost believed she could touch the dark hair that glinted in the sunlight of the room, and she reached toward it. Her fingers came into contact with the thick, heavy strands, and Allie jerked her hand back. The quick movement caused a resumption of the pounding in her temples that had dulled her senses for so long, and she squinted against the pain.

"Allie?"

A large, comforting hand took hers. She recognized its contours and looked up, only to become lost in a glowing translucence that seemed to consume her.

"Don't be afraid, Allie."

"Wh . . . what happened?" Her voice a hoarse, unrecognizable croak, Allie searched the room around her for something familiar.

"A train wreck. You were hurt and I brought you here."

"Here?"

"To my house."

Total recall returned with unexpected sharpness, and Allie briefly closed her eyes against the memory of grinding wheels, screeching whistles, terrified screams, and the breathtaking impact of collision.

"Margaret! Is—"

"She's fine, Allie. She's sleeping in the room down the hall. She hardly has a scratch. You were the one who was injured. You've been unconscious for a few days."

Still uncertain of the reality of the specter with whom she conversed, Allie questioned tightly, "Where's James?"

The gentle hand cradling hers stiffened. "Wherever you left him."

Her head was beginning to throb again and Allie squinted as much against the pain as with confusion. "Is he with Margaret?"

"Margaret's asleep down the hall," he said again.

"Does James know about the accident?"

"I don't know."

"I have to tell him. He'll be worried."

"It doesn't matter."

The lines of Delaney's face tightened in an expression Allie remembered well. She didn't know why he was angry with her, but the threads of their conversation were becoming lost in the shadows closing in around her. She raised her hand to her head, finding a bandage there.

"I—I'm tired. My head aches."

"Then close your eyes, Allie." The hand holding hers squeezed comfortingly. "I'll take care of you. Don't be afraid."

Allie was drifting away from the large, handsome room again, back into the darkness that had been her refuge. She was unable to respond, but she wanted to tell Delaney she wasn't afraid, that she knew he'd take care of her. Hadn't he always?

chapter

twenty-one

"I'm afraid, Mama."

Margaret's whisper was muffled as she pressed her face into the pillow beside her mother's head, but the anguish in her barely discernible statement tore at Allie's heart. She wanted desperately to wrap her arms around her frightened child and hold her close, but the simplest movement caused a resumption of pain, and she was incapable of the simple effort. Instead, she responded softly, managing to raise her head and press her cheek against her daughter's pale hair in a weak effort at reassurance.

"You don't have to be afraid anymore, darling. We had a terrible fright, but we're both going to be fine. I'll be on my feet soon, and we'll—"

"I want to see Papa." Margaret's tear-streaked face turned toward hers. "I don't want to stay here with Mr. Marsh. He doesn't like me."

A silent torment touched Allie's mind as she attempted to calm her disturbed child. "Of course he likes you, dear."

"He hates me, Mama." Tears spilling anew, Margaret nodded, insistent. "He does. He frowns every time he looks at me, and his eyes make me feel cold deep inside. He doesn't want me to stay with you. He always tries to make me leave your room.''

"Mr. Marsh is . . . an old friend, Margaret.'' Forcing a smile, Allie continued with difficulty, "You shouldn't feel that way. He's trying to help us.''

"I want Papa. I want to go home.''

Allie attempted to quell the waves of weakness sweeping her. This was all so difficult. There were so many things she still did not understand. She had awakened only a few hours earlier from a prolonged, frightening darkness filled with confusion. Delaney had seemed more dream than reality when she opened her eyes and found him beside her, but she was now painfully aware that he was only too real. The silent animosity between Delaney and Margaret, which had become apparent the moment her daughter entered the room, was far too debilitating for Allie to deal with in her weakened state.

"Margaret, dear, we'll only be here for a little while, just until I feel well enough to take care of things.''

"I want to go home now, Mama.''

"Your mother isn't well enough for this conversation, Margaret.''

The deeply voiced interruption from the doorway made Margaret and Allie turn toward Delaney as he entered the room. Allie's heart stirred at the familiarity of his towering height and tightly muscled physique, never more imposing than when he was casually dressed as he was now. But it was the severity of his tone to which her daughter responded as she hastily brushed the tears from her face and raised her firm chin.

"Your mother needs her rest," Delaney continued, "and I think you should leave. If you're at a loss for something to occupy your time, you can go downstairs and help Olga fix something for your mother to eat.''

"I want to stay here.''

Allie's gaze moved tensely between Delaney and Margaret. She was deeply aware of the irony of the quiet confrontation—two faces so dissimilar in appearance, yet so similar in expression; eyes diverse in color, yet reflecting the same unyielding determination, which was only one of the character traits they shared. But she did not have the strength to meet the strain of the moment.

"Please, darling, do as Mr. Marsh asks." Despising the weakness in her voice, Allie continued with determination, "Maybe you could make me some of your cinnamon toast." Margaret's frown darkened with marked resemblance to that of the man who watched her disapprovingly, and Allie's throat tightened. "Please, dear."

After taking only a moment to consider her mother's request, Margaret pulled herself to her feet. Her quiet "Yes, Mama" was accompanied by a glance toward Delaney, which was as frigid as the gaze that met it.

Closing her eyes, Allie listened as Margaret's uneven step sounded in the hall. When she opened her eyes again, Delaney was standing beside the bed. She did not have the strength for wasted words. "Have you notified James about the accident?"

Delaney did not respond.

"Delaney . . ." James's name on her lips had tightened lines of resentment in Delaney's face in a way that was achingly familiar, and Allie was swept with a brief bittersweet nostalgia. How many times had she attempted to deal with that same resentment in the past? How many times had she sought to soften the anger in Delaney's pale eyes? How many times had she been touched to the heart when that cold blue ice melted with a glowing warmth reserved for her alone?

"There's little point in contacting James now, is there?" Allie blinked, confused by Delaney's response, and Delaney took the opportunity to continue. "It could be dangerous for you to be moved. Dr. Willis made that very clear, and since James can't do anything to help you right now, I don't think there is any need to notify him."

Allie's mind was beginning to whirl. "I—I told James I'd write to him when I arrived. He'll be worried."

"He wasn't worried when he sent you and his daughter to the city unprotected."

"He couldn't come, and Dr. Lindstrom is going to be in Chicago for a limited time. Margaret must see him."

"Margaret told Dr. Willis about her hip. I'll make sure she sees Lindstrom."

Things were moving too fast for Allie to comprehend them clearly.

"But if James—"

"James will only get upset if he knows you're here."

"You don't really care if James becomes upset."

"I don't, but you do, and Dr. Willis said it wouldn't be good for you."

"But . . . but I can't stay here!"

"Do you have a choice?"

Allie allowed her eyes to close momentarily. When she opened them again, her voice reflected her growing weakness. "I do have a choice about whether James is informed or not . . . don't I, Delaney?"

Delaney's lips snapped tightly closed at her weakly voiced challenge. His jaw hardened as he fought to restrain an ire that touched her with a physical presence. But she had always been sensitive to Delaney's emotions. She had always felt his frustration, anger, and pain as deeply as her own, and she regretted that it had to be this way. But the time was long past for regrets.

"All right. I'll notify him."

"Delaney—"

"I said all right."

His light eyes frigid ice, Delaney turned toward the door.

Clutching his suitcase, James walked briskly, depending on the experienced passengers with whom he had arrived in Chicago to lead him through the confusing train station. On the street a short time later, he perused the hectic scene of impending arrivals and departures as he allowed himself a few moments to get his bearings and gather his thoughts.

The message in the wire delivered to his kitchen door had struck him with the force of a blow. The name signed at the bottom had been doubly startling: Delaney Marsh. Almost eight years, and the feelings of anger, loathing, jealousy, and distrust that he had experienced the first moment he saw that damn prison boy had surged to life again. But Delaney Marsh was a homeless prison boy no longer.

Searching the street for transportation, James remembered the details of Marsh's wire: a train accident; Margaret was fine but Allie was injured; they were both in Marsh's home and would stay there until Allie was well. The wire had not contained an invitation, but he had not needed one.

Carefully controlling his anger, James raised his hand toward

an approaching hack. He was certain there was a more econom-
ical way to the address Marsh had provided, but money was not
important right now. His first priority was, as it had always
been, Allie.

The hack that drew to a halt beside him was well tended, and
the powerful gelding straining impatiently at the traces was well
groomed. It was obvious this particular vehicle normally trans-
ported affluent customers. The well-dressed driver's speculative
expression confirmed his thoughts, and James felt a flash of anger.

"Wabash Avenue and Peck Court."

James settled himself on the spotless velour upholstery, and
the carriage jolted into motion. The elegant address Marsh had
supplied had not really surprised him. James had made it his
business to keep track of Marsh in the time since he had left the
farm. Marsh's continued contact with Max Marshall until the
editor's death had provided a flow of information about the success of his journalistic career. It was only after Marshall's death
that James had learned that Delaney had also maintained contact
with one of his less respectable associates in town. He supposed
it gave Lil Trevor great pleasure to pass along information about
Marsh's financial success now and again. They were, after all,
birds of a feather.

James frowned with a familiar resentment. He had long ago
given up trying to understand the twists of fate that had continued to rain financial misfortune on him even as Marsh became
more successful each year. He supposed the irony of it was never
so clear as now, as he made his way in his worn Sunday best to
the posh address of the prison boy to whom his family had once
given a home. Still, he knew that Delaney's wealth would not
bother him at all if it wasn't for Allie.

But Allie loved him, of that James was certain. He had seen
her change as the years passed, and he knew she had put Delaney
Marsh behind her. She was his wife, and she had made a commitment to him. There was no way in the world Marsh would
make her compromise that commitment.

Impatience edged James's thoughts as the hack continued its
steady pace through the crowded streets. Lifting his hat, James
ran his fingers through his damp fair hair in an anxious gesture.
The facilities on the train had been inadequate, and he was less

than fresh. He was also aware that he needed a haircut, that his clothes reflected the abuse of travel, and that the sleepless nights he had spent since receiving Marsh's wire had left visible marks of strain on his face. He was not at his best, and were he not so anxious to see Allie, he would not allow Marsh the advantage of seeing him this way. But he could delay no longer in seeing Allie. He needed to know she was all right, that she would soon be well. He needed to hold her in his arms and assure them both that whatever strange twist of fate had again touched their lives, she would soon return home with him.

And when Allie and Margaret did return home, James was determined to work every waking hour of the day toward giving them the life they deserved, even though he did not fool himself that he could ever match the affluence Marsh was rumored to have attained. He consoled himself, however, with the knowledge that he offered Allie something Marsh was incapable of giving—the security of love. He knew Allie had come to that same realization the day Sarah revealed that she, too, carried Marsh's child.

The hot rage of hatred James had experienced in that moment of revelation, years ago, was still alive and strong within him. Knowing Allie, loving and understanding her, James knew she might one day forgive Marsh for what he had done. But she would never forget.

The hot spring sun beating down on the stuffy carriage raised a flush of perspiration on James's brow, and he wiped it away with the palm of his hand. The carriage had turned onto a quiet tree-lined street of well-built, graceful homes. Low, elaborate iron railings separated the entrances from wide sidewalks shaded by new foliage, which lent a sweet scent to the air. It was serene and lovely, but James frowned as the driver drew the carriage to a halt.

Withdrawing the fare from his pocket, James stepped down from the carriage, paid the driver, and picked up his suitcase. The carriage continued down the street as he crossed the sidewalk, pushed open the gate, and started up the stone steps toward the carved oak door.

Taking the brass knocker in his hand, James rapped sharply. His gaze flicked over the gray-haired woman who opened the door, then rose toward the handsome, light-eyed man who had paused on the staircase behind her to stare coldly in his direction. Returning his stare, James stated flatly, "I'm here to see my wife."

The well-accoutred carriage that had followed James's hack down the street at a prudent pace drew to a halt a short distance away from Delaney's house. Leaning toward the window, Sybil felt a hand on her elbow as a low voice cautioned, "I thought you didn't want to reveal yourself in this surveillance, dear."

Annoyed, Sybil jerked her arm from the man's grasp. "This is none of your affair, Harriman. I informed you of my intentions before I consented to lunch with you today, and I told you I would not accept your invitation if you had any intention of interfering."

Harriman Bain's narrow, intelligent face moved into a faint smile. "You're correct, Sybil. It's to my discredit, I suppose, that I'm so much a fool over you that I'll agree to almost anything that will enable me to enjoy your company for a few hours, even something as foolish as helping you spy on an old lover."

"Harriman, please!"

"You know Delaney Marsh was your lover, and I know it. As a matter of fact, there are few people in our set who don't know about the affair, with the exception of your father. And the only reason he doesn't know is because no one has the courage to tell him."

"It would make little difference to me if he did know."

"It might make a difference to Marsh."

"Never! Delaney isn't afraid of him. That's why Father dislikes him so."

"Oh? I thought your father disliked him because Marsh all but accused him of being a hypocrite and a crook."

"I don't want to discuss it! I'm interested in something else right now, and you're distracting me."

Leaning his slender, perfectly tailored form forward, Harriman watched Delaney Marsh's front door as a fair-haired, commonly dressed fellow with a suitcase in his hand ascended the front steps. He turned back to Sybil's beautiful face, his jaded heart leaping in a way it did for no other woman. He supposed he would never completely understand his love for her. Sybil had been a willful, spoiled girl of fourteen when he had first met her, but, six years her senior and considerably indulged by parents wealthy enough to make them social equals with the Davidsons, he had found her amusing. Her aggressive pursuit of life had often mirrored his own youthful experimenting, and he had experienced both admiration and unexpressed dismay as he listened to the tales of escapades she boastfully recounted only to him. His response to her confidences had earned him the position of friend and confidant, which had become the bane of his existence as his own wild youth had slipped away and he had begun to view the beautiful, desirable woman Sybil had become in a different light. But despite his most diligent attempts, he had been unsuccessful in persuading her to take him seriously. Totally subservient to his passion for her, he had temporarily accepted the role Sybil chose to foist on him, but not without considerable impatience and occasional irritability.

Despairing once more at her malevolent chuckle, Harriman followed Sybil's gaze as she motioned toward the man standing at Delaney Marsh's front door.

"Rather common-looking, wouldn't you say? You do know who he is, don't you?"

"No, I don't. Nor do I care."

Sybil gave him an impatient glance. "That fellow is the husband of Delaney Marsh's latest amour, the woman he found at that stupid train wreck and took home with him."

"Sybil, really. You're making up a story to suit your own purposes. It's a well-established fact that the woman Marsh took into his home was injured in the wreck and is too ill to be moved."

"No one will ever make me believe that's all there is to it! I know Delaney, and I saw the change in him the moment he stepped out of that woman's bedroom. You should have seen him! He told me to keep my voice down, and he propelled me down that staircase like . . . like—"

"Did it ever occur to you that you had gone too far by forcing your way into Marsh's house and attempting to oust his invited guest?"

"Don't be a fool, Harriman! My behavior was high-handed and foolish, but I've been high-handed with Delaney before. Previously, my antics amused him, and I was able to get my way in spite of them. Under other circumstances, I would have been able to get out of the situation, but he was a different man that day. The look in his eyes when he came out of that woman's room was possessive, protective, almost fanatical! I think if I had taken one step closer, he would have dragged me away by the hair!''

Harriman's smile bore an incredulous light. "Sybil, you amaze me. I would think you'd be humiliated to admit the fellow threw you out.''

Sybil hesitated, considering his remark. "I've never hidden anything from you. I suppose I've never felt the need. You're always on my side, and no matter how outlandish my antics, you never disapprove.''

"Oh, but I often do.''

"Well, you never show it.''

"That's because I love you, and I know it would alienate you to show you how jealous I am of your lovers.''

Sybil cast Harriman a slightly amused glance. "Take care, Harry, dear. One day I may decide to take you seriously, you know.''

"I wish you would.''

Her gaze lingered briefly on Harriman's pleasant face; then Sybil turned abruptly. "You're distracting me. Now, look at that fellow. What do you suppose he does for a living? He's from Michigan someplace. You don't suppose he's a farmer?''

"A very honorable occupation.''

"Really, Harriman, be serious! Wait, look! The door is opening. It's Olga. It doesn't look like that old witch is going to let him in. Damn her, she'd better. The sooner he gets in, the sooner I'll be rid of that easy piece in Delaney's bed.''

Harriman shook his head, incredulous. "Think what you're saying, Sybil! You're one of Marsh's former lovers yourself, but you don't have the sense to see that he's finished with you. Now you've completely overstepped the bounds of accepted behavior by paying someone in his house to spy on him and report back to you.''

The polished oak door opened wide and the fellow on Delaney's doorstep stepped in. Releasing a satisfied breath as the door closed behind him, Sybil sat back and gave her companion her full attention as she spoke with a confident smile.

"Well, it won't be long now until Delaney is free and missing me desperately. In any case, I'm sure I'll find out tomorrow exactly what happened from the moment that unappealing fellow stepped into the foyer.'' Sybil was obviously pleased. ''You may tell your man to drive on, Harriman. I've suddenly developed quite an appetite for lunch.''

Suddenly serious, Harriman studied Sybil's beautiful face. ''Must you always get your way?''

''Yes.''

Harriman shook his well-groomed head. ''I'm sometimes appalled by my complete fascination with you, Sybil. I've become so sensible in all other aspects of my life. You are quite ruthless, you know.''

''Perhaps.'' Sybil held his gaze. ''But you've maligned me, unfairly in one respect, Harriman dear.''

''Have I?''

''Yes. I can't take credit for hiring a spy in Delaney's household, when the truth is simply that the temporary maid Delaney's housekeeper hired is a busybody and fond of gossip. Neither can you hold me responsible for the coincidence that finds her using the same greengrocer my maid uses.''

''Coincidence! Sybil, you live miles from here!''

Sybil lowered her heavily lashed eyelids seductively. ''Well, perhaps I am responsible, then.'' As Harriman raised his eyes to the ceiling of the carriage in disbelief, Sybil slid her arm under his. ''Anyway, I'm ravenous. We'll have a delicious lunch together, and a very entertaining time. You know I always enjoy myself when I'm with you, Harriman.''

Snuggling down at his side, extremely satisfied with herself, Sybil directed her gaze again toward the street as the carriage jerked into motion.

Sybil's carriage turned the corner and disappeared from sight, and a small man discreetly hidden on the opposite side of the street heaved a sigh of relief. He turned his attention back to the stone facade of Delaney Marsh's home, slapping at an insect that buzzed annoyingly at his pockmarked cheek.

He didn't like being in this part of town, and he was anxious to see this job come to an end. Sybil Davidson, nosy bitch that she was, was only making things harder by getting in his way, and he was glad to see the last of her for the day.

The man who had gone into Marsh's house a few minutes ago was a stranger to him. The way he looked and walked made that fellow seem as out of place in this neighborhood as he was. Something was going on in Marsh's house, and it was only a matter of time until he found out what it was.

Finding out was his job, and he was good at what he did.

His gaze intense as James stepped into the foyer, Delaney felt the stir of old animosities. He knew instinctively that his feelings were returned in kind and that time and circumstance had changed little between them. This man could never be his friend.

That thought causing him little regret, Delaney was acutely aware that this confrontation would be different from those in the past. James was now in his house, needing something from him. The reversal of their roles gave Delaney particular satisfaction, as did the realization that James would have to seek *his* goodwill now. Delaney's expression tightened with the silent acknowledgment that no goodwill would be forthcoming.

He assessed James through narrowed eyes. Case hadn't changed very much. There were new lines in his face and his clothes were a bit seedier now, but his self-righteous judgmental attitude was still apparent and still managed to get Delaney's back up. But whatever his personal feelings about James, he knew the fellow's feeling for Allie had never been in question. There was no denying Case's concern or his right to be in Delaney's home—but that did not mean he had to like it.

Dispensing with the amenities, Delaney said concisely, "Allie's upstairs."

Fully aware that he had not invited James to follow, Delaney turned and started up the staircase. A muscle ticked in his cheek at the sound of James's step behind him. Waiting on the upper landing, Delaney turned, unsmiling.

"There are some things you should know before you go into Allie's room. The first is that Allie has a severe concussion and Dr. Willis feels she shouldn't be moved. Her other injuries aren't serious but they're painful and they compound the dangers of her concussion, as do any agitations she might suffer. The only treatment the doctor has prescribed is rest and quiet." Delaney's frown tightened. "There's no love lost between us, Case. There never has been, but whatever you think of me, or whatever your objections to Allie's presence in my house, you'll do well to keep your thoughts to yourself for her sake. If you doubt the truth of anything I'm telling you, you can speak to Dr. Willis yourself when he arrives. Until then, you have no choice but to accept what I say and conduct yourself accordingly.''

James remained silent, his face flushing with resentment. Experiencing a heightening of his dislike for the man, Delaney took a firm hold on his control at Case's intentionally noncommittal response.

''Which room is Allie in?''

Bastard.

Delaney took the few steps to Allie's door and rapped lightly. At a soft response, he pushed the door open.

''Papa!''

Margaret's joyful exclamation echoed in the silent room as she limped past Delaney and threw herself into her father's arms. Delaney saw Allie's face whiten. Concerned, he went immediately to her side.

''Are you all right, Allie?''

''Y—yes.'' But Allie was breathing unevenly, and had obvious trouble with her simple response.

''Mama, Papa's here! Now everything is going to be all right.''

The happiness in Margaret's voice cutting deeper than he cared to admit, Delaney turned as the child pulled her father toward the bed. The silence while James stood motionless at Allie's bedside was broken by his low voice murmuring her name as he crouched beside her and drew her into his arms.

A familiar pain stirred anew inside Delaney, cutting deep into his heart as Allie closed her eyes and slid her arm around James. With supreme strength of will, Delaney turned and walked out into the hallway and pulled the door closed behind him.

Delaney disappeared through the doorway as Allie looked up into James's emotion-filled face. She saw the love there. She had felt it in his kiss, still warm on her lips, and heard it in his voice. Myriad emotions assailed her, confusing her. In the few moments James and Delaney had stood side by side in the doorway, she had sensed the tension between them, and a familiar despair returned.

"I'm sorry, James. I don't know how this all happened. There was an accident, and when I woke up, Delaney was there. Margaret said I was pinned by some wreckage, and when she went to find help, he was the first person she saw. She led him back to help me, but—"

"I wish I never saw him. I hate him, Papa."

"Margaret!"

Ignoring her mother's gasped reaction to her impassioned statement, Margaret continued with a heated fervor, "And he hates me, I know he does. You're going to take us away from here, aren't you, Papa? I don't want to stay here anymore. I want to go home with you."

The irony in James's glance was almost more than she could bear, and Allie turned toward her daughter's flushed face.

"Margaret, your father's tired and hot. Why don't you go down to the kitchen and bring him back something cool to drink?"

"Mama, I want to stay here."

"I *am* thirsty, Margaret"—James's soft interjection turned Margaret toward him—"and your mother and I need a few minutes to decide what's best for all of us. Do as your mother asks, like a good girl."

Accustomed as she was to obedience, Margaret moved reluctantly, halting at the doorway. "I'll be back in a little while, Papa, and when Mama has to rest again, you can come to my room."

James's smile touched Allie's heart. "That'll be just fine, dear."

Waiting only until Margaret had cleared the doorway, James turned back to Allie. There was only a moment's hesitation before his mouth found hers in an unrestrained kiss and Allie closed her eyes to its deepening warmth. His hands cupping her cheeks, James kissed her again, more passionately, his breathing ragged as he drew back with a low murmur of apology.

"I love you, Allie. When the wire came and I read you were injured, I was never so frightened in my life." James touched the bandage on her forehead lightly. "This is all my fault. I never should have let you and Margaret travel alone."

"It was no one's fault, James. We didn't have a choice. It's just that the situation is so complicated now."

The sound of a step at the doorway interrupted Allie's statement and made James turn toward Dr. Willis's stooped figure as he entered the room. The doctor approached the bed, Delaney a few steps behind him, and extended his hand in greeting.

"My name is Dr. Willis, Mr. Case. I've been treating your wife. It's my guess you'd like to know more about her condition."

James shook Dr. Willis's hand as the older man continued. "Your wife's condition has improved considerably since she first arrived in this house. I must say I credit Mr. Marsh's quick action with saving her life. By the time she arrived here, she was suffering serious reaction to the trauma. Had she remained at the site of the wreck unattended for any period of time, she might not have survived."

James's face whitened, and Dr. Willis patted his arm consolingly. "You needn't worry about that now, Mr. Case. That's all in the past."

"I want to take her home."

Dr. Willis shook his head. "I wouldn't advise it at present."

"But—"

"Mr. Case, your wife's concussion is improving, but she's not entirely stable. She still has moments of disorientation, dizziness—lapses—and her strength is only gradually returning. That should be apparent to you. What you cannot so readily see is that she is severely bruised, has a broken ankle, a traumatized shoulder—all injuries, that while they are more painful than dangerous, contribute to the seriousness of her condition."

"What are you trying to tell me, Doctor?"

Dr. Willis smiled at James's confusion. "I'm sorry, Mr. Case. I've said too much too fast. Suffice it to say that Mrs. Case cannot be moved at the present time."

James's sharp glance in Delaney's direction did not go unnoticed by Allie.

"When do you think I'll be able to take her home?"

"Mr. Case, I realize you're anxious to get your wife back to the safety of your own home, but it's impossible to answer you precisely. A few weeks, perhaps a month, maybe more."

"My wife can't stay here that long!"

Dr. Willis darted a confused glance at Delaney and then at

James, seeming to notice for the first time the tension between them.

"It would be inadvisable for Mrs. Case to travel at this time, even as far as a few city blocks. Mr. Marsh has agreed to oversee her care. He has also asked me to contact Dr. Lindstrom for a consultation regarding Margaret's hip."

James's response was immediate. "He has no right to act in Allie's or Margaret's behalf!"

Looking toward Allie with concern, Dr. Willis shook his head. "It won't do to upset your wife, Mr. Case."

Realizing for the first time that she was trembling, Allie attempted a smile. "I'm all right. I'm tired, that's all."

Dr. Willis touched Allie's cheek lightly. "Yes, I suppose you are. We'll continue this discussion outside, shall we, gentlemen?"

Allie shook her head. "No, please, I'm fine."

Dr. Willis squeezed her hand lightly. "My dear lady, you may rest assured this dispute will be settled expeditiously because I will counsel these two foolish fellows who are both so concerned about your welfare that they risk your health in debating the best way to care for you."

"I haven't said a word, Doctor." Speaking for the first time, Delaney held Allie's gaze as she glanced toward him. "I'm satisfied to follow your advice as to what's best for Allie."

James's sharp glance caused Dr. Willis to take a quick step between the two men.

"Outside, please, gentlemen. I'll be finished here in a few minutes, and then I'll join you."

When the two men had disappeared through the doorway, Allie turned toward Dr. Willis as he picked up a pitcher and filled a glass with water. He shook the contents of a medicine packet into the glass. Her heart pounding so rapidly that she had difficulty catching her breath, Allie attempted to ignore the growing pain in her temple.

"Dr. Willis, I would like to leave here as soon as possible."

"All in good time, dear." His voice gaining a firmness she had not heard before, Dr. Willis raised Allie gently on his arm. "Drink this. It'll calm you and allow you to rest."

"But, Doctor—"

"Drink."

Realizing she had little choice, Allie emptied the glass, her gaze fixed on Dr. Willis's sober expression as he lowered her against the pillow and ordered softly, "Now go to sleep."

Allie closed her eyes, her hand unconsciously seeking the comfort of the medal beneath her sleeping garment as the sedative began taking effect. The throbbing pain in her head and images of tense, angry faces vied with a slowly encroaching stillness. She saw a familiar outline in that silence. It was the Lady's face. She saw her smile as a voice crept into the darkness that was overwhelming her.

"Downstairs, gentlemen. We have some things we must discuss."

The sun was past its zenith when Dr. Willis walked out of the house at last. The front door clicked closed behind him and he released an exhausted sigh as he started down the steps. The unexpected animosity between Delaney Marsh and James Case had made matters extremely difficult.

Shaking his head as he turned toward his home a few houses down the street, Dr. Willis was grateful that he did not have far to walk. The antipathy between the two men had gone unexpressed, but its presence was almost physical, inhibiting their power to reason. The only common ground between them appeared to be their mutual concern for the lovely Mrs. Case. That concern had finally convinced Mr. Case to entrust his wife to Delaney Marsh's care and to abandon his plan to take her with him when he returned home in a few days.

Pushing open the gate in front of his residence, Dr. Willis climbed the steps to his front door. A pensive expression on his lined face, he shook his head. After all these years, the vagaries of the human spirit still continued to amaze him. One clear but unspoken fact had emerged from the discussion that had just ended. Both of those men loved that woman.

It was unfortunate, but only one of them could have her.

Delaney glanced at the clock in the foyer, then opened the front door and looked out into the street. His attention drawn by the hack pulling to a halt in front of the house, he paid little attention to the bright sunlight which etched a lacy pattern on the sidewalk and responded with absentminded courtesy to a strolling couple's greeting. Signaling the driver of the hack to wait, he started up the staircase to the second floor, his brow knitting in a frown as snatches of a soft conversation from Allie's room met his ear.

He strode toward the voices, aware that this was the first time in the several days since James's arrival that he had not deliberately avoided the room while James was present. Pausing in the doorway, Delaney said, "The hack has arrived."

"I'll be there in a minute."

His gaze on Allie's pale face, Delaney gave a perfunctory nod to James. He didn't like the way Allie looked. Miss Hatcher said Allie hadn't rested well or slept through the night since James arrived, and it was for that reason as much as his own desire to have James out of the house that he was glad James had to return to the farm. The situation was too much of a strain for Allie in her weakened state. Once Case was gone, Allie and he would be able to assume a comfortable relationship that would not impede her recovery.

At present he could not and would not think any farther than that.

Looking toward Margaret, who sat at her mother's side, Delaney saw open dislike in the child's eyes as she returned his glance. The girl looked like Allie, but she was obviously her father's daughter. She was not about to let him forget it.

Turning on his heel, Delaney left the room. In a few minutes his patience would be rewarded and James would leave. It could not be soon enough.

Delaney was standing by the front door a short time later when muffled voices on the upstairs landing drew his gaze to James as he emerged from Allie's room. Margaret was clinging to his side, obviously upset, and he crouched down to speak to her in a soft tone. Straightening up after a last good-bye, he came downstairs and picked up his suitcase. He turned to Delaney and spoke.

"There are some things I should say to you before I leave, Marsh. I don't suppose I'll ever understand you, much less trust you, but you saved Allie's life, and for that I owe you my thanks. You know I don't want to leave her here with you, but I don't have any choice. I've told Dr. Willis to send me the bills for treating Allie and arranging Margaret's appointment with Dr.

Lindstrom. I want you to know, too, that I intend to pay you back every cent you've spent.''

"I don't want your money."

James's eyes hardened. "Maybe not, but you might as well make up your mind that money's the only return you'll get for your efforts.''

His contempt returning full measure, Delaney gave a short laugh. "You haven't changed a bit in all these years, have you, Case?''

James's gaze remained steady. "Strangely enough, I've been thinking the same thing about you.''

Allowing a few moments for his words to register, James walked out of the house. Within moments his hired carriage had rounded the corner and disappeared from sight.

Delaney closed the front door with distinct relief, but he had taken only a few steps into Allie's room before he realized upon meeting Margaret's gaze that Case had not really left at all. James's hostility shone from the child's eyes, which were so similar to Allie's in every other way. His own animosity renewed, he frowned darkly.

"Margaret." Allie spoke, and Margaret turned toward her. "Mr. Marsh and I have some things to talk about. Please leave us alone for a little while.''

Her resentment obvious, Margaret followed her mother's request. Waiting until Margaret had limped out of the room, Allie turned to Delaney. Her distress started a small ache inside him.

"I haven't had an opportunity to talk to you in the past few days, Delaney. My head is a little clearer now, and I realize I've never thanked you for saving my life." Stiffening as he approached her bedside, Allie determinedly continued, "You've been very kind, and I—''

"What's all this talk about my being kind, Allie?" Aware that her expression of gratitude was an effort to put distance between them, Delaney took her hand in his own. The warmth of it was balm to his troubled spirit. "Didn't you tell me that I'd always be your friend?''

Allie's hesitation deepened the ache inside him to the point of pain. "That was a long time ago. A lot of things have happened since then.''

His gaze dwelling on the uncertainty in Allie's dark eyes,

Delaney nodded, resisting the memory of other, more intimate emotions he had seen there. "A lot of things—but whatever has happened to us and between us, one thing hasn't changed. You're still special to me, Allie. You always will be. There's no kindness involved. You need someone to take care of you right now and I'm here. That's the way it should be."

The glitter of tears appeared in Allie's dark eyes as she attempted a smile. "Eight years is a long time, but in some ways, it's no time at all. You're everything you ever said you'd be, aren't you, Delaney? You've worked hard, and you're successful and wealthy. I'm very proud of your success."

"Are you?" Delaney gave a short laugh. "So is James."

The lines of strain returned to Allie's brow and Delaney instantly regretted his sarcasm. "I'm sorry, Allie."

"I think we're all sorry—for a lot of things."

Suddenly unable to face his feelings as he sensed a deeper meaning to Allie's words, Delaney stroked back a wayward wisp of hair from Allie's face. His touch lingering, he cupped her smooth cheek with his palm, then spoke a truth that came from the bottom of his heart. "I think it's time to bury the pain of the past, Allie. Too much time has passed for us to waste any more on useless regrets."

"Delaney—"

"It's time to remember the good things, Allie. Think back. When you were alone and needed someone a long time ago, you took my hand, and everything was all right. It was good for you then, and it was good for me, too. I want to take care of you again. I want to make sure you'll be all right and to see you well and strong. Take my hand again, Allie. Trust me to make things right for you."

A shadow flicked across Allie's face.

"What's wrong, Allie?"

"Nothing."

The shadow remained and resentment stirred within Delaney as a voice in the back of his mind taunted that it was he who had cause for grievance, not Allie. She had promised to love him all her life, but her love had not included enough faith for her to wait a few short months for him to return for her. Instead, she had married James, borne James's child, and put James irretrievably between them.

But he didn't want to look back on the past with bitterness now. He just wanted to be Allie's friend again, to have her close to him the way she was a long time ago. He wanted to help her, and he wanted to feel her warmth. That was all he wanted. Why was she resisting him?

"Tell me what's wrong."

Averting her gaze, Allie removed her hand from his grasp. "I'm tired, Delaney. I'd like to sleep for a while."

Delaney drew himself slowly to his feet, steeling himself against the pain of Allie's withdrawal. She was ill, confused. When she was well again, she would be able to think more clearly. He would be here for her then, just as he had always been. And when she turned to him with warmth in her heart, the spot inside him that was hers alone would come alive again. He needed to feel that life. His heart had been cold and dead for too long.

But Allie had already closed her eyes, and Delaney walked quietly to the door.

Delaney's footsteps retreated down the hall, and safe at last from his scrutiny, Allie opened her eyes. His soft request echoed in her mind: "Take my hand again, Allie. Trust me to make things right for you."

Those words stirred a pain that was almost more than she could bear as Allie's mind shrieked in silent response.

How can you make things right for me, Delaney? Can you change the past? Can you change the night you told me you'd always love me, then walked away without turning back? Can you change the reality that the child who hates you, and whom you dislike so strongly is really your own? Can you erase the aching truth from my mind that you never really shared the joy and beauty I experienced in our joining? Can you make me forget that despite your beautiful words of love, it all meant so little to you that even while I cursed myself for causing the rift between us, Sarah was lying in your arms?

Closing her eyes, Allie took a ragged breath.

I've forgiven you, Delaney. A part of me will always love you, but I cannot forget what you did that night. The pain of your betrayal cuts me still.

Take your hand? I dare not.

Trust you? Never again.

Lost in despair, Allie turned to her side, the movement causing a physical pain to equal her mental anguish. The chain around
her neck slipped outside her nightdress, and the medal caught
her eye.

Allie closed her hand around the medal, breathing deeply until the painful images within her mind slowly began changing.
She was a child again, and she saw the handsome youth with
bitter eyes staring down at her as the rail car in which they
traveled shook and rattled its way through the night. His gaze
altered, softening unexpectedly. He slipped the medal into her
hand, and she felt its outline against her palm. It warmed her
heart, and she closed her eyes. She remembered the comfort of
his arm around her as she slipped off to sleep. She remembered
the peace, the love.

It was with her still.

chapter

twenty-two

DELANEY STRODE DOWN Wabash Avenue, his haste apparent. He silently assessed the mild May weather, satisfaction bringing a faint smile to his lips. Time had seemed to stand still for the past few weeks while spring regressed and the weather turned cold. The unseasonable bite in the air had abruptly halted the budding of trees and foliage. Flowers had maintained their semi-bloom as if all action had been stopped by the wave of a great, unseen hand. But now, as he headed home from the *Tribune* office, the bowers of the trees lining the street seemed lush, and the midafternoon air was heavily scented. The weather was actually balmy, and he was going to make the best of it.

Nodding to a neighboring matron and her giggling daughter as they strolled past, Delaney lengthened his stride. Giggling women . . . they still annoyed him no end. Allie had never had that propensity, and she had not changed in the time they had been apart—not in that way, at least. There had been other changes, however, almost intangible, keeping a distance between them in the two weeks she had spent recuperating in his home.

The silences that developed between them—ironically, when

they were closest to recapturing the spontaneity of the past—
were the most difficult. Allie would drift away from him then,
despite his efforts to bring her back. Somehow he did not believe
she thought of James in those moments. He sensed that something else caused the tension between them, but he did not feel
free to explore those silences with her. As if by mutual consent,
they had both avoided mentioning their last night together and
the painful events that led to their separation.

As for himself Delaney acknowledged that his bitterness, so
strong during the years they had been apart, mysteriously faded
the moment he saw Allie again and took her into his arms. He
had never been more aware of that than he was at this moment
as he hastened homeward after rushing through the day's work
to reassure himself that she was still there. It had been that way
for him since he had returned to work—the nagging fear that he
would one day return home to find James waiting to take Allie
away.

James had returned only once to visit Allie and Margaret.
Delaney supposed he should be grateful that James could not
afford to come to the city very often. But James kept in touch
with Dr. Willis and wrote to Allie and Margaret every day.

Delaney reminded himself that despite James's influence, Allie was still Allie. That fact became clearer each day as her
health improved. Her joy was still alive, apparent in her dark
eyes, if a trifle subdued. The spontaneity was there, occasionally
bubbling to the surface in their conversations, despite her effort
to contain it. Her interest in Delaney's work was difficult to
conceal, as was her pride in his accomplishments, and she appeared content to listen for hours on end as he discussed the
vagaries of his journalistic career, his aspirations, his concerns.
Their closeness, their similarity of spirit, had not changed, and
Delaney cherished it.

Time and again Allie astounded him with her comprehension
of the complicated issues they discussed, occasionally causing
him to reassess his thinking when she exposed him to her clear,
humanistic point of view. The warmth between them grew
stronger each day, with each touch, with each reminiscence, and
he took consolation in the fact that although the bond between
them had suffered through the years, it had not been severed.

It had become painfully clear to Delaney that he could not get enough of Allie these days. He supposed the fact that her stay with him was to be limited stimulated the desperation he felt each time she retreated from him. He silently cursed James for the hesitation he sometimes saw in Allie's eyes, for the lapse of trust occasionally visible there. He wanted her to be his ally, his friend.

Remembering James's parting admonition, Delaney gave a short, scornful laugh. Case had never understood the scope of feelings between Allie and him. They transcended the common physical relationship between a man and a woman, and if a part of him still longed for Allie in that way, he had stricken that possibility from his mind. He knew Allie. He loved and respected her for the importance he knew she attached to her wedding vows. Fidelity was an important part of her makeup. She had chosen loyalty to the Case family over him and he would have to accept her decision. He would be satisfied now to have a small part of Allie back. He had not realized how very much his life had been lacking without her.

Women, after all, were easy to find. Sybil had been haunting his trail for days, and he knew he had but to crook his finger and she or some other woman would come running. At present he had neither the interest nor the inclination.

Entering his home a few minutes later, Delaney tossed his hat on a chair and started across the foyer without a break in stride. He stripped off his jacket as he ascended the staircase to the second floor, dropping it on the hall table even as he pulled off his cravat, unbuttoned his shirt collar, and stepped up to Allie's bedroom door.

The door was open, and Delaney caught Allie's eye as she held a finger up to her lips in an unspoken request for silence. Glancing at the chaise beside the bed, he saw Margaret was asleep. Delaney walked to the girl's side, a familiar distress stirring to life inside him as he looked down at James's child. Firmly forcing it aside, he snatched up Allie's wrapper from the foot of the bed and sat beside her. Without a word of explanation, he raised her carefully to a seated position and helped her into the garment. Her whispered protest elicited from him the same unspoken request for silence she had given him moments before.

Standing up, Delaney scooped Allie into his arms. He ignored her wagging head and hushed objections, meeting them with a firm "shhhhh!" as he carried her out of the room and down the steps.

Allie's arm tightened around his neck as he reached the foyer and turned down the narrow hallway toward the rear of the house. Ignoring curious glances from Olga and the temporary maid, he carried Allie through the kitchen and into the back-yard.

He paused briefly when the sun touched Allie's pale skin and she emitted a soft gasp of pleasure. His reward complete, Delaney watched as Allie's dark eyes appreciatively surveyed the garden just bursting into life around them. His gardener's meticulous preparations were evident in the newly turned earth of rose beds and flowering shrubs, and he silently applauded the talent that had arranged to have daffodils nod in cheery greeting as he carried Allie along the path, and a bed of violets in full bloom encircling the bower toward which he headed. A chaise was lightly shaded by an oak tree and heaped with pillows and a coverlet in expectation of this afternoon's outing.

Lowering Allie gently onto the chaise, he adjusted the pillows behind her back, carefully slipping another beneath her splinted ankle before covering her legs. When he had adjusted the coverlet around her, he raised his eyes to find her studying him intently. He sat on the chaise beside her and brushed back a wisp of hair from her cheek, the uncomfortable thought registering in the back of his mind that he had used the wayward strand as an excuse to touch her.

"I thought you might like some air today. You haven't been out since the accident, and this afternoon was too good to waste."

Anxiety touched Allie's expression.

"Is something wrong, Allie?"

"I get confused sometimes, Delaney. Things are foreign and yet familiar in so many ways. It's been that way since I woke up after the accident. Everything still seems unreal sometimes. I have the feeling I'm going to wake up and find out this has all been a dream and I—" Allie shook her fair head. "Dr. Willis says this occasional bewilderment will pass, but it leaves me uncertain at times."

"Uncertain about what, Allie?" Concerned, Delaney reached

for Allie's hand. It was surprisingly cold, and he enclosed it in both of his, his gaze intent on her pale face.

"Uncertain about what's real and what isn't."

Delaney gave a short laugh that belied his concern. "That's easy to clarify. You're here with me now, in the garden. You've been in my house for two weeks, and you're getting better every day. The doctor says your shoulder is all but healed, your bruises have faded, the worst of your concussion is past, and in a few more weeks your ankle will be as good as new." Delaney touched the small, ragged mark on her forehead. "You may have a small scar . . ."

Suddenly realizing his hand had lingered longer than necessary, Delaney dropped it to his side, releasing her other hand as well. "But you'll still be beautiful."

"Beautiful?" A familiar disbelief replaced the uncertainty on Allie's face. "I'm no more beautiful now than I ever was. You're the one who's beautiful. You were when we were children, and you're even more beautiful now that you're a man. I remember thinking when I was a child that it was all right that I was plain, because you were beautiful, and that made me beautiful, too. But I'm long past the fancies of childhood, and beauty isn't important to me anymore."

His smile reflecting a sudden sadness, Delaney shook his head, his gaze moving to the chain barely visible at Allie's neckline. "So you've buried the past. . . . Is that why you still wear the medal I gave you?" At the unexpected glimmer of tears in Allie's dark eyes, Delaney reached out for her.

"Oh, Allie . . ." Drawing her against his chest, he held her comfortingly close and stroked her hair as he had when she was a child. "You'll always be a part of me, Allie, just as I'll always be a part of you. We were bonded long ago by everything that happened to us, by the medal, by what it means to you and what it means to me. It's all mixed together for us, and no matter what else changes, that never will. I tried to deny that a long time ago, but it wasn't any good. It isn't any good now, either."

Drawing back, Delaney smiled down into Allie's sober face.

"I want to help you, Allie, you and Margaret. I promised myself a long time ago that I would take care of you, that I'd never let anyone hurt you, but something went wrong. I still don't quite understand what happened, but even if it's too late

for us in some ways, it's not too late to make other things right.
When we part this time, Allie, I want to know things didn't go
all wrong again. I don't want my memories tarnished with bitterness and pain this time. James will never understand, but I
think you do. Don't pull back from me, Allie. Let me take care
of you. Trust me. That's all I ask."

Allie's sober expression flickered momentarily and Delaney
held his breath. He saw the final barriers she had erected between them waver, and an intense, aching need rose inside him.
He wanted, he needed—

"Mama!"

Margaret's voice reverberated in the stillness of the garden
and her step resounded on the path in the moment before she
burst into view.

"Mama, I woke up and you were gone! I was afraid something had happened to you, but Olga said you were in the garden." The glance Margaret turned toward Delaney was almost
accusing, and Delaney experienced a familiar irritation. He
turned back toward Allie as she spoke quietly to the agitated
child.

"Mr. Marsh thought I might benefit from fresh air and sunlight, Margaret." Allowing Delaney an unreadable glance, Allie
continued quietly, "But he was wrong, dear. I'm not feeling at
all well, and he's decided to take me back to my room so I may
rest. Isn't that right, Delaney?"

Startled at Allie's withdrawal, Delaney remained motionless
for a moment before slowly drawing himself to his feet. Feeling
a deadening sense of loss, he responded with a nod as he picked
Allie up in his arms and started back toward the house.

The last bold streaks of the setting sun were fading from the
twilight sky as silence finally settled over Allie's room. The door
had closed behind Margaret a few minutes before, and Allie
knew her daughter would soon be asleep in her room down the
hall.

Allie faced the thoughts she had kept at bay while her daughter claimed her attention for the major part of late afternoon.

Uninvited, pale blue eyes, almost translucent, again invaded
her thoughts, the plea in their depths touching her heart: *Let me
take care of you, Allie. That's all I ask. Trust me.*

Each word had struck Allie's heart with longing. She would never be able to tell Delaney how dearly she wished she could erase the pain of the past from her mind. She loved Delaney in so many ways that it hurt her to refuse him. She did not doubt that he loved her, in his way. It was the quality of that love she questioned.

Love you, Delaney? How could I not?

Trust you? My dear Delaney, can't you see? You ask too much.

Unconscious of the passage of time, except as a steady ticking emanating from the timepiece on the mantel, Delaney paced the floor of his bedroom. It was dark, and he was suddenly aware of the silence of the house around him. A quick glance toward the clock revealed it was a little past two in the morning, and a low sound of disbelief escaped his lips.

Was it possible that almost ten hours had passed since he had carried Allie back from the garden that afternoon? He had walked out of the house after that, his sense of loss acute. He had wandered the streets for hours, returning home at twilight to have Olga tell him that Mrs. Case was sleeping and did not wish to be disturbed.

He had then retired to his room, and Olga had brought up a tray. He glanced toward the nightstand. The tray was still there, exactly as she had left it.

The heat in the room suddenly oppressive, Delaney stripped off his shirt and threw it onto a chair. He was stiff, his body aching as if from strenuous exercise. He ran his hand through his hair in an anxious gesture as he attempted to gather his thoughts.

What had gone wrong between Allie and him in the garden? He had sensed the final barriers between them falling and joy had begun to swell within him. The fragile moment had been shattered by Margaret's appearance, but he had not expected Allie to become distant, shutting him out even more effectively than before.

Why was Allie holding back? He knew he couldn't blame James's disapproval or Margaret's dislike of him. Allie had gone against disapproval and popular opinion too many times in his defense. It was something else.

His agitation increasing, Delaney walked to the door of his

room, stepped into the dark hallway, and headed toward Allie's room. Alert to the silence within, Delaney entered the room and approached Allie's bed. The lamp on the night table was turned low and she was asleep. He looked down at her clear, beautiful countenance unmarked by the anxiety of their encounter in the garden that afternoon. Beautiful—how she fought that description of herself. Why couldn't she understand that she was incomparably beautiful to him, that she always would be? Why couldn't she accept that truth from his lips? Why couldn't she read it in his eyes?

His gaze lingered. The soft glow of the lamp lent faint shadows to the fragile contours of Allie's face. The pale gold of her hair strewn across the pillow was a matchless halo; her delicate features were composed, serene.

Delaney's heart began a ragged pounding. Allie was small, vulnerable, helpless—and he wanted her with every ounce of strength in his body.

The shock of his sudden realization held Delaney momentarily immobile. Lies, all of it! Everything he had said to Allie, everything he had told himself was a lie fabricated to escape a reality he could not face. He had never stopped loving or wanting Allie. He never would.

Delaney closed his eyes against his anguish. The ragged fabric of the life he had woven and named contentment had started unraveling the moment he had seen Allie again. The loose threads now littered his mind with lost dreams and broken promises, and a love that was so much a part of him that it would not die without taking his life as well.

Had Allie read in his eyes the truth he had denied even to himself? Was that the reason she held back from him?

Shaken, Delaney turned abruptly from Allie's bed. He walked back out into the dark hallway and closed the door behind him. In his room moments later, he felt a sudden, wild urge to laugh. Delaney Marsh had set stringent goals in his life. He had wanted success, and he had achieved it. He had wanted wealth, and he had attained it. He had wanted respect, and it was his. But Delaney Marsh had been too much a fool to realize that everything was nothing without the woman who gave life to his soul and joy to his heart.

But Allie had chosen another man over him, and Delaney

knew that his distress would only cause her grief. There had been too much grief between them. He could not be responsible for more.

Lying abed in his darkened room, Delaney stared at the shadowed ceiling over his head. Allie's image was clear before his eyes, her pale hair glowing, her dark eyes sober. She suddenly smiled, filling his heart, and he smiled in return, despite the choking thickness in his throat.

He would take care of Allie, just as he had promised. And when she no longer needed him, he would let her go. He loved her. It was the least—and the most—he could do.

chapter

twenty-three

"YOU'RE IN TROUBLE, Marsh."

Delaney frowned at Mulrooney's harsh words as he approached the scowling man's desk. The editor stood as he neared, drawing his impressive bulk erect, glaring, but Delaney was not surprised at his reception. The message to see Mulrooney had been waiting for him when he arrived at the office at an unusually early hour. Taking into consideration the articles he had been writing for the past few weeks, Mulrooney was probably upset. "I've been in trouble before," Delaney said.

"Not like this."

Delaney stood before the older man with growing impatience. He definitely was not in the mood for guessing games this morning. "Get to the point, Mulrooney."

"A messenger delivered some papers late yesterday—legal papers." Picking up a packet of papers from his desk, he shoved it toward Delaney, waiting only until it was in his hand and he was scanning the top sheet before continuing. "Otis Davidson is threatening to sue us."

Delaney shrugged. "So? The *Tribune* has received legal threats before. He's bluffing, but it doesn't really make much difference, you know. Every word I've written about him and his business dealings is true, and I can back it all up with evidence.''

''That's not the point.''

Delaney raised light eyes bright with anger to Mulrooney's unyielding countenance. ''What *is* the point, then, Mulrooney?''

''The point is, your attack on Davidson's management of his holdings in Conley's Patch and Healy Slough was supposed to be your cover for a bigger and a more important story about murder and a white slave prostitution ring, but you're letting it get out of control. Davidson is *not* our target here! We've been printing your articles, but that's all come to an end. I don't know what's gotten into you in the past few weeks, Marsh, but you've thrown your objectivity to the winds, as well as your common sense! Your original assignment was to bring to the public consciousness the need for fireproof buildings in Chicago, and you were supposed to start with large real-estate holders like Davidson, remember?''

Delaney fought to suppress an angry retort. His reaction did not go unobserved.

''That's right, you'd better hold your tongue. If I didn't know better, I'd think this thing between Davidson and you was a personal vendetta.''

''I don't give a damn about Davidson as a person, Mulrooney, and you know it.''

''Yeah, I know it. Maybe that's the point. You've got a bad case of tunnel vision, Marsh. While your investigation into the prostitution ring is floundering—''

''It isn't floundering, dammit! I've spent the last four days down in Conley's Patch, and people are really beginning to open up to me. In a few weeks, I'll have everything documented and I'll be ready to break the story. I might even have a witness who'd be willing to testify about the murders.''

Mulrooney's expression changed dramatically, and Delaney felt a flash of satisfaction. The old news hound smelled a big story in the wind. Now it was just a matter of how much pressure he was willing to take to get it.

Mulrooney's face drew into lines of concentration. ''I know you better than to think you're making all this up just to get out of a tight situation, Marsh, so I'll ask you a question: How much longer will you need to get everything firmed up?''

"A few weeks, just as I said."

Mulrooney nodded his shaggy head. "In the meantime I expect you to take it easy on Davidson."

"No chance."

"Dammit, Marsh, you—"

"If I start taking it easy on Davidson now, the people in the Patch won't believe a word I say to them. The attack on Davidson gives me credibility down there. They think if I'm not afraid of him, I'm not afraid of anybody else, either."

Mulrooney pointed to the legal papers in Delaney's hands. "And in the meantime, what am I supposed to do with those?"

Delaney carefully folded the papers in half and tore them in two. Then, leaning over Mulrooney's desk, he dropped them into the wastebasket.

"You're an arrogant bastard, Marsh."

"I've heard that before."

Mulrooney lowered himself into his chair, an action Delaney recognized as a ploy to gain time. Seated, he raised his frown to Delaney, regarding him with a narrowed, assessing gaze.

"I'll give you the time—a few weeks—to get this Conley's Patch thing straightened out. In the meantime, I want you to be careful what you write about Davidson."

"You're wasting your breath, Mulrooney."

Mulrooney's face flushing, he was on his feet again in a move that was surprisingly swift for a man of his bulk. Dwarfing his desk, he leaned forward on his wide palms to emphasize his softly spoken words. "I'm the boss here, remember, Marsh?"

Delaney's answering smile held no trace of warmth. "And I'm the man you hired to get your work done. I'm telling you it'll get done—all of it. I'm also telling you not to tell me how to do my job."

Slowly straightening, Mulrooney stared into Delaney's belligerent expression. "If you've got personal problems, Marsh, I don't want them impinging on your professional life. I expect you to use professional judgment at all times. Is that clear?"

Damn Mulrooney and his astuteness. "It's clear."

The editor nodded his unkempt head once more. "Then you're on your own again for a few more weeks." Glancing toward the wastebasket, he shrugged his beefy shoulders. "I suppose it'll take that long for Davidson to get another set of legal papers in motion." Mulrooney looked back to Delaney. "Go, Marsh. Get to work."

"I'm taking a few hours off this morning. A private matter."

"Go, Marsh! I don't want to hear any of this. I just want to hear you've got that story ready a few weeks from now. And I'm telling you, it'd better be good!"

Not bothering with assurances, Delaney turned toward the door. In a few minutes he was in a hack on his way home.

Turning to the passing street, Delaney saw little as his mind worked in familiar, disturbing channels. He might have been able to avoid this confrontation with Mulrooney if he had not left a few papers on his desk that he would need later in the day, but he would only have been putting off the inevitable. The heated exchange with Mulrooney was the culmination of the extremely difficult week that had passed since his nighttime visit to Allie's room. During that time, he had thrown himself into his work in an attempt to distract his mind. He had spent hours in Conley's Patch, interviewing residents surreptitiously, and had spent even more hours back at the office producing the articles to which Otis Davidson had reacted with legal action. Delaney was very close to getting enough information on the prostitution ring and the murders to bring the whole mess out into the open, but that realization provided him little satisfaction.

Even now, countless tormented hours after he had faced his true feelings for Allie, his anguish had not subsided. A smile fraught with pain touched Delaney's lips. He had never loved anyone but Allie. It was a bitter irony indeed for him to realize that, because he loved her, he would have to let her go.

Allie's ankle would soon be healed. Dr. Willis had reassessed the injury since the swelling had lessened and now saw the problem as a severe sprain rather than a fracture. The doctor had already started Allie up on her feet, and he maintained it would only be a little while longer until she was completely ambulatory.

But Delaney knew he was not yet prepared to face Allie's leaving, and he realized the appointment he was scheduled to keep with Margaret a short hour from now would determine how soon that time would come. He frowned, realizing Dr. Lindstrom, a man who was merely a name to him, would soon take the matter out of his hands. At best, he would have a few more weeks while Margaret recuperated from an operation, but that time would be a parting gift he would always cherish.

Delaney's carriage turned onto Wabash Avenue. He stared in the direction of his home, waiting for it to come into sight. It was still early and the streets had not stirred fully to life, but he knew Allie and Margaret were waiting.

"Sybil, I'm beginning to feel a bit ridiculous."

Sybil flicked Harriman Bain a glance filled with disdain as he sat in the carriage beside her, parked a discreet distance from Delaney's door. "I don't feel in the least foolish. As a matter of fact, I'm distinctly angry."

His hand moving to Sybil's shoulder, Harriman caressed her gently, in his mind reliving the sensation of her smooth flesh under his palm. He didn't suppose he would ever forget the previous night, which they had spent together. In light of the passion Sybil had exhibited in his arms, he found himself incredulous at her present preoccupation with a former lover.

Harriman sighed. Unfortunately, Sybil did not realize that having become accustomed to the character of the spoiled child produced by a wealthy environment, he was far better equipped to make her happy than Delaney Marsh was. But she did not, silly child that she was, and he supposed he would have to patiently educate her to that reality. However, patience was difficult when he had to conceal his jealousy or run the risk of losing her. With that thought in mind, Harriman questioned Sybil lightly.

"Why are you angry, dear?"

"Because, damn him, Delaney never had time for me, but he *makes* time for that country bumpkin he now has in his bed! He spent no more than a few minutes in his office this morning before racing home to her."

"Sybil, how do you know he is 'racing' home to her?"

"Harriman, don't be a fool! Why else would he come home so early in the day? It's obvious that last night's passion was not enough and he—"

"It was not enough for me, either, darling."

Sybil's tirade halted abruptly as she turned to observe the

earnest gleam in Harriman's eye. A faint smile flickered across her lips. "I confess, I did not believe you could be such an insatiable beast."

"Beast, darling?"

"Well . . . perhaps that wasn't the right word."

Leaning forward, Harriman pressed a lingering, questing kiss on Sybil's parted lips, and she raised a well-shaped brow in amusement.

"Harry, dear, you can't be serious. I must go home. Father will return at noon, and I must make it appear I slept in my own bed while he and Mother were away for the weekend."

"That leaves us several hours, dear."

Her beautiful face suddenly losing all trace of levity, Sybil looked into Harriman's warm gaze with vexation. "This situation between Delaney and me is a joke to you, isn't it? It isn't for me. Delaney Marsh is the only man I have ever loved. I want to spend the rest of my life with him, and he threw me over for a little farm chit. I intend to win him back . . . or exact my revenge. That need is very strong, Harriman. It can't go un-filled."

Harriman was suddenly as serious as she. "And if Marsh proves unattainable, how do you intend to get your revenge?"

"I haven't decided yet." Sybil's frown reflected her distress. "That talkative maid, Mary, said Delaney cannot seem to keep his hands off the sickly Mrs. Case. She said that when the woman was unable to get around, he carried her everywhere, sweeping her into the garden for outings and . . ." Her voice trailing away, Sybil bit her lip to restrain her distress at that thought. In control of herself once more, she met Harriman's gaze. "Evidently the woman's daughter is quite upset over the relationship between her mother and Delaney. It's my thought that stupid farmer she's married to would be very grateful to learn what's going on while his wife is 'recuperating.' "

"You wouldn't do that, Sybil!"

"Oh? Why not?"

"Because everything you're saying is either gossip or conjec-ture. You don't know if there's a word of truth in it."

"Don't I? Well, I tell you this, Harriman, whether there is truth in it or not, if Delaney doesn't see the error of his ways soon—"

"By 'error of his ways,' you mean . . . ?"

"I mean, if he doesn't wake up to the fact that I'm the woman for him, that I can do more for him than—"

"I've heard this speech before, Sybil."

Giving Harriman a deadly look, Sybil continued resolutely, "If he doesn't wake up soon, he'll find out he made a mistake in choosing that woman over me."

Sybil was trembling with distress and jealousy, and unable to bear her anguish, Harriman slid his arms around her in a comforting embrace. Damned spoiled woman. Why did he love her so?

Intensely aware that his own passion was an ungovernable as Sybil's, that the similarity of their natures made him view her excesses with more latitude than probably was wise, Harriman pulled her closer. "That may be so, dear, but in the meantime you may console yourself with me. And I'll amuse you in return. We do make such lovely playmates."

Sybil's shuddering slowly ceasing, she raised her glorious blue eyes to his. A pensive smile touched her lips. "I suppose we do, Harry."

Allowing her time for no further response, Harriman raised his voice in brief command. "Home, Orsen."

The carriage snapped into motion.

Bloodshot eyes observing from across the street blinked as the sleek Bain carriage moved forward. A low growl escaped the small, wiry fellow's throat as he watched from his position of concealment. Damn that persistent rich bitch! Always hanging around Marsh, always following him. She made such a show of herself that he had seen Marsh looking over his shoulder several times, watching for her. She made it damned hard for him to keep out of view of them hard, light eyes, and he knew damned well what would happen if Marsh realized he was being watched.

Well, one thing was for sure. The way things were going, he wouldn't be bothered with this job much longer, and he'd be damned glad to see the end of it. A low snicker escaped his long, bony throat, and his protruding Adam's apple bobbed with the next thought he savored so pleasurably. The hardest part would be over for him then, but for Marsh, it would be another story.

* * *

Allie raised a shaking hand to her head in an effort to still its reeling. It had been stupid of her to expect her ankle to support her weight the first time she attempted to walk by herself. But the error in her thinking had quickly been revealed to her when a stabbing pain had immobilized her at her first step. It had only been with the sheerest luck that she had managed to keep from falling.

A long strand of hair fanned Allie's neck, and she groaned in annoyance. She had struggled to pin up her hair in a semblance of order, but it was already slipping loose. Not only that, but the dress Olga had helped her into had become wrinkled and she still had not managed to reach the wardrobe to retrieve her shoes. She had hoped to look presentable when Delaney returned, but getting herself on her feet and remaining there was harder than she had thought it would be.

She had been so encouraged when Dr. Willis had told her that he no longer believed her ankle was broken. A sprain sounded so much less serious than a break, but his comment that there was a possibility of tendon damage had put a damper on her spirits. She was impatient with lying in bed and she wanted to be on her own as soon as possible. Unknown to Delaney, James had found a boardinghouse near the hospital where she and Margaret could stay if Dr. Lindstrom decided to operate. The boardinghouse had several things to recommend it. Its location would allow visits from hospital physicians who would follow through on Margaret's case after Dr. Lindstrom left the city; it would free Delaney of the burden of their care and presence, and it would spare James the agitation of knowing she and Margaret were under Delaney's roof.

Everything hinged on the extent of her mobility, for Margaret would be bedridden for an indeterminate time, and the speed of her recuperation would depend on the quality of care she received. However, it had taken Allie only a few moments on her feet to realize that there would have to be a miraculous improvement in her ankle if she was to accomplish the heavy nursing chores she would face.

Breathing deeply, Allie prepared to stand again. Smoothing the skirt of the pale blue foulard afternoon dress, she frowned at the realization that Delaney had personally selected this dress for her. She had immediately recognized its striking resemblance to a dress she had owned years ago, one Delaney had said made her look like a small ceramic doll he had once seen in a store window in New York. He had said he always wondered how it would feel to hold something that valuable and fragile. He had given her a hard, enthusiastic hug then and laughed, saying it felt pretty good. But his clear-eyed gaze had communicated a far deeper message the first time she had worn this particular dress.

Her thoughts strengthening her determination, Allie swung her feet to the floor and attempted to stand up. Gasping with pain as she put weight on her injured ankle, Allie lurched helplessly toward the nearby nightstand. Missing as she grasped the edge, she fell, striking her head as she hit the floor. Disoriented, she was startled as Delaney appeared at her side, his anxious gaze searching her face.

"What happened, Allie? Are you all right?"

"I . . . I'm fine."

Lifting her cautiously, Delaney carried her toward the bed, but Allie protested sharply.

"No, I don't want to lie down, Delaney. I was getting dressed. I'm going with you when you take Margaret to see Dr. Lindstrom."

Delaney paused, his light eyes studying her. "So that's it." He lowered her to the bed and sat beside her, then took her hand.

"I'm sorry. I should've realized you'd be apprehensive about this consultation with Dr. Lindstrom, but everything will be all right. You don't have to worry about Margaret. I'll make sure Dr. Lindstrom sees her and gives me a full explanation of his findings. If he decides he can help Margaret, I'll have him talk to you before anything is done. Will that satisfy you, Allie?"

The throbbing pain in Allie's ankle had returned, but she still hesitated in response. How could she explain to Delaney that the more he did for her, the more uncomfortable she became? How could she tell him that she needed independence from him so she could assess the conflicting loyalties, which were so mixed up inside her that they were tearing her apart?

"Allie?"

"Of course, you're right." She attempted a smile. "But I'd

like to talk to Margaret before you go. Would you ask her to come in here, please?''

Delaney nodded and rose to leave. She saw hesitation in his eyes. He sensed something and was uneasy, but she could not allow it to affect her. She knew what must be done.

Delaney attempted to make himself more comfortable on the seat of the rented hack, but it was a wasted effort. Silently accepting that his present unease was not physical, he glanced once more toward Margaret, who sat stiffly beside him, her head determinedly turned toward the window and the streets through which they passed.

Delaney followed her gaze, wondering at the perversity that had made him instruct the driver to use an indirect route to the office Dr. Lindstrom was using in the Marine Hospital. He supposed he should be grateful that Dr. Willis had persuaded Dr. Lindstrom to see Margaret, since the railroad accident had caused the famous surgeon to cancel all other appointments during his stay in Chicago. But somehow, at the present moment all he felt was uneasiness.

The pace of the hack changed, the reverberating sound of hooves against the cobbled street altering as the horses negotiated a corner to bring the sparkling surface of the Chicago River into view. Millions of tiny ripples raised by the brisk breeze danced in the sun, turning the surface into a fluid blanket of diamonds studded with graceful masts of swaying ships. A cool wind brushed Delaney's face, carrying the familiar odors of fish and moisture-laden air so characteristic of the docks, in a total assault on the senses to which he had never become inured. Glancing toward the silent, unsmiling child beside him, Delaney realized if he had hoped to elicit a reaction from her, he had failed miserably.

Delaney studied Margaret's rigid form. The breeze lifted her pale hair from narrow shoulders covered with a lightweight pink dress and wrap. The ensemble complemented the child's fair coloring. He had seen the dress when he purchased the blue foulard for Allie. He was well aware that Margaret would resent wearing the outfit if she realized it was his money that had bought it, but Olga had been only too accommodating in twisting the

truth enough to make both Margaret and Allie believe that James
had left a sufficient sum to replace the clothing lost in the wreck.

Not for the first time it occurred to Delaney as Margaret sat,
her posture rigid, her small chin fixed with determination, that
she was the image of Allie as he had first seen her. He supposed
that accounted for his conflicting feelings with regard to the child.
There was no denying the anger she aroused in him with intense
perusals and accusing glances so reminiscent of her father's, but
there was something else, a feeling to which he could not put a
name, which would give him no rest. Whatever it was, he had
a strong inclination to—

"Sir, this is the hospital coming up on our right."

At the driver's call from atop the carriage Delaney turned to
the three-story brick building coming into view. An effort had
been made to relieve its cold, institutional appearance with wide
wooden porches extending from the first and second floors and
with abbreviated lawns on either side of the front entrance, but
the building projected little of the appeal intended.

They were drawing steadily closer to the imposing edifice
when Delaney was startled by a tremor that unexpectedly shook
Margaret's rigid posture. He was more startled still by a low,
almost indistinguishable sob that escaped her throat in the moment before she raised her chin a fraction higher with a small
sniff.

Reacting instinctively, Delaney curved his hand around her
cheek and gently turned Margaret's face toward him. Tears
welled in her great dark eyes in a way that touched his heart.

"What's the matter, Margaret? Don't you feel well?"

Margaret remained silent. Her attempt to brush away a tear
brought her hand in contact with Delaney's long fingers as he
smoothed it from her face.

"Tell me what's wrong, Margaret."

The child shuddered again, and Delaney turned to give the
driver further instructions.

"Drive around the block again."

Delaney looked back toward Margaret with concern.

Abruptly brushing away his hand, Margaret gulped back her
tears. "I don't want to see that doctor with you! You don't like
me and you don't care about me. You're only taking me because
Mama can't go and Papa had to go home."

Delaney shook his head. "That's not true, Margaret. I do care what happens to you."

"No, you don't! You never liked me, and you were mean to Papa, too. You only like Mama."

Margaret's perceptiveness and distress were unanticipated, and Delaney was at a loss for a response. Distressed to recall his previous callous disregard for her feelings, he realized her agitation touched him more deeply than he had thought possible, and he took her arm gently, refusing to allow her to shake off his touch.

"Margaret, there are so many things you don't understand—things that happened before you were born."

"I don't care. I don't want to go with you. I want to go back to Mama."

"Margaret, listen to me." Realizing the situation was quickly progressing out of control, Delaney gripped both Margaret's arms firmly, holding her immobile. When she attempted to break free, he spoke in soft reprimand. "Your mother put you in my care today, Margaret. She expects me to take you to see Dr. Lindstrom, and she also expects you to behave. She would be very disappointed in you and very upset if you didn't keep your appointment." Margaret's struggle came to an abrupt halt, and Delaney continued quietly, "But I realize your reluctance isn't entirely your fault. I'm to blame, too, and I want to tell you some things that might help you understand the way I've been acting. Will you listen, Margaret?"

Her eyes still averted, Margaret gave a reluctant nod.

Encouraged, Delaney began softly. "Your mama and I are old friends, Margaret. I've known her since she was a little older than you are now. We were both alone, with no family and no home when we met. Your mama was frightened, just as you are now, and I was very unhappy. We became friends, and when your grandmother and grandfather took us into their house to live, our friendship became stronger. Your papa didn't like me, Margaret, and I didn't like him. We both had a lot of reasons why we felt that way, but Mama liked us both. It made her unhappy to see two people she liked always arguing, and when I left the farm, I suppose she was unhappy because even though it was a relief not to be torn between us, she knew she would miss me, too."

Delaney noted that Margaret's trembling had ceased. She turned toward him with a speculative gaze as he continued, "I came to Chicago to live, and I hadn't seen your mother since that time. But I missed her, Margaret. I missed her very much, and when I saw her injured in the wreck, I was afraid I wouldn't be able to help her in time. I couldn't think about anything else but helping her to get better, and I didn't want anyone to get in the way. I was selfish about wanting to keep her to myself after all the years that had passed without seeing her. And I was jealous of the time you had with her while we were separated, so I wasn't very pleasant to you.

"I'm very sorry for that, Margaret. I hope you can forgive me." Realizing he meant those words sincerely, Delaney watched as Margaret's dark eyes flickered, but she made no response, and he continued, determined. "Then your papa came here, Margaret. Nothing had changed between us. We still disliked each other, and we still argued. But that didn't stop your papa from doing what was best for your mama and you. So he went back to the farm and left you here until your mama could get well. Your papa and I will never be friends, but he knew I would keep my word to take care of you both."

Margaret was listening attentively, and Delaney's hopes rose. "Your mama and your papa want you to see Dr. Lindstrom today. They want him to fix your hip so you can walk more easily—and I want it, too." Raising his hand to Margaret's cheek, Delaney brushed a wisp of pale hair out of the path of her tears, his voice deepening with the previously unacknowledged truth he was about to speak. "I want the doctor to help you because your mama's my friend and I love her, just as I love you because you're a part of her."

Delaney attempted a smile. "Do you believe me, Margaret?"

Withholding response, Margaret looked hard and deep into his eyes, and Delaney's anxiety mounted. Suddenly realizing how much he needed and wanted this child's acceptance, he could hardly bear her silence. He prompted softly, "Can you forgive me?"

Tears brimming in her eyes once more, Margaret gave a short nod.

Delaney slid his arms around Margaret and hugged her close, an unexpected thickness appearing in his throat as her arms moved lightly around him in return. Drawing away as the carriage drew to a halt in front of the hospital, Delaney was about to speak when Margaret stiffened.

"I don't want to go in," she said. "I—I'm afraid."

Delaney smiled in an attempt at comfort. "Dr. Lindstrom won't hurt you, dear."

"But . . . but what if he can't help me? Mama and Papa will be so unhappy, and I don't want to disappoint them."

The full reason for Margaret's reluctance was clear at last, and Delaney was touched by her unselfish concern for her parents. But he would have expected little else from Allie's child.

"Your mama and papa could never be disappointed in you, Margaret. And neither could I." The last sentence increased the tears in Margaret's eyes, and Delaney enclosed her small hand in his. "Let's go in now. I promise you, everything will be all right."

Delaney walked up the path toward the hospital with Margaret at his side, her hand in his. She was still tense as they approached the entrance, and he cast her an encouraging glance. A shadow of a smile touched her lips, and Delaney's aching spirit swelled.

chapter

twenty-four

THE STENCH OF sweating bodies, sickness, and human waste was overpowering. It had struck Allie the moment Delaney carried her through the doors of the hospital a few hours earlier and had grown increasingly potent as they progressed through the colorless corridors of the massive institution. The wave of nausea it had initiated did not subside as they sat on the hard bench awaiting word of Margaret's operation. Grateful that she had not been made to suffer the rigors of this place, or one like it, after being injured in the train wreck, she realized Delaney had spared her yet another hardship for which she would never be able to adequately express her gratitude.

Retching spasms threatened again, but Allie knew that anxiety was more responsible for her unsettled physical state than the pervading odors and the dismal atmosphere of the waiting area. She glanced at the large clock on the wall. Was it possible they had only been here three hours? It seemed like a lifetime.

"Allie, are you all right?"

Allie turned at the concern in Delaney's voice. She nodded, unable to speak over her physical discomfort. The darkening of Delaney's brow was clear indication that she had been unsuccessful in concealing her distress.

"Would you like a glass of water? Do you want to lie down for a while?"

Delaney covered her hand with his, and embarrassed at her show of weakness, Allie forced a smile. "No, I'm fine. It's just that it's very stuffy in here." Her smile slipped. "And I hadn't realized the operation would take so long."

Delaney slid his arm around her shoulder and drew her supportively against his side. Accepting the comfort of his strength, Allie restrained the desire to curve her arm around him in return. Her fears for Margaret were making this day a living nightmare. How fervently she wished James could have been here with her, but Dr. Lindstrom's crowded schedule had allowed only overnight notice of an opening, and she had had no choice but to accept it.

But one thing had been accomplished during this uncertain time while they waited for Dr. Lindstrom's calendar to clear. The relationship between Delaney and Margaret had improved immeasurably, and a cautious friendship had grown between them.

A bittersweet pain had touched her heart as she watched her daughter warm to Delaney's kindnesses, and as she had seen his response. But she was no stranger to the warmth he showed once his heart had become engaged, and it was a great comfort to her that the antipathy between them had finally been put to rest. Her pledge to James that Delaney and Margaret would know each other only as friends had been a heavy burden, and she was only now feeling some relief.

A footstep in the hallway brought Allie back to the present. She rose to her feet, grimacing with pain as her ankle failed and Delaney rose to her support. The light pounding in her head increased to a painful drumming, but the person approaching proved to be neither Dr. Lindstrom nor Dr. Willis.

Her torment apparent, Allie turned with a single, broken word: "Delaney—"

Delaney drew her into the comforting circle of his arms, and Allie closed her eyes against her fears. The medal lying against her skin warmed in a silent consolation that had eluded her until now as Delaney's whispered words of reassurance brushed her ear.

Yes, everything would be all right. It had to be.

Allie's breath caught in her throat when Dr. Willis finally appeared in the doorway. The pounding in her head becoming acute as he approached, she searched the aging doctor's fatigued expression.

"Is it over? Is Margaret all right?"

Dr. Willis's brief nod allowed a choked sound of relief to escape Allie's paralyzed throat. Not quite laughter, not quite a sob, it tightened Delaney's arm around her as Dr. Willis managed a tired smile.

"I've never seen anything like it. Dr. Lindstrom performed a miracle. Barring unforeseen incident, Margaret will be as good as new."

"When can I see her?"

His weary smile fading into a frown, Dr. Willis appeared to notice Allie's pallor for the first time. He took a short step toward her, his gaze assessing as he spoke. "Not for a few hours. Dr. Lindstrom likes to maintain tight control over circumstances immediately following an operation of this sort. Go home now, and when—"

"No, I'll wait. I want to see Margaret."

"Allie, dear." Slipping into a form of address with which he had become more comfortable, Dr. Willis wagged his graying head. "Don't waste your strength in protests. You're still recuperating, and you must not weaken yourself at this point in time. Margaret has not yet regained consciousness, and she won't be aware of your presence in any case until later in the afternoon. Go home. Take one of the powders I left you and get some rest. Come back later, when you're feeling stronger. Your daughter will need your help in the coming weeks, and you will want to be up to it."

The wisdom of Dr. Willis's words overcoming her objections, Allie nodded, startled as Delaney swept her up into his arms. Her short protest was answered by Dr. Willis's weary chortle.

"I wouldn't complain, my dear. I wager there are many women who would wish to command such special treatment from this fellow. Mr. Marsh knows what you need, and right now you need rest. Do that, my dear. I'll expect to see you back here in a few hours."

As Delaney strode rapidly down the corridor, Allie assessed his tense expression. It suddenly occurred to her that his concern was twofold: He worried about her as well as Margaret. Allie squeezed his shoulder lightly, drawing his attention to her face. Her attempt at comfort emerged as a wobbly smile.

"Margaret's going to be all right, Delaney."

Delaney's light eyes dwelled for long moments on her face before he carried her outside. Undisturbed by his silence, Allie relaxed against his chest, her tension draining away at the silent communication between them. There was no more need for words.

"Did you see him carrying his pale, fainting swan?" Her voice a harsh jeer, Sybil choked back the tears brimming in her glorious blue eyes as she turned to the man seated beside her. Their carriage shuddered into motion as she continued, "He treats her as if she's something precious, instead of the common tart that she is. What does he see in her, Harriman? She's a drab stick of a woman with no appeal at all!"

Harriman Bain paused, his distinguished face sober as he concealed his impatience with difficulty. "I happen to disagree with you, but that makes little difference, because you refuse to acknowledge a very important point, Sybil. Delaney Marsh doesn't see that woman through your eyes. He sees her through the eyes of love."

Sybil stiffened, paling. "Rot! That's nothing but foolish nonsense!"

"You've lost him, Sybil. Face it now before you make a bigger fool of yourself than you already have. You don't realize how very fortunate you are, my dear."

"Fortunate! How did you come to that brilliant conclusion?"

"You're fortunate because I view you in the same way that Delaney Marsh views Mrs. Case. You should realize that nothing else would have permitted me to endure your behavior of the past few weeks without turning my back on you and leaving you flat."

"You could never do that, Harriman." Her beautiful face reflecting a self-assurance totally absent a few moments before,

Sybil managed a knowing smile. "You could never turn your back on me."

Witnessing a new light in Harriman's eyes, Sybil felt a small flutter of anxiety as he raised a well-tended hand to her cheek.

"For the first time, I find that I'm not so sure," he said. "Fair warning, dear. I will not be party to any malicious machinations. You're pushing me very close to the edge. I suggest you not take further liberty with my affection."

The peculiar sense of loss Harriman's words evoked was fleeting, and Sybil dismissed it as Delaney's carriage slipped out of sight ahead of them on the street. Her jealousy flamed anew.

"Perhaps you're right, Harriman darling. Perhaps I have lost Delaney, and perhaps I wouldn't want him back now even if he came to me on his knees, begging for a reconciliation."

"I'd say the possibility of that eventuality is nil."

Sybil looked at Harriman with impatience. "Then I'll rule out my first choice and prepare for the second."

His expression hardening, Harriman stared directly into Sybil's narrowed blue eyes. "I warn you now, Sybil. Leave the fellow alone and forget any twisted notions of revenge you might be entertaining."

"I shan't bother to confirm or deny that intention. It's really none of your affair."

"You've made it my affair."

"That's where you're wrong." Sybil looked out onto the passing street. "Can't you get this fellow to drive a little faster? I'm fatigued. I think a nice hot bath will relax me quite well. And then a short nap." Turning back to Harriman, Sybil continued, "And when I'm my old self again, I will welcome your call. Shall I expect you this evening, darling?"

Startled at Sybil's about-face, Harriman remained silent. Not quite able to trust her, he was unable to resist her as well.

"Shall we say eight?" she prompted.

Sybil slid her arm around his neck and drew Harriman's mouth down to hers. Regret for the love he bore this beautiful, headstrong woman was soon overcome by the familiar taste of her, and Harriman consoled himself with the thought that in a few more moments he would no longer care.

* * *

The sedative had begun to take effect and Allie was drifting off to sleep. Seated on the side of her bed, Delaney curled his hand around Allie's, smiling as she fought to raise her eyelids one last time.

"You won't let me sleep too long. I must see Margaret."

"I promise to wake you."

But Allie's hand was already limp, and Delaney realized his response had gone unheard. Gently he raised her palm to his lips. Holding it to his mouth for long moments, he tasted her skin, his eyes closing at the bittersweet pain of the subtle intimacy. Leaning forward, supporting himself on his hands, he looked down into her face, certain that he never had, and never would, see another woman as beautiful as she. He ached with love for her.

Halting his painful thoughts, Delaney forced the lump from his throat with sheer force of will. The truth was that Allie was beyond his reach. He would never again know the ecstasy of holding her in his arms, feeling her flesh against his. He would never again know the fulfillment of two parts of one spirit totally converged into a whole by the act of love. He would never again feel her heartbeat echo his own, breathe her fragrant scent, hear the soft, gasping cries of passion that still resounded in his dreams.

His eyes intent on her face, Delaney lowered his lips lightly to the scar on Allie's forehead, loving it because it had restored her to him, if only temporarily. He trailed his lips across her eyelids, knowing it was through those eyes he had first seen love. He pressed his lips against the gentle pulse in her temple, grateful for the life throbbing there. He touched her delicate ear with his mouth, wishing he could whisper the words of love that so filled his heart. He followed the curve of her proud, determined chin. He paused at her lips.

Her lips were still, slightly parted, her breath lightly fanning his mouth. He rested his mouth lightly against hers, allowing her breath to mingle with his, tasting it, warming to it, his hunger growing. His hands slipped into the pale silk of her hair, cradling her head as he was overwhelmed by a deep, painful yearning.

"Allie—" His whisper a soft hiss in the silence of the room, he grazed her lips with his words. "That night so long ago when you lay in my arms, I became angry when you said the Lady had brought us together. I didn't want to hear you say she made us part of each other, that it would always be that way. I was jealous of her. I wanted there to be only us—no one, nothing else, to share what we had. But things are different now. If I believed in the Lady, if I thought she could hear me, I would ask her to send my words into God's ear the way she sends yours. And those words would be a plea that you would never leave me.''

His lips touching hers in a fleeting kiss, Delaney drew back just far enough to look into Allie's still face once more as he continued. ''Do you still talk to the Lady about me, Allie? Do you still see her sweet face and ask her to—''

A loud pounding at the front door drew him up sharply. The movement caused Allie to move restlessly in her sleep and Delaney whispered a soft word of reassurance as he reached for the coverlet at the foot of the bed. The pounding sounded again, more frantically than before, and he stood up, annoyed that the few quiet moments he had stolen with Allie had been interrupted.

He heard a woman's voice at the front door, slightly raised, mingling with Olga's. He recognized that voice and hurried down to the foyer, his eyes on the young redhead standing there.

''What are you doing here, Mae? Don't you know it's dangerous for you?''

Running toward him as he reached the foyer, Mae Brewster clutched his shirt, her broken fingernails digging into the spotless fabric. Her breath was ragged, her eyes frantic. ''They know, Mr. Marsh! They know everythin'!''

''What do you mean?''

''One of the girls told me Mr. Paynter knows you've been tryin' to find out who killed Selina and the other girls. He knows I've been talkin' to you. He'll kill me just like he killed her, and nobody'll care—just like nobody cared about them!''

''I care, Mae, or I wouldn't have gone down to Conley's Patch, would I?'' Carefully extricating himself from Mae's clutching fingers, Delaney glanced at Olga. ''Is anyone else in the house, Olga? Is Mary here?''

''No, she's gone for the day, Mr. Marsh.''

Delaney looked into Mae's frightened face. He had seen faces like this on the streets of New York those long years ago. Some were younger, some older, some prettier, and some no longer pretty at all. They all had one thing in common: The acceptance of their hard lot in life was visible in their eyes. But this girl's eyes also reflected terror.

Realizing that Mae was shaking so badly she could hardly stand, he grasped her wrists firmly and led her to a chair.

"Sit here for a few minutes, Mae. I'm going to hail a hack and take you someplace where you'll be safe. When you're settled, I'll finish my investigation. We'll get Paynter and the others who are responsible for the killings and for forcing girls into his houses. When it's all over, I'll see to it that you have enough money to start all over again, someplace else, wherever you want to go. Do you believe me, Mae?"

Mae, still quaking, cast Olga a quick, uncertain look.

"Olga has been with me for six years, and she's completely trustworthy. Will you do as I say, Mae?"

Gulping audibly, Mae nodded, and Delaney released her wrists. He snatched a jacket from a hook near the door and hurried down the front steps toward the street. A short time later he reentered and motioned Mae to her feet.

"The hack is waiting." He took the shuddering young woman's arm as she walked toward him.

Her smeared makeup stood out brightly on her pale skin—a travesty of its former attempt at appeal—and her revealing dress hung loosely on her thin frame. The girl looked exactly like what she had been forced to become, a panic-stricken whore, young and pathetic.

Delaney slipped an arm around her. "I'll take you where you'll be safe until I'm ready to come and get you. Will you wait for me, Mae?"

The girl nodded, and Delaney led her to the door with a glance toward Olga's unrevealing expression.

"Dr. Willis recommended I give Mrs. Case a powder. She's sleeping. I'll be back before she awakens. Watch over her for me, Olga."

The woman's nod all he needed for reassurance, Delaney took Mae's thin, trembling arm and walked her down the steps and into the carriage. With a short command to the driver, he drew the curtain across the window and settled back beside the frightened woman. He realized the full implications of this situation for the first time and he frowned. He was running out of time, and if he wasn't careful, he would be in more trouble than Mulrooney ever dreamed.

The small, rodentlike fellow concealing himself on the opposite side of Wabash Avenue laughed low in his throat as Delaney's carriage moved briskly down the street. Following it with his eyes until it turned the corner and moved out of sight, he slipped from hiding and emerged on the street with a brisk step.

He had a lot to thank Mae Brewster for today. The girl had cinched things for him, and Mr. Paynter would pay him plenty when he came back with this information. The way things looked, Marsh was taking the girl somewhere. It didn't make much difference where. He'd find her pretty quick, and Mr. Paynter would see that somebody else took it from there.

That was the way he liked it. Nobody ever got away with snitching on Mr. Paynter. He shook his head. Nobody.

chapter

twenty-five

JAMES HELD THE scented pink stationery in his hand. The elaborate script and the obviously expensive envelope were intriguing. He had no doubt that was the reason Rob Miller had gone out of his way to deliver it to him on the way back from town. James had not enjoyed disappointing the fellow, but intuition had caused him to delay opening the letter until Rob had given up and gone home. He was exceedingly glad he had.

Suddenly angry, James looked again at the letter in his hand, rereading the message for the third time. The pain caused by the written words did not lessen.

Mr. Case,

You do not know me, but we have an acquaintance in common—Delaney Marsh. I do not know your opinion of Mr. Marsh, and for that reason I hesitated to write for fear you would give this note little credence. But time has worsened the situation to the point of scandal, and in good conscience I can no longer keep silent.

Mr. Case, it pains me to inform you that Mr. Marsh and your wife are conducting a flagrant affair that is the disgrace of the good people of Wabash Avenue. They have

*been seen in each other's arms in full view of the neighbors
in the garden behind Mr. Marsh's home and in public places
where such behavior is entirely unsuitable. I feel it is only
fair to add that your young daughter appears to be suffering
as a result of the conduct of Mrs. Case and Mr. Marsh.
She has been seen on more than one occasion to be considerably ill at ease in his presence.*

*I write you, Mr. Case, in the hope that you will see fit
to take proper action. It is always difficult when a man is
informed his wife has taken a lover, but I believe you will
agree it is your duty to see that this dishonorable conduct
is brought to a halt.*

*I hope you will forgive me for being the bearer of such
unwelcome news. I do consider myself*
A Friend

His complexion grew pale beneath his sun-darkened skin, and
James closed his eyes briefly. In his heart he could not believe
a word of this well-written note. Not Allie . . . his Allie. She
would not betray anyone, especially him.

The wrinkled letter in his hand seeming suddenly to burn his
palm, James rolled it up into a ball and tossed it on the ground.
Stepping off the porch, he hesitated a moment longer before
grinding it into the dirt of the yard with his foot. Turning, he
walked back into the house. He would leave first thing in the
morning.

Foremost in his mind as he entered his bedroom and started
to pack was his realization that someone in that city, possibly
living near Allie, hated her enough to attempt to incite him
against her.

Panicking at his sudden fear for Allie's safety, James knew
only one thing. He had to see Allie, to convince himself she
was truly all right. He loved her and missed her terribly. He
wanted her home but, most of all, he wanted her safe. He would
not leave Chicago again until he was certain she was secure.

Bending low over the silver teapot in her hand, Sybil allowed
Harriman a teasing view of her generous bosom, quickly raising
her glance to catch the appreciation in his eye as she asked

lightly, "Do you want some more, Harry?" At his startled glance, she added innocently, "Tea, that is."

The brief discomfort visible on Harriman's distinguished face appearing to amuse her, Sybil lowered the pot gracefully to the tray and added two teaspoons of sugar to the steaming cup. "You like it sweet and hot, isn't that right? Tea, that is."

Sybil handed Harriman the cup, all but laughing aloud as he mumbled an unintelligible reply. Casting her a warning glance, Harriman reached for a biscuit, his eyes scanning the small, elaborately furnished parlor.

"I admit to considerable surprise when I arrived here and found your mother at home, Sybil. As fond of her as I am, I'm also grateful that the dear lady saw fit to leave us alone for a little while so we could talk." Harriman paused, his aristocratic brow rising as he asked a short direct question. "What are you up to, Sybil?"

"Are you always so perceptive, Harry dear, or is your perception only so accurate with me?"

"Sybil dear, I see through you as I do a pane of glass. I'll ask you again. What are you up to?"

"Nothing at all." An expression of supreme contentment moving over her lovely face, Sybil took a casual sip of tea. "I've decided to put aside my 'jealous fury' and go on with my life and the sweet games we play—and to see where they lead, Harry dear."

Harriman's narrow, distinguished face went still, and he lowered his cup to the table. "You're saying you've finally conceded that Delaney Marsh is beyond your reach."

The tic in Sybil's cheek was more revealing than a response, and the slow dawning of hope in Harriman's gaze faded. "What have you done, Sybil?"

Sybil set her cup noisily in its saucer. "I will not be interrogated by you, Harriman! What I have or have not done is not your concern!"

Harriman rose angrily to his feet. Not to be outdone, Sybil rose and faced him, only to have him clamp his smooth hands on her shoulders and give her a hard shake.

"I asked you what you've done to make you so smug and self-satisfied. Damn you, if you've—"

"What do you think I've done? I'm not about to let Delaney Marsh toss me over for a country slut!"

"Sybil! What did you do?"

"I wrote her husband a letter, that's what I did!" Her eyes blazing azure fire, Sybil spat heatedly into Harriman's darkening expression, "And you needn't look so disapproving, because I don't care a damn! By now that skinny little bitch's husband has read that letter and is on his way here to take his wife home with him where she belongs."

"What did you write in that letter?"

"The truth! I wrote that Delaney and his wife are having an affair, and that Delaney can neither keep his hands off her nor bear to part from her! I wrote that the relationship is an open scandal!"

"That's not true."

"I don't care! I will have that woman out of Delaney's house, now and forever!"

"And when she's gone, you'll conveniently show up on his doorstep."

"If I feel the inclination!"

Harriman's face went white. He dropped his hands from Sybil's shoulders, turned, and strode toward the door.

"Harriman, where are you going?"

Harriman's expression was frozen as he turned in reply. "I've decided to leave before I lose what's left of my honor. A man can only be pushed so far, Sybil. You lost the man you wanted because you pushed him beyond his limits, and as inconceivable as it may seem to you, you're now losing me for the same reason. I told you, I wouldn't be party to your revenge scheme."

"But you aren't! You have nothing to do with it!"

"That's where you're wrong. By my silence, by my presence, I've lent you support. I told myself there was no true malice in you, that you'd come to realize the value of my affection for you in time, but I realize now that I've been just as great a fool as you. There's one difference between us, however. I will be a fool no longer. Good-bye, Sybil."

"Harriman, you can't leave!"

"Can't I? You're wrong again."

Turning, Harriman pushed open the door and left Sybil standing in incredulous silence. His footsteps echoed in the empty hall, and it was only after the click of the front door had ceased reverberating in the silence that Sybil finally believed he was gone.

Relieved to be back in familiar surroundings and away from the discomfort of the Wabash Avenue post where he had kept watch so diligently, Weasel wound his way through the narrow gaslit streets of Conley's Patch. He turned his head in quick, jerking motions, his small slitted eyes sweeping the area as he continued his rapid, silent step. But it was more than physical appearance that had earned him the nickname by which he was known throughout the patch, and Weasel was about to prove how well the label suited him.

Weasel smiled, his uneven rotting teeth glinting in the light of the street lamps, his protruding Adam's apple bobbing as he swallowed. He was glad to be called back to Mr. Paynter's office. Mr. Paynter was an important man. He ran the Patch and everything that went on in it, and Delaney Marsh hadn't fooled him for a minute when he came sniffing around, pretending to investigate Otis Davidson's holdings. Mr. Paynter knew Marsh's reputation and suspected Marsh was looking for a story on him and the whores he had gotten rid of. And then Mr. Paynter sent for Weasel.

He gave a low, self-satisfied snigger. He had shown Mr. Paynter that he could be depended on to do the job for him. He had followed Marsh, dogging his heels, watching his house. He had done little else for the past few weeks, but it had all finally paid off with the appearance of that redheaded whore, Mae.

Weasel smiled again. Everything was going just as he had thought it would, and he liked being able to anticipate what his boss would do. Mr. Paynter had been furious when Weasel told him that Mae Brewster had shown up on Marsh's doorstep a few nights ago and that Marsh had whisked her away. Mr. Paynter had checked the house where Mae worked, and she had not returned. Weasel had known she wouldn't be there, and he had experienced a familiar thrill at the murderous gleam in Mr. Paynter's eye.

Served the damned whore right that Mr. Paynter finally found out she was the one who was rumored to be giving Marsh information! It wouldn't be hard to find that hack driver and get

the address where Marsh dropped Mae. Weasel assumed that
Mr. Paynter had sent for him to tell him one of the other fellas
had already done just that.

Weasel paused in front of a familiar frame building, his eyes
darting to a lighted window on the second floor. Mr. Paynter
had a business to run, and he wouldn't let anything or anybody
get in his way. Mae would be taken care of soon, and then it
would be Marsh's turn. Weasel had no doubt Mr. Paynter had
also sent for him because definite plans were being made to take
care of Marsh and he was the best person to point him out. He
didn't mind. He liked being in on the excitement.

It would be like the last job he had helped finish for Mr.
Paynter—quick and fast, probably on a crowded street. When
this job was done, Marsh would be dead, and Mr. Paynter would
be in the clear again with nobody looking into his business and
everybody more scared than ever to cross him.

Yeah, he liked that.

His uneven lips twitching with anticipation, Weasel knocked
on the front door of the house. The door opened a cautious
crack.

"Mr. Paynter wants to see me."

The door opened wider and Weasel stepped inside, nodding
at the curt reply: "Mr. Paynter's waitin' for you."

Weasel walked up the staircase, pleased with himself and his
importance and excited at what was to come.

James peered out the window of the railway car, scanning the
terminal with a tense glance as the train drew to a screeching
halt. He was impatient with the delay caused by a last-minute
switching of tracks, and he was driven by his certainty that Allie
was in danger. That certainty had grown stronger inside him
with each mile he had traveled.

Snatching up his suitcase, he left the car, hurried across the
platform, and pushed his way through the milling throng.
Emerging on the sidewalk outside, he glanced anxiously around
the crowded street, paying little attention to the chilling damp-
ness that hung on the heavy air and the gray, overcast sky threatening rain. Spotting an approaching hack, he raised his hand,
catching the eye of the driver, his anxiety growing as the carriage
made its way toward him.

Not taking the time to examine the strange panic all but overwhelming him, James gave Delaney's Wabash Avenue address to the driver with an admonition for haste. A tense frown lined his face as the carriage moved into motion.

Her expression sober, Allie glanced briefly toward the overcast sky as Delaney lifted her into the rented hack and climbed in beside her. She shivered as the carriage lurched forward, concerned that this was not an ideal day to bring Margaret home. Amending that thought a moment later, Allie realized she should be grateful that Margaret was well enough to be discharged from the hospital for recuperation at home after such a limited stay. She knew she also should be grateful her own ankle had improved so dramatically in recent days that she was managing to get around quite well on her own. Delaney's assistance was a precaution on which he insisted, but she had already decided that as soon as full strength returned, she would take the rooms James had found for them and relieve Delaney of the burden of their care.

Refusing to submit to the disturbing feelings that thought evoked, Allie shivered again as the carriage negotiated a turn in the road and a gust of moist air brushed her face. But she knew instinctively this most recent decision had little to do with the uneasiness that had plagued her since awakening. Her peculiar inability to define the cause for that uneasiness heightened her tension.

"Are you all right, Allie? I have to make a brief stop at the printer's along the way, but it shouldn't take long."

"I'm fine, just a little chilled."

Delaney's assessing gaze moved over her face. He reached out to cover her hand with his, and Allie realized it was useless to attempt to conceal her anxiety from him.

"I'll be finished with the assignment I've been working on at the newspaper soon. Everything will settle back to normal once we have Margaret back with us again."

Lines of concern tightened between Delaney's eyes, and Allie's disquiet deepened. Except for the time he had spent with her at the hospital each morning, she had seen very little of Delaney in recent days. He returned home late each night, exhausted and tense, and she suspected he was working on something very difficult for the newspaper. She had the feeling it was all drawing to a head, and although she realized it had little to do with her, she was concerned.

She also realized that the unspoken ties between Delaney and her grew stronger each day, and she feared—

Determined to evade the thought which followed, Allie responded with a soft statement. "You're right. In a little while everything will be as it should again. I suppose I can be patient a little longer."

Delaney slid a reassuring arm around her shoulder. It was a natural gesture of comfort, and Allie accepted it. It would only be a little while longer.

Olga jumped at the unexpected pounding at the front door. The delicate teacup she held slipped from her fingers and crashed onto the kitchen floor, and she frowned at the shattered pieces as the frantic pounding continued.

She hurried to open the front door, angry words freezing on her lips at the panic apparent on the face of the familiar red-headed woman standing there. Shoving past her into the foyer and pushing the door shut behind her, Mae Brewster demanded breathlessly, "Where's Mr. Marsh?"

Olga's reply was cautious. "He's out this morning."

"Where is he, damn you!" Desperation touched Mae's voice as she gripped Olga's arms. Her small hands were surprisingly strong, and her rough nails dug into the older woman's skin as she shook Olga with growing hysteria. "They came after me— Mr. Paynter's men! They said they was goin' to kill me for talkin' to Mr. Marsh, but I got away! They said some others was goin' to kill Mr. Marsh, too. Tell me where he is!"

Bewildered by the girl's statement, Olga shook her head. "Mr. Marsh went out with Mrs. Case. They went to—"

"To the hospital?" At Olga's nod, the girl went still. Her hands dropped to her sides and she stepped back. "Then it's too late. They said some of Mr. Paynter's men was waitin' for Mr. Marsh to show up at the hospital like he does every mornin'. They're goin' to kill him, and I ain't goin' to be able to do nothin' about it."

Olga's lined face paled. "The police—we can tell the police!"

"No, I ain't goin' to no police. They'll arrest me, and then when I get out of jail, Mr. Paynter's men will be waitin'. It's too late anyway—too late."

Mae pulled open the door, pausing on the doorstep, tears brimming in her frightened eyes. "Mr. Marsh treated me nice, and I wanted to save him. But now I gotta save me."

Biting her lip against her tears, Mae turned to go down the steps, but collided with a fair-haired man who had walked up behind her. Freeing herself from his supporting hands with a gasp, she brushed past him and was out through the gate as he turned a sharp, inquiring glance toward Olga's white face.

"What happened, Olga?"

"Mr. Case!" Trembling so violently she could hardly speak, Olga gasped, "Some men—they're going to kill Mr. Marsh!"

"Where's Mrs. Case?"

"She's with him! They went to the Marine Hospital to pick up Margaret. That girl—Mae—she said some men are waiting there for Mr. Marsh to arrive, and then they're going to kill him. She said—"

Without a word, James started back down the steps. His shout halted the hack that had brought him as it pulled away from the curb. Covering the distance to the carriage within seconds, he barked an order as he jerked open the door. "The Marine Hospital—quick!"

The carriage lurched forward even as James secured the door behind him. Sitting back in the seat, he closed his eyes at the horrifying realization that he was in danger of losing Allie in a way he had never dreamed.

The Marine Hospital—it could not be far! He must get there in time!

Allie looked at Delaney. He was silent, appearing lost in thought as he stared at the hospital, which was coming into view. His hat lay on the seat beside him, and his profile was clearly outlined against the street beyond. His serious brow, the straight, strong bridge of his nose, the chiseled contours of his cheek, the well-shaped lips and strong chin—it was a picture that had filled her dreams, waking and sleeping, for most of her life. It was etched into her soul, never to be displaced.

But it gave her little peace this day. Instead, it seemed to accelerate her anxiety, driving all anticipation of Margaret's impending release from her mind. Something was wrong. Something . . .

Allie's fingers sought the outline of the medal beneath her bodice, her hand dropping away as Delaney turned toward her with an encouraging smile.

"Dr. Lindstrom has probably already signed Margaret's release. It's my bet she's ready and waiting for us to pick her up right now."

Delaney turned as the carriage drew up at the curb, and Allie frowned. Something felt very wrong.

Delaney pushed open the door. He reached toward her, but she shook her head. "I don't need help. I can get down by myself."

Determined not to allow Delaney's frown to deter her, Allie waited until Delaney stepped down onto the curb before taking the hand he extended toward her. Wincing at the pain in her ankle, Allie stepped onto the curb, suddenly grateful for the support of Delaney's arm.

There was a rush of footsteps to her right, and Allie turned to see several men running toward them. Delaney's head jerked, and she heard his low grunt of surprise, saw the alarm in his clear eyes in the brief second before he pushed her roughly behind him. She heard a familiar voice shout her name as the men neared, saw a familiar fair head briefly cross her line of vision. A gunshot, and Delaney flung her to the ground.

A scuffle—Delaney and a man with a gun!

Allie was struggling to her feet when James suddenly appeared at her side. He pushed her back down on the sidewalk and spoke in a harsh, breathless rasp. "Stay down, out of the way! There are a few of them but I think—"

Another gunshot, and James jerked suddenly upright. A startled expression crossed his face in the brief second before he fell to his knees beside her. Momentarily motionless, his eyes on her face, he slowly crumpled to the ground.

Incredulity held Allie motionless as a third shot rang out and the struggle behind them ceased.

The thud of a body hitting the ground and the sound of running footsteps made her raise her terror-stricken gaze to the man standing over her. Her eyes met and held Delaney's for the briefest moment before snapping back to James, lying so still beside her.

Male voices shouting . . . more people running, scuffling, carriages arriving . . . confusion . . . but Allie saw none of the furor around her. Moving as if in a dream, she touched James's cheek.

"James—" Her voice was a low whisper, building in volume as she repeated his name over and again. "James, look at me. Talk to me!"

She was kneeling on the muddy walk, struggling to raise James's head to her lap when strong hands aided her effort. She stroked James's face, pressing light kisses against his cheek. She whispered his name over and over against his ear, pleading with him to open his eyes. She became angry when he failed to respond. She shook him violently, her ire growing when he remained limp and motionless in her arms.

"James, wake up! Open your eyes . . . please open your eyes!"

She felt hands on her shoulders, attempting to raise her to her feet, but she shook them off, cradling James in her arms, pressing her face tight against his cheek.

"James, I love you. I need you. Please don't leave us. James . . ."

"Allie, get up."

"No!" Suddenly viciously angry, Allie pulled back from Delaney, pushing at his hands. "Leave him alone! I'll take care of him! I can—"

"He's dead, Allie."

"No!" Her eyes wide with horror, Allie looked back at James's still face. Fear a hot, white heat inside her, she grasped James's coat, shaking him with all her strength. Suddenly realizing that her hands were wet and sticky, she lifted them to stare at her palms. They were red with blood. She shook her head, frowning. She wiped her hands against her skirt.

"Allie—"

"No! He's not dead!"

Suddenly she was fighting Delaney as he drew her to her feet, struggling against him as he sought to restrain her. From the corner of her eye, she saw a policeman kneel beside James. She saw him shake his head. She saw a blanket descending over James, being pulled up over his face.

She screamed. An endless shriek, the scream went on and on inside her mind, continuing after the staring faces faded, echoing after all sound dimmed. The memory of the sound was the only reality remaining after the light darkened and faded away.

The air was sweet with the scent of new bloom and freshly turned earth. Bumblebees, their furry striped jackets fresh and new, buzzed among scattered wildflowers with a soft, comforting sound natural to the sunlit, quiet morning. A faint breeze stirred the warm air, loosening a wisp of hair from the tight bun secured atop Allie's head, whipping it against her pale cheek as she stood beside the open grave. Unconscious of the silent circle of people around her and of the strong male presence at her back, she watched in silence as James's coffin was lowered into the gaping hole in the ground.

A sharp tremor shook Allie's body, and she closed her eyes. This was not really happening, she told herself. This was a cruel dream from which she would awaken. She had not returned to the land she loved so well, to the only true home she had ever known, to bury the man who had loved her more than his own life.

Supportive hands closed on her arms, drawing her close, but she resisted them. She took a few steps closer and watched with a strange fascination as the wooden coffin was slowly lowered. The Reverend Mr. Whittier's deep, solemn voice echoed in the back of her mind, but she could not seem to comprehend his words.

She stared at the sober faces encircling her. Elmer Winthrop, Elizabeth Morley Grimes, Charlie Knots, Amory Bishop, Mosley Rourke, Rob Miller, Dr. Peters, Homer Trace, others . . . many others. They had come to say good-bye.

They were silent, looking toward her, and she knew what she had to do. Stepping forward, Allie took a handful of the warm earth from the mound nearby and threw it into the grave. The dirt struck the lid of the coffin with a hollow, echoing sound and Allie felt a sudden urge to laugh. It was almost like a party, with all of James's friends attending, only there was nothing to celebrate.

The circle around her began to dissipate with mumbled words of sympathy, and a strong hand gripped her elbow in an attempt to guide her away. Allie turned to Delaney. His face was sober, unreadable and she shook her head. She didn't want to leave yet.

She saw a sudden movement from the couple standing slightly to Delaney's rear and turned toward Sarah as she left Bobbie's side and walked closer. Halting a few feet away, Sarah looked up into Delaney's face, and Allie was struck with the thought that nothing had really changed. Almost eight years had passed and Sarah was married and the mother of two children, but she was still startlingly beautiful. And she still wanted Delaney.

"It's been a long time, Delaney. I never expected to see you again, after the way you left Cass County."

Allie did not have to look at Delaney to know he was frowning as he said, "I guess you were wrong."

Sarah stiffened at Delaney's response, casting Bobbie a harsh glance as he extended his hand toward Delaney with a quiet word of greeting. She frowned as Delaney accepted his hand warmly, and she addressed Delaney again as if Allie did not exist. "I suppose you'll be going back to the city now that you've paid your respects here."

Delaney's hand slipped to Allie's arm as he took a step closer to her, backing her up with the strength of his body.

"That's up to Allie. If she needs a few more days here to straighten things out, we'll stay, but she—"

"Allie, Allie—it's always Allie, isn't it!" Sarah stepped forward, her beautiful face contorted with jealousy. "You don't even have the decency to wait until my brother is cold in his grave before you put your hands on his wife! But you never did have much decency, did you, Delaney? You never even—"

"Sarah!" Grasping his wife's arm, Bobbie drew her back, turning her toward him. "I think you've said enough. It's time to go home. The children are waiting."

Sarah gave a short laugh. "Yes, the children." Turning to address Allie for the first time, Sarah smiled tightly. "You really must bring Margaret home soon, Allie. My son misses her so. They have so much in common."

Sarah's cruel words rocked her, and Allie took a short step backwards. Stiffening as Delaney's arm moved around her, she swallowed once, and then again. Still unable to respond past the sudden constriction of her throat, she closed her eyes briefly as Delaney spoke in her stead.

"Allie's exhausted. We're going back to the farm now. Bobbie . . ." Addressing the silent young man, Delaney continued quietly, "I've arranged to have Homer look after the farm for a while. If you should need Allie for anything after we've gone, I'll leave an address where you can reach us."

"Reach *us*?" Sarah repeated. "Isn't that convenient!"

Allie shook her head. "No, it isn't like that."

"You don't have to explain anything to us, Allie." Casting an angry glance at his wife, Bobbie gripped her arm more firmly. "Let's go, Sarah."

Turning without another word, Sarah followed her husband's lead.

After watching their wagon move down the cemetery road, Allie turned to Delaney.

"I want to go back, Delaney."

"Back where?"

"To Chicago. I want to be with Margaret."

Delaney nodded in silent acceptance of her decision.

As she turned toward the wagon, Allie heard the first shovelful of dirt hit James's coffin. The second struck it as she started to walk away. The steady scraping sound continued as Delaney lifted her onto the wagon. It echoed in the silent field, heard above the wagon's groaning creak as Delaney settled in beside her. The sound reverberated endlessly inside Allie's mind, and as they pulled away, she knew she would never forget it.

chapter
twenty-six

TORMENTED, DELANEY PACED the floor of his room. A month had passed since James's death, and summer had begun making itself felt in the lengthening of bright, sunlit days and warm, humid nights, but he was well aware that this night's sleeplessness was not due to physical discomfort. He had retired to his room a few hours earlier after a difficult evening during which he had again failed to penetrate the barrier that Allie had built around her heart.

Delaney raked his fingers through his hair in a characteristic gesture of frustration. Ironically, everything was going wrong between Allie and him just as many other aspects of his life were falling neatly into place.

The men who had attacked him and killed James had been identified and arrested. No one was surprised to learn that they were Moss Paynter's men. One of the most feared men in Conley's Patch and other sections of the city where immigrants suffered the effects of poverty and ignorance of their new country's ways, Moss Paynter had been the object of Delaney's investigation from the first. However, it had not been until Mae Brewster showed up at his door and agreed to testify against Paynter that

Mulrooney had agreed to go ahead with his exposé of Paynter's illegal activities in Conley's Patch and his connection to the murder of several young prostitutes.

Everything had caved in after that, collapsing like a great house of cards, and Paynter had been buried in the debris. The white-slave prostitution ring, the killings he had ordered to keep his people in line, the bribery of public officials, countless petty crimes connected with the illegal empire he had established in that ramshackle section of town, had all been exposed, and Paynter had been arrested.

Delaney's reporting had been showered with critical acclaim, and his prestige had risen enormously. He had even managed to smooth the breach between himself and Otis Davidson II, a surprising success, which he owed largely to Sybil's unexpected efforts in his behalf. It appeared Otis Davidson would do just about anything his darling daughter asked since she announced her engagement to Harriman Bain. Delaney could certainly understand Davidson's relief that Sybil appeared to have found the right man at last. As for Bain himself, he appeared to be a decent sort who had considerable influence over Sybil, and who Delaney suspected was behind the change in her attitude toward him. He supposed he would never understand why either of them should feel a need to make something up to him, but he was grateful to have Sybil out of his hair. He wished Bain luck. He had a feeling the fellow would need it.

Those concerns behind him, Delaney was now actively involved in the *Tribune*'s campaign to make Chicago a fireproof city—with Otis Davidson's full cooperation. It was an assignment he had considered dull only a few months earlier but for which he was presently grateful, since his personal affairs were in such disorder.

The only aspect of his private life that had shown marked improvement was his relationship with Margaret. Strangely, in light of Allie's aloofness, she had encouraged her daughter's confidence in him. It was through Margaret's quiet reminiscences of her father that Delaney had begun to appreciate James for the first time. Although his own feelings about the man had not changed, he had learned to be grateful that James had been a devoted father and a loving husband.

But the past was dead, and it was time to look to the future. Or was it?

Again running an anxious hand through his hair, Delaney walked to the window and looked out into the dark shadows of the garden. He breathed deeply of the moist night air, turning back to slant a glance toward the clock on the mantel. Three o'clock. His short laugh reflected little mirth.

He had not had a woman in his bed since Allie reentered his life, and he was only too well aware that the coldhearted womanizer he had been in recent years had received his comeuppance. The man who had claimed he neither needed nor wanted more than physical satisfaction from any woman now ached with wanting one woman alone. But Delaney knew the throbbing urgency inside him was not stimulated by mere physical desire. There was so much more he wanted to give Allie, to share with her.

The direction of his thoughts suddenly changing, Delaney frowned. On the countless occasions when he had imagined Allie free of James, he had neither envisioned nor desired seeing him lying dead in Allie's arms. The memory of that morning still clear in his mind's eye, he acknowledged again the debt of gratitude he owed James for shielding Allie from the bullet that had taken his life. He supposed it was that realization that had finally allowed him to make his peace with James's memory.

Delaney's frown darkened. Allie had not made her peace, and their future together depended upon her doing so. Telling himself he was expecting too much too soon, Delaney still found that, in silent hours such as these, he was more terrified than he dared admit that Allie's acceptance of that last, harrowing caprice of fate would never be accomplished.

That thought was almost more than he could bear, and Delaney turned toward his bed. Not bothering to strip off his trousers, he lay down, only to be bothered by a thought that had given him little rest in recent days. Persistent, nagging, it was the feeling that more than James's memory stood between Allie and him. He sensed it, saw it occasionally—a silent, fleeting accusation in Allie's eyes in those rare moments when her gaze was unguarded.

Questions, unending and without answer, assailed Delaney,

and his frustration grew. He wanted Allie. He needed her. He could not lose her again.

The image of the medal came to Delaney's mind, and he felt a moment's consolation. Allie's belief in the Lady and everything the medal represented to her was strong. That medal was the one firm link between them.

The image on the medal suddenly clear in his mind's eye, Delaney felt the whisper of a soft plea rise inside him. Immediately regretting his momentary lapse, he turned on his side. With great determination he forced back further thought and attempted to ignore the sounds of a restlessness similar to his own coming from the room next door.

Tortured thoughts—painful, poignant, merciless. Allie moved restlessly as fragmented, haunting images continued to fill her mind.

James, his expression sober as she emerged from the chicken coop as a child, her face streaked with tears. His face relaxing into a faint smile, freckles dark against his sunburned skin, as she took the newborn kitten into her hands.

James, his face flushed with fury as he came over the sun-warmed hill to find Delaney pinning her against the grassy slope with the weight of his body, his mouth close to hers.

James, the pain in his eyes as intense as her own as he followed her into the frozen stillness of the yard where she had fled Sarah's stunning announcement that she, too, carried Delaney's child.

James slipping the medal into her hands as she resisted Margaret's birth, allowing her a consolation she had forbidden herself out of loyalty to him.

James, loving her, taking her gently, tenderly, never asking more than she was willing to give.

James, forgiving, enduring with understanding the love for Delaney she sought to suppress, the part of her that could never be his.

James, tense, shoving her to the sidewalk outside the hospital to save her life, shielding her from the bullet that took his own.

James, still, lifeless, unresponsive to her pleas, his blood on her hands, a stain she knew would remain there forever.

Tears, sobs, regrets.

James, why did I never explain to you that I loved you in a way I loved no other? Why did I take for granted that you understood my feelings for you had progressed past affection, past gratitude, past all the lesser emotions that were a prelude to love? Why did I not tell you that despite the love for Delaney which would always be a part of me, I was your wife, faithful to you, loving you in a way I never loved him. Why did I never tell you that I would hold my marriage vows sacred and never defile them, no matter how much I longed to be in Delaney's arms?

But I longed to be in your arms, too, James. I longed to feel your selfless love encircle me, to hear your whispered words of devotion, which shielded me from images of light, piercing eyes I could not elude. I yearned to look into your eyes, to see the love there, to feel its safety protecting me from the myriad unnamed dangers of Delaney's anger, of Delaney's bitterness, of Delaney's love.

But I can look into your eyes no longer, James. They're closed forever, and I mourn their loss as I mourn the loss of your gentle strength, your understanding, your love, constant, never failing—a love free of betrayal.

You never forgot or forgave Delaney for that last night. I forgave him, James, but I cannot forget.

Hear me, James. Please hear me as I add one more pledge to the many honored between us. I'll hold true to my word, as you were true to every promise made to me. I won't deprive you of your daughter because you're no longer with us. Margaret will always be yours, and no word other than that will ever pass my lips.

I miss you, James. I love you. Hear me, James. Please hear me.

There was no response, and Allie closed her eyes.

Sounds of restlessness from the room next door caused a new anxiety to touch Allie's mind. She knew the danger in that restlessness, and she was suddenly aware that the time for mourning had ceased. She knew what she had to do.

His shaggy gray brows tightly knit in a frown, Dr. Willis scowled in Allie's direction. The bright sunlight of midmorning was at her back where she stood opposite him in the hallway, outside Margaret's room, and he strained to read her expression. The attempt proving futile, he gave his head a short negative shake.

"It's my opinion that it would be a mistake to take Margaret home to the farm at this time, Allie. She's coming along very well, but she still needs careful observation and treatment."

"We have a very competent physician at home, Dr. Willis. Surely Dr. Peters will be able to follow through with the care Dr. Lindstrom has prescribed."

"Allie . . ." Dr. Willis took her hand. "You've asked my professional opinion, and I've given it to you. The operation Dr. Lindstrom performed on Margaret is extremely new, and its results are still unpredictable." Pausing again as Allie's fine lips compressed in a straight, unsmiling line, he slid his arm around her narrow waist, coaxing her along with him as he turned toward the staircase. It occurred to him that her waist was not much broader than her child's, and he marveled again at the petite stature of this lovely young woman.

They neared the head of the staircase and Dr. Willis turned Allie toward him, grateful that the light streaming through the transom over the front door was bright enough for him to see her face more clearly as he inquired, "Allie dear, it isn't difficult to see that something is worrying you. Can't you tell me what it is?"

Her unusual dark eyes were troubled, and Allie avoided his gaze as she replied. "I've been in this house too long, Dr. Willis. It's been a month since James's death, and it's time for me to go home. Margaret and I are a burden on Delaney. I don't want it to be that way. I have my own life and Delaney has his."

"I doubt that Mr. Marsh considers either you or Margaret a burden."

Allie's frown darkened, and Dr. Willis had the impression his well-intentioned words had not reassured her. Despairing at his clumsiness, Dr. Willis urged Allie down the staircase beside him, turning toward her when they reached the front door. He gave a short sigh.

"If you're uncomfortable here, dear, I'm certain I can find accommodations for you near the hospital."

Immediately realizing the error of his words as an embarrassed color touched Allie's pale cheeks, Dr. Willis again cursed his stupidity.

"At one time that might have been possible," Allie replied, "but my financial affairs are in disorder right now. I'm not certain I have sufficient funds to allow it."

Knowing instinctively any offer of aid would be resolutely refused, Dr. Willis shrugged. "Then I don't see that you have any choice but to remain here for another few weeks at least. It won't be that difficult, will it, dear?"

Instant denial of his casual assumption flickered in the depths of the dark eyes holding his, and Dr. Willis became acutely aware of the control behind Allie's short reply.

"No, I suppose not."

A few moments later, his footsteps echoing against the sidewalk as he made his way home, Dr. Willis found himself frowning once more. Tipping his hat to a passing matron, he climbed the staircase to his front door.

It occurred to him that he really must be getting old if he had forgotten how very difficult and painful the intricacies of life and love could sometimes be. But he was not too old for one thing to be very clear. Delaney Marsh would have to tread very lightly with the lovely Mrs. Allie Case right now. If he did not, he just might lose her.

chapter

twenty-seven

AT THE SOUND of Margaret's soft laughter, Allie raised her head from the mending in her lap and looked toward her daughter's bed. Margaret turned her head from the book in front of her with another short exclamation that elicited a chuckle from Delaney, who sat beside her. The quiet exchange between them continued, and a sharp bittersweet pain squeezed at Allie's heart.

The old animosity and resentment between Margaret and Delaney were a thing of the past. Unobserved, Allie allowed her gaze to linger on the two heads almost touching over the brightly illustrated pages of the book. The contrast between Margaret's silver-blond hair and Delaney's thick ebony mane was as extreme as the comparison between Margaret's delicate bone structure and Delaney's broad masculine frame. No one would ever suspect the blood of one ran in the veins of the other.

And no one would ever know.

The flood of sadness following that thought snapped Allie from her reverie, guiltily restoring to her mind the decision she had made only a few nights before. She and her daughter would remain in Delaney's house only until Margaret was officially released from the care of Dr. Lindstrom's assistants. It would not be much longer.

That thought afforded her little consolation as harsh memories returned. The dimly lit hallway of the Case farmhouse was as clear in her mind's eye as was the image of Sarah, stepping out of the shadows to confront James and her as they returned from the snow-covered yard. Sarah's biting words again spilled across her mind, a virulent tirade that cut her still. She closed her eyes at the picture of Sarah's bitter fury as she pushed her apron aside to expose the swell of her distended abdomen.

Delaney's child.

Allie's world had crumbled around her then, and she was acutely aware that had it not been for James, she would not have survived.

Another bubble of laughter brought Allie back from her sober memories, turning her toward the bed where Delaney patiently awaited his turn to read. Deeply engrossed, he did not see the pain in Allie's eyes as he gently smoothed a wisp of hair from Margaret's cheek. Delaney's tenderness was a drug that became vital to life. It created a dependence that weakened the spirit. But that tenderness did not change the basic truth that if she could not trust Delaney's fidelity, she could not trust his love.

Margaret read the concluding lines of the familiar story, and Allie fought to shake the effects of her sobering thoughts. Forcing a smile to her face, she placed her mending on the table beside her and drew herself to her feet. The flicker of concern in Delaney's gaze as he turned toward her revealed only too clearly that she had not been entirely successful in chasing shadows of the haunting memories from her eyes as she spoke.

"Have you thanked Delaney for reading that book with you, Margaret?"

"Yes, Mama."

"Then it's time to go to sleep."

Taking a moment to adjust the coverlet across her daughter's chest, Allie leaned down and kissed her cheek with a soft, "Good night, dear."

Allie's throat tightened as Delaney leaned down to kiss Margaret as well, and she was acutely aware of the hand Delaney rested at her waist as he guided her toward the door.

In the hallway, Delaney turned her toward him. Her emotions unsteady, Allie averted her gaze only to feel Delaney's hand cup her chin, raising her gaze to meet his. She resisted his touch and his eyes clouded.

"Allie, what's the matter? I know something's wrong. You slip farther and farther away from me each day. Can't you talk to me?"

Allie's smile was stiff. "It's nothing, Delaney. I'm tired, that's all. I'm going to bed."

Delaney nodded as she turned toward her room. Her conviction firm, she closed the door behind her.

Casually dressed in shirtsleeves, his head bared to the growing warmth of the early morning sun, Delaney turned down another nameless street. He had been awake most of the night. Finally giving up in his efforts to sleep, he had slipped out of the house at dawn with no particular destination in mind. He had been walking ever since, the turmoil in his mind fueling his rapid step.

He was losing Allie.

A knife of pain twisted again in Delaney's gut at his acknowledgment of that reality, and he felt the press of panic. He recalled the previous night and the sudden distance Allie had forced between them as they left Margaret's room. He had searched his mind in an attempt to recall a word or an action that might have triggered her withdrawal, but he had been unsuccessful.

He was helpless against her coldness, the impenetrable barrier Allie had erected between them, and he knew with an instinct that was inborn that time was running short. If he didn't identify the cause for her withdrawal soon, it would be too late.

Raking his hand through his hair, Delaney rested his palm at the base of his neck, massaging the knot of tension there. What had happened between them? Allie and he had never had trouble talking. Allie's heart had always been open to him. But somehow he knew that the change that had come about in her since James's death wasn't due to grief alone.

A gradual anger infusing his mind, Delaney slowed his step. The hardening of his features as he drew himself erect, the growing determination obvious in his stance, attracted cautious glances from passersby, but Delaney was unconscious of their stares.

Turning abruptly, he headed home, covering the sidewalk in long, rapid strides. He had come to a decision. He would put to rest the discomfort between Allie and him today—this morning—or he would know the reason why.

The house was unnaturally quiet as Allie slipped another pin into her hair and gave her reflection in the bedroom mirror a quick glance. A pale, stubborn wisp slipped free from the tightly bound coil, and she experienced a familiar annoyance. Finally securing the wayward strand, she turned away from the revealing glass.

She was too pale, and she was too thin. Her black mourning dress covered her from her throat to the toes of her narrow leather slippers, its short sleeves partially baring arms that looked like two white sticks protruding from the dark fabric. The sight was unappealing, but she spared it minimal concern. She had more important things on her mind.

Taking up a packet of papers from the nightstand, she made another attempt to decipher the complicated legal terms that so confused her. It seemed somehow profane for the total sum of James's life's work to have been reduced to an endless progression of legal papers. Allie shivered at the thought. She was too far away from the warm earth of the farm, the sweetly scented air, and the quiet beauty that surrounded it. She needed to return and allow her memories to take on a physical presence so she might find a peace that was absent here.

Her mind returned to the previous night, and Allie felt a familiar tension. The silent appeal in Delaney's eyes had almost been her undoing. She was too close to him. His distress inflicted painful wounds inside her, but it had always been that way. She had always suffered Delaney's pain, and she supposed she always would. But there had only been one time that she had not believed she would survive the pain her love for Delaney had caused her, and she was determined she would never suffer that anguish again.

Forcing her mind back to the papers in her hand, Allie strained over the unfamiliar terms, knowing Margaret's and her future hung in the balance. A sudden noise from below startled her from her thoughts, and she walked swiftly into the hall. She jumped with a start at Delaney's unexpected appearance halfway up the stairs.

"Oh, Delaney! You frightened me. I heard something and I knew no one was home."

Continuing toward her, Delaney stepped up onto the landing, his dark brows knit in a frown. "Where is everyone?"

"Dr. Willis came by and took Margaret for an outing in his carriage. He said she needs some diversion and some air. Mary's off today, and Olga is out shopping. I've been going over some legal papers that just arrived in the mail."

Delaney's frown darkened, and Allie's heart began a ragged beat as he walked closer. He halted abruptly within a few feet of her, and Allie steeled herself against his visible torment.

"Allie, we have to talk."

Knowing a sudden need for escape, Allie shook her head. "I . . . I'm busy now, Delaney."

Her attempt to turn away was halted by Delaney's sudden grip on her arm. Forcing herself to remain calm as he turned her back toward him, Allie met his pensive scrutiny without a smile.

"Why are you doing this to me, Allie?"

The pain in Delaney's voice squeezed her heart. "Please, Delaney, I'd like to finish reading these papers."

"Dammit, Allie, stop hiding! Something's wrong. Don't deny it, because I know it's true. You're treating me like a stranger. You're closing me out and I don't like being an outsider. I want you to let me back in."

"I don't know what you mean."

A new despair touched Delaney's face. "Why are you lying to me, Allie? You're trying to put distance between us, but I'm not going to let you do it. Something is bothering you. Tell me what it is so I can make it right."

"There's nothing wrong."

"Allie, look at me." His hand cupping her chin, Delaney turned Allie back toward him. His gaze was riveting. "Allie, I want you to think back and remember how good it once was between us. You told me then that we were part of each other, that we always would be. You said you would always know my pain—feel it deep inside you. Well, I'm hurting now. I don't know what this barrier is between us, but I want it to be gone."

"Please, Delaney—"

"No, Allie, it's my turn to ask you please—please tell me what's wrong." Suddenly slipping his arms around her, Delaney crushed her close as he continued his ardent plea. "Allie, don't you know I love you? Don't you know it's tearing me apart to know that even while I'm holding you in my arms, the distance between us remains? What happened? What did I do to make you turn against me this past month?"

Maintaining control with sheer strength of will, Allie attempted to draw back from Delaney's embrace. When he refused to release her, she looked up, her expression unyielding.

"Let me go, Delaney."

"No, not until you tell me what's wrong."

"I'm going home."

"Home!" Delaney paused. "You *are* home."

"No, I'm not!" Allie's response was instantaneous. "Home is where James and I made a life together."

"James is gone, Allie. My quarrel with him is over, and I don't want to fight anymore. I want to know why you're angry with me, so I can make it better. I want to take care of you, to keep you with me the rest of my life."

Sincerity shone from his eyes, and Allie fought to retain her resolve. Words—they were only words. Delaney had shown before how easily he forgot similar words spoken with the same fervor. She could not let herself believe him again.

She shook her head. "I'm going back to the farm."

Delaney's reaction to her flat statement was a tightening of his embrace. He swallowed deeply, and she could feel his strong body tremble as his voice emerged in a ragged whisper.

"I said before that it's my turn to say please, so I'll say it again. Please let me love you, Allie. Please let me take care of you. Please let me keep you with me the rest of my life. Now that you're with me again, I can't let you go. Allie, please . . ."

Allie closed her eyes, bleeding inside at Delaney's despair. She could feel the wall around her heart crumbling, its roar echoing in her ears with the wild drumming of her heart. Her proud, independent Delaney was begging her to love him! Didn't he know—couldn't he see that she had never *stopped* loving him, that loving him was as spontaneous as each breath she breathed?

Able to bear the torment no longer, Allie struggled to free

herself, rasping a low "Let me go!", only to feel her struggles slowly die at his whispered appeal.

"Don't pull away from me, Allie. Try to remember how it was. I remember. You lived within me even when I was empty inside. You smiled, and I was happy. You laughed, and I found joy. And when you spoke, my heart responded with a voice so clear that it still resounds in my mind. You loved me once, Allie—you made me love you then. I still love you."

Delaney's eyes burned with intensity, and the misery visible in their clear depths increased her distress. She ached to assuage that pain that wounded her so deeply as well. The brush of Delaney's lips against hers was balm to her distress as he continued.

"I remember our last night together, Allie. I've relived it countless times in my dreams. I remember holding you in my arms, feeling you beneath me. I remember realizing I'd never felt really alive before that moment. I remember knowing I was whole at last, with you the most important part of me. You're my heart, Allie, and if I have a soul at all, it's you. You taught me how to love again. Let me do the same for you. Let me love you."

Delaney's voice reverberated in her mind as his lips caressed her brow, her cheek, the line of her jaw. He brushed her mouth with his, and Allie's breath caught in her throat as his mouth settled on hers, more firmly than before. She stood motionless, powerless to resist their hungry seeking as he separated her lips with his.

Yes, she remembered. The urgency rapidly building inside her as Delaney's passion deepened was familiar. That same need now drew her arms around Delaney's neck to clasp him close. The myriad colors inundating her mind as her tongue met his in loving response bore a reminiscent hue, and as Delaney melded her to him, her heart raced with long-absent joy.

But it was a debilitating joy that robbed her of the strength to protest as Delaney lifted her into his arms and carried her into his room. It made her gasp with rapture as, his hard body warm upon her, his welcome weight holding her firm against the bed, he sought the comfort of her body. It made her glory in his response as she met kiss with kiss, caress with caress, indulging the wonder that raged between them.

Her flesh bared against Delaney's at last, Allie shared his passion. He entered her, and she gasped her bliss as he overwhelmed her slender form with his power. Her mind echoed his words as he rasped, "I love you, Allie."

She was unable to speak past the exhilaration that filled her as the rhythm of their lovemaking grew more intense, as she gave to him fully. Her joy swelled at the loving litany Delaney breathlessly whispered as they neared culmination. Gasping, she shared his fulfillment, the soft sound joining his low cry to linger in her mind long moments after all was still.

But reality returned. With it came a devastating rush of shame at the ease with which Delaney had slipped behind her defenses, and Allie closed her eyes against the pain of that realization. She opened them a moment later to find Delaney studying her face, his expression concerned. His eyes were filled with tenderness, the same tenderness that had so easily defeated her resolve. She steeled herself against it.

His gaze slipped to the silver disk lying between her breasts, and he took it into his hand as he looked back up into her face.

"Do you remember what you told me a long time ago, Allie? You told me that the Lady brought us together. I've never believed it, but I know that this medal binds us, whatever the reason. It always will."

He lowered his head to kiss her once more. He frowned when she averted her face and whispered, "Margaret will be home any minute."

Silent at her response, he studied her expression a moment longer before nodding and standing up beside the bed. He pulled her to her feet beside him. She resisted when he attempted to draw her into his arms again, and she felt his eyes upon her as she turned to pick up her black mourning dress. They were both fully dressed when Delaney tilted her face up to his. His gentleness tore at her heart as he whispered, "I love you, Allie. I can wait a little longer if you need time. Just don't shut me out, darling. That's all I ask."

Olga's voice sounded in the foyer, saving her the need for response as Delaney walked quickly out into the hall.

Alone in her room a few minutes later, her agonized regrets overwhelming, Allie knew what she must do.

* * *

The warm breeze from the river carried a familiar stench, interrupting his thoughts as Delaney walked along the crowded street, and he marveled at the odors genteel women shoppers would endure in order to patronize this popular Lake Street shopping district. But he supposed a street bursting with shops, stores, and wholesale warehouses and teeming with stevedores, sidewalk peddlers, and fishmongers was irresistible to an experienced shopper's discerning eye.

Delaney raised his gaze to the numerous signs displayed under and above the colorful awnings that lined the street on both sides, advertising rare books, hats, caps, furs, dry goods, and carpets, but his objective was none of those fine establishments. He had in mind a dressmaker's shop at the far end of the street, which had served him well since Allie reentered his life.

Slowing his brisk step to avoid colliding with a pair of matrons taking advantage of the mildness of midday to stroll at a snail's pace past the attractive store windows, Delaney fought his impatience. He took his first opportunity to slip past them, his mind filled with the plans he had made since Allie's and his loving encounter that morning.

A small discomfort returning, Delaney frowned. He regretted the disquiet Allie had displayed when the heat of their loving was over, but his selfish heart felt little remorse. He loved her, and he could not make himself regret their lovemaking. It had been a beautiful, natural joining of two parts of a single human spirit, and it had renewed him. He consoled himself that time would heal Allie's unease. When that time came, he knew she would be happy. But in the interim, he had decided to progress with plans that had already been delayed too long.

The brightly striped awning he sought came into view at the end of the street, and Delaney hastened his step. The proprietress of the shop, a small, smiling Frenchwoman, had proved her patience was without end and her skill unmatched, and he had work for her this day.

Striding to the door of the small shop, Delaney entered and waited impatiently until the curtains at the rear of the store parted and Madame Denieve stepped through.

"Ah, Monsieur Marsh! I am most pleased to see you. How may I help you?"

Delaney's handsome face was sober, his eyes direct as they

dwelled momentarily on the dark-haired woman's inquisitive expression. A smile flickered across his lips as he responded quietly, "I've come with another commission for you, Madame Denieve. I'd like you to make a wedding gown."

Margaret's voice rose from the foyer below, announcing her return, and Allie anxiously smoothed the skirt of her fresh mourning gown with a nervous hand, then walked swiftly to the door of her room. Stepping into the hall, she crossed to the railing as Dr. Willis and Margaret raised smiling faces toward her.

"Mama, Dr. Willis and I had a wonderful time. We took a long ride and we—"

"Margaret dear, I'm sorry to interrupt you, but we haven't much time. We must leave immediately if we're to make the afternoon train."

"The afternoon train?" Dr. Willis's response reflected his surprise.

"Yes, Margaret and I are leaving. We're going home."

"Mama!"

"Margaret, I'm sorry this is so unexpected, but I don't have time to explain. Everything will be all right, dear. I've packed your things." Turning her gaze toward the startled doctor, Allie attempted a reassuring smile. "I'll make certain Dr. Peters keeps a close eye on Margaret, Dr. Willis, but if I could ask one thing more of you?" At Dr. Willis's nod, Allie continued, "If you could summon a hack and help me lift Margaret into the carriage . . . ?"

Ignoring Dr. Willis's obvious disapproval and Margaret's bewilderment as they stared up at her in silence, Allie turned abruptly and walked back to her room. She approached the dresser, seeing in the mirror there the reason for Dr. Willis's concern. Her face was pinched, unnaturally white, her dark eyes shadowed, her lips unsteady. But her appearance was of little consequence.

Emptying her mind of thought, Allie picked up her small dark hat and secured it atop her neatly bound hair. The white envelope on the corner of the dresser was reflected in the glass, and she picked it up with a trembling hand. The paper seemed to scorch her palm as she walked to the bed and placed the note on the pillow.

Her throat tightening, Allie closed her eyes briefly as a great swell of regret swept her mind. She swallowed against her anguish and raised her hands to the neckline of her dress. Slowly, with fingers made clumsy by distress, she withdrew the medal and slipped it off over her head. She clutched it tightly, myriad emotions assailing her as she opened her hand to stare down at it for the last time. The Lady's dear face was exquisitely clear to her as Allie's voice emerged in a low, trembling whisper. "Forgive me."

Unable to bear any more, Allie placed the medal beside the envelope and picked up her small traveling case. With a rapid step she walked to the door and descended the stairs to the first floor.

Dr. Willis's lined face was grave. "Are you certain you're not making a mistake, dear?"

Allie's short response—"I'm sure"—was choked with emotion.

Allie walked through the doorway toward the carriage where Margaret awaited her. Aware that Dr. Willis was close at her heels, she turned toward him as she reached the curb. Unable to speak, she pressed a kiss against his cheek before assuming the seat beside Margaret. Seconds later the carriage lurched into motion.

Delaney stared with a deepening sense of unreality at the small white envelope on the pillow of Allie's bed. He snatched it up and tore it open, gripping the thin sheet inside with a trembling hand. The neat script was achingly familiar to him and he swallowed at the painful constricting of his throat as he started to read.

Dear Delaney,
    This is not the way I prefer to say good-bye, but it is the only way open to me. I truly doubt that I would be able to make you understand my reasons for leaving, so I won't try.
    Instead, I ask a favor of you. I ask you to remember you said you love me and want me to be happy. If that is so,

you will accept my decision to leave. I'm a changed person,
Delaney. I'm no longer the young woman you left in Cass
County years ago. I've grown older, matured, and much
has happened that I cannot forget. These things are a part
of my life as you can never be.

You'll do well without me, Delaney. You have before, and
you will again. Margaret and I will be well, also. Don't
worry about us.

If you truly love me as you say you do, you will let me
go. I could never be truly happy with you, and I would not
be able to live with the heartache of trying.

I'm leaving the medal for you, Delaney. The bond be-
tween us is finally severed. You are free.
                        Allie

Delaney stared with disbelief at the sheet of paper in his hand.
Only this morning he had held Allie in his arms and loved her.
And she had loved him back!

Turning to the gleaming medal and chain lying on the pillow,
Delaney felt the significance of Allie's final gesture cut merci-
lessly into his heart. Allie was gone. She would never come
back.

A slow rage consuming him, Delaney snatched the medal up
into his hand. The image etched on the shining disk was as clear
as it had ever been, and just as meaningless. The kind, benevolent Lady did not exist! He had always known that, hadn't he?
Then why had he begun believing she might truly be there,
somewhere, listening, watching, guiding Allie's life and his with
whispered words into God's ear? Why had he come to accept
that it was she who had given Allie into his care when they were
children, and that it was she who had allowed them to find each
other again?

There was no Lady, and no such thing as love! This ache, this
burning desire deep inside him was a damnable emotion without
name. It was a grievous wound that would not heal. It had
plagued him most of his life, but it would plague him no more!

He would grant Allie's request. She had walked out of his
home and out of his life. Love? He would show her what he
thought of love.

Delaney hurled the medal against the far wall. It struck with a loud crack and bounced onto the floor out of his sight.

Turning sharply on his heel, Delaney left the room. He was determined to keep the medal and the woman connected with it out of sight, out of mind, and forever out of his heart.

chapter

twenty-eight

THE ROLLING LANDSCAPE Allie viewed through the kitchen window was warmly familiar. Summer scents were heavy in the air—sweet honeysuckle from the bush beside the porch, occasional whiffs of mint from the herb garden beyond, and barn odors, always strongest in the heat of the afternoon sun. A hint of a smile touched Allie's lips. All familiar scents, but some not particularly pleasant.

Strange, the pungent smell of the barn had completely escaped her notice in recent years. It had become a part of her life, a reality she accepted without thought. Only since her return had it again come to her notice, as her mind seemed to assess every aspect of her life as if it were new. But she had been away for months, and had been home only a few days. She was still adjusting to the changes in her life.

She was grateful that Homer Trace had consented to work a few days a week for as long as she could afford to pay him. He had evidently done his work well since James's death, and she had been inordinately pleased to see the farm in such excellent condition when she returned. James would have been happy to see the healthy crops in his fields, the well-tended animals in his barn, and his family at home again. But James was not here, and Allie was acutely aware that she could not continue on as if he was.

A warm gust of air from the open window loosened a strand of hair against her neck, and Allie made an attempt to smooth it back into place. Shaking her head at the futility of the effort, she reached for the drying cloth and picked up the first of the plates draining in the sink. Her hands moving by rote at a task to which she was well accustomed, Allie glanced around the familiar kitchen. Everything was the same—the same stove at which Mother Case had stood for long hours cooking for her newly enlarged family, the same table and chairs where that loving woman had drawn them all together at mealtime in the hope that the diverse personalities of those sitting around it would eventually accept one another enough to act as one. Allie's smile was bittersweet. Even the dishes she now dried were the same.

Her task finished, Allie stacked the plates neatly on the side-board. She folded the drying cloth and hung it on the rack by the window, absentmindedly drying her hands on her apron, which was worn to a comfortable softness, much like the patterned cotton dress beneath. But a frown slipped across her face with her silent admission that her attempt to surround herself with familiar things had turned out to be a wasted effort. Everything and nothing was the same.

Allie looked toward the staircase. All was quiet upstairs, and she supposed Margaret was sleeping as was her custom in the afternoon. Dr. Peters had come out the day after they arrived, and had seemed very pleased with her progress. He had told Margaret that he thought she would be able to attend school in the fall, and Margaret had smiled. She had not smiled very often since their return, and Allie realized it was far more difficult for her young daughter to accept James's death here, where memories were so strong.

Allie turned toward the sideboard and began paring potatoes. She knew she had to keep busy if she was to survive the long, empty days and nights filled with painful memories.

Two men she loved were lost to her, in vastly different but equally irrevocable ways. She loved James and he was gone, but thoughts of Delaney taunted her with the happiness just beyond her reach.

She missed Delaney. She missed his voice, his touch. She missed talking to him, their exchange of thoughts, the way he listened, concentrating, when she spoke, as if he were devouring every word. She missed the pride in his glance when he looked at her, the love she had read in his eyes. She knew she would continue to miss him for the rest of her life. But despite her loneliness and the uncertainty of her future, she did not truly regret leaving him.

The relief she had felt after leaving Delaney was mixed with confused feelings which she had not yet resolved. No longer was she subjected to the daily assault of his masculine presence, the tenderness and hunger in his gaze, which had become more potent with each passing day. Here, at a safe distance, it was easier for her to remind herself that too many things had happened between them, things that could never be forgotten. Her own deceit in hiding the truth of Margaret's paternity from Delaney weighed heavily on her conscience, another impediment between them, but James's death had not negated the promise she had made him. She would not be able to live with a broken promise, especially to James.

But even if that were not true, she could not reveal the truth about Margaret for she was certain Sarah's jealousy would compel her to disregard the consequences and reveal the truth about Jeremy as well. Too many lives would be affected by that revelation. Jeremy would learn that the father he loved was not his own, and his life would be changed forever. The truth would also rebound on Margaret, and Allie could not force her daughter to face the truth that Delaney had fathered both her and Jeremy on the same night, and then calmly walked away.

Pain stirred anew within her. She had fled Delaney and she had hurt him. But she had had no choice.

Allie blinked away the tears brimming in her eyes. She had shed enough tears to last a lifetime. She was determined to shed no more.

A sound in the hallway broke into her sober thoughts, and Allie jumped as Sarah appeared in the doorway. Her expression feral, Sarah faced Allie with a hard smile.

"He's not here, is he? I knew it!" Sarah's laughter held a shrill note of victory. "Delaney didn't come back for me, and he won't come back for you, either!"

Her patience at a low ebb, Allie responded sharply, "What are you talking about, Sarah? What do you want?"

"Our hired man said he saw a man who looked like Delaney heading this way over an hour ago. I told him he was a fool, that Delaney would never come back here again, but I wanted to be sure. I finally managed to sneak away, and it's worth all my trouble to see you standing here alone now that Delaney's finished with you. That's why you came home, isn't it? Delaney's finished with you."

"I asked you what you want, Sarah."

"Stupid question! I want what I've always wanted. Delaney, of course."

"Sarah!"

"Oh, don't pretend with me! I knew what was going on between you and Delaney while you were in Chicago! My brother was a fool, and I told him so! I told him he was making a mistake leaving you in Delaney's house, no matter how badly injured you were. I told him to find another place for you to stay in Chicago, but he wouldn't listen. He said you couldn't be moved. He said you were safe and well cared for, and that he wouldn't risk your safety for petty jealousy. He said he trusted you! Only you and I know what a fool he was, isn't that right, Allie?"

"No, it isn't!"

"You never could be trusted, could you? First you stole my mother's love from me—made her love you more than she loved her own daughter. I hated you for that. I always will. Then you tricked my brother into marrying you and paid him back by cheating on him. All the while you were in Chicago you warmed Delaney's bed while my brother was faithful and lonely in his."

"Get out of here, Sarah!"

"But the truth is, my brother was a fool! He got what he deserved for marrying you—a cheap street trollop my mother took from the gutter!"

"I said get out!"

Sarah took another step forward, her green eyes gleaming maniacally. "But it didn't work out the way you planned, did it, Allie dear? All of a sudden you're back at home in this dreary kitchen, wearing an apron and a faded dress. And you're alone, except for your pitiful little bastard upstairs."

Allie took a threatening step forward, rigid with anger. "Get out of here now, Sarah, before I do something I'll be sorry for."

"Oh, I forgot! You're the lady of the manor now, and this beautiful castle is all yours!" Sarah flicked a deprecating gaze around the simple kitchen. "Quite a comedown from Delaney's home on Wabash Avenue, isn't it?" At Allie's obvious surprise, Sarah laughed aloud. "I've made it my business to keep up with the news on Delaney since he left. I know Delaney's wealthy now, that he's a successful journalist, that all of Chicago is talking about the work he did recently in exposing a ring of murderers. He's everything he ever said he'd be, and you thought you were going to share it with him. You threw yourself at him again, just as you always did, but it didn't work, did it? Delaney got tired of you and tossed you out! He didn't even wait until your crippled brat could walk out the door!"

Allie closed the distance between herself and Sarah in a few rapid steps. She faced the taller woman squarely, her voice low and shaking with fury. "Get out! I don't want you in my house! You're a malicious, jealous woman who doesn't have the sense to be grateful to Bobbie for—"

"For what! For living a boring life on a farm where the highlight of my week is a trip to town to buy groceries, where my greatest accomplishment in recent years was getting my youngest child to stop wetting her pants? I should be with Delaney, sharing his life! I should be living in his mansion and sleeping in his bed! You never belonged there. You're not worthy of him. You, with your pale, sickly face and puny body. Delaney and I are two of a kind. We think alike and look alike. Together we could have set Chicago on its ear, but you fixed that for me, didn't you? You turned Delaney against me!"

"I didn't!"

"But I got even! I showed you I'm more of a woman than you'll ever be! You gave Delaney an undersized crippled daughter, but I gave him a beautiful, perfect son."

"Sarah! Damn you, that's a lie!"

Turning at the sound of her husband's voice, Sarah swallowed convulsively. Her eyes widened as Bobbie entered the room and walked toward her, his face white with rage.

"Chester said he saw you slipping off into the woods behind the barn, and I knew where I'd find you. You had to see if

Delaney really did come back, didn't you? What were you going to do if you found him here? Tell him the same lies you told Allie? Jeremy is *my* son! You know it and I know it, Sarah! And I curse my own stupidity in not suspecting the lie you've made everyone believe all these years!''

''No, Bobbie, you misunderstood!'' Sarah took a wary step backward. ''I didn't tell Allie that Jeremy was Delaney's son.''

''Liar!'' Turning to Allie, Bobbie continued hotly, ''What did she tell you, Allie? That she was with Delaney that last night before he left, and that she conceived his child then?'' Not waiting for Allie's response, Bobbie shook his head. ''Not a word of it is true! I know because I stayed in town that night after the dance. I was so damned angry and disgusted with the way things were going between Sarah and me that I was determined to get drunk, but my heart wasn't in it. I was standing outside Delaney's rooming house, crazy with jealousy. I had decided to go in and have it out with him when Sarah came running down the back staircase, crying. When she raced out of town, I followed her. I caught up with her and made her tell me everything that had happened.

''She said she went to Delaney's room and told him she was going away with him. He laughed at her! He said he was drunk, but not drunk enough to saddle himself with a selfish, spiteful bitch just because the woman he wanted didn't love him enough. He said he wouldn't touch Sarah with a ten-foot pole, and if she didn't get out of his room fast, he was going to call the house down on her. She told me he ran her out, actually pushed her out the door and slammed it behind her.''

Bobbie turned to glance at his wife's pale face. ''Stupid fool that I was, I felt sorry for her. I loved her, and I wanted to comfort her. I took her in my arms and I rocked her like a baby. I told her that Delaney was a damned fool, that I'd give my right arm to have her. I kissed her, and she kissed me back. I kissed her again and she slid her arms around me. I made love to her, Allie. We were together until almost down. Then all of a sudden she got up and dressed. She looked at me in a strange way and said she never wanted to see me again, that if I came to the farm, she'd have her pa run me off. She said she didn't want me, that she had never wanted me, that the only man she wanted was Delaney, and if she couldn't have him, she didn't want anybody.''

Bobbie shook his head, incredulous even in retrospect as he faced Allie's silence. ''I was furious and hurt, and for a while I was determined never to look at Sarah again. But that didn't last long. I tried to talk to her, but she wouldn't see me, so I gave up. Then one day Sarah showed up on my doorstep. She told me she was going to have my baby. Damned fool that I was, I was actually happy, Allie! I knew it was the only way I was going to get her, so I married her and took her home with me. I never told anybody any of this because I didn't want to humiliate her. I never dreamed she was passing off my son as Delaney's—that she was holding it over your head all these years! I knew Margaret was Delaney's child. I knew there was no way James would have waited until you were so far along before marrying you if he had been the father. I'm sorry, Allie. James didn't want anyone to know Margaret wasn't his, and I never would have mentioned it, except to explain.''

Incredulous at these disclosures, Allie stared at Bobbie's earnest expression. ''But how can you be sure Sarah wasn't lying to you? She's good at it. She—''

''Because she was a virgin, Allie. I was the first man for Sarah, damn her, and whether she likes it or not, I'm going to be her only man.'' Bobbie directed a hard glance into Sarah's glazed green eyes as he spoke in a low, rigidly controlled voice. ''Delaney doesn't want her now any more than he ever did. I'm the only one who wants her, God help me. She's my wife, and I'm going to keep her—Saturday shopping trips, baby's wet pants, and all.''

Bobbie's expression was severe when he addressed Sarah directly. ''I won't tell you to apologize to Allie, Sarah. You wouldn't mean it, and I have a feeling Allie couldn't forgive you anyway.''

Bobbie's face was deeply flushed, and Allie knew his wife's humiliating behavior had taken a heavy toll. Appearing to read her thoughts, Bobbie cast her a bitter smile as he grasped his wife's arm firmly. ''Don't worry about me, Allie. I have what I want, even if things aren't exactly the way I want them. Sarah isn't going anywhere. She isn't a complete fool. She knows I'm all she's got left, and she's too much of a coward to try to make it alone. Isn't that right, Sarah?''

Sarah pulled free of Bobbie's grip and started toward the doorway. Halting suddenly, her body rigid, she stared at something just beyond Allie's range of vision. Again grasping her arm, Bobbie propelled her into motion and out of the room as Delaney stepped into view.

His handsome face frozen with anger, Delaney advanced into the room. He stood towering over Allie, his eyes frigid as he spoke. "I never realized how big a fool I was until this moment. I suppose I should be grateful my horse pulled up lame, allowing Sarah to get here ahead of me, but right now all I want is for you to tell me everything I overheard isn't true. Tell me Margaret isn't mine, that you didn't keep my daughter from me all these years so James could raise her as his own! Tell me it isn't true that you hated me so much that you wouldn't even tell me she was mine after James was dead! Tell me you didn't do this to me, Allie. Tell me!''

"Sarah told me that you and she . . . She said the child she was carrying was yours, too, and I—''

"And you believed her?'' Delaney was incredulous. "You thought I could make love to Sarah after we had been together, that I could soil what we meant to each other out of spite?''

"She was pregnant, Delaney! I knew she loved you. She had told me a hundred times she'd never be with anyone but you. I knew she meant it.''

"What about what *I* had said? Didn't you believe me, when I told you I loved you, that you were a part of me, that I wanted to take care of you the rest of my life?''

"You left me!''

"You were the one who made that choice. You walked away and left *me*.''

"Mother Case was sick. She was dying, Delaney!''

"So was I, Allie, without you.''

"Oh, Delaney, I didn't think you'd leave. I thought you'd wake up the next morning and decide to wait a little longer. I didn't believe it when that train left and you were on it.''

"When I think what a fool I was . . . I waited for you to come. I stared at that platform, expecting you to walk around the corner right up until I stepped on that train. Now I know it was all a damned waste of time! You never believed me. You believed James—everything he told you. And all that talk, about the medal and belonging to me, it was nothing but talk to you then, just as it's all talk now.''

"No, Delaney. No!''

"What is it, then? Don't tell me it's the truth and you love me. Love means trust, doesn't it, Allie? Love means giving yourself to the person you love, being willing to sacrifice everything, even your pride. I was angry when I found that note on the bed, Allie. For a few days I hated you and everything that was yours, and then I started to think. You said if I loved you, I'd let you go, but that was nonsense. I loved you too much to let you go, and I knew my pride was keeping me from coming after you.

"Then I remembered that pride had made me leave without you that first time I went to Chicago. And I remembered that when I finally admitted my mistake to myself and came back to get you, you were married to James and it was too late.''

"Oh, Delancy, I waited. I believed you would come back until Sarah told me—''

"And you believed her.''

Allie paused, a wealth of misery in her single, anguished word of response. "Yes.''

Delaney stared down into Allie's white face. When he finally spoke, his voice was flat, emotionless. "Well, I suppose there's nothing more to say.''

Reaching into his pocket, Delaney withdrew a familiar medal and chain. Expressionless, he dropped it into her hand. "You might as well keep this. It doesn't mean anything to me.''

As her hand closed around the medal, Delaney turned and walked out of the house. The realization that he was walking out of her life forever held Allie immobile as the sound of his horse's hooves echoed against the hard-packed road and slowly faded into the distance.

Allie fought the despair that threatened to overwhelm her. So many mistakes, so many misunderstandings, so many deceits that had gone undiscovered until it was too late . . .

Opening her hand, Allie looked at the medal Delaney had dropped so coldly into her palm. She stared down at the familiar image of the Lady, a spontaneous whisper rising to her lips.

"You sent Delaney to me. I always knew you did. So why did I stop believing?"

The stark, empty silence was filled with aching regrets as Allie slipped the medal over her head and let it drop against her breast. Clenching it in her fist, she turned to the staircase, glancing up toward the second floor where Margaret slept. She had taken the first step when a voice from behind her froze her into immobility.

"Allie?"

Unable to turn toward the sound, Allie waited an eternity until Delaney's arms slipped around her from behind, until she heard his deep, earnest voice in her ear.

"Forgive me, Allie. My damned pride wouldn't let me accept the thought that you could doubt me. I was halfway down the road before I realized I was making the same mistake I had made once before. I love you, Allie. We've lost so much time, and I've lost the first seven years of my daughter's life. I'm not going to lose the rest of it, and I'm not going to lose you, Allie. I told you once that I'd make you forget the pain of the past, and I will. If you can just believe in me again."

Delaney turned her toward him and Allie saw love, commitment, and myriad other tender emotions reflected in his eyes. Her love for him rose in a great overwhelming swell.

"Oh, Delaney . . ."

Enveloping her in his arms, Delaney buried his face in her hair with whispered words of love that echoed in her heart, and Allie slid her arms around him.

She was home, at last.

Conscious of the medal lying against her breast between them, Allie closed her eyes, silent words of thanksgiving forming in her mind with the certainty, again so clear, that this was meant to be.

Wrapped in each other's arms, Allie and Delaney were oblivious to a sound at the window, a fluttering that accompanied the flight of a small gray dove as it took wing. The bird soared upward into the limitless sky like a brief, whispered prayer, winging, fading, blending evermore.

Dear Friends,

WINGS OF A DOVE was a particular pleasure for me to write. Allie and Delaney immediately came alive for me upon reading the story of the first orphan train, and as their story unfolded in my mind, it touched my heart. I hope you feel the same.

Thank you for your letters in the past, and I hope to hear from you again. I enjoy your comments and your friendship.

Sincerely,

Elaine Barbieri

Elaine Barbieri
P.O. Box 536
West Milford, NJ 07480

Elaine Barbieri

WINGS OF A DOVE

Allie and Delaney met on a harrowing train ride, along with hundreds of other orphans, travelling from the rough tenements of nineteenth-century New York City, to the vast farmlands of the Midwest, their friendship soon blossomed into starry-eyed romance. And as they grew into adulthood, so did their passion...
__WINGS OF A DOVE 0-515-10205-9/$4.50

Also by Elaine Barbieri

__TARNISHED ANGEL 0-515-09748-9/$4.50
Devina Dale--beautiful, defiant. An adventurous pioneer who dares to face the wild West. She will allow nothing to stand in the way of her dreams. Not even the handsome outlaw who kidnaps her for revenge--the enemy she cannot help but love.

For Visa and MasterCard orders call: 1-800-631-8571

FOR MAIL ORDERS: CHECK BOOK(S). FILL OUT COUPON. SEND TO: **BERKLEY PUBLISHING GROUP** 390 Murray Hill Pkwy., Dept. B East Rutherford, NJ 07073	POSTAGE AND HANDLING: $1.00 for one book, 25¢ for each additional. Do not exceed $3.50.

POSTAGE AND HANDLING:
$1.00 for one book, 25¢ for each additional. Do not exceed $3.50.

BOOK TOTAL $ ____

POSTAGE & HANDLING $ ____

NAME_____

APPLICABLE SALES TAX $ ____

ADDRESS_____

(CA, NJ, NY, PA)

CITY_____

TOTAL AMOUNT DUE $ ____

STATE_____ZIP_____

PAYABLE IN US FUNDS.
(No cash orders accepted.)

PLEASE ALLOW 6 WEEKS FOR DELIVERY.
PRICES ARE SUBJECT TO CHANGE WITHOUT NOTICE.

287